Praise for *Coyote*

"A wonderful historical n
defiance, war and peace, a desire to belong. The characters feel
at once familiar and new, ordinary and complex, and so
marvelously alive. A treasure of a book."
— Kristina Gorcheva-Newberry, author of *The Orchard*

"The Vietnam War rages through Amanda Cockrell's masterful
novel *Coyote Weather,* a story about young love in an
impossible, chaotic, fear-driven time. A poignant,
compassionate, and suspenseful read, I couldn't put it down."
— Elizabeth Poliner, author of *As Close to Us as Breathing*

For Amanda Cockrell's previous novels:

"I loved this story with its deft use of magical realism, its
wonderfully quirky yet believable characters, and its honest
portrayal of relationships, good and bad."
— Han Nolan, author of *Dancing on the Edge*
and *What We Keep Is Not Always What Will Stay*

"A lively and diverse cast of characters, credible people as
surprising and memorable as the pilgrims in Chaucer's
Canterbury Tales...Amanda Cockrell is a master magician and
this novel is a pleasure to read from first to last."
— George Garrett, author of *Death of the Fox, The
Succession, Entered from the Sun, Pomegranate Seed*

COYOTE WEATHER

COYOTE WEATHER

a novel of the 1960s

Amanda Cockrell

NORTHAMPTON HOUSE PRESS

CIP data TK

COYOTE WEATHER. © 2023 Amanda Cockrell
Jacket art and cover design by Naia Poyer.
ISBN 978-1-950668-16-8 (print edition)
ISBN 978-1-950668-15-1 (ebook edition)
Library of Congress Control Number: 2023902066
Published by Northampton House Press, www.northampton-
house.com. Franktown Virginia USA.
Printed in the United States of America
10 9 8 7 6 5 4 3 2

For Tony, always and everything

PROLOGUE
1967

The banner read GOOD LUCK, RANDY in gold letters. It hung from the curtain rod above the picture window and the curtains were open so everyone inside could see the newly-installed flagpole in the front yard. The flag was new too. It shone in the winter sun against the bright blue of the sky and the mountains that ringed the valley. It was a sign the Ottleys were patriotic, and proud to have their son serving.

His mother put a plate with more cake in his hands and one of his father's friends slapped him on the back. "Army's gonna be good for you," he told him jovially. "You'll see. You're a good boy, not like these punks trying to get out of their duty."

"You'll get to see the world," another older man said. "I envy you, son."

To Randy Ottley the room felt claustrophobic, small and suddenly airless. When their guests had left, his father would drive him to the Los Angeles induction center and he wouldn't be able to come back. His sister Mimi, Ellen Callahan, Martin Alvarez, and a handful of other high school friends stood awkwardly around the cake, now a half-eaten jumble of crumbs with icing letters and half the Stars and Stripes.

"Time to go, Randy," his father said, and the guests began to make their goodbyes. His dad picked up the suitcase and motioned him toward the waiting car.

"Good luck, man," someone called.

"Give the Viet Cong hell."

"Take care of yourself."

"Come home soon, man."

I
SOMETHING IN THE AIR

When Randy Ottley first began trying to come home that summer the people who felt his presence were never sure what they had seen, if anything. He was more a breath on the back of the neck, a flicker out of the corner of the eye, an urge to open the window and call out for whoever was late getting home that night.

The coyotes saw him in the distance, floating toward the valley above the Channel Islands, a spectral translucent shimmer in the darkness, and they puzzled over him. For one thing, he was going the wrong way, not out to sea. The Chumash, the people who'd been there first, had worn the path over the dark water between the islands, and even now most of those departing followed it, trailing footsteps of faint blue light behind them. But this one was trying to get into the valley, and he didn't seem to be dead, not in the way humans usually were.

At night he closed his eyes, stopped his ears to the screaming voice of the drill instructor, the humiliation, the insults, the exhaustion of running until his legs gave way under him, the ridicule for questions to which he knew no answers. Then he could lift out of his physical self, a soul departing a body it was no longer tethered to. Furious, desperate concentration would lift him above the barracks the way he'd lifted over his back yard as a dreaming child. Once he was well up it was easier. He drifted south along the coastline, like floating in a pool, cutting through the night, a silent plane homing.

As always when he neared his goal, he lost his balance and slowed, tipping precariously above the humpbacked forms of the Channel Islands. He righted himself, face down, yearning and determined. It was harder going and the salt air was thick, like pushing through a bubble. It clung to him as he followed the highway past the oilfields, passing above the refinery lights, a spangle of stars masking the solid ugliness of tanks and pipes, a fairy castle that would vanish, like his flight, with the sun.

Closer. Up the grade past the apple orchards, following the train tracks that went to the packing sheds at the end of the valley. The air grew thicker and more elastic as he tried to turn off toward the cul de sac where his mother's house would be, with the flagpole in the yard.

"There's something in the air, man." Jerry Manoury scratched the back of his neck. He kept feeling like something was crawling there.

"It's dry." Aaron pinched out the end of his joint and slid it carefully into his jeans. "Coyote weather. We're gonna have a fire sure as shit. I saw Char Man last night."

Jerry figured Aaron might have seen anything last night.

"No shit, man," Aaron insisted. "Kind of hovering over Creek Road, bigger'n life, all burned black."

Jerry scratched his neck again. Char Man was a local legend, subject of ever-evolving campfire recitations. Something *was* out there, but it wasn't Char Man. Probably just the Santa Ana wind. It always made his skin crawl. It had been coyote weather all summer—dry, brown and ready to catch fire. All anybody could grow was foxtails, and the stream that ran along Creek Road had shrunk to a few puddles between the stones where the long green moss was drying out like moldy beards. The wild peacocks in the East End flew into town to roost on the red-tiled roof of the Arcade and drink out of the fountain in the park. Jerry heard their screams echoing in the bougainvillea. The air was dry with static electricity, and the gray-brown coyotes came down out of the foothills and ate people's cats.

There were more coyotes than usual that year. Jerry saw them at dusk, scrambling along a ridgetop where a new house was going up, nosing through the debris, or trotting under the live oaks, ears pricked like radar receivers, tuning in the evening news. They watched the war in southeast Asia through living room windows, on televisions flickering bluely in the dim light. They sat outside City Hall and cocked their big ears toward the City Council's efforts to chase the hippies out of the park. They stuck their noses into overturned garbage cans and read the draft board's memos. Jerry had a letter from the board in his dresser drawer. He looked at it occasionally but there wasn't any point in opening it because he knew what it said.

"Char Man," Aaron said again, "I swear," and Jerry shook his head.

"You'll see." Aaron ambled up the street to some dubious appointment Jerry would just as soon not be involved in and Jerry looked up at the sky again. A big fat moon hung over the eucalyptus trees, overlaying their pungent scent with a milky haze. Up the street, Irish dance music unwound from the open door of the Ayala Art Center. He felt at a loose end tonight, like most nights. Might as well dance as anything else. It was one of the few things so far that gave him any sense of

5

accomplishment. He had been no good at math in high school, but he could see the complicated geometry of the dances like blueprints in his head.

Inside the Art Center the dance had just ended and everyone was sorting themselves out for the next one: kindergarten teachers in embroidered peasant skirts and leotards, Hollywood types in polo shirts earnestly slumming with the locals, and the usual assortment of teenagers with nowhere else to go.

The instructor, a storklike figure in ballet flats, dropped the needle on the turntable with a mild *skrawk* and a fast Russian dance started up. Two people Jerry knew opened up the line and hooked him in. The music was like the crack-the-whip at a fair, a line of flying feet in a snake shape on the polished floor.

As the snake's head wove past its tail, he spotted a girl across the room. She had a curtain of long brown hair, and was dancing between Martin Alvarez, a boy he knew vaguely, and a stunner of a girl. The stunner looked dangerous to him, too beautiful for mortal man, but the brown-haired girl might be approachable, and he had a thing for long hair.

He caught her eye as they danced past each other and he smiled, just because she was cute, and she smiled back, startled. Then she was gone, dancing down the room near the head of the line. He broke loose with a flying leap into the air, landing on the balls of his feet, dancing backward into the line again, while it opened up to take him in, showing off even if the chances she would be interested in him were slim. Still, when the dance ended, he headed for the corner where she and Martin and the stunner leaned against each other, panting.

"Hey, man," Jerry said to Martin. His eyes slid to the girl.

"Hey." Martin brightened. "This is Ellen."

She was little, with that cloud of long hair and a jawline that looked like she could be stubborn.

"Do you, uh, want to go someplace?" Jerry said to her. He

figured he sounded like a goon. "Just down the street," he said to Martin.

Martin nodded. He and the stunner faded away.

"Third wheel," Ellen said. "I'd probably better."

"My luck," Jerry said. He held out his hand.

She grinned and took it. "Teak's staying with me for the weekend. You'll have to take me back to them at some point."

"I'll only carry you off a few blocks. He'll know where to collect you."

"What is this place?"

"Secret refuge."

He led her down the steps and up the sidewalk under the whisper of the eucalyptus leaves. "So where have you been?" he said after half a block. "I don't know you."

"Actually I don't know you either. Name?"

"Jerry Manoury."

"Ellen Callahan. I've been at college in Virginia. And I went to Apple Valley so nobody knows me."

Apple Valley was the lefty private school where film business kids went. No wonder she could folk dance. He wondered how far out of his league she was.

"Are you in school?" she asked him.

"Sort of." Meaning no, but he didn't want to admit it. "Ventura JC. I'm there for the summer to flunk calculus again." And try to keep the draft board off his ass, which would have worked better if he'd actually been going to class.

"Sounds dismal," Ellen said. "I actually picked my college because it doesn't have a math requirement. Well, partly."

"Seriously? Can I go there?"

"It's a girls' school."

"Ouch." He turned them up the steps of a tiny house with an arched door. *The Place*, read wavy letters over the arch. It was just a couple of rooms, a stucco storefront that belonged to

7

"Robert's mom," Jerry explained. "She used to have a beauty shop out here."

Robert, in residence, was tall black guy with glasses even more owlish than Jerry's and a khaki shirt with a patch that said AGUILAR AUTOMOTIVE. He looked surprised at their entrance but bowed at Ellen as Jerry led her through the door, appearing to approve. "Welcome to our lair. Not fancy but our own."

The walls were brown and a travel poster of Mont St. Michel tacked over the coffee pot provided the decor. The cable-spool tables had candles in raffia-wrapped chianti bottles. Most of the handful of kids there weren't old enough to drink, but the faint, sweet, burning-leaves scent of pot smoke mingled with tobacco and burnt coffee grounds.

Jerry poured Ellen a cup of coffee. He put his elbows on the table, unsure quite what to do with her now. He took his glasses off and peered at her. "What do you do in the daytime?"

"I have a summer job at the paper in Ventura."

"Covering fires and murders and stuff?"

Ellen looked wistful. "Fashion shows. They don't let girls work in the newsroom."

"Bummer."

"I know. If I could bring them a good story on my own, they might actually pay attention to me instead of treating me like some kind of pet."

"Ayala's not exactly a hotbed of breaking news," Jerry said. "It's a big night when someone knocks over the Shell station."

"Fourth of July's coming up. Maybe one of the floats will catch fire again."

"You were here for that?"

"Two years ago, front row, while the padres and their mission went up in flames."

He remembered it. "Unintentional auto da fe." He smiled at her, hooked. "I should have met you then, before you took off for the East Coast. Don't vanish on me now, okay?"

She cocked her head, as if she were trying to decide if he was serious. "No," she said thoughtfully.

Later Martin and Teak drove Jerry home in Martin's old Bel Air, with Ellen beside him in the back seat. The Bel Air's enormous fins gave it the look of a B-movie rocket ship cutting through the dusty night. Whatever had been in the air earlier was gone. Jerry pointed past the folded top to where the moon glowed like a potent headlamp on the edge of the valley.

"Look at that." He nuzzled Ellen's ear. The foothills were limned in silver, and maybe she'd let him kiss her. He'd try, anyway, in case she did disappear. She lived in the Arbolada, for Christ's sake, her father was a screenwriter.

When he bent his head down she was looking right up at him. The full moon was split into two white marbles in her eyes, and her long hair was blowing in a spill of heavy brown silk over her shoulder. Eucalyptus and oranges scented the wind. She tasted like coffee.

When they dropped him off, Jerry watched Martin's car until he couldn't see its tail lights anymore, then trotted up the walk and let himself in.

"I'm home, Ma." It was two in the morning.

His mother looked up from a sociology text at the kitchen table. "Did you go to class today?"

He didn't answer. He didn't go for the same reason he'd flunked the first time. Except that the desks had ashtrays, it was just like high school, where he'd not lived up to his potential, according to baffled messages from the vice principal. Now that he'd turned eighteen, he was skating on the thin edge of a student deferment. When he did go to campus, he spent the day in the library, reading. His mother, on the other hand, had unexpectedly decided to go to college herself, and was relentless about education, even if she couldn't manage his.

Jerry went into his room and shut the door. His father was asleep. His little brother might still be out. He stretched out on the unmade bed and looked at the ceiling, thinking.

He spent a lot of his time doing that. He hadn't slept more than two or three hours at a stretch since he was a kid in L.A., when he'd lain awake listening to the roar of rocket engines from the desert. When he was old enough to realize that his father helped design them, about the time of the Cuban missile crisis, and it became clear the next standoff would blow the world to hell, they'd said something to him about the unwisdom of counting on much.

Tonight he felt as if maybe something had shifted. Something in the pattern had changed. He'd like to think it was this girl, but he wanted that too badly, and he'd learned not to want things that way, not specifically. When you wanted something that was so defined, what you always got was a thing that was just enough amiss to make the difference painful.

II

UN-AMERICAN ACTIVITY

Ellen's mother radiated polite misgivings the first time she met Jerry.

"We're going down to the park, Mom," Ellen said and scooted out the door before Lily had a chance to ask questions. She was supposed to meet some nice boy at college and marry him, the way her mother had done. She knew that. Instead when she wasn't working at the newspaper she was trading books with Jerry, learning to smoke pot, and today, hanging out in the arroyo behind the park, with Jerry and Robert and their friend Aaron.

Aaron was tall, with a thick shock of black hair that stood straight up as if he was perpetually electrified. He had a guitar and Jerry had brought a flute. They were noodling through some tune she didn't recognize. Jerry sat cross-legged on a flat rock, red sandstone warmed by the sun, his feet tucked lotus-fashion. His brown hair curled around his ears, and the dark flying brows gave him an oddly alert look even when he was sleepy. His shoulders were muscular, and his bare feet were wiry with high arches and narrow heels. He wore faded jeans, a string of red and blue beads, and a blue work shirt with the sleeves rolled up. His eyes were closed and he looked dreamy and blissful.

When they broke Jerry opened his eyes and asked Aaron, "When did you get back, man?"

"Yesterday," Aaron said. "Bad food, bad company. Some dude had a cough, went on all night like a bullfrog."

"Aaron just got out of jail," Jerry explained.

"Oh," Ellen said. She couldn't think of what else to say. It probably wasn't polite to ask why.

Jerry grinned. "He's not dangerous."

Aaron seemed to know what she was thinking. He waggled his eyebrows at her and bared his teeth. "Vagrancy, loitering with intent, and copping an attitude."

"Criminal nature." Robert shook his head and they all laughed.

Above them, through the contorted branches, a red-tailed hawk was riding the thermals against a blue-white sky. The arroyo was dry unless it rained, and shaded by live oaks that shed their leaves in a prickly carpet. One was biting into her bare thigh and she shifted uncomfortably on her perch on the rock.

Jerry put his flute down. He pulled his shirt off and spread it out. "Sit on this."

"Walter Raleigh," Robert said. "Rides again."

"Shut up." Jerry put his arm around her. "My mom wants to meet you. She thinks you're a good influence. So far, Robert's the only other good influence I know, so you represent a one hundred percent increase."

"Hey, *I'm* an influence," Aaron said.

"That's what the cops said," Robert told him.

"Asshole." Aaron dumped a handful of leaves on Robert's head and rubbed them into his hair.

Robert rolled into a crouch. "Come on, motherfucker."

Aaron leaped on him with a shriek, spread-eagled, and they rolled in the leaves and foxtails in the dry bed of the gulley, howling with laughter.

"Don't mind them," Jerry said. "They don't get out much."

They sat and watched Robert and Aaron thrash in the oak leaves as if they were spectators at some unorthodox wrestling match. When they finally sat up, Aaron said he had to see a man about a delivery.

Robert pushed his glasses up his nose. "I'm glad you've finally learned your lesson," he remarked. "I myself have to go to work."

They clambered out of the arroyo and ambled off in opposite directions.

Jerry kissed her on the ear, then sat back and peered at her with a kind of earnest hunger. "What the hell are you doing, going to school in Virginia?"

She didn't want to say, *My mother sent me there so I wouldn't go to Berkeley and meet someone like you.* He probably knew that already. For her part, she was secretly terrified, because she knew he was casual about going to class. When she flew home from Carter Randolph the airports were full of khaki-uniformed soldiers who looked younger than she was, and seemed confused about how they'd got there. Of the boys she'd gone out with in high school, Randy Ottley had been drafted and his father had made him go. Carl Leeman had volunteered and had his picture in the paper. It was as if they were fading into transparency or halftone dots on newsprint, all those gone-away boys.

Jerry tilted his head back, watching the hawk. "Wouldn't you like to have wings?" he asked, possibly because he guessed what she was thinking and wanted to forestall it.

"What kind?"

"Hawk wings," Jerry said.

Ellen leaned against his shoulder. She'd never thought of herself as a hawk. A robin, possibly. Not a guided missile with feathers and mad yellow eyes. "Would I have to eat shrews?"

Jerry grinned at her. "Part of the deal."

She was beginning to suspect that might be the case.

Mimi Ottley sat under a purple sombrero on the restaurant wall, where it made a gaudy silver-spangled halo around her head. Her expression was severe, blond bangs cut precisely across her forehead, hair a perfect lacquered flip. "You aren't ever even home," she said to Ellen.

"I'm working," Ellen said, wolfing tacos. "I'm supposed to go take pictures of some women's club at two."

"You're out with that hippie," Mimi said. "I know a girl who went to school with him. She says one whole year he never went to gym class. They almost kicked him out."

Ellen didn't say anything.

Mimi sighed. "People like that are just making everything worse."

"You can't keep getting mad at me for seeing boys," Ellen said. "Randy and I weren't a good match."

"It has nothing to do with your breaking up with my brother."

"*He* broke up with *me,*" Ellen pointed out. "We were fifteen. And then you got upset at me for going with Carl Leeman."

"Carl was setting fires and just wild," Mimi said. "My father says now he's in the Army it'll make a man of him, just like Randy."

Ellen had known Randy as someone with his head firmly in comic books and the chess club. He'd looked like a hamster under a cat's paw at his going-away party. 'Making a man of him' seemed like a horrible idea. "How?" she demanded. She was feeling argumentative, even though she knew it was mostly that

Mimi's feelings were hurt. They used to spend a lot of time together, when neither had a boyfriend or Ellen was going with Randy. Mimi was dating a boy from college now, but he was in ROTC and the Young Americans for Freedom. He and Mimi seemed to take the antiwar movement as a personal affront, and Jerry felt much the same way about the war.

"My brother is defending his country," Mimi said stiffly.

"Well, wouldn't you rather have him home?" Ellen wasn't even sure how the country had gotten into that war. First there'd been military advisors to keep the communists out, then suddenly there were troops, and more troops, most of them drafted, and the evening accounting of the dead, American bodies versus Vietnamese. Or maybe it hadn't been sudden. Maybe she just hadn't been paying attention, until Randy was drafted.

"He did what he had to," Mimi said. "He didn't burn his draft card or go hide in Canada and leave someone else to fight in his place. That's why Mother put the flagpole up, because we're proud."

Ellen sighed. They weren't going to see eye to eye. "Jerry has a student deferment. He's not in Canada. And I don't know what we're doing in Vietnam. The Viet Cong haven't attacked the U.S. and they aren't likely to." She scraped the last of her beans onto her fork.

"Well!" Mimi smiled brightly. "Martin Alvarez's band is playing at that new coffee house they're opening at the Inn next weekend. Maybe we'll see you there." She didn't suggest they go together.

"Sure," Jerry said. Jerry would go pretty much anywhere with her; last week she'd dragged him to a formal dance held by the Women of the Moose, forty or fifty women in tight curls and evening dresses, with their Moose husbands in tuxedos. Ellen wore an evening dress her mother had bought her, hopefully, for college dances, and Jerry wore his father's blazer and tie. He'd observed the Moose contingent with the eye of an anthropologist on an isolated island while Ellen took pictures and wrote down who poured the punch.

The Riverbottom Ramblers' coffee house debut was more promising as a date. The Oak Grove was the Ayala Inn's attempt to get with the times, a room in the basement of the main club house, with candles and red-checked tablecloths and framed concert posters of Joan Baez and Bob Dylan. It was a nice safe place for Ayala's teenagers to go. It was supposed to keep them from wanting to go to Los Angeles.

Ellen snuggled against Jerry while the Ramblers, two guitarists and a banjo player, got into the mournful strains of "Five Hundred Miles."

It was crowded and they had ended up scrunched around a tiny table with Mimi Ottley and her boyfriend Don but Jerry and Don hadn't either one of them said a word about the war. The Riverbottom Ramblers weren't going to play anything too controversial. Martin had told her the Inn manager would let them sing "Blowin' in the Wind" and that was it.

Ellen could feel the shape of Jerry's arm against her cheek, feel the dark curve of his hair brush her head. The Ramblers sang "The House of the Rising Sun" and "The Midnight Special" and "The Tennessee Stud," and Mimi's boyfriend was tapping his fingers on his knee to the music.

The band finished its last set with "Didn't He Ramble," their signature song, and took a bow. Martin stepped to the microphone again. "That's all for tonight, brothers and sisters. If you liked us, tell the management they don't pay enough. And since the night's still young, if you're wondering where to go from here, I've been asked to tell you there's a vigil happening downtown, in front of the wall by Libbey Park. Nothing out of hand, just a quiet expression of concern about the war. We'll be down there and we might play some more."

There was another round of applause.

"Far out," Jerry whispered. He'd slipped Martin a note earlier, but they hadn't known if Martin was going to be able to slide the announcement past the management.

People were standing up, putting on their coats. "I guess we won't be seeing you there," Mimi's boyfriend said to Jerry. He put his arm around Mimi as if she were in direct danger from the counterculture.

"Somebody oughta run those cowards off the streets," an older man said. Two boys with him said "Damn right" and shook his hand.

"Fascists," someone else said back to them, and there was a tense silence. Some differences could be transcended, but the dividing line was the war. It scraped everyone's nerves raw.

"Maybe we'll go to the pinko vigil," one of the boys said. "Who wants to come?"

The coffee house manager edged into the crowd. "Take it easy, folks, this isn't a political meeting."

The tension relaxed a degree, like someone easing back the rubber of a slingshot. "Riot at the Ayala Inn," Jerry whispered in Ellen's ear. He flicked a glance at the boys. "Those two were assholes when we were in high school and they're assholes now."

They inched through the lower level doors with the rest of the audience, out onto the patio and a double set of stone steps to the cars.

A hand spun Jerry around and the boys bracketed him, one a

step above, the other two steps below.

"Going downtown to wave a candle around?" The one below reached up and grabbed Jerry by the shoulder. "You're a fag, Manure." They ignored Ellen, elbowing her out of the way.

Jerry didn't move. She was suddenly frightened. They didn't see her, their eyes were fixed on Jerry.

The guy with his hand on Jerry's shoulder stuck his face in Jerry's. "I'm gonna teach you something, hippie, 'cause you haven't got the balls to fight back."

Jerry kept looking at him. His hands were at his sides.

"Stop it!" Mimi's boyfriend Don was there, authoritative, like a high school principal.

One boy said, "These creeps're all afraid to fight."

"So you're going to make a fool of yourself trying to make him?" Don looked at Jerry and Ellen. "You two better go now."

Jerry turned on his heel without speaking. Ellen ran after him down the steps to her car.

"We'll see you downtown," someone shouted.

She jammed the key in the ignition, hands shaking. She backed the VW out of its spot and slammed it into first gear.

Jerry's jaw was set. He didn't say anything. By the time she got downtown and found a parking place by the old Spanish-style tower of the post office, he was acting as if it hadn't happened, but something in his movements looked precarious.

An adobe wall bordered Libbey Park. Open archways that matched the red-tiled Spanish arcade across the street stood along the curb, and the sidewalk ran between the arches and the wall. Overhead a long arbor laced with wisteria whispered in the dry breeze.

About thirty people were already lined up on the wall, swinging their feet, candles cupped in their hands. More stood along the sidewalk with placards.

"Want to be on the barricades, or just support the

movement?" Jerry asked her.

"Support the movement," she said, still shaken, and he boosted her up on the wall.

"Are you okay now? They're just morons. They think they're still on the football team."

One of the organizers, a woman with thick dark curls pulled back with a clip, came up to them and handed Jerry two candles in paper cups. He gave one to Ellen. "Some idiots who were at the gig at the Inn are thinking about seeing if they can make trouble," he told the woman. "How high is the asshole quotient on our end tonight?"

The woman inspected the vigil. "High." She bit her lip.

"So where's the Chief?" Ayala's Chief of Police could generally be counted on to be wherever something was likely to get started.

"He came by a minute ago and said we couldn't sit on the wall."

The wall was a source of contention. The hippies liked to sit on it and unnerve people with their long hair and bare feet. The City Council was getting touchy and had recommended draconian measures. Jerry thought half the people there tonight were more interested in pissing off the Council than they were in protesting.

"I doubt Chief really cares where we sit," he said. "As long as we keep it together."

"That was my thinking," the woman said. "Is your mom coming tonight?"

"I don't know." Jerry tucked Ellen into the crook of his arm. "Judy, this is Ellen."

Judy gave Ellen an uninterested once-over and a nod and went off to talk to a balding man with a placard. Ellen hadn't mentioned to her parents going to a protest after the show. She'd never been to one before; it wasn't the sort of thing she would do alone, or it hadn't been. There were placards along the street: WAR IS NOT HEALTHY FOR CHILDREN AND OTHER LIVING THINGS — BRING BACK OUR BOYS — GIVE PEACE A CHANCE. One was pasted with a photograph of exploding jungle, the fire frozen in black and white. Cars were rolling slowly past, some of the drivers shouting things out of rolled-down windows. Martin and the Ramblers were singing "With God on Our Side" and it was hard to tell who was who over the music.

It was like being at a fair, or a festival. A girl in a short white dress and long blond hair that hung in tight crimps down her shoulders danced on the sidewalk, a candle in each hand. The man on the wall next to Ellen had a wreath of wisteria in his hair. She didn't notice for a while that the people on the sidewalk and the wall were shouting back at the cars. Then she saw that the cars were closer together, jamming the street. People were starting to get out of them, shaking their fists at the protesters.

"Aw, man," Jerry said. He sounded disgusted.

All around them people were jumping off the wall. The night crackled with possibility.

"My camera's in the car," Ellen said. "I want it." If she got the city editor film of whatever was going to happen, maybe he'd let her cover news stories.

Jerry hesitated and finally shrugged. "Okay."

They slid off the wall and ducked through the park to the lot behind the post office. Sirens wailed, coming up the street. Ellen grabbed her camera and stuffed a flash bulb in the holder and the rest of the pack in her purse. Whatever was going on under the streetlights along the wall was murky, a jumble of shouting faces and raised fists. The police were there now, pulling people apart, and someone had jumped on the hood of a car and was trying to hammer the wooden butt of his placard through the windshield.

Ellen aimed the camera at him. The flash went off, a bright flare of light. She popped the dead bulb out and fished for another. The woman who'd organized the vigil was screaming at the protesters to get back on the sidewalk, not to fight, but no one was listening. Martin and the Ramblers must have packed up their instruments while they were still undamaged, and now were trying to wade through the jam in the street to their car.

Three men in the bed of a pickup piled out while the driver leaned on the horn. They wore crew cuts and there were beer cans in the back of the truck. They grabbed the first hippie they saw and kicked him while his friends swung at them. The protesters screamed at the police, "Get 'em off us!" while the cops looked as if they didn't know who to fight.

More protesters surged past Ellen and Jerry, throwing their candles on the sidewalk, just wanting to get in it, to let loose with all the anger that had been bottled up while the assholes in pickup trucks called them faggots and creeps and cowards.

Jerry grabbed Ellen by the arm and pulled her through the gates into the park. "You aren't a war correspondent," he said. "This is gonna get worse." He grabbed Judy too. "You won't get anywhere now. Let the cops do it or they'll pick you up."

Judy looked terrified and ready to cry. This kind of thing didn't happen in Ayala. Berkeley maybe, or L.A., not Ayala. "Bastards," she said. "Pig bastards."

"They're just trying to stay above water," Jerry said. But now there were more sirens and two county patrol cars rolled up. The deputies waded into the crowd, and they weren't paying any attention to the local cops. They swung nightsticks at the protesters, even the ones who'd been beaten up. People began to scatter as the deputies looked around for anyone with long hair.

"That's it," Jerry said. "Outta here."

Ellen snapped one more shot of a deputy with his nightstick raised before Jerry yanked her away into the dark. She heard running feet behind them. Now she was scared to death, maybe not such a hotshot fearless journalist after all. But the feet went on by, it was just someone else getting the hell out. The screaming from the street and the sirens blocked out any other sound. A red light went round and round like a wash of blood over the path.

"Where's your car?" Jerry asked Judy.

"Back there." She looked over her shoulder at the street.

"Leave it. We'll take you home." He pulled open the door to Ellen's bug.

They got in without arguing. Judy gave Ellen directions and they took her home. When they pulled up outside Judy's house, Judy looked at Jerry. "I'll come by tomorrow. We've got to decide what to do next." She squeezed his shoulder. "Thanks for the ride." As if he'd been driving, or it was his car.

Ellen glared at her back as she left.

"Christ," Jerry said. "I'm sorry I got you into that. I didn't think things would get that heavy."

"Why are you sorry?" she demanded. "Don't you think I belong there? Don't you think I can deal with things?" She glared at him too in the dim light from the street lamp, nerves shredded with the suspicion that maybe she couldn't.

"I was trying to take good care of you," Jerry said, stung. He wondered how Daniel Callahan was going to like having his daughter involved in a riot.

"Well, don't worry because apparently nobody can see me," Ellen snapped. "Women who have the hots for you, guys who want to beat you up. I appear to be transparent."

Jerry laughed. "Judy doesn't have the hots for me. She's my mom's friend."

"The hell she doesn't." Ellen refused to believe he didn't know it either. She flicked an eye at him as she started the car. "I'm taking you home next. While you're planning the revolution tomorrow, I have to go to work."

Farther up the valley the ghost floated, the piece of Randy Ottley that had learned to detach itself, trying to go inside his house, inside his room with the chess club jacket on the wall, his model trains waiting on the table he'd built for them, where his mother dusted them every morning. His feet were blistered raw inside boots he had polished incorrectly and been made to run in another two miles, and then another five for going to sick call. He tried to blot out the never-ending fear, that he would vomit again or cry exhausted over a hole to be dug just to be filled in, of the drill sergeant, of night fire practice in the darkness. The flagpole swam in his vision like a beacon. Beyond it he could see the orange groves and the coyotes trotting along the ridge line, brushy tails carried low.

A voice cut through the thick air, "Hump it, Ottley!" A boot connected with his ribs and he clung frantically to the fading vision of the flag on its pole. The coyotes raised their rifles and fired at him.

Jean Ottley heard the sirens and stood on the front lawn looking past the street lamps. The night felt restless and unhealthy. The sirens got louder. Jean tipped her head back so she could see the flagpole, upright against the sky, and leaned her cheek against the cool metal. The sirens rose and fell and the wisps of cloud overhead looked curdled in the red glow of the lights from downtown, as if they were trying to spit something out.

III
ELLEN AND THE PILL

I took this last night." Ellen set her roll of film on the city editor's desk. "There was a big scene in Ayala with an antiwar vigil and some local pro-war people and the police. I thought maybe you could use it."

He looked at her blankly.

"I'm Ellen Callahan."

"Oh, the summer hire in Soc." He pronounced it "Sock," short for Society. He shook his head. "We didn't have anybody up there. You don't expect riots in Ayala." He chuckled.

"*I* was up there."

"Oh. Yeah."

"The sheriff's department got called in. Not just the local police. They were going after people with nightsticks."

The city editor smiled at her. "Well, I'll look at your pics, hon."

"He threw my film in the wastebasket!" Ellen said. "I *saw*

25

him." She smacked her fist on the steering wheel. "He didn't even have it developed! As soon as I went back to my desk he tossed it."

"They don't want to hear about the fuzz being bad boys," Jerry said. "It might make the antiwar movement look good."

"He didn't want to look at it because I'm female! We don't get to do anything but write up Luci Johnson's wedding. I spent all *last* summer describing her goddamn dress!" Every society section in the country had swooned over a White House wedding. Ellen's department had devoted an entire breathless page to the trousseau while the men in the newsroom were reporting on the space program.

"Maybe you're in the wrong profession," Jerry suggested. His opinion was that most of what the papers printed was either fatuous or a flat-out lie. It was one of the arguments they entertained themselves with late at night, sitting in her car.

"Maybe I'm the wrong sex," she said.

"Not for me." Jerry leaned over and bit her ear, his hands up under her blouse. The emergency brake dug into her thigh. They couldn't do this at her house unless her parents weren't home, and she hadn't the nerve to do it at his parents' house, although he assured her it would be cool. Jerry's mother Dreama was going to college too. Ellen had never talked about philosophy and art with anyone's mother before. She hadn't met his father yet, only knew that he was Austrian, another thing beyond her experience.

Jerry's hand was up under her skirt now, and he was trying to pull her into his lap. She kept getting stuck on the gear shift. "This is an awful car to make out in," he said. She wouldn't get in the back seat with him because what if a cop came along, but all the same for the last two months they'd spent most of their time in her car.

"If you got your license," Ellen said, "you could get a car

that didn't have bucket seats." He knew how to drive but had never bothered with a license.

"No bread," he said into her ear.

"How do you get to school?"

"Hitchhike. If you will get off the subject of the damn car, I will promise to take you on an actual date. How's that?"

"A real date?"

"Truly. Dinner. At the Firebird. I will look respectable enough to please your mother."

"Did you get a job?" Jerry's friend Robert worked evenings at the Firebird.

"Sort of. Enough for a dinner." He bit her ear and she knew something would happen after that dinner. They'd been working up to it for a while. Unexpectedly, he whispered, "I love you."

"I love you too," she said. She snuggled against him, resisting the temptation to ask what they were going to do about that in the long run.

A breeze came up, blending the eucalyptus with the warm scent of sage from the chaparral on the hills. This month's moon had waned to a curved dish above them. Jerry pulled her to his chest. He did love her, so much that sometimes he thought it would stop his heart, but he didn't know what to do about it either, besides the obvious. "These days I can sleep at night," he offered. "I think that's because of you."

"You're really serious about this guy, aren't you?" Teak sounded envious.

"There's no way I can go to a doctor in Ayala." Ellen was running her finger down the listings in the Yellow Pages. Ayala was tiny, a combination of intellectual retreat, bedroom town for Hollywood, and haven for Theosophists and folk dancers. Her parents seemed to know all of them. LA was blessed anonymity.

"There's a clinic on Fairfax," Ellen said. Teak pushed the telephone at her. That was what she liked about Teak. No matter what she was going to do, Teak never made her feel it was ill-advised or a nice girl wouldn't do it. Teak had been taking birth control pills for two years.

Ellen had a story prepared, about being engaged. She couldn't summon up the nerve to just come out and say she wanted to sleep with her boyfriend. Taking the Pill at all was controversial. Some doctors wouldn't prescribe it for anyone. Apparently if you were female it was immoral to want to have sex just for fun, even if you were married.

She dialed the number and the woman on the other end listened patiently as she babbled earnestly into the receiver. She couldn't tell whether the woman believed her story or not, but she got an appointment for the afternoon.

She hung up and grinned at Teak, feeling giddy. "Oh, my God, what if some old lady my mother knows happens to be driving down Fairfax and sees me?"

"You could wear a disguise. Dark glasses. A trench coat."

"Oh God, I know they're going to want to call." She wasn't eighteen yet, she'd skipped sixth grade and her birthday wasn't until September. "The appointment's for three o'clock. *Please* don't forget and let somebody else answer the phone." Teak was a receptionist, she was supposed to answer the phone, but what if— "You can't even go to the bathroom. Not till they call you."

"Fear not," Teak said. "Yes, indeed, doctor, this *is* Mrs. Callahan, although I have to pee. You may certainly prescribe birth control for dear Ellen, we wouldn't want her to get knocked up, now would we?" She gave it a snooty accent and a quaver as if she were about ninety years old.

"Oh, shit, they won't believe you. They'll put me in jail or something."

"You could wait till September," Teak said.

"I have to go back to school then." She wasn't going to wait until September, not now that she had made up her mind.

Teak was dressing to go to work. "What does your mother think about him?" she asked, pulling a black silk blouse past her curlers.

"She'd rather I went out with some nice boy who wears shoes."

Teak chuckled. She wriggled into a pair of pantyhose and pulled on a suede miniskirt and high heels and disappeared into the bathroom to brush her hair out. Just now, aside from Martin she was going out with her boss, who she said looked like a toad, and wanted her to marry him and bear his toadlets. Teak seemed to take up with rich older men or lost young ones. Martin was the most normal of her men. She gave Ellen a thumbs-up sign and sailed out the door, a fringed leather bag swinging from one shoulder. After a minute Ellen heard her car start up. Teak's apartment was up a side road in Laurel Canyon, a postage-stamp house clinging to the hillside. The tiny bathroom had deep purple walls and a strange assortment of souvenirs: feathers, drawings, painted rocks. The main room had a record player, cinder-block shelves, and Teak's bed with a llama-skin blanket on it.

Ellen sat on the llama skin and worried about public humiliation until two-thirty. Then she got in her car and drove down Laurel Canyon into Hollywood. The landscape on Fairfax was a mix of palm trees, dusty bird-of-paradise, strip joints and Hebrew bookstores.

The clinic was shabby and made her feel furtive. She sat in an orange plastic chair with her ankles crossed and made sure the little diamond her godmother had given her showed on her ring finger.

"...And well, my mother thinks I should, because we might get married pretty quickly." Was she talking too much?

The doctor looked attentive but suspicious, with some kind of form in his hand. "What is your fiancé's name, please?"

Ellen froze. Was he going to write that down? She couldn't tell him, Jerry. What if somebody saw that? She blurted "Carl Leeman." He was safely distant. The backs of her thighs were sticking to the plastic chair. She felt light-headed. What if she fainted in the examining room? She imagined dropping, sweeping with her the glass jars of cotton balls and tongue depressors, a whirlwind of glass settling on the greasy rug.

"Of course, you understand we'll need your parents' permission to prescribe," the doctor said.

"My parents are divorced," she said. Her parents had been married forever. "You can call my mother at work. She's expecting the call." She gave him Teak's number.

"I see." The doctor turned it over in his fingers. "Tell me, what does your fiancé do?"

"He's in school," Ellen said, panicked. "At Stanford." Why had she picked Stanford? Nobody would believe Carl had gotten into Stanford. Was he going to want an address?

The doctor stuck his head out of the examining room, possibly to call in a fearsome nurse, the woman Ellen had seen in the hallway, who had a permanent wave like her P.E. teacher and would disapprove of premarital sex. "Call Mrs. Callahan at this number for permission to prescribe for her daughter," he said.

Ellen held her breath. "I'll be back in a moment," the doctor said.

He was back in twenty minutes, long enough for Ellen to decide he was calling the police, he'd gotten her parents' real phone number from Information, she ought to climb up on the examining table and crawl out the one high window. But it had chicken wire in the opaque glass and looked as if it was painted shut.

"These'll start you off." He placed a cardboard disk with twenty-one pills in individual bubbles in her hand, along with a prescription slip. "You can take this to the pharmacy next door. They'll give you a six-month supply." He patted her hand absently and left. He hadn't examined her or even asked any questions about her periods.

She drove back to Ayala and hid the pills in her dresser drawer. The doctor hadn't believed a word she said, she realized. He didn't care if she was sleeping with her boyfriend. If he thought premarital sex was immoral he wouldn't be running a birth control clinic.

Jerry had some suspicion as to why Ellen had gone to see Teak on a day that required her to call in sick to the newspaper, but he wasn't going to tip the balance of their relationship with clinical questions. Whatever came along, or didn't, would be worth it. Which was funny, he thought, because the world hadn't changed and it was still likely to blow itself to hell at any given moment and take him with it, but until it did, he had this.

As if to prove the fleeting moment, the day's mail was spread out on the kitchen counter. He crumpled the new letter from the draft board and put it in the trash can. Its contents seemed as incomprehensible as a communiqué from the moon.

"I need a tie again," he told his father.

His father raised one eyebrow. "A tie?" Raymond Manoury still had the accent, the Viennese articulation that lent importance to anything he said. It was very hard for Jerry's father to sound frivolous.

"Yeah. I'd ask Ma, but she doesn't wear them."

"This is serious, this girl." His father smiled and picked out a navy blue tie with thin yellow stripes. Jerry suspected he was also hoping Ellen was going to be a good influence.

Jerry buttoned his good white shirt and knotted the tie.

"You look as if you are about to strangle. Here. Wear this, too." Raymond handed him the dark blue blazer. "If this keeps up, we will have to buy you one."

Jerry's younger brother gave him a wolf whistle as he went through the living room when Ellen knocked. His mother shot him a speculative look from the kitchen. His father, having provided suitable attire, was now reading his newspaper and didn't look up.

Jerry wondered, not for the first time, how the two of them ever got together. Raymond and his grandmother had fled Vienna just ahead of the Germans, and Raymond had tried to join the Army and kill Nazis but they wouldn't take him because he'd had TB. Dreama had left Iowa for California and Raymond was probably the first Jew she'd ever met. As Jerry understood it, he and his brother had been baptized because Dreama's mother wouldn't shut up until they were, but God hadn't given either of his parents much reason to be religious. Jerry wasn't entirely sure what he was. Agnostic might sum it up. He couldn't bring himself to believe in much, but he couldn't give up hope entirely either. Ellen seemed a form of hope.

Ellen smiled when she saw the coat and tie and he took her hand and hustled her out before anybody had any comments.

At the restaurant they sat stiffly, pretending to be grown-ups. They were both too young to order wine. Ellen had bought a new dress for the night, with a high waist and pale flowers like a Jacobean tapestry printed on some wispy material. Robert was clearing one of the other tables. He grinned at them and shook his head, as if Jerry had done something unexpected and possibly mad or dangerous. They ordered T-bone steaks and took the leftovers in a white doggy bag with a poodle on it, for Ellen's actual dog. As they were leaving, Jerry said quietly, "There's a place I want to take you."

He gave her directions out to the East End. It was dark now and the road they turned onto wound through an avocado orchard. A pair of coyotes trotted across in front of them, eyes gleaming in the headlights. The road turned to gravel and ran between oak trees, then ended in front of a fieldstone house with a Chinese lantern vine over the door. Its pale pods rustled against the torn screen.

"Who lives here?" There were no lights on.

"A friend of mine rents it," Jerry said. "Looks like he's not home tonight, though." She looked at him with growing suspicion, and he grinned. "Come on."

He took her hand, and she thought, *Well, I said I was going to. It's what I got the pills for.* Only what if he thought her body was ugly, once he saw it? What if she wasn't any good at this? She assumed that Jerry had had plenty of practice.

The coyotes yipped in the orchard and when he opened the door, which wasn't locked, a tiger cat, who had been hanging around on the porch, whipped in past their ankles.

"Not a good night to be out, Lunchbucket," Jerry said, scratching its ears.

The tiger cat jumped up on the wide window ledge, and sat looking out, ears flattened.

The front room had an old sofa and a stone fireplace. A guitar leaned against the wall, under a lamp with a torn shade. On the bar that separated the living room from the kitchen was a glass ashtray with a joint and a note that read ENJOY. Jerry peered at it and raised his eyebrows at their unexpected good fortune.

Over his shoulder she saw an open doorway and the foot of a brass bed. He lit the joint and she took a long drag. When she blew the smoke out, Jerry kissed her and it was hard to tell what was the pot and what was Jerry. They went into the bedroom, taking the joint and the ashtray with them, and pretty soon the ashtray and Jerry's glasses were on the floor.

"Jerry, whose house is this? What if they come home?" Ellen sat up, suddenly panic-stricken. She looked around for her dress, wondering how fast she could get it on.

"He won't be back till morning," Jerry said. He was pulling his pants off.

"Who?"

"Aaron. It's cool. He won't come back."

She remembered the boy with the bushy dark hair. He'd made her uncomfortable, and she still wondered what he'd been in jail for.

"Hey, honey." Jerry had stopped suddenly, his hands on her shoulders. He was looking in her face. "If you don't want to do this now, it's okay. I don't want to do anything too soon."

"No! No, I do want to." She put the thought of Aaron coming home early out of her mind. Jerry slid out of his jeans and she tried not to let him catch her staring, though she suspected that without his glasses he couldn't tell what she was looking at.

He shifted her gently so that her head was on the pillow, and she forgot to be embarrassed and worry about what she looked like because Jerry so plainly thought she was beautiful.

She'd heard that the first time wasn't supposed to be much fun, but somebody had been wrong about that.

IV
GODDESS OF MERCY

Quit that!" Ellen looked around guiltily. They were sitting on the sofa in her living room while they waited for dinner and Jerry was biting her ear. She'd invited him even though it felt like sitting on a bomb to watch Jerry and her parents make small talk. Especially when he was wearing only jeans and a denim vest and a string of beads.

Lily Callahan had refrained from asking Jerry why he wasn't wearing a shirt, but Ellen knew she wanted to. Especially now they'd found out she was downtown while Ayala was having its only riot. Lily had called Martin's mother and Martin's mother had said someone broke Martin's guitar case and he had a black eye and one of the other boys had a cut on his head. Ellen's father had applauded her initiative in taking photographs. She hadn't told him nobody wanted them.

Now they both had to explain exactly where it was that Ellen was going to stay when she and Jerry went to San Francisco together.

They both thought of this trip as their big adventure, a last chance before Ellen went back to school. They'd been to L.A. twice to stay with Teak, though Ellen's parents hadn't known Jerry was staying there too. He had a convincing number of friends in Los Angeles. Now they planned something better.

35

Ellen would quit the paper a week early and they'd stay with a respectable woman friend of Jerry's mother in Berkeley.

"It's cool," Jerry said confidently. "Ana's my mom's old friend. She'll be glad to have us."

"Who else will be there?" Ellen's father asked.

"Robert may come along," Jerry said.

"Maybe Martin," Ellen said.

"Well...." Lily said. Ellen had gone to school with Martin Alvarez and Ellen knew she approved of Robert as long as Ellen wasn't dating him. Mixed-race couples were just asking for trouble all their lives, Lily had said, casually, to Ellen, just in case.

"Mother, I'll be fine," she said, trying not to say it through gritted teeth.

"It's not that we don't trust you, dear," Lily said.

"It's that you don't trust anybody else, and who knows who I may meet up there." She could recite her mother's reasoning by heart, but the dangers that worried Lily seemed so foreign to the real dangers that her mother didn't even know about that Ellen felt as if she were reading "Advice To My Daughter" from a vintage copy of *Ladies Home Journal.* There was no way even to explain that she'd be better off with Jerry, because he knew where to stay away from, the places that might explode under your feet, than she would be with a bevy of her equally naive girlfriends, which had been Lily's first suggestion.

"Well..." Lily said again.

"We'll expect you to leave phone numbers," Daniel Callahan said. He bent an interested eye on Jerry. "How's summer school?"

"Like being trapped in a bad training film," Jerry said. "To be honest."

"What are you going to do when you finish with that?"

"I don't know." He shrugged and gave Ellen a smile. "Go check out the scene, I guess."

"Not much future in checking out the scene," Daniel commented.

Ellen looked at her hands. Why couldn't he just lie, for God's sake? She'd already had this argument with him. She didn't want to listen to him have it again with her parents.

"There's not much future in anything if you don't know what you want," Jerry said. "I can't see going to college just to go to college, just to have *been* to college, so that I'm a good boy and some corporation will graciously hire me."

"I see. And what do you think you'll do instead?" Daniel gave Jerry his full attention.

"That's what I need to find out."

Ellen's father shook oil and vinegar onto his salad. "You're very intelligent," he commented. "Don't you feel the most intelligent ones in a given population have an obligation to use their intelligence for the betterment of the rest of society?"

"It depends on how long you expect the rest of society to last, man," Jerry said. "And what you think of it to start with."

"I think it's better than any of our current alternatives," Daniel said.

Ellen drew a pattern in the condensation on her water glass. She never managed to get the better of her father in these discussions, though they had been good training for arguing with Jerry.

"Then maybe we should be changing the alternatives," Jerry said, "instead of wringing our hands and saying, 'Oh, no, we couldn't possibly live a different way, we couldn't possibly be fair to *everybody*, that would take something away from *me*!'"

"That's what people run for public office for," Daniel said. "To change the system."

"In other words, I can change the system, but first I have to go to college and run for office and make compromises and be co-opted by the system." Jerry pushed his glasses up on his nose.

37

"No way, man."

"Do you want dessert?" Ellen said, irritated with both of them. They'd be at it all night while she pushed cherry tomatoes around in her salad.

"Sure," Jerry said. "Now, look—"

"The system's only the sum of its parts." Daniel waved an arm to encompass whatever parts might be within reach. Lily took his plate out from in front of him while he did.

"The democratic ideality," Jerry retorted. "I bought into that when I was little. I bought into Kennedy's speech—before they offed him. 'Ask not what your country can do for you.' I got goose bumps. I bought into the civil rights movement and the Peace Corps. I figured we were going to change the world." He leaned back while Ellen slid peach pie in front of him. "I thought we were the good guys," he said with disgust.

"And how have you earned the privilege of deciding what the common good is?" Daniel inquired. "That generally requires the paying of some apprentice fee. Some dues, if you will." He stuck a fork in his pie.

Then after dessert Ellen's parents both went off to play poker with friends and left them alone in the house.

Jerry was still trying to figure it, decide if there was some trap. The Callahans' house made him uneasy, as if the snare might be physical, some trap door under the Chinese rug, ready to suck him down through the furnace duct and deposit him outdoors, safely outside the princess's tower. Ellen's parents were unfailingly kind, which was also outside his experience of parents of girls who were interested in him. Sometimes he thought they liked him. At other times, though, he thought they just came from a place where you were nice to people whether you liked them or not.

Robert, Martin, and Ellen took turns driving Ellen's VW north since Jerry's lack of a license had convinced her they'd all get tickets if he got caught driving without one. They stopped to wade in the tide pools near San Simeon, wiggling bare toes in the frigid, crystalline water. They folded the top down and put their faces to the sun and the salty wind along the Big Sur coast, where the road wound like a goat track above aquamarine coves and the jagged brown basking places of the seal rocks.

Hitchhikers flocked along the Pacific Coast Highway, in fringed vests and dirty jeans, with knapsacks, guitar cases, and signs that read SAN FRANCISCO or SEATTLE, part of the endless migration that summer to wherever something interesting might be happening.

To Jerry, despite his cynicism, it still seemed a sign that something was happening that might not come again, some way of living that might even bring to fruition their parents' and grandparents' ideas of utopia. He watched the red and white signs ticking past them on the highway:

OTHERS THINK
THEIR PRODUCT GOOD
BUT OURS DOES WHAT
YOU THINK IT SHOULD
BURMA SHAVE

They'd left at dawn and it was evening when they came into San Francisco, then across the Bay Bridge while Jerry read directions to Ellen. She took the wrong ramp and they found themselves driving along the Oakland mud flats past a field of driftwood sculpture backlit by the bay and the red sun— airplanes, running men, women holding flowers, all made of planks nailed together, floating above the mud. They looked as if they might keep going, striding across the bay.

She slowed the car and stopped in a rutted, half paved square that might once have been a gas station. They loped across the mud flats, giddy with discovery, to stand peering up at the statues. Each figure was nailed to a post so that it lifted above the ground, already on its way.

They stayed until the sun fell behind the skyline across the bay and it got suddenly cold, a sandy, estuarine smell rising from the water.

Ana's place proved to be an old wooden house on Shattuck Avenue and Ana Salazar a willowy woman in her thirties in an apron and a long paisley dress with trailing sleeves. She met them at the door with a joint in her hand.

"Welcome, good people." She took a closer look at Jerry. "Hey, you grew."

"This is Ellen," Jerry said. He tucked her into his arm. "And Martin, and Robert."

"Wow," Ana said, looking at Martin's guitar case. "Music. Far out." She waved them all into the house and drifted back to the kitchen, visible through a doorway from the living room.

Jerry dumped their bags on a sofa covered with an Indian bedspread that looked like Ana's dress, while Ellen craned her neck around, taking in books and a tumble of laundry on the floor.

Ana was making soup. She called over her shoulder, "I have to go to work at eight, but Starsong and Mickey are supposed to be here. Do you remember her? She used to be Susan."

"Little thing?" Jerry called back. "Big eyes like an owl?"

"Yeah. Mickey's her old man. They're on their way to Tucson. She does charts, you should let her do yours."

"Actually we thought we'd go back out and see the sights. I want to go to North Beach," Jerry said. "See City Lights Books. Walk in the footsteps of the great."

"Sure," Ana said. "Go to the Hungry i so you can tell Dreama you've been." She cocked her head at Martin. "There's usually good music."

Martin shook his head. "I'll pass. I need to see a guy up here. I'll catch you in the morning," he said to Jerry.

Robert had gone to sleep on the couch, his head tilted back against the wall.

"You two have fun," Ana said.

"What does she do?" Ellen whispered to Jerry as they went out the door.

"Bartender," Jerry said. "Some club in Oakland. She just got divorced again and she's trying to get it together." Lately it seemed to him that everybody was trying to get something together; either that or letting it hang loose enough to be dangerous.

In North Beach they walked hand in hand past Italian eateries, through the smells of tomato sauce and red wine, to the Hungry i, as hip and smoky and closet-like as they'd both imagined.

"Hip was here before hip got hip," Jerry said. Since the late forties, North Beach had been the home of poets and dreaming malcontents. He suspected there wasn't much that the hippies, dewy-eyed and fresh from Omaha and Bakersfield, could teach the old guard.

"Martin should have come," Ellen said. She couldn't imagine why Martin had passed up the Hungry i.

41

"He's got something going," Jerry said. "I don't know what. Or maybe he always looks that knotted up. I don't know him."

"No, he looks funny to me, too." They chewed on that thought for a few minutes and then gave it up while a girl with long black hair and thin white hands like birds' feathers sang huskily in the dim light under a blue spot.

When it was late they walked down Columbus Avenue to City Lights Books, open all night and owned by Lawrence Ferlinghetti. Happy tourists, they lost each other in its claustrophobic warren of nooks and crannies, stairs and unexpected small balconies, browsing through poetry and philosophy, Anaïs Nin, Sartre and Beauvoir, Hesse, Kerouac, Ginsburg and Corso, Edward Albee, James Baldwin, Eldridge Cleaver, Norman Mailer, Ken Kesey, Tom Wolfe, books on how to avoid the draft and how to grow pot, all the revolutionaries and troublemakers past and present.

He could live there, Jerry thought. He could live in a bookstore; have a little room in the back, with a cot and a hot plate, make just enough money to buy more books. It seemed a fantastic notion, as distant and seductive as paradise. "What do you want?" his high school counselor had kept asking. But living in a bookstore seemed an inadequate answer.

Ellen was yawning when they got in the car, sleepy enough to let him drive. She woke only once on the bridge to ask if he'd remembered to flip the reserve lever over when he filled the car.

"It's fine," Jerry said. "Go back to sleep." He eased the Volkswagen around a lumbering bread truck. The car had no gas gauge. It had a second tank that held a gallon and was opened by a lever on the floor. When you ran out of gas, you flipped the lever. Then you had thirty miles to find gas. If you didn't flip it back, the reserve tank drained too, and when you were out, you were out.

German engineering at its finest, Jerry thought, and then as always there was that little twitch when he thought of Germany, or Austria. One half of him had something in the blood, some racial memory that would always be there, that would not be washed away by baptisms or atheism or ignorance. His grandmother had cooked the traditional food, braided loaves of challah, matzoh ball soup, and tzimmes, but no one had ever said they were Jewish. No one talked about Vienna, or leaving it. Or who had not made it out. Had there been more, Jerry wondered, had they died in the camps? Aunts and cousins he hadn't known about? He'd never been able to ask his father.

He woke Ellen up outside Ana's house, and they tiptoed in to find the lights off, except for a lamp in the kitchen and a note from Ana: THE ROOM NEXT TO THE BATHROOM IS YOURS. THERE MAY BE SOMEONE ELSE IN THERE TOO. PEACE. ANA.

Ellen looked too sleepy to protest, and he pointed her at the bathroom and then the room beside it. He dragged her suitcase in from the living room. A mattress by the door was empty, but they could hear faint breathing from the other side of the room.

"Who is it?" Ellen whispered.

"Robert?" Jerry suggested. "Or Martin?"

"Robert's asleep in the living room and the way she was looking at Martin, I bet I know where he is." Ellen pulled her nightgown on over her head and began taking her clothes off under it.

"It's J. Edgar Hoover," Jerry said. "It's Richard Nixon in disguise. It's a nun."

She yawned. "Maybe I'm too tired to care who it is."

Jerry lay down next to her until he could hear her breathing deepen into sleep. He knew if he left her there alone she'd freak, but this was a night he wasn't going to be able to sleep. When he thought she was out good, he kissed her forehead and got up again.

Robert was indeed asleep on the couch but Martin wasn't in

Ana's bed. He was sitting up in the dark living room. Jerry caught the brief flare of a cigarette, and Martin's silhouette in the light from the street lamp outside.

"Hey, man," Jerry said quietly.

Martin followed Jerry out onto the porch. He sat on the railing and swung his feet, staring at them as if they kept some internal, involuntary rhythm. "I need a ride into the city in the morning," he said.

Jerry lowered himself into a battered wicker chair by the front door. It listed to the left when he put his weight in it. "So what's happening?"

"Got a letter from the draft board." Martin looked up now, staring at the bell beside Ana's door, where the button dangled from its wiring, as if the nakedness of its exposed workings matched his own. "They turned down my C.O. case."

"Ah, shit, man." Jerry thought about his own letter. He'd tossed it, but he could still feel its presence, like a tarantula, furred legs testing the surface of his skin.

"I talked to a friend at Berkeley tonight," Martin said. "He turned me on to an agency in the Haight that does draft counseling."

"Six secrets to a better C.O.," Jerry said with a ragged grin. "Six proven ways to demonstrate your sincerity without getting ordained." Maybe he should try for a conscientious objection. But you were supposed to believe all war was wrong. Just thinking *this* war was immoral and stupid didn't count.

"He talked about a mental," Martin said. "If you can prove you're crazy. Or homosexual. I heard about a guy who wore women's underwear to his physical, but I don't think it got him off."

"How do you prove you're crazy? Do they give tests?"

"Yeah, but they're hard to fake. If you act too crazy, they know you're not crazy."

"What if you act just a little crazy?"

"Then you're not insane enough. They have rules about it, but only the board knows the rules."

Jerry pulled a joint out of his pocket and lit it. "Want some?"

Martin sucked smoke in and stared at the doorbell. "You can try to prove you're a big time drug addict," he said. "Show up with needle tracks. A pin works. But that seems like a hell of a thing. I heard about a dude who actually did heroin the day of his physical and damn near OD'd. Does that thing actually ring?"

"If you put rubber gloves on," Jerry said, turning to look at the loose wiring. "Otherwise the current goes through you into a metal plate in the floor and powers Ana's sewing machine." He could see the voltage, gold with overtones of tangerine, curling off the doorbell like a slinky and sinking through the porch floor. Or maybe that was the smoke. He leaned back in the chair. "You'd think the Army'd get tired of trying to draft people who're just going to screw up their program."

"It's a matter of discipline," Martin said moodily. "We can't have people running around loose thinking they can run their own lives, decide not to shoot people they never met. It would undermine Society." He passed Jerry the joint.

"Ah, shit, man," Jerry said. "They're gonna yank my 2-S. They said I'm not matriculating at the proper speed, whatever that means."

A car came slowly up Shattuck and Jerry put the joint out in his hand. They stiffened, watching it slow further, then speed up again.

"God," Jerry said. "I feel like some narc is watching me behind every bush anymore. Or the FBI. Robert knows a guy at UCSB who's putting himself through school reporting things he hears people say. Everybody knows who the guy is. Now I'm thinking there have got to be some of those at Ventura, and wondering what I've said." He was silent, cogitating. "I haven't told Ellen any of this."

"Is that fair?"

"Maybe not." Jerry squinted his eyes at the dark yard, determined to see through the complacent laissez-faire of the pot to reality, however unpleasant. Even the air looked tired, as shabby as Ana's porch. "I'll tell her when something happens. Jesus, let us have one summer. Have you told Teak?"

"Yeah. But I don't know what she thinks. I told her I might go to Canada."

"No shit?" That sounded like going to Antarctica, or hell. Irreversible.

"It seemed like an idea at the time." Martin looked bleak. "My old man would shit, though. He already doesn't like the C.O. business."

"Does he figure you should be a patriot?" Jerry was suddenly grateful for his own old man, who'd wanted to fight the Nazis, but didn't see any percentage in fighting Vietnamese.

"I think he's just embarrassed," Martin said bitterly. "It's about what the fellows at the office would say. 'Your kid's a coward, Alvarez.' Randy Ottley's old man is lording it over him because Ottley went in before they dragged him off bodily. I saw him before he left though. I never saw anyone look that green."

The city of night. Ruled by what the fellows at the office would say. Jerry closed his eyes. When he woke, Martin had gone in the house, and the milkman had left two glass bottles by his feet.

"Jerry?" Ellen stuck her head around the door. She was in her nightgown, a kimono wrapped around that.

"Oh, babe." Jerry yawned. "I'm sorry. Did you wake up and worry?" He picked up the milk bottles and came inside. Ellen narrowed her eyes at him.

Ana was at the stove in a chenille bathrobe, frying bacon.

Robert stood beside her, rubbing his eyes. Martin sat at the kitchen table eating corn flakes. A clock on the water-stained wallpaper said 9:25.

"You should go to Sausalito this morning," Ana told him. "There are all these black guys drumming in the park every Saturday. It's wonderful."

"Cool." Jerry's fingers rippled along his thigh in a silent beat, eager to be out of there. The kitchen was gray and gritty, depressing as last night's conversation about how to prove you were a heroin addict, and Ellen was pissed at him. "We need to run into the city first, though."

"One of the people sleeping in our room has a blue penis tattooed on his arm," Ellen informed him.

"That's Mickey," Ana said. She yelled, "Mickey, put your shirt on!"

"It was just an art update," Ellen said. She punched Jerry's arm. "I thought maybe you'd like one, too. Where did you go?"

"I went to sleep on the porch," Jerry said. "Honest."

She disappeared into the bedroom and a minute later went into the bathroom with her clothes under her arm. She emerged in a green silk skirt and a white Mexican blouse. Her hair stood out around her face stiff with static electricity. He wondered if she'd manufactured it personally when she found out he wasn't in bed with her.

"Starsong says men who are born under Scorpio have a very earthy sexuality," she informed Jerry breathlessly.

"He was on the porch," Martin said. "Talking to me. You can ask the milkman if he sleeps with his mouth open."

"Jesus, I must have been a sight." Jerry caught Ellen when she didn't think he was looking, and saw her laughing at him. While he watched, the morning flowered into semi-liquid light that poured through the windows like marigolds, like little butter-colored snowflakes. He grabbed her and kissed the back of her neck, burrowing his face into her hair. "I'll get a blue arm tattooed on my penis," he said in her ear. "How's that?" He'd heard obscene tattoos would keep you out of the Army, but what if they didn't think it was obscene enough? Would you have to keep adding things? And have to live with it afterward.

"We're going to go see a draft counselor in the Haight," he told Ellen and Robert as they got into the car. Martin slid into the driver's seat.

Ellen snapped her head around at Jerry now, eyes wide. "I thought you were 2-S."

"Nothing's permanent," Jerry said. He gave it as much nonchalance as he could manage.

"I lost my C.O. case," Martin said.

"Oh, *no*." Ellen gripped Jerry's arm.

"We're nonessential personnel," Martin said, driving. "The last thing this country needs is more pinko artists. Send 'em off to the Army."

"Well, who's essential?" Ellen demanded.

"Rocket scientists. Fat generals," Martin said. "Corporate typhoons."

"Lady Bird Johnson," Jerry said. "Truman Capote. Hope Cooke."

"Tiny Tim."

"Tiny Tim's not essential," Ellen said.

"Neither are real estate agents. Let's get rid of them." Robert polished his glasses, ready to take his part in the revolution. "And lodge members with stupid hats."

"People who try to sell you *The Watchtower*," Ellen said. "Hare Krishnas in airports."

"Chihuahuas," Martin said.

"No, you have to be human."

Martin crossed the Bay Bridge and threaded the VW through the Financial District.

"Gray flannel suits," Jerry said. "Ties narrower than your nose."

Martin turned off Sansome onto Sacramento and then Grant. In Chinatown traffic slowed to a crawl. The streets were jammed with children and women with baskets of fish, men reading incomprehensible newspapers.

"Do you know where you're going?" Ellen asked him.

"I think I'm lost."

"Stop here," Jerry said as a minuscule parking space appeared.

Martin pulled the car into it, wheels nearly over the curb. "This may not be the best place to ask directions."

"They probably have them pre-printed for every silly hippie who hits town," Jerry said. "'Go to the Haight, don't camp here, please.' Anyway, I'm going to buy something."

They shrugged and followed him, craning their necks at green pagoda roofs climbing the sky like stylized fir trees, and balconies strung with crimson lanterns. The air was a mixture of unfamiliar herbs, noodles cooking, incense and dried seaweed. They peered at the vegetables displayed in grocery windows as Jerry led them beneath a balcony that leaned precariously over the street, and into a narrow shop under a ceiling hung with butterfly kites. Barely navigable passages wound between shelves filled with ivory temples and jade dragons, silk trousers embroidered with red and yellow fish, and paper parasols with red lacquer handles, strung among the kites.

"What are you looking for?" Ellen whispered to Jerry.

"Magic," Jerry said. He inspected an array of seated Buddhas and good luck cats, and turned to the man behind the counter. "Do you have Guan Yin?"

"Guan Yin." The storekeeper bustled to the back and produced an ivory statuette of a standing goddess, one hand upraised. "A very good choice."

"Who is she?" Ellen asked.

Jerry turned her in his hand. "Goddess of mercy," he said. He dug in his pocket for his wallet.

V
BRIGADOON

The draft counseling office was in the bottom of a Victorian row house on Stanyan. Its peeling paint was touched up here and there with yellow brighter than the original, which gave it the air of a raffish marigold. Jefferson Airplane spilled out an open window above the office, where a black and white cat slept on the sill.

The office was staffed by two women in jeans and cotton sweaters and a younger man in a clerical collar. He looked over Martin's C.O. form while Ellen, Jerry and Robert waited on folding chairs with two other long-haired boys and a third who looked out from under a close-cropped thatch with a kind of defiant terror at everyone who came in the door.

He's a deserter, Ellen thought suddenly. She almost said it to Jerry but bit the words back. The room was small. They could hear everything that the counselor was saying to Martin. Would the counselor take him into a back room? She hoped so; his fear saturated the air.

"To be honest, I'm not surprised they turned you down," the counselor said to Martin. "You wrote a good statement here—" he tapped his finger on the form. "But it's the same statement they hear from everybody. The draft boards are flooded with these applications. You practically have to be a member of one of the established peace churches to get C.O. status now."

"Peace churches?"

"Quakers, Amish, Mennonites. Denominations that have traditionally been pacifist." The counselor smiled wryly and touched his collar. "Catholics aren't pacifists, I have it from the local draft board who want to know what the hell I'm doing counseling draft resisters."

"What else can I do?"

"Have you received your induction notice yet?"

"No."

"Good. First you can appeal. If you get turned down again, you can appeal to the state board. You can make that take quite a while. If they give you thirty days to appeal, appeal on the twenty-ninth day."

"What if I get turned down all the way?"

Jerry, listening more closely than he wanted Ellen to know, felt as if they had all somehow put a foot in glue. There seemed no way to cut loose entirely from the government's right to take over their lives at any moment.

"Well, preemptive enlistment is a possibility," the counselor said. "In the National Guard or Reserves or the Coast Guard, although those spots are very hard to get. You generally have to have some connections. And in any case you'd have to do it now because they won't take you if you've already got an induction notice."

"I don't want to go into the military at all," Martin said.

"You can enroll in school, and apply for a deferment. Although that may not last. The 2-S is stinkingly discriminatory in favor of rich white kids. One of our goals is to eliminate it."

"I don't want to go to school either," Martin said. "I'm an artist. I have work to do."

"Then try for a medical exemption. If you have enough money you can find a doctor who can find something the matter with you. Allergies. Chronic athlete's foot. There's a long list of physical peculiarities in the regulations your induction physical won't turn up but theoretically will get you out."

"I don't have any money," Martin said. "It goes with being an artist." He shrugged. "See statement above. Oh, and I play in a band. That makes even less."

The counselor nodded. "I rarely see anybody who has financial resources. They already know how. Or their parents do."

Ellen watched a fly circle the counselor's head like a halo. She clutched the red paper bag with the Guan Yin in it, praying it really was a talisman, a mercy to protect them all.

The counselor tapped his fingers on the papers. "Here are your other options. You can try for a mental but it's not easy and it can haunt you for the rest of your life. Once you've proved you're crazy, it's not easy to prove you aren't, later. And if they give you a 1-Y, they'll make you come back every six months and prove to *them* you're still crazy. Or you can go to Canada, although you must understand that I am *not* counseling you to do that."

There must be regulations, Ellen thought, about how you could legally suggest that someone do something illegal.

"If you did," the counselor was saying carefully, "the Committee To Aid American War Objectors in Vancouver would help you get settled and guide you through the immigration process. But you should know going in you might never be able to come back."

"I'm not ready for that," Martin said. The others waiting in the folding chairs shuffled their feet uneasily. The boy who might be a deserter put his face in his hands.

"No. It may be the hardest route." The counselor rearranged the pencils on his desk, making a neat corral of four of them. He looked up finally with nothing new to say, nothing he probably hadn't said to ten boys already that day. "You can stall and try to wait out the war, or hope they screw up and lose your file somehow. Ask to have your case transferred to another city, then back again. And never try for more than one deferment or exemption at a time. When they turn you down on that one, you wait till the last minute and then try the next. Each time you do that, it'll eat up several months.

"Or you can make a nuisance of yourself and hope to convince them you'd be more trouble than you're worth. Send statements written on bricks or old tires or a banana peel—the draft board has to keep anything you send it for your file, it's the law. Tell them you're a communist. Protest the war publicly, and convince them you'd infect all the other recruits in boot camp. The risk there is that it could backfire and they'll decide to draft you anyway, right away, punitively. You can't tell."

"Jesus," Martin said.

"If it gets down to it, you can refuse induction."

"And go to jail?"

"Usually they give you a second shot at accepting induction. After that, prison terms vary. It's shorter than life in Canada, but you'll have a record and prison's no picnic. I can't advise you to do that. I can only tell you it's a possibility."

Martin's chair scraped slowly on the old carpet, like a ragged breath.

The counselor spread his hands. His fingers had the same marigold-yellow paint in the creases as the house. "Come back when you've reached a decision, and we'll help you with whatever way you want to go."

Martin stood and the other three assembled themselves around him. Ellen shot a last glance at the boy with the cropped hair. He flinched when he saw her looking at him and she turned away.

The morning overcast had burned off when they stepped out

into the street again, and they paused, startled by the crystalline light. A woman in a cerise shawl sat nursing her baby on the stoop next door, beside a man carefully painting a mandala onto his bare left foot. Down the street the Panhandle, the narrow end of Golden Gate Park, was jammed with people amid a jumble of kites and tents. Harmonica music, bells, incense and pot overlaid an earthier smell of dogs and garbage.

"You could get lost here, couldn't you?" Martin said. "Just sink into the surf and disappear." He looked out at the crowd. A pair of cops were wading into it.

"Too lost," Robert said.

"It's like Brigadoon," Jerry said. "You couldn't stay."

"For a while," Martin said.

"Yeah," Jerry said wistfully. "For a while."

Ellen put her arm through his. If Martin and Jerry went into the park, she and Robert would never get them out again. It would be like stepping in a fairy ring. "What about Sausalito?" she asked him.

"Sure," Jerry said. "Too many freaks for you?"

"Mmm."

They walked slowly back toward the car, veering across the street to a head shop with a three-foot Buddha with electric blue eyes in the window. Ellen was willing to shop, Jerry noticed. The head shop smelled like tobacco, pot, and patchouli oil. Every available surface was stacked with Indian bedspreads and blacklight posters, sieves and scales, a wooden salad bowl full of roach clips, and water pipes sitting fatly on their shelves. Rolling papers were available at the cash register, and in the glass case below was a display of stash boxes in sandalwood, lacquerware, cinnabar, even carved jade. The main activity for which the shop sold equipment was illegal, and the accoutrements themselves belied the theory that material possessions were unimportant. The effect was surreal, in a neighborhood in which comparative surreality was hard to achieve.

They bought some incense and a hash pipe as bread-and-butter presents for Ana. On the way out, Ellen saw another Guan Yin in the window, sitting on a red and yellow flower pot beside the electric-eyed Buddha. This one looked alarmed, she thought.

At the end of the Golden Gate was Fort Baker, startling in its proximity as northbound cars came off the bridge. For an instant Ellen looked onto the grounds, and then the highway dived through a huge painted rainbow, and at the end of the tunnel Sausalito nestled on the edge of the Bay, brown and green hills rising at its back. It looked Mediterranean, bathed in a dusty white light, with houses perched on the cliffs above the street. The air smelled like salt and baked bread and diesel oil.

Ana was right about the drummers. In a flat courtyard at least twenty men were beating on African drums, hands flying like birds over the drum skins. Jerry's eyes gleamed and he hunkered down as near as he thought they would be willing to let him get. His hands hovered over his thighs, beating out a soft counterpoint on his jeans.

Ellen curled up a little farther away in the grass and Robert folded himself up beside her. He watched the drummers, like Ellen not ready to be caught up in it, holding back and suspicious. "You know why these guys live here?" he whispered in her ear.

"They don't just come for whatever this is?"

"No. Sausalito's where there are no rules, sexually speaking." He sounded like the sociology student he was, safely enrolled at

UC Santa Barbara for the fall. "Most of these guys have white old ladies. How many mixed couples did you see in the Haight? Or how many black people for that matter?"

"Not many," Ellen said.

"They live here because nobody gives them any shit here," Robert said. "Most of the rest of the guys here go for guys, so no one's in a position to get snotty."

A place for everybody, Ellen thought. The Haight for hippies, Sausalito for mixed couples and homosexuals. Neat boxes, keeping everyone from stoning each other to death. Despite its lefty politics, her private school had been entirely white. Robert was almost the only black guy she knew. And where did the lesbians live, she wondered. Ellen had never met a lesbian as far as she knew, and wondered what could possibly be fun about sex with a girl.

The curve of human desire seemed to be wide and almost incomprehensible. Looking at the drummers, she couldn't tell which ones lived here for love of some white woman and which for lovers of their own sex, black or white. Their hair grew wildly in afro bushes, their torsos clothed in red and green dashikis. Their skin color varied from sandstone to ebony and they looked like a visual poem in shades of brown. They were very beautiful. Martin had got his sketchbook out.

She saw that Jerry had edged closer and one of the drummers was grinning at him and holding out his drum. Jerry jumped up and knelt in the circle with the others, hands skimming the drum. He closed his eyes and Ellen could see the sound wash over him like surf, like breaking spray.

"He's in heaven," Robert said. He smiled and tucked his arm around her shoulders. The beat caught them up too and they let go, swaying on the grass.

It was a sitting dance, a celebration that washed away the war for an hour, the drummers shaking their wild hair, seeming to lift off the ground, so that Ellen wouldn't have been surprised if the park had lifted too, revolving in the air above the bay, borne on the drums. If you really wanted to levitate, she thought, you might do it here.

It was evening when they started back, gratified that no one had seemed to mind the three white kids in their midst, convinced that civilization was possible after all. The Golden Gate swam with fog now, fat furry clouds like caterpillars crawling through its rust-red tiers. Ellen drove and Jerry sat in the front seat drumming his fingers on his knees. His dark hair curled around his ears. His eyes watched the fog caterpillars from behind his glasses.

They would stop in Berkeley and get something to cook for dinner at Ana's, maybe spaghetti, and maybe there wouldn't be anyone in their room tonight. She looked sideways at Jerry. The drumming fingers slid off his thigh onto hers.

By mutual, silent agreement, Jerry and Ellen cleaned Ana's kitchen together before they cooked. The air was thick with chlorine and Pine-Sol and Ana seemed gratified. Martin gave her a sketch he'd made of the drummers and she taped it to the kitchen wall. Mickey and Starsong appeared and hovered in the doorway. Starsong was elfin, reedy and pale with wide protuberant, brown eyes and a fall of dark hair. Mickey was thick-shouldered, with the muscular aggressiveness of a young bull. He wore his t-shirt with the sleeves rolled up to show his tattoo. The penis had balls attached and appeared to be racing down a highway. It had a cloud of dust behind it.

Through the kitchen window, Ellen saw a butter-colored

Cadillac pull up in front of the house. Mickey went out the front door to talk to whoever was in it.

"I don't eat meat," Starsong told them apologetically as Ellen's hand hovered above a skillet, balancing two pounds of hamburger.

"I'll make meatballs. You can pick them out." Ellen dropped wads of the hamburger in the skillet.

"I could do your charts," Starsong said. She seemed to want to stay in the kitchen. "I have this theory—"

Mickey came back. "We're splitting in the morning. Bring me a beer." He disappeared into the living room.

"Nice," Ellen said as Starsong got the beer and trotted after him.

"That's just Mickey," Ana said. She was ironing a red miniskirt in the corner of the kitchen. "Starsong says he gets uptight around new people."

"He's an asshole," Jerry said.

Ana shrugged. "She didn't have to get him the beer. Starsong and Mickey are like completely free people. They don't even have a house."

In the living room, Mickey was sitting on the sofa with his feet on a table. Ellen ransacked Ana's spice rack and tipped oregano, basil and marjoram into the sauce on the stove. A cloud of tomato/basil steam bubbled up from the pot, eclipsing the Pine-Sol. Jerry, who had a thing for train wreck ballads, was singing a gruesome example and chopping onions.

"Murdered upon the railway, and laid in a lonesome grave..." He wiped his eyes with the back of his hand.

Starsong pattered in again. She glanced at the cooking meat and a grimace of nausea crossed her face. "Mickey wants another beer," she whispered. She sidled closer to Jerry and kneaded his shoulders. "You're all tense," she said. "I'll have to give you a back rub."

Jerry's eyes flicked toward Ellen. "Got to chop my onions," he told Starsong. "Otherwise we don't eat."

Ellen poked the meatballs around in the skillet and Starsong disappeared. It was like playing house, Ellen thought, with people you didn't know well whose habits were uninviting.

When they had eaten, Robert and Martin did the dishes with Ana, passing Ana's new pipe back and forth between them. Ellen and Jerry stayed for what seemed like a decently polite interval and then raised their eyebrows at each other with suggestive smiles. They tiptoed down the hall.

The lights in their room were off, but when Ellen opened the door she found Mickey and Starsong having a tight-faced, hissed argument in the corner. She started to back out again, but Jerry slid in behind her and they had their own *sotto voce* argument by the half-open door.

"Isn't there anywhere else we can stay?" Ellen whispered.

"You'll hurt Ana's feelings." Jerry looked at her anxiously. "Babe, what's eating you?"

She wondered if they could possibly be participating in the same conversation. "I'd like to be *alone* with you for more than two minutes at a stretch."

"Oh." Jerry eyed the couple in the corner. "They're about to crash."

"That doesn't help if they do it in here!"

He snuggled his hands around her waist. "I want to get laid too," he whispered. He tugged at her until she was sitting down on the mattress with him.

"Not in a room with them in it!" she hissed.

"Not even if they're snoring? Old Mickey's gonna topple in a minute. He's had about too much party. He's gonna be blue for true when he wakes up."

She felt Jerry's hand slide up under her blouse. "Quit it! I can't make love with you in front of other people!" From the other end of the room came the angry murmur of slurred voices and then the smack of a hand and the crash of breaking glass. They both started to get up.

Before they could stand, Mickey stalked past, lurching. Starsong followed him, whispering venomously, "You just want to go to Tucson by yourself and fuck everything there while I'm doing charts for some fat old pig in a suit! It *is* charts, isn't it? It *better* be charts."

Mickey rounded on her in the hallway and they both slammed against the wall. "It's good bread. We need it for me to get us set up in Tucson. Shut up."

"Fuck you."

"Jesus," Jerry said. He pushed the door closed and felt for the key that hung on a shoestring from the doorknob. Ellen heard it turn in the lock.

After a minute someone tried the knob and swore.

"Jerry—"

"The hell with him, he can sleep on the porch."

They heard Mickey grumbling in the hall, and Starsong's angry whine. Martin was playing his guitar in the living room. He and Ana were singing. Jerry started working on the waistband of Ellen's skirt again, and she let him. At least they weren't right in the same room. Starsong and Mickey had made love in there just before dawn with *her* in it, noisily. She had lain there frozen, wondering where the hell Jerry was. And then Starsong had sat up and started a *conversation* with her. She was an old friend of Jerry's, so she said.

"Who *is* that woman?" Ellen asked Jerry.

"Who? Lift your butt so I can get your skirt off."

"*Starsong*, or whatever her real name is."

"Just someone my mom knew. She stayed at the house a while back."

"Did you sleep with her?" she demanded.

"Does it matter?" He sounded as if he hadn't thought of that, as if there was no reason for that to make a difference. He took his hand off her leg.

"Theoretically, no."

To Jerry, Ellen didn't sound as if theoretically meant actually. "Yeah, once," he admitted. "Neither one of us had anything else going. It was before I met you."

"Then why didn't you tell me?" They were each propped on an elbow now, arguing in whispers.

"I didn't think you'd care."

"Oh, right."

He sighed. "Look, if you want to just give up on this and go out there and socialize, it's okay. I'll understand."

"No," Ellen said, pigheaded now. There was no noise in the hall. Everyone in the house knew what they were doing, but at least they weren't in here with them. She felt as if she'd been sucked into some demented alternate universe. She buried her face in Jerry's chest and wrapped her arms around his back, hanging on.

In the morning Robert was in the kitchen, eating cold spaghetti, and Mickey and Starsong were sorting clothes into two packs. (Jerry had unlocked the door around midnight.) Martin and Ana were nowhere to be seen. Ellen thought indignantly of Teak, but she didn't know what she could do. She wasn't the chaperone. And she had all she could do lately to figure out her own love life.

Starsong was packing rumpled clothes that might have been anything at all. Her hands were spidery with splitting nails. Every so often she looked at Mickey and made a sort of hiss and he lifted a hand and let it drop back again. She had a thin blue bruise under one eye.

"I told you, there's no place for you to stay," Mickey said.

Jerry made coffee and Ellen fled to the front porch with hers. Jerry sat next to her on an old sofa and picked up the newspaper that lay rolled on the floor. A tortoiseshell cat came from somewhere and stretched its toes in front of them in a pool of sun. The morning began to slide toward normality. The butter-yellow Cadillac pulled up in front of the house and a scream from the living room flung her against Jerry.

"You motherfucker!" Ana yelled. "Son of a bitch bastard, *hijo de la chingada!*" She appeared in the doorway in her robe with Martin behind her. "Get out!"

Mickey and Starsong came through the door, dragging duffel bags.

"Get *out!*" Ana screamed at Mickey again.

Mickey didn't look at Ana. Starsong looked blank, an almost botanical inertness, both arms wrapped around her pack. They went down the steps to the Caddy. An arm reached out the driver's window and handed Mickey something. Even at this distance Ellen could see it was money. Mickey stuffed it in his pocket. Starsong got in. Mickey glanced back at Ana's porch for a moment as the Cadillac pulled away. Then he slung his duffel over his shoulder and walked off down the street.

Ana said, "So I was wrong." Her mouth twisted and Jerry and Martin eyed her uneasily. She looked explosive. "Stay out here," she told them, "and kill that *pendejo* if he comes back."

So much for the new utopia. Ellen looked at the paper abandoned in Jerry's lap. On the front page a plane slid sideways through the air in a cloud of fire, while below the fold, Governor Reagan was planning to clean up student demonstrations on college campuses.

VI
SIX O'CLOCK NEWS

When Ellen got back to school for her sophomore year, the student revolution appeared to have taken a detour past Carter Randolph and headed up the road to New York, where it was occupying the president's office, smoking his cigars, and planning the insurrection. At Carter Randolph, students were required to attend chapel on Sundays and sign out with a housemother when they left the campus. The Fall Cotillion Committee had a ticket booth in the post office. And there was a letter from Jerry in her box, decorated in brilliant scarlet, persimmon, and green, psychedelic letters spelling out LOVE all around her name and address. What if she brought him to Cotillion? She envisioned them surrounded by all those girls in pearls with their tuxedoed dates and boys in dress uniform from Virginia Military Institute—and Jerry in his father's blue blazer, glasses, his endearing and slightly goofy smile, probably stoned.

"You don't want to go to Cotillion anyway," Linda said scornfully. "It's like a horse show—who has the most expensive dress, and the date with the most money. Then you get drunk and throw up in the social room." Linda had recently read Betty

Friedan, gone home to Davenport for the summer, refused to make her debut, and upset her mother. She was angular and intense, with hair the color of maple syrup clipped into a sleek, chin-length bob.

"Well, I'm going," Maggie said. "Even if I have to take that dumb bunny Bob. Nobody ever said it's unliberated to have a good time." She lounged on Ellen's top bunk, expensive little blue-and-green Pappagallo flats dangling from her toes. Maggie wore perfect make-up, even for classes, and had a carefully coiffed tawny mane like a collie. She spent most of her time in Ellen and Linda's room because her intended roommate had suddenly gotten married instead over the summer, and the college had assigned her a shy biology major who went to bed at nine.

"You'd go anywhere if it was with a boy," Linda said. She sat cross-legged on the floor in cut-off jeans, playing solitaire. Bob Dylan was on the record player.

"I would not. I told Chip Sorenson I wouldn't ever date him again if he was the last man on earth, and the species could just die out for all I cared, after he took me to that party at the cabin and we ended up shooting rats at three in the morning." Maggie's Atlanta drawl was theatrical. She peered at the picture of Jerry on Ellen's dresser. "And just who is this boy?"

"I met him at home," Ellen said with her mouth full of pins. She was making a tablecloth out of the Indian bedspread she'd bought in San Francisco. Pretty soon their room would look like Ana's house. "We were folk dancing," she added.

Maggie whooped.

"Shut up," Ellen said, grinning.

"And you went to bed with him?" Maggie and Linda were intent in their interest, and maybe a little envious.

"Yeah." Ellen blushed.

"Lord, child, you had a summer," Maggie said. "But what are

you going to *do* with him?"

She was silent. That question had occurred to her too. She got up and peeled off her jeans and rooted around in the closet for a skirt. They had to wear skirts in the dining room at night. And stockings, or knee socks. Ellen wouldn't have been caught dead in knee socks. Students at Berkeley were rioting, and at Carter Randolph you had to wear knee socks.

"She doesn't have to do anything with him," Linda said. "You don't have to marry everybody off and give them three kids and a membership in the country club."

"I'm not going to worry about that right now," Ellen said, unwilling to admit that she was. "I'll take what I can get." That was Jerry's motto, but then he thought the world was going to blow up next week. She found optimism harder to shake.

"God, Ellen, you're such a hippie," Maggie said.

Linda stood up in one motion, like a heron getting out of its nest, and pulled a cotton Villager miniskirt that predated Betty Friedan on over her cut-offs. "There's an anti-war march on the Pentagon next month."

"They aren't going to let you go to that," Maggie said.

"We aren't going to sign out saying we're going to march on the Pentagon," Linda said. "We're going to sign out saying we're going to the Library of Congress."

Maggie shook her head. "You are crazy."

"Us," Linda said. "You."

"Oh, no."

"You're going," Ellen said abruptly, having made up her own mind. "You have to have some principles."

"Daddy would just die," Maggie said. That seemed to amuse her. "He's on the Selective Service board at home."

When they left for Washington, cutting their Friday classes, Maggie was supposedly restricted to campus as a result of her cheerful determination to upend dormitory closing hours when she felt like it. "I don't know why they gave me a first floor room if they didn't want me to come in the window," she said, scrunching herself out of sight on the floorboards in the back of Linda's Austin.

They might as well all have climbed out the window, Ellen thought, out of Carter Randolph's antebellum green quad and red brick buildings, white columns and balconies. She and Linda had solemnly declared the purpose of their trip to be research for mid-term papers, their destination a Holiday Inn in Washington. It was an adventure, like going to San Francisco with Jerry, barreling along the humpbacked curves of Route 11, listening to the Beatles on the radio.

"We all live in a yellow submarine—" Linda drummed her palms on the steering wheel.

They drove north through the Shenandoah Valley, past little towns all painted from the same palette, white farm houses with red and green tin roofs, brick buildings made from the local red clay, weathered gray barns and white pasture fence, green fields and trees going rusty with the autumn chill. The cadets from Virginia Military Institute had marched down this road in 1864 to be killed at the Battle of New Market. What did all those ghosts think of three women going to Washington to protest a war on the other side of the world? Could you say to them now, *We're sorry, what a stupid thing to have made you die for?*

At New Market, they turned east but didn't seem to lose the ghosts. Ellen could feel them clinging like leaves to the roof of the car, singing "Yellow Submarine" in whispers while they cut straight through Manassas Battlefield.

The Army helicopters were the first thing Ellen noticed, hovering like malevolent horseflies over the sprawl of demonstrators coalescing around the Lincoln Memorial. She stood jammed between Maggie and a tall, cadaverous black man in fatigues and a daisy-chain necklace with an empty cartridge belt across his chest. Linda was in front of her. Ellen wanted to grab Linda's belt and hold on, the way they used to do in kindergarten so no one got lost. Her feet hurt. They'd gotten up at dawn to find a parking place, and still walked for miles. She wondered how much farther it was to the Pentagon.

The crowd spilled away from the Memorial into the gardens, and lined the edges of the reflecting pool. Occasionally someone in high spirits fell in, but mostly they listened to the speeches and watched the helicopters buzz back and forth overhead as the government prepared to confront seventy-five thousand angry members of its own citizenry. No one knew what was going to happen. Army patrols circled major buildings. The House of Representatives had shut down for the day in fear of invasion. Troops of the 82nd Airborne were prepared to defend the Pentagon.

Ellen felt as if she were inside some large, living thing, listening to its various organs and parts trying to get coordinated. Over the speeches, they could hear shouts from different groups attempting to keep their contingents in line: black nationalists in afros, Vietnam Veterans against the War, Women's Strike for Peace waving placards, Communists handing out pamphlets and red and blue Viet Cong flags, and the Capitol's entrepreneurs selling souvenirs and lunch to everyone. The air smelled of hot dogs and smoke and the acrid odor tension lent the body.

Toward the front of the crowd were the bigwigs of the National Mobilization Committee and behind them was everyone else, representatives of a hundred peace groups. None of them had been able to agree on tactics and the Mobe had settled on compromise—a rally at the Lincoln Memorial to protest the war, then a march on the Pentagon to challenge it directly. Of course they were going on to the Pentagon, Linda said when Maggie pointed out that that was where people were going to get arrested.

"There are people on the roof there with guns."

"How do you know?" Linda demanded.

"I asked a soldier," Maggie said. "He was real nice."

The crowd began to move. Some people were falling away, but the rest, nearly half, linked arms and surged toward the Arlington Memorial Bridge. You couldn't turn around now if you tried. The bridge was thick with people, like milk pouring out of a bottle, flowing across the Potomac. Ellen linked arms with Maggie and Linda, carried on the current. At the other end of the bridge the marchers swung left past the gates of Arlington Cemetery. Robert E. Lee had owned Arlington, Ellen remembered, before the Union had buried all its dead soldiers in his front lawn. What would happen if they buried all the soldiers who came back from Vietnam in front of the Pentagon? But you couldn't, you'd need jackhammers.

Behind them Washington had looked white and faintly magical in its sunlight, and not unwelcoming, full of marble and statues, bronze trim weathered into soft greens, marble tinged by age with a purple blush. The Pentagon was stark, a five-sided warehouse, squat and businesslike. It rose out of its parking lot like a concrete rhinoceros.

The Yippies had parked a flatbed truck with a sound system in the lower lot. They were, they said, going to exorcise the demons of the war generals and levitate the building. The crowd had thinned out along the road, but now everyone jammed together again, bunching up as they pushed against the line of federal marshals and paratrooper MPs blocking the main steps. They had come, someone from the Episcopal Peace Fellowship shouted through a bullhorn, to disrupt the center of the American war machine. Ellen looked up at the Pentagon-rhinoceros and wondered how anyone could. Its hide was solid concrete. And Maggie was right; there were riflemen on the roof.

The demonstrators filled the wide steps that led to the upper lot in front of the main entrance. More were coming behind them. Ellen was jostled along, up one step and then another, while the ones in front taunted the MPs. A boy in a turtleneck sweater was solemnly sticking carnations in their rifle barrels. Something was building, some final pressure being reached. From the lower lot she could hear faintly the sounds of the Yippies' program of monkey theater—The Fugs, a rock band composed mainly of left-wing poets, were chanting away "the cancerous tumors of the war generals." On the steps, someone let out a howl of bravado and charged the MPs.

The rest poured after him, pushing through the soldiers, who staggered against the weight of the onslaught and tried to close ranks again, too late. The demonstrators dived between them and raced for the entrance. Ellen was flung forward, pounding across the pavement, past the MPs now and blinded suddenly, eyes streaming tears, an acrid smell in the air. The marshals were swinging truncheons, and when someone reached out and grabbed her by the hair, she spun around screaming at him and found herself face to face with a television camera. The marshal pulled her away with his other hand; she felt his fingers digging into her wrist, and tangled in her flying hair. He let her go and she flew sideways into the crowd. Hands grabbed her, set her on her feet, pulled her into their midst beside a screaming boy with his fist clenched in the air.

More troops came running from inside the building, firing tear gas and wielding truncheons. The demonstrators fell back, shouting at them, then charged forward again, heads down, bulling their way through with sheer numbers. Someone in an Indian costume and an Uncle Sam hat stood astride a toppled barricade. He had wild black hair and he tipped his hat at her. Then they were running for the doors and she had no idea where Linda and Maggie were. A middle aged man in glasses and a tweed jacket was running beside her, puffing to keep up. As Ellen hit the top step, the doors opened and people came flying out, thrown by the soldiers massed in the hallways inside.

A helicopter went by overhead, its dull roar pounding at her ears. Her eyes were still streaming and she squinted at a federal marshal standing by one of the fat white columns that adorned the entrance. He jerked her forward by her jacket, twisted her arm behind her, and threw her down the steps.

Ellen rolled three steps, hitting each marble corner with her ribs. An elderly man in a clerical collar picked her up and she started to scream at him too, before she realized he was on her side. She tasted blood in her mouth.

"Go back," he shouted at her.

The protestors were retreating down the main steps, battered and angry. They sat down at the feet of the MPs in the upper lot and refused to move. Ellen sat down too, curling herself into a corner between the concrete steps and the retaining wall that bordered the upper lot. The helicopters were still droning back and forth overhead like wasps. She hurt all over, ribs, eyes, feet. Her mouth was gritty. She touched her face. There was a sore spot on her cheek that was probably a bruise, and her lip was puffy and felt tight. She'd seen people hit on the head with clubs, up on the steps. She crouched, bewildered. Was this how those boys from the Virginia Military Institute had felt at New Market? Bewildered as to how it had come to this? She sat there until the sun went down, wondering vaguely where Maggie and Linda were, too depressed to go find them.

All around her everyone was chanting: "Hey, hey, LBJ, how many kids did you kill today?" interspersed with pleas to the soldiers, most of whom were no older than the demonstrators, to "Join us, join us, we love you." In the twilight at the top of the steps, someone held up a burning draft card. Hundreds more followed, little lights like candles flickering through the dusk. There were still reporters in the crowd, and the bright lights of the TV crews blazed out of the dark and blinded her as she looked for Maggie and Linda. Someone came by with a basket of sandwiches and she took one.

An odd sensation of camping out settled over the crowd. The protestors began to sing. The soldiers were stone-faced, ignoring the taunts and invitations. Ellen wondered what Jerry would think of it all. Then she saw Maggie and Linda, looking for her, stumbling over seated bodies.

"My Lord, where've you been? We thought you'd been arrested and thrown in the pokey." Maggie inspected Ellen's face by the flame of her cigarette lighter. "What hit you?"

"The steps mostly." She fingered her mouth gingerly.

"I saw you screaming 'Fuck you' at a marshal," Linda said. "That was the last we saw of you."

"He grabbed my hair," Ellen said, still outraged.

"There was a reporter right there. You were probably on the six o'clock news."

Ellen groaned.

"Relax," Maggie said. "You didn't look like yourself at all. You looked like a lunatic. No one would recognize you."

Ellen sat down again and made room for Maggie. Linda had already squeezed onto the steps beside a couple who looked like anybody's nice schoolteachers. Reunited now, Maggie didn't say anything else about leaving and looked content to huddle in her car coat and sing "Masters of War" with everyone else. There were more sandwiches, and someone passed a joint along the line and Ellen showed Maggie how to inhale and hold the smoke down.

The deadline for the late night news approached. The reporters read their stories with the singing protestors in the background, looked around hopefully to see if anything else exciting was going to go on before deadline, and when it didn't, packed their lights and gear and left.

Now it was going to happen, Ellen thought. She shivered. Despite Jerry's opinion, the press was a light bulb that, if nothing else, illuminated the bald truth when it was held under its filament. She looked around uneasily in the darkness and started to stand up.

The demonstrators were still crooning, "Join us, join us," when the paratroopers from the 82nd Airborne formed a wedge and drove its nose into the crowd in front of the steps. As the demonstrators stood or rolled out of the way, the marshals reached for them through the line of paratroopers and yanked them through, clubbing them, passing them backward hand to hand to be booked.

"Run!" Ellen yelled, and they pelted across the dark parking lot, with the furious shouting of the demonstrators and the barked orders of the paratroopers and the marshals following them. Three or four bullhorns were bellowing against each other like competing elk, shouting incomprehensible orders to go, to stay, to sit down, to disperse.

They fled across the bridge, dodging police. When they got to their car, the Capitol streets were full of people, walking aimlessly, eyes bright with the excitement of violence in the air, of trouble that was not of their making. They eyed Ellen's bloody face with a frightening avidity and she flung herself into the car.

The street was spotlighted briefly by a helicopter above them, its beam cruising the night. Ellen looked at her battered face in the rear-view mirror and wondered how much of it makeup would cover.

Unfortunately, she actually had been on the six o'clock news. The telephone was ringing when she and Linda walked into their room the next afternoon, and Charlotte Latimer, the dorm president, followed them in without knocking and glared at them.

It was Jerry on the phone. "Hello, lover. I called to make sure you're not in jail."

Ellen sank down on the bed with the receiver to her ear, its cord stretched precariously from the desk. She dumped her suitcase on the rug. "I'm all right. How did you know?"

"You were on Channel 2, bigger than life."

"Oh, God."

"We're tired," Linda hissed at Charlotte. "It'll keep till tomorrow."

"I'm expecting you to report yourself to Judicial Court by tomorrow morning," Charlotte said.

"Are you really okay?" Jerry sounded worried. "I can't tell you what I've been thinking since I saw you on TV with that jerk grabbing you by the hair."

"I'm okay," Ellen said. "Why should I report myself? You saw me. *You* go report me."

"What's going on?" Jerry's voice said in the telephone.

"We don't take this lightly, Callahan," Charlotte said.

"Go away!" Ellen said. "No, not you. Jerry, hold on." She put her hand over the mouthpiece and said between her teeth, "Go send me a summons or a government warrant or whatever it is, but *leave me alone!*"

Charlotte blinked at her, lips tight, and turned on her heel. The door closed behind her with a smack.

"I told you it could wait," Linda said to Charlotte's departing back.

The chairman of the student Judicial Court tapped her pencil on a legal pad and looked severely at Ellen. Buffy McKeever wore a white turtleneck and a gray tweed miniskirt. Her blond hair was pulled to the nape of her neck and tied with a gray silk scarf. "Callahan, was your roommate involved in this—this fiasco?"

"Certainly not. She was involved in the Library of Congress." Ellen looked at Buffy blandly.

"She claims she wasn't," Buffy said. "She claims she was at the demonstration as well."

"Then ask her about it!" Ellen snapped. "I wasn't monitoring her."

The eight other members of the court, two of them Ellen's classmates, wrote that down on their legal pads. Charlotte Latimer sat to one side, ex-officio. Ellen waited for Buffy to pound on the table and order her head cut off, but Buffy said, "What about Maggie Berringer?"

Ellen widened her eyes. "Maggie's on strict campus. She couldn't go anywhere."

Buffy tapped her pencil slowly three times, regretfully. She took off her tortoiseshell glasses and polished them on her sleeve. "Callahan, you are not taking this seriously. I should advise you that is a big mistake."

Ellen laid her ears back. "There isn't anything in the student handbook that says I can't go to the Pentagon if I want to." She knew the dean was going to write a letter to her parents, but her parents knew about it anyway, since they'd also seen her on television. She'd called them collect from a pay phone in Washington so they wouldn't worry, and her mother, who would never have approved of Ellen going in the first place, was now furiously angry with Lyndon Johnson personally.

Buffy opened the handbook. "'Any conduct causing criticism of Carter Randolph or endangering the life, property, or the reputation of the College,'" she read, enunciating clearly. "I would call yelling 'Fuck you!' pardon my language, at an official of the United States government on national television endangering the reputation of the College. As well as participating in a riot. And conspiracy against the government. And violating the Honor Code by refusing to report a fellow student."

Charlotte Latimer closed her eyes sorrowfully.

"We are all very disappointed in you, Callahan," Buffy said. "You owe yourself more respect than this." She leaned earnestly toward Ellen, glasses on the end of her nose. "Everyone here is entitled to her political convictions, and I'm sure yours are very different from mine, but the whole college suffers when students behave like hooligans in expressing them. You devalue your degree and mine when you call ugly attention to the college. Now I want you to think about that."

Linda, who had turned herself in by confessing when no one had seen her, and hadn't been on television, got campused for two weeks. Ellen adamantly refused to turn herself in, on the grounds that any idiot could have seen her on television, and had, so Buffy vengefully gave Ellen and Maggie both social probation, which meant that they couldn't leave campus until Christmas. As a result, they got wonderful grades on their semester finals.

By Christmas, Ellen longed for Jerry so strongly that it amounted to the physical sensation of having some body part missing. Her parents brought him with them to meet her plane in Los Angeles and she spent the ride back to Ayala cuddled into his arm in the back seat. "It's making your mom twitch not to look in the rearview mirror," Jerry whispered.

It wasn't until the next day that she learned with a lurch in her stomach that he'd quit school.

"It was hopeless," he said. "I couldn't stick it."

"They'll draft you," she said, terrified. She grabbed his arm. They were sitting in a patch of winter sun on a brick wall under the live oaks in her back yard.

"They wouldn't want me," Jerry said confidently, and she thought that they wouldn't, but they were stubborn enough to take him anyway. Insubordination was part of his skeletal structure. They would grind him down somehow or send him home crazy.

"Aaron's going in, though," Jerry said.

"They took *Aaron?*" Aaron had real needle tracks on his arms.

"He's cool with it," Jerry said. He picked an oak leaf off the wall and dug at his fingertip with the spines, making it hang from the tip of his forefinger. "He says he'll learn a trade in the Army."

Jerry took Ellen to Aaron's farewell party. "I'm gonna learn heavy equipment mechanics," Aaron said. He smiled his wild-eyed smile and popped a beer. "I keep telling Manoury here he oughta come in with me. But he has this authority problem." He guffawed.

"I've started a C.O. case," Jerry said. "And you love authority figures about as much as the coyotes out there."

Aaron tipped his beer. "No, man. I just want to be one, for a change."

"Why don't you just go back to school?" Ellen asked him.

"Jeez, I'd rather be in the Army," Aaron said.

"Well, *you* wouldn't," Ellen hissed at Jerry. She knew she was wheedling. What was he going to do with his life if he didn't go to school?

"I'd rather be self-educated," Jerry said. "And not get what I read bent through the learned professor's prism to support his own trip. What's wrong with earning bread actually doing something? I learned to pour concrete last week."

The house in the orange grove looked much as it had the night Jerry had brought her there. Aaron didn't have many possessions, and most of the furniture belonged to the house. Tonight it was full of people in odd finery. Jerry wore a blue chambray work shirt with an orange and yellow sunburst embroidered on the back. Dreama had on a knitted lace vest over a green velvet tunic. She had given up telling Aaron how stupid he was, and was smoking a joint. She had brought a carrier to collect Aaron's cat. A fire blazed in the old stone fireplace, and a woman Ellen had met at Dreama's house was playing Aaron's guitar. Jerry wandered over to sing with her. Ellen tried to imagine what Aaron would look like with his wild brush of hair subdued in a military buzz cut. "I hope you find what you want," she told him.

"Me too," Aaron said. "Got to get it together sometime." He swigged his beer. "You take care of Manoury. He gets in trouble too easy." He wagged his head solemnly. "You gonna be his girl, you got to watch out for him."

"I thought you didn't approve of me," Ellen said. Aaron left her less apprehensive than usual tonight. Maybe it was the beer.

Aaron bent down to peer at her, brows knitted. "You want to give him what he wants, or you want to change him to suit you, dress him up in a coat and tie, get him a job with your dad?"

"My father's a screenwriter, he doesn't hire people. And why do I have to be the one to change?" She glared at Aaron. I got my mouth busted open in a riot, she wanted to say, and you still think I'm a snotty little rich girl. And she got good grades at Carter Randolph and they all thought she was a hippie. She saw Robert lounging by the fireplace in a red velvet jacket, a Greek fisherman's cap pulled over his brow. He was at UC Santa Barbara. It would have been simpler to have fallen in love with Robert, despite her mother's warnings about mixed race couples; she thought he was half in love with her. Maybe she could have done it if Jerry hadn't been there.

"Well, shit," Aaron said. "Ol' Jerry wants you, that's all I know. He's in love. It's a groove to watch." He gave her an avuncular pat on the shoulder. "You're okay. Don't let any of those bitches his mom hangs out with give you any shit."

Ellen looked sideways at Aaron. "Women have this thing for Jerry," she commented. "Sometimes I feel like I have to get in line."

"That's 'cause they know he won't hurt 'em." Aaron scratched his head, standing his hair up higher, like someone wearing a bird's nest. "They don't know that about me." He nodded regretfully. "But Manoury treats 'em right."

Ellen ran her finger around the edge of her beer can. "Does

he go out with people while I'm gone?"

"Jesus," Aaron said. "What do you think?"

Ellen wondered who had embroidered that sunburst.

"Hey, lover." Jerry bounced up and kissed the back of her neck. He grabbed her hand and pulled her into the living room where people were starting to dance to the Doors on a tiny record player in front of the fireplace. The fire sent their shadows careening along the walls, blending and separating like smoke. Jerry's eyes were half closed, lost in the music. *Love me two times...* She watched him and a tide of love flooded over her. It would have to be enough to know that while she was here, there was no one else for him; to know that Martin had appealed his C.O. case and got a hearing scheduled; to have Robert safe at UCSB; to say goodbye to Aaron with some hope that the Army actually was the right move for him. To dance their way maybe, into hope.

VII
YOU HAVE BEEN
RECLASSIFIED

On January 30, during Tet, the Vietnamese New Year, the Viet Cong launched an offensive that took them all the way into the grounds of the U.S. Embassy in Saigon and made it clear that the White House and the Army had been lying to everyone. "What the hell is going on?" Walter Cronkite demanded on the evening news, "I thought we were winning!"

The pandemonium shook Randy Ottley out of the sleep that came rarely now and the nightmares that came with it, and flung him from his bunker. Then somehow he was in a helicopter above a crescent-shaped ridge. Encapsulated in noise, he crouched frozen in the doorway, wild to escape the claustrophobia of the chopper and shying from the chaos below.

"Ottley, go, goddammit!" the sergeant screamed, and pushed him, and he dropped waist-deep into muddy water. He staggered drunkenly through bullets and the smoke from mortar shells and the stink of high explosive. A spray of mud and steel shards rained down from a mortar round. A man fell forward in the water, raising another spray of mud, and two more vanished in a *crump!* and a cloud of smoke. The helicopters lifted off and the planes came in, skimming the trees, dropping napalm canisters.

It billowed up out of the trees in a ball of fire, and the enemy mortars ceased. He blundered from the mud into the village, hacking at the hedgerows that blocked his way with the fire at his heels. Flakes of burning phosphorus landed in the thatched roofs and the village went up in flames too, while the jungle went on burning around it. Three women ran out of a house, screaming, a mother and grandmother and adolescent girl. The grandmother's hair was on fire. The mother saw him and stopped to scream at him and spit.

"No!" cried the girl when he raised his rifle. "No VC!"

He fired anyway because anyone could be VC, and kept on running, sobbing, plowing through the burning village. He clawed desperately for the refuge of his waking dream, a shelter from his constant terror, a barrier against fire and blood and guilt. His mind hammered at the burning air that held him until it parted and he could lift over the oily smoke, homing. His body stumbled earthbound, rifle in hand, while his ghost fled across the ocean until the air above the valley snapped shut like a rubber band and flung him back.

Jerry saw the Saigon police chief fire a bullet through the head of a Viet Cong prisoner on the *Huntley-Brinkley Report*. He heard an American major at Ben Tre announce that it had become necessary to destroy a town in order to save it. In the last war, news had come slowly, filtered through newsreels and copy editors. In this war you could watch American soldiers and Vietnamese civilians dying on your TV screen.

In April, when Martin Luther King was killed in Memphis, Jerry typed up his own C.O. appeal and watched the rioting that followed on his parents' television. In the morning he walked to the draft board and found it in a state of terrified siege, the sidewalk in front milling with screaming protestors.

"What do you want?" The secretary looked past his shoulder to be sure there was no one with him. She was popeyed with fright behind her teardrop glasses.

"I'm here to appeal my Conscientious Objector case," Jerry said.

The secretary pointed to a chair. While he waited he thought about Martin Luther King and how things were going to go without him now, and how a crazy person or an evil-hearted one could just take anyone out.

Through a half open door he could see five people shuffling papers at a long table in a room behind the secretary's desk. When he'd had enough time to get completely depressed, she showed him in and closed the door behind her with the air of someone putting the dog out.

At the table were a bonily thin man in a bolo tie, a pudgy one with a pink, balding scalp, an elderly man with a hearing aid, the barber who cut his father's hair, and a middle-aged woman in a matching pink sweater set.

"So, son, why do you think you want to be a conscientious objector?" the pudgy man asked, not looking at him.

"I don't believe in killing people," Jerry said. He handed them his statement and a sheaf of letters from character witnesses. The skinny man peered into the envelope and set it aside. No one else looked at it.

"Never?" the skinny man said. "Under any circumstances?"

"Never," Jerry said, knowing that the minute you said killing might be justified sometimes, you were in the Army. Selective objection was not an option.

"Son, you need to step up," his father's barber said. "Make your dad proud."

83

Jerry thought of old man Ottley, waving Randy's enlistment picture around to anyone who'd look at it, bragging about patriotism.

"Son, let me write you a little scenario," the skinny man said while Jerry wondered if they were going to read anything in his envelope. "Supposing you're home with your family, and someone breaks down the door and starts to rape your sister—"

"I don't have a sister," Jerry said.

"Then your mother. He has a knife to her throat. What do you do?"

"Is this guy a Viet Cong?" Jerry said.

"No, he's a robber!"

"Then why does he want to rape my mother?"

"I don't know why," the skinny man said. "Because he's bad. The point is, what would you do about it?"

"I guess I'd punch him," Jerry said.

"Oh, for heaven's sake, Alvin, let me," the woman said. She looked understandingly at Jerry. "Just stop and think about how you really feel. Suppose you were in a room with your grandmother, say, and you had a gun in your lap—"

"I don't own a gun," Jerry said firmly. "And my grandmother's dead."

"Pretend you do," the woman said. "And someone breaks the door down, and he has a machine gun in his hand. What would you do?"

In order to be a C.O. it looked as if you had to be willing to let someone machine gun your grandmother. "I'd talk to him," Jerry said. It seemed as reasonable as anything else in light of the conversation. They weren't going to give him the exemption. They knew they weren't, that was what all the stupid questions were for, so they could find something to point to and say, Aha, this kid doesn't object to killing, he'd shoot a crazed machine gunner to protect his grandmother.

"Son, just why aren't you willing to serve your country?" his father's barber asked him.

Jerry shook his head, goaded now and furious. "Because the bitch went and turned on me, that's why."

There was a collective hiss of indrawn breath.

"My country is killing innocent civilians in somebody else's country, and the citizens here are killing their heroes, and I don't want any part of it." He slammed his chair back and shoved the interview room door open while the secretary scurried out of his way.

You have been reclassified 1-A.

Jerry balanced the letter in his hand, as if it were a brick he might throw. He felt overwhelmingly angry that they should decide this, decide that he had to give up privacy, self-determination, all rights to exist as an individual, just because they said so. He'd seen the recruits in L.A. waiting to get on a bus, a drill sergeant screaming in their faces. Had seen the major at Ben Tre. They expected him to do that?

Raymond Manoury poked a finger at the letter in Jerry's hand, prodding the stiff white paper with his nail. "Well, son, what are you going to do now, about this?"

"I don't know," Jerry said.

"Well, I would suggest you decide."

He didn't offer any further suggestions, and Jerry took the letter into his room and stared at it some more. This was not a battle his father was going to fight. Raymond Manoury had a job with a security clearance at the Naval Air Station at Point Mugu, but Jerry actually had no idea whether his father wanted him to join the service or not. Personal responsibility and making your own decisions were the child-rearing theories Dreama and Raymond espoused. They wouldn't make his choices for him, even now when he halfway wanted them to.

Jerry closed his eyes, but he could still see the letter under his lids. It felt like sandpaper there, like some disease he'd contracted. How much point was there in appealing his case again? He wouldn't win. And more and more he felt slimy trying, telling blithe lies about his respect for all human life. If he had been his father, if it had been 1942, he would have enlisted and killed Nazis without a qualm. Maybe his father knew that, and his silent disapproval stemmed from the fact Jerry was lying, and not from the fact that he wouldn't fight this war.

He went in his parents' room and sat down at his mother's typewriter. Maybe he'd see where honesty got him. Dreama had always said that if you were doing what you knew was right, you were powerful.

Dear Draft Board,

I am somebody you do not want. Although I cannot honestly claim to believe that killing is always wrong, I believe this war is immoral. Because of that, I cannot allow myself to participate in it. I will exercise my right of free speech by voicing this opinion to everyone around me, which will not have a good effect on your recruits. If I am drafted, I will refuse to fight or to cooperate in any other way in what I believe to be an immoral undertaking. I understand that these views do not qualify me as a Conscientious Objector, but I think you should consider them before you put me in your army, where I will cause you untold trouble. Furthermore, I do not respond well to authority. The administrators at my high school will corroborate this. I will really be more trouble to you than I am worth. Please consider leaving me alone.

Yours respectfully,
Gerald R. Manoury

Ellen came home for the summer in May and in June Ellen and Jerry, and Dreama and Raymond Manoury, sat together in a line on the Manourys' sofa and drank coffee and watched the Democratic primary returns.

It was the kind of dusty California night where doors stood open, letting in the smell of wet grass from the neighbors' sprinkler systems, and the coyotes carried on a conversation down in the riverbed. There had still been little rain and thus fewer rabbits and the coyotes compensated with chickens when they could. Jerry honestly liked the bastards; they were inventive and curious and almost as indestructible as cockroaches—the ranchers who tried to get rid of them just ended up with more coyotes—but they didn't have any business in people's chicken coops any more than his country did in Vietnam. They seemed to him a metaphor for both the war itself and for the American brass frantically ordering gadget after gadget from the Acme Company. Jerry was pinning his hopes on Bobby Kennedy, whose platform emphasized non-aggression in foreign policy and a peace settlement between North and South Vietnam.

Dreama kept the coffee pot going in the kitchen, and the table was sticky with rings of milk and sugared coffee. They picked at the last of a pan of macaroni and cheese and watched the percentages tick up. California had become crucial. Whoever won tonight would challenge Hubert Humphrey and the Johnson political machine at the Democratic convention in August. To Jerry it seemed the last chance at proof that government by the people was possible.

"Kennedy will win it," Raymond Manoury said. He sat

upright on the sofa with his tie loosened and Aaron's cat in his lap. A folding slide rule, two pens and a pencil stuck out of his pocket.

"How do you know?" Dreama pushed her sandals off and rubbed her bare toes on the rug.

"Because he is a Kennedy, for one thing," Raymond said.

Dreama was rooting for Eugene McCarthy, and even some of the scruffier of the anti-war faction had gone "clean for Gene," cut their hair and canvassed voters. But Robert Kennedy was the remaining half of the radicals' idealized "Liberation Ticket" of Kennedy and King, and when he decided to run, McCarthy paled next to him. He lacked Kennedy's impassioned rhetoric and burning intensity. Maybe because of that, Dreama supported him stubbornly.

Jerry was engrossed in the numbers on the screen, his elbows on his knees, eyes pensive behind his glasses. Ellen remembered what he'd said to her father about watching John Kennedy and buying into Kennedy's idea of America. Robert Kennedy had the same pull, stirred the same hope that the world could be remade for the better.

The ballroom of the Ambassador Hotel in Los Angeles looked like a birthday party. Balloons bobbed over the heads of Kennedy campaign workers, and a surge of silly hats skimmed back and forth through the crowd. The reporters liked Kennedy too. Whatever was in the air came through the little screen of the television, potent and seductive, as the votes came in and Kennedy stayed ahead. It seemed to Ellen there might be hope that they knew where they were going after all.

"He's gonna do it," Jerry said. His hand grasped hers.

The world, which lately had flopped so wildly on its axis, a top with a bad spin on it, might yet stabilize. Life might be what she'd been led to believe it should be. She squeezed his hand back.

Dreama was making another pot of coffee. "The last returns are coming in, Ma!" Jerry yelled. Dreama hurried back, wiping her hands on the back of her shorts.

The coverage had cut back to the studio. The results were running along a banner behind the announcer's head: forty-six percent for Kennedy to forty-two for McCarthy. McCarthy had conceded.

The crowd in the Ambassador ballroom exploded, cheering and screaming. Campaign workers kissed each other to the rapid-fire pop of champagne corks. Reeling from one disaster after another, they had something to hang onto again, someone to pin hope on. They shouted his name over and over.

It was infectious. Jerry pushed his glasses back and grinned. "He's gonna do it, Ma."

Victory was more than political, Kennedy was saying now, talking to supporters, talking out of the television to Jerry and Ellen, Dreama and Raymond sitting on the sofa. It was the proof we could end the cataclysm, the disenchantment within society, the distrust between black and white, between poor and rich, between generations, the bitter splintering of the war.

"I think we can end the divisions within the United States, the violence," Bobby said. He was Bobby to everyone tonight, and it was impossible not to think so too, caught in the moment, boosted up with the balloons and the chanting campaign workers.

They kept watching, even though nothing much interesting was going to happen now. "It's like seeing a torch passed," Jerry said. "Pretty hokey shit, I know, but that's how I feel."

"Clichés are clichés because they have been true for a long time," Raymond said.

Kennedy waved at his supporters and turned away, a man who was buoyed up on the same emotions as the rest of them, who was tired and wanted to go to bed, a man who still had a press conference waiting for him. The cameras followed him, squeezing through a crowd in the serving pantry behind the ballroom. Hands reached out to touch him, to congratulate him.

Then a scuffle, a flurry of bodies. It was hard to tell what on the little black and white screen. Someone shouted: "He's been shot! He's been shot!" The camera tilted crazily. An announcer's face filled the screen, wavered and disappeared again. The room came back, with people milling frantically in it. In the center, in a suffocatingly still hollow, Kennedy lay on his back with blood around his head. A busboy knelt staring, transfixed.

"Oh, my God," Dreama said.

Ethel Kennedy came out of the crowd, almost out of the screen, mouth twisted, eyes unbelieving, her hand pushed against the camera lens, shoving all those people back. Shoulders in suit jackets filled the screen.

The studio announcer told them what had happened while they sat frozen. Bobby had been shot in the head. A gunman in the crowd had been apprehended. Kennedy had been taken to the hospital, where he was still breathing, or dead on arrival, or had tried to speak in the ambulance, or was still alive but not expected to live. No one knew. The announcers looked shell-shocked.

Jerry stood up with an angry howl. "They've done it again! What the hell *use* is anything?" He turned on his heel and flung the screen door open. It slammed into the wall and bounced closed again, quivering.

Ellen looked uneasily at Dreama and Raymond.

"The world is full of pain," Raymond Manoury said.

Ellen found Jerry sitting in her car, smoking angrily, staring out the windshield at the darkness.

"Are you all right?" It seemed a stupid question. Who was all right tonight? She slid into the driver's seat.

"I thought," Jerry said between his teeth, "there was some

kind of hope. I thought he was going to pick up what his brother left and carry it for us. And they wasted him—again!"

"The television said it was some Arab."

"They, them, whoever. The forces of evil, if you want to call them that, all right?" He pounded his fist on the dashboard. "The motherfucking forces of evil, the business as usual people, the people who want to pick up everything good and valuable and throw it in the fucking furnace so they can melt it down and make another rifle out of it, or another tank, or more things to own, more televisions, more swimming pools, more fucking plastics companies."

He was shouting. She laid a hand on his arm. "Do you really think it was that? Some conspiracy? How can you know that yet?" She felt somehow compelled to be orderly in her thinking, too tidy for chaos to take an interest in.

"How can I know anything?" Jerry said caustically. "How do you look the universe in the eye and say this was just chance? We should have known better than to believe we had a prayer."

Ellen tried to sort out her own emotions, and found numbness. If she thought too hard about the gun, about Robert Kennedy's eyes staring blankly from the floor, she was filled with terror. "Do you want to go back in and watch?"

Jerry shook his head. "They were just doomed," he said. "Bobby and his brother. They didn't fit the pattern. They actually had this stupid idea that the words were real—that this really is the land of opportunity. That we really do have a right to pursue happiness. They couldn't even wait for this one to get the Presidency. They wanted him offed before he got there."

"*Who?*" Ellen said.

He shrugged. "The forces of darkness." They seemed real tonight.

"He might live," she said.

"No. Not to be President. Not with a bullet in his head. If he hasn't died, he will. He might as well." He put his hands over his face and began to cry.

Ellen held him. She didn't know what else to do so she wrapped her arms around his shoulders and let him cry into her blouse, deep strangling sobs that shook his whole chest. His anger was something she could feel on his skin, like someone running a fever.

When it abated, they got out of the car without saying anything and went back in the house. The living room was dark. They went through it to Jerry's room, and locked the door. Ellen undressed and got in bed with him and they made love fiercely and silently to hold back the darkness, the bottomless, boundless empty place, a black hole where all the heroes had winked out like suns falling.

Kennedy died the next day. His family took his body back to New York and a weeping, endless line of mourners paraded by his casket in St. Patrick's Cathedral while the country watched on television. Andy Williams sang "The Battle Hymn of the Republic" at the funeral, and Ellen never heard it afterward without a quick stab of memory, another permanent hole in the heart.

Through June, the Poor People's March on Washington went on, without Martin Luther King and without Robert Kennedy, from a rain-soaked and miserable camp called Resurrection City. In July, desecrating the United States flag became a federal crime, a law that had never seemed necessary before. At work, Ellen restlessly read every inch of copy that came over the AP wire, trying to make sense of the world and failing.

Near the end of July she came home in the late afternoon to find Martin sitting on cardboard boxes in her driveway, accompanied by Jerry and Teak, all manically stoned.

"I'm going to Canada," Martin said as she got out of the car. "Can you send this shit after me when I get an address?" He made a sweeping gesture at the boxes.

Canada, Ellen thought, stomach buckling. Teak had an arm across both boys' shoulders, her bare legs stretched out in front of her, digging channels in the gravel with her sandals.

"No good," Teak said, shaking her head at Martin. "Can't make art without your stuff. Got to have your stuff."

"Customs won't let you cross the border without a job offer if it looks like you're trying to move in," Martin said. "Lots of people moving in." He shook his head back at her. "Crashing in Canada's living room. Eating everything in the refrigerator. Poor old Canada. And anyone might, for instance, be somebody they don't want. An undesirable. I might."

"Hippie communist revolutionary," Jerry said solemnly. "With a purse."

Ellen took note of the next-door neighbor on her porch, clipping geraniums. "Come inside," she hissed. They were as unruly as drunks, and her parents' car was in the driveway. She pushed them through the back gate to the guest cabin under the live oaks, and Martin and Jerry carried the boxes.

Jerry staggered sideways with his. "Jesus, what is in this?"

"Lithography stone."

"I have to say Hi to Dan and Lily," Teak said.

"Later," Ellen said.

The cabin was old and ratty and served mostly as a retreat for anyone who wanted to get away from the rest of the family. They set the boxes down in the middle of the frayed rug.

"They turned down my C.O. appeal," Martin said, suddenly

lucid. "I filed a change of address just to stall the paperwork till I can get out of the country."

"Are you sure you can't appeal again? What about a lawyer? Do your parents know you're going?"

"My mother knows. She'll tell my old man after I'm gone. I got a lecture from him last week about patriotism. Herb Ottley was lording it over him at the Elks about how Randy was serving."

"He doesn't even know where he's going," Teak said.

"I'm going to Vancouver."

"When?" Ellen asked.

"Tonight. I got an induction notice and my *pendejo* landlord saw the envelope. He's a frothing rightwing patriot. He told me once that if he thought I was dodging the draft he'd call the FBI."

"He wants me to come with him," Teak said. "I've never done anything like going to Canada. That's another country. That may be too stupid. My shrink says I have to quit doing what men tell me to."

"Damn it, I've already told you that!" Martin said. "But this is a hell of a time to stop."

"Got to stop sometime," Teak said reasonably. She wrapped her arms around herself. "Not Canada," she said. "I'm afraid to go away like that. I might not get back."

"*You* can come back," Martin said.

"I don't know," Teak said. She shook her head. "I think this place you're at is a place where you, you know, stay. You were in it when I got here. I don't want to be in it."

Ellen looked from one to the other. She doubted there was anything any of them could do that wouldn't eventually turn out to have been the wrong thing. She went out on the porch, and Jerry followed her. The knotted branches overhead made a fine dusty shade, and they sat on the step under it and waited for

Teak and Martin to strike whatever bargain they were going to. They were each afflicted with a sick relief that it wasn't the two of them in there.

VIII
NIGHT MUSIC

The next month Ellen's mother, looking for a stash of old photographs, found Martin's boxes in the cabin. "Do you know where he's gone?" she demanded. "Why didn't you tell me they were there? I feel like I just found a snake. His mother is perfectly distraught."

"Then she knows where he's gone," Ellen muttered.

"He called her," Lily admitted. "His father was threatening to call the FBI, but Sally told him she'd divorce him if he did that. I didn't think she had the gumption. Ed couldn't have really meant that."

"He wants me to send him the boxes later." Ellen looked around her parents' living room, wondering how someone she'd known since fourth grade could be in Canada, hiding.

"Maybe you shouldn't tell anyone you have them. I didn't tell Sally." Lily bit her lip and Ellen could see tears starting. "Poor Sally! I'm so glad you're a girl!" Her mother flung her arms around her. "I wanted a boy, too, after I had you," she said into Ellen's neck. "Besides you, I mean. But I'm glad I didn't have any more. I don't think I could bear it now."

Jerry tapped on the front door, which stood open, with only the screen latched. Lily looked at him with some new insight, said, "Ohhhh," and fled.

"What was that about?"

"She's just realized *you* might get drafted," Ellen said tightly. "She's feeling sorry for boys."

"I might," Jerry said.

Ellen didn't answer him. She stalked to her car, feeling precarious, as if pieces of her might begin to separate themselves, like Martin's boxes, alighting in bus stations and strangers' closets. Jerry followed her, sliding into the passenger seat as she put the car in gear. She swung through town, down to Creek Road where the dairy cows grazed.

Abruptly she stopped the car in the shade of the trees that overhung their fence. There was just enough room to pull off the road, and hardly any traffic. They sat and watched the cows silently while she tried to figure out how to persuade Jerry to do what she wanted, and Jerry waited while she thought about it. The cows were black and white and boxlike, ambling heads-down, half grown calves at their heels. They wouldn't get to keep them, Ellen realized. Only the girls.

"You've got to go back to school."

"Wouldn't do any good," Jerry said. "I'm 1-A now, love." The draft board's demand to report for his pre-induction physical had contained no response to his letter. They didn't care.

She put her knuckles in her mouth. "Why didn't you tell me?"

"I was sort of waiting for a good time."

"How can you be so stupid?" she screamed, and the cows flung their heads up, ears twitching. She burst into tears. "They're going to draft you!"

"Not me." Jerry put his hand on her arm. "Hush. You're scaring the cows."

She jumped out of the car, slamming the door behind her. She glared at him in furious misery and stumbled away through the wild fennel and nettles that grew along the verge between the road and the thin strands of barbed wire. The nettles raked her arms and legs and she shrieked.

Jerry floundered after her. He had on jeans and he held his arms high, over his head. He caught her by the wrist where she stood sobbing and rubbing her arms. "You're in a nest of the stuff, honey. Come on. Back up. This way."

Gulping sobs, she let him ease her back out of the nettles. He opened the passenger door and put her in that side of the car, got in and put it in gear. She didn't ask where they were going.

They pulled onto Ayala Avenue again and headed west through town and then up Highway 33. Ellen didn't say anything about his driving, still without a license. What difference did it make if he got a ticket when they were trying to draft him? And then she thought that if he called himself to their attention, they might draft him now, right away, and she grabbed at his arm, panic-stricken.

Jerry just said, "Quit it," and kept driving, pushing the little red bug up through the tawny, lion-colored foothills, the gears whining. The highway bordered a stream for a while, steep bluffs rising above it over a bed of rounded brown stones. Then it came out into a high meadow, lit with yellow branches of Scotch broom. They bumped over a narrow road, and then a dirt one and then he parked, high up in the gray-green ridges, somewhere Ellen didn't remember having been before. A trail led off from the end of the road through the brush—crackling, dusty clumps of sage and the big white ruffled cups of Matilija poppies, between outcrops of pale stone.

"Come on," Jerry said.

She got out, dubiously, sniffling. He wiped her face with his fingers and she batted them away, so he reached out and took her hand instead. She thought he was going to lead her up the trail, but a few steps onto it he pushed his way into the scrub, leaving behind a sharp scent of sage and a scattering of purple petals, and tugged her after him.

"Are there snakes up here?"

"They rattle," Jerry said. "Quit it. You're too mean to bite."

"I hate hiking," Ellen said rebelliously. Bugs, not resonant enough to be snakes, chirred in the brush.

"I want to show you something." He sounded elaborately patient, as if he was working at it. She bit her lip and decided not to prod him any further, a resolution that lasted five minutes while they trudged uphill, through foxtails and poison oak.

"Where are we going?"

"You'll see."

"Jerry, we need to talk."

"Not now."

She stumbled after him, trying to think how to explain what she meant, how to make him see she was right, that the situation could still be salvaged, if he'd just go back to school. Her father knew lawyers, he played poker with one. They could find out what to do.

"Here." Jerry stopped abruptly in front of a cliff of sandy soil and white stones. The rocks here looked like huge slabs of bone or ivory, slantwise in the hillside like the skeletal remains of mastodons. He put one foot on the slope and pulled himself up by a manzanita bush. When he had a solid footing, he turned and held his hand out for Ellen. She let him drag her up the slope, slipping in loose stone and scratching her arms on the dry scrub that grew between the rocks.

"Come on. Up here."

She clambered the rest of the way after him and turned to see what he was looking at. She'd thought it would be the view, the foothills spilling away below them, studded with the dark green of pine trees and the flat white slabs of stone, repeating themselves endlessly until they came to the bowl of the valley. But Jerry had wedged himself under an overhang of rock and was looking up. Ellen ducked in beside him and followed his eyes. On the roof of the overhang, above their heads, was an animal, scratched into the stone, with bits of old russet paint still clinging to its crescent ears and tail. It was sinuous and cheerful, with round eyes and whiskers like the bristles of a brush. It looked as if it wanted to play.

"Somebody made him a long time ago," Jerry said. "The Chumash probably. They lived all over these hills. Not many people know about him."

Ellen was aware that this was a kind of gift, an apology for her misery. "Is he a fox?"

"He's an otter. See how long he is, and look at his paws. There used to be otters in the Sespe. I always wanted to be one when I was little."

You would, she thought. What would they do with an otter in the Army?

"Jerry, what are we going to do?"

"You're going to go back to school." He kissed the end of her nose.

"What are *you* going to do?"

"I can have them transfer my file to Berkeley, to Ana's address. Then when they send me a notice there, I can transfer it back again, and then somewhere else. It'll work for a while."

"For a while. And you didn't answer my question. What are *we* going to do?"

He ran his hands through his hair. It was down to his shoulders now, dark and wavy. "Babe, I don't know. The whole world's going up in flames and you want me to make plans."

"People who make plans don't go up in flames," she said stubbornly.

"Ah, shit, I'm only nineteen. The government wants my ass,

you want me to get with your program—"

"If you got with my program, maybe the government would leave your ass alone! That's the point!" She glared at him, stubborn and desperate.

"I don't want to get with a program." He sounded as desperate as she did. "I want to be nineteen. I don't want people trying to ship me off to shoot people, and I don't want people trying to marry me off either," he added, goaded.

"I never said 'marry'." She looked away.

"I could hear you thinking it."

"I didn't *say* it."

"Babe, it doesn't matter. I know you want to." He pulled her close to him and held her with her face against his chest. If she tipped her chin she could just see the otter over his shoulder, frisking eternally in the rock. "I don't blame you. You want what you want. And I love you. But I think about things like bringing kids into the world and I get the shakes. The world's enough of a mess."

"My father says the people who are intelligent and care about things are the ones who should reproduce."

"We aren't cows," Jerry said. "Planned breeding is bullshit."

"I didn't say planned breeding. I just said, if anybody ought to have children, intelligent people should. Otherwise we leave it up to the idiots. And the world just gets dumber."

"It's hard to decide who's an idiot, though."

"No, it's not."

"Couldn't you just be an otter for a while, babe? Sworn to fun, loyal to none?"

"I *am* loyal," she muttered. "That's the trouble. You're the one . . . Aaron says you see other people while I'm not here."

"There are people all over the place."

"You know what I mean. Sleep with them."

"Who? How many?" He leaned back and saw her expression

and quit joking. "Not many. Not often. It's lonesome out. Sometimes it just seems like, you know, a good idea. You keep going back to college."

"I have to."

"I don't love anybody but you. They don't love me either," he added, as if that made it all right. Otters.

Ellen looked at the little otter gamboling on the ceiling. She wondered how long he'd been there, caught in the stone, and if there was some other otter waiting for him to come home.

When they came back her parents were watching the Democratic convention. The Chicago amphitheater was ringed with barbed wire. Daniel was grim-faced. Lily sat frozen with hands to her mouth. On the screen a furious man screamed "Oink, oink!" at a cop just before a billy club came down on his head, splattering his eyes with blood. Whatever else he had said was bleeped out.

"Democracy at work," Jerry said as he sat down cross-legged on the floor beside the sofa. Ellen huddled next to him. Her father's hand touched her shoulder briefly. She'd read the stories on the AP wire at the paper in the afternoon, and the day before, but the still photos the wire disgorged didn't carry the angry terror of the moving screen. There were ten thousand people in the park now, outside the hotel where Hubert Humphrey and Eugene McCarthy had their headquarters. A young demonstrator in an army helmet began to climb a flagpole. Chicago police charged and dragged him off. When more demonstrators pulled the flag down and replaced it with a red t-shirt, the police went berserk. A frightened reporter inside the barbed wire talked of numbers beaten and arrested, of Mace and tear gas in the park, while the angry blood-covered demonstrators threw bricks and eggs and balloons filled with paint and urine, and police pulled press and bystanders out of the crowd and beat them too.

"This must be what Prague was like," Jerry murmured. A week before, Soviet tanks had rolled into Prague and over the Czechoslovakian experiment. "Those kids worked within the system too," he muttered, with an eye on Daniel Callahan.

"This is not how the system is supposed to work," Daniel said.

"This has been going on for three days," Jerry said. "The system better figure it out fast."

The network cut to Senator Abraham Ribicoff, who'd taken the podium to nominate another alternative to Humphrey. "With George McGovern as president we would not have to have such Gestapo tactics on the streets of Chicago," Ribicoff said over the uproar in the background.

The camera cut again, a close-up on Chicago's mayor, Richard Daley. His voice was drowned by convention noise, but lip-readers all over the country saw him scream "Fuck you" at Ribicoff.

Jerry didn't say anything else.

Lily made a plate of sandwiches and they went on watching. The peace plank had already been defeated in the afternoon and the end seemed inevitable, but no one turned the TV off. The vote count was interspersed with scenes of rioting outside. Police waded into the kids in the park again, and they chanted back venomously, "The whole world is watching!" The radicals had been joined by the bitter supporters of Eugene McCarthy, whose campaign was sinking. Kennedy might have taken it, but now it was clear that Humphrey, Johnson's heir apparent, was going to be nominated.

"Linda's there," Ellen said. "She's with McCarthy's people."

"You'd never see her in all this mob."

Linda had been campaigning furiously for McCarthy all summer, had called Ellen and wanted her to come out to Chicago with her. Remembering Washington, Ellen had been guiltily glad to say she couldn't leave her job.

Humphrey's nomination was official before midnight. For the benefit of the press, McCarthy's supporters staged a funeral march for peace. The next night the Democrats ran a filmed tribute to Bobby Kennedy that got more applause than their candidate.

Ellen went back to school amid a bombardment of Nixon and Humphrey campaign ads. Jerry moped for a week. He thought of hitching out and surprising her, of going back to school and getting his degree, and of buying a kilo of weed and just staying stoned till she got back so he wouldn't miss her. None of those avenues looked promising, even the last one, since he didn't have any money, so when a friend of Robert's old man offered him work cutting trail for the Forest Service up in the Sespe watershed, he took it. It would at least keep him from screwing around with other girls.

Two months into the job, lonesome and feeling sorry for himself, he climbed the ridge behind the camp and went to see the otter. It was a moonshot November night a week before Thanksgiving, a holiday that Ellen couldn't afford to fly home for, with Christmas coming up so soon after.

He lay under the overhang and watched the otter dance across the stone, thinking about the people who'd carved him with a flint blade. He had his flute in his jacket pocket, in a flannel bag. He fitted the pieces together and began to play. The moonlight eddied on the Scotch broom and the brittle stems of Matilija poppies gone to seed. He didn't know whether those grew anywhere else. Matilija was a local name. They seemed a part of the valley magic to him, like Scotch broom honey and the small horned toads, soft as glove leather, that came out to sun themselves on warm stones in the afternoon. The little otter climbed off his ledge and danced through them, where a stream had flowed once.

The night was still except for his flute. If he could make the otter dance, maybe he could weave some spell to stop the world from spinning off into calamity, like an oil drum rolling downhill, gathering speed, flattening whatever got in its path. Ellen wanted to get married and have babies. Jerry was fairly certain the world was going to blow up and spatter them across the universe, babies and all, any day now.

In grade school they'd made him practice nuclear war drills, crouching under his desk, hands folded across his head to keep off the fallout. Raymond Manoury designed missile guidance systems. Jerry had known even then how much good a desktop and folded hands would do. Not much less than the backyard fallout shelters stocked with food and water, so terror-stricken suburbanites could survive six months underground like moles before they had to come out and die of radiation poisoning.

He wanted to do things before that happened. See things, try things out. Ellen wanted him to get a degree and teach other idiots who wanted to get their degrees. It seemed more important to do something, make something, leave something behind. They'd had a silly argument about the dignity of manual labor versus an intellectual life. Jerry knew he'd been pompous but he still thought he'd been right. Intellectual life had gotten everyone where they were now. Universities had produced the professors who had produced the bombs.

The flute song faltered, weighed down with knowledge. If magic had worked here once, it didn't anymore.

It was daylight, fourteen hours away. Quivering with terror, what was left of Randy Ottley shot a woman because he thought she had a bomb in her shawl. She was tiny. In America he would have thought she was no more than twelve. It didn't matter. Yesterday, another woman had handed a soldier a market basket full of fruit and before the sergeant could shout at him to put it down, it had exploded. Shreds of his body hung in the blackened tree above where he had stood.

Randy backed away from the dead woman now because her bomb might still go off. He staggered up the road after his unit through the charred huts that had been the village, through the stink of napalm and burned flesh, and saw her get up out of the mud and follow him. He crouched, head between his knees, eyes closed, conjuring home, conjuring the flagpole and his trains and his letter jacket while the sergeant kicked him to his feet again. The ghost fled from the sergeant and the dead woman both, pulled like a compass needle toward the valley half a world away.

A shrill, thin sound like gulls, like fingernails on a blackboard, screeched across the flute's voice. Jerry thought at first it was the East End peacocks, their cries carrying through the cold night. But it came again, not strident enough for peafowl. Not coyotes either. He craned his neck at the sky, navy blue above the stone roof of the otter's cave, spattered with stars. An uncertain light appeared to be wandering in them, homing on something in the hills.

He froze. The thing coalesced, still transparent but more substantial, a shape he could almost see if he looked at it peripherally. Looked at straight on, it faded into the hillside, disappeared in the gleam of moonlight on the dry stems of the poppies. The otter saw it too. It stopped cavorting in the old stream bed and went back in its stone, where it watched the sky, eyes bright as nickels.

The light hovered above the ridge. Its insubstantiality beat against the air like someone outside a door that wouldn't open. Around it the sky undulated, shimmered like a web with a fly in it.

"Go away," Jerry said to it, uneasy. The luminescence hung above him, whimpering.

"I mean it, man. Go away." He pulled his knees up and backed himself into the otter's alcove, the flute across his knees. A rising shriek hung on the wind.

"Shit." Jerry put the flute in his pocket. The presence lurked among the stars, elongated and transparent as a ripple. He buttoned up his coat and set off down the ridge, homing on the trail camp and the fire. Behind him in the night he could hear someone crying.

"Hey, Callahan, there's an FBI man in the social room to see you." Maggie propped one hand on her hip. She looked interested and mildly shocked.

Ellen stuck her head up from the pile of history texts on her desk. "Me?"

Linda's dark head popped up from her pillow on the top bunk. "They want Callahan?"

"That's what he says. Mrs. Henn thought they must want Linda, but he said he wants you. Mother Henn is having palpitations, you can imagine."

Eileen Henn was the housemother and Ellen thought she was probably a match for an FBI man. She got up with a nudge of fear in her chest that it was about Jerry. She'd just talked to him on the telephone, one of their rationed weekly long distance calls, but maybe he hadn't told her something. Surely he would have told her if the FBI were after him. He'd probably be proud of it. Maybe it was about Martin. But they'd already come to see her about Martin, last summer, when he hadn't shown up for induction.

"You want moral support?" Linda was sitting up now.

Maggie groaned. "Don't take *her*. She'll have you in handcuffs before you can say you don't know anything about it." Linda had been among the McCarthy supporters hauled from their beds at midnight and beaten by hysterical police because someone had thrown something from the hotel balcony. She was now notorious at Carter Randolph.

"I *don't* know anything about it." Ellen combed her hair in the mirror over her dresser and went down to the social room. She could hear Maggie and Linda lurking in the hall behind her, trying to eavesdrop.

Mrs. Henn was waiting with the FBI man. She wasn't going to hand one of her charges over to the government without supervision. Her magenta hair looked as if she'd just taken it out of curlers and the chain on her black harlequin glasses hung over one ear.

"I apologize for troubling you so late, Miss Callahan. I'm Agent Torgerson." The agent wore a dark suit and a plain blue tie. He had sandy hair cut short and slicked down firmly and a nose dusted with freckles. He showed her an ID, a quick flip. It could have been a secret decoder badge.

Mrs. Henn looked pointedly at her watch: 10:00 p.m., dormitory closing hours on a weeknight.

Ellen swallowed the lump of terror in her throat. "I don't know why you're here." *Please, not Jerry.*

"Do you know a young man named Randolph Ottley, Miss Callahan?"

She blinked, off balance. Randy Ottley was already in the Army. Why was he asking about him? Maybe he'd been killed and they wanted her to tell Mimi. But that didn't make sense. "I know his sister and I went out with him in high school. He's in the Army."

"Do you know his whereabouts at the moment?"

"He's in the Army," Ellen said again. Didn't *they* know where he was?

"Has he been in contact with you?"

"No."

"But you dated him? He never asked you to mail letters for him, or send packages? Did he ever ask you to keep his whereabouts a secret?"

"I don't *know* his whereabouts! He's in Vietnam," she said. "Why are you asking me?"

"Has Martin Alvarez been in contact with him?"

"I don't know! I haven't been in contact with Martin Alvarez."

Agent Torgerson muttered, "Denies contact," and wrote in his notebook.

She glared at him. "I told that other man who talked to me last summer. I sent Martin some boxes he left with me. He said that wasn't illegal."

"Aiding draft evaders is illegal."

"I didn't know anything about that," she said, tight-lipped. "What do you want with Randy? He won't know where Martin is."

"Where did you spend Thanksgiving, Miss Callahan?"

"*Thanksgiving?*"

"With her friend Maggie Berringer in Atlanta," Mrs. Henn said. She seemed worried Ellen would incriminate herself if not assisted.

"Thank you, Miss Callahan." The agent stood. He made a courtly bow to Mrs. Henn. "I'm sorry to have troubled you so late in the evening, ma'am."

When Ellen got back to her room, Maggie and Linda were back there, too. Linda pulled her inside. "Your mom's on the phone."

"Oh, Ellen," Lily said over the long distance line. "Linda said an FBI man was talking to you."

"I still don't know what he wanted," Ellen said. "I think maybe he's looking for Martin."

"He's looking for Randy Ottley," Lily said, her voice quavering. "He's deserted."

"Oh, my God." Ellen remembered Randy the last time she'd seen him, hair cut short, face scrubbed pink, standing in Mimi's living room at his going-away party. The brother who was doing his duty. His mother had put a flagpole in the front yard.

"He had R and R in Hawaii over Thanksgiving," Lily said tearily. "But he never went back to his unit."

"Are they sure he deserted?"

"He checked out of his hotel but he didn't get on the plane

back to his base. No one knows where he went. He must have."

Ellen thought about the boy she had seen in the draft counseling office. She thought about Randy in Hawaii, in the middle of the Pacific Ocean. Where would he go?

"Couldn't something have happened to him?"

"Oh, I don't know! Jean and Herb are just distraught."

"I've got to call Mimi. Is that okay?" Long distance calls were expensive.

"Of course. But I'm not sure that's a good idea." Lily paused. "I think everybody's gone crazy," she said.

When the operator rang Mimi's house and a voice she didn't know answered the phone, Ellen thought maybe she should have called person-to-person to be sure she got her, but the voice said, "Wait a minute," and Mimi picked it up.

"Hi, it's Ellen. I—"

"I can't talk to you now."

"I know, hon. I'm so sorry. I just called to tell you I—"

"You've done enough!" Mimi's voice hissed into the receiver. "My mother's having a nervous breakdown!"

"I'm sorry. I—"

"This is your fault! I can't talk to you!" The telephone rattled as if she had dropped the receiver.

"I think it would be better if you didn't call Mimi again," the first voice said. It sounded like Don the boyfriend. The telephone clicked and then hummed a dial tone in Ellen's ear. She stared at it, bewildered.

"What's the matter?" Linda and Maggie were looking at her with concern.

"This boy I know deserted." She picked up the telephone again and dialed the operator. "I want to make a person–to-person call to Mr. Gerald Manoury."

Jerry answered on the second ring. "He isn't here just now," he told the operator gravely. "But we expect him back in a few minutes." Person-to-person calls were more expensive, but if you didn't get the person you were calling for, you didn't have to pay.

"Thank you, Operator. I'll call back." Ellen waited, tapping her fingers, in case she got the same operator. She counted to ten and asked for Jerry's number, station-to-station.

"What is it, babe?" Jerry said as soon as he picked up the phone again.

"I just talked to Mimi Ottley."

"Yeah, I know."

"What do you mean, you know?"

"I mean I know what's gone down. So you talked to Mimi?"

"You knew about Randy?"

"You know what the valley's like. Pretty much everybody in Ayala knows by now."

"She wouldn't talk to me. She said it was *my* fault! And then that boyfriend, Don, hung up on me."

"Of course it's your fault. The poor bastard deserted. You hang out with dangerous elements like me and Martin Alvarez, it must be your influence." Jerry's voice sounded tight, as if he was talking between his teeth, or trying not to cry.

"Oh, that doesn't make sense. I went out with him for a while when we were in high school and Mimi got mad at me when we broke up, but that doesn't make any sense."

"Doesn't matter now, babe. They're hurting. If they can blame it on somebody, they don't have to blame themselves for shoving the poor bastard into the infantry."

"But how is it *my* fault? I called her up to tell her—"

"To tell her what?"

"To tell her I was sorry? I was thinking about her? To tell her I *cared*? And her idiot boyfriend hung up on me." She started to cry.

"Better not to call her for a while, maybe."

"I'm not going to call her at all!"

"Give her a while, then call."

"And why are you so goddamn sympathetic?" She was suddenly unreasoningly furious. Her mother was right. Everyone had gone crazy.

"'Cause it could have been me, I suppose." Jerry sounded subdued. He paused. "'Cause all the poor bastard wanted was to go home."

"How do you know?"

"I saw him. Me and the otter."

"What?"

"Up on the ridge. I went up there to look at the otter one night while we were cutting trail, when I was feeling really bummed, and missing you. I just sat and played my flute, and something sort of came floating over the ridge, crying. It gave me the creeps."

"Were you stoned?"

"No, officer. But I really do think it was him. It felt like whatever it was was trying to get into the valley and couldn't somehow, you know? I reckon he's been trying to get home for a long time. That was the best he could manage."

"Well, he can't go home at all now, ever. Where's he going to go?"

"I don't know, babe."

"Oh, God, it's horrible."

"He's not the first poor bastard to do it."

"Everyone's lost their mind," she said. "Mimi thinks it's my fault her brother deserted, you claim you saw some sort of astral projection up in the hills, and an FBI man interrogated me in the social room tonight."

"What did he want?"

"He wanted to know where Randy Ottley was! Why do they think I'd know?"

"They don't. They just fish."
"I want to come home!"

Ellen lay in bed that night trying to go home, trying to do whatever Randy Ottley, if that had been him, had done. She conjured up her childhood flying dream and got as far as the Mississippi, but she couldn't remember what the land looked like after that, between the river and the Rocky Mountains. When she tried to form the valley all she saw was mist and she ended up sobbing in her pillow while Linda and Maggie patted her and looked at each other with worried glances and wondered whether they ought to call Mrs. Henn.

IX
FREEWAY CHICKENS

Christmas trees always gave Jerry the creeps, although he kept trying not to tell Ellen that because she so obviously got off on Christmas. The multicolored flashing lights and the tinsel and the snow-colored angels made him twitch. Last year Dreama had given him ten dollars and told him to buy Ellen a present, so he had, a hand-carved wooden hair clip she exclaimed over until he couldn't tell whether she liked it or just the fact he'd given it to her. This year he'd made her a pair of earrings, spiderwebs of copper wire with a silver-solder fly in the center. She gave him a secondhand copy of Thorne Smith's *The Stray Lamb*, that she'd had some store search for, and they sat together out on the brick wall under the live oaks in her back yard, watching the stars while her folks and her folks' friends from L.A. and her thousands of cousins ate dinner and played poker and the kids ran around being Batman and flying plastic airplanes.

Apollo 8 floated above them, circling the moon. They couldn't see it, but the idea of it was there, a tiny capsule like a top flung into the sky with three actual humans inside.

Teak and her parents were there for dinner, and Ellen and Jerry watched Teak and one of Ellen's boy cousins walk out into the back yard together.

"I wish she wouldn't do that," Ellen said.

"Martin didn't own her," Jerry said.

"No, but he had to go to Canada, and Mike has a deferment. It isn't fair."

"Take a bet," Jerry said. "She doesn't marry any of them. She marries an obscure Austrian rocket scientist and goes to live in middle Europe. He's probably a cousin of mine."

"She marries a dentist. Why does it matter who she marries?" Ellen demanded, disgruntled.

"I don't know. Because you owe Martin something?"

She kicked the brick wall with her heels.

"You just want everybody organized. Watch the sky instead. You never know what's going to be up there these days." He pulled her head back against his shoulder and they squinted at the moon.

"Mimi's talking to me again," Ellen said. "She came over this afternoon with Don as if nothing had happened and never mentioned Randy. Mother says Jean doesn't talk about him either. They've just made him nonexistent." She brooded. "I suppose I might too if I had FBI men looking up my skirt with a periscope. I feel— hounded. And they only came to see me once. The Ottleys must be going mad." She stared at the moon. "I thought they'd take that flagpole down, but they didn't."

"It looks patriotic."

"Mother says Sally Alvarez says Ed's sort of coming around. He let her send Martin some money. Do you think the Ottleys really know where Randy is?"

"I think Herb Ottley would turn in his grandmother. You haven't seen this." Jerry pulled a clipping out of his jeans pocket. "It ran in the *Ayala News* last week. I don't imagine your mom felt like sending it to you."

Ellen unfolded it. It smelled like pot and she sniffed it and grinned at him.

"Just read it."

It was from the editorial page, an ostensible letter to the editor, titled, "Open Letter to My Son."

Dear Randy,

What can a mother say to a boy who is a deserter and a traitor to his country and his family and friends? I know you read the Ayala News and will have it sent to you if you can, by someone who is helping you disgrace yourself and us. I don't want to know who they are. But I want you to read this so you will know what you have done to your father and your sister and me. We were so proud of you. We thought you were a man. But a man does not run away from his responsibilities. Mimi was so proud of you, but now she just hopes you are dead because that would be better than what you are. And your father has a heart condition, but I am sure you are not bothered by that. Maybe you will be bothered by the fact that you can never come home again, but I doubt it.

If you do want to come home, there is only one way you can do it. You can get back to your unit while you are only AWOL and not a deserter. Your father will come and get you if you tell us where you are. But we will not be a part in your becoming a traitor. I hope you will decide to do the right thing and tell us where you are so we can tell your commander.

Love,

Mom, Dad and Mimi

Ellen felt as if the Christmas turkey were going to come back up. She pushed the clipping away from her, back at Jerry, as if he could undo it by putting it in his pocket again.

"Ah, shit," he said, contrite. "I shouldn't have showed you that. My old man may be a little weird, but he beats Herb Ottley hands down."

"Jean wrote that letter," Ellen said.

"Under whose influence?"

"Women are capable of being vicious on their own."

"Think your mom would feel that way? Or you would, about one of *your* kids?"

"Neither would my father. And assuming I ever have any," she muttered.

"Come on. I told Robert we'd come by later if we could." Jerry dragged her off the wall. He wasn't going to fight with her on Christmas. He shouldn't have shown her the damn clipping and he didn't really know why he'd been carrying it around in his pocket. Maybe to remind him when he was well off, the difference between his father and Herb Ottley.

He put her in her car and she drove obediently over to Robert's house. The Hutchinsons' front windows were outlined with big multicolored lights and the tree in the front room was draped with tinsel and sprayed with fake snow. It never snowed in Ayala except on Christmas trees.

Robert's father was settled in a new recliner that still had *Merry Christmas, Dad* pinned to the arm. He waved them toward a spread of cookies, fruitcake, a glass bowl of eggnog, and cut-glass dishes of candy.

Robert looked like an ad for J. C. Penney in a new yellow sweater and a red and blue tie. His mother was taking his picture with a Polaroid camera. Robert had an apartment at UC Santa Barbara now, the family's first college student, and everyone was proud of him. The Polaroid slowly spat out the picture. It was stiff, and ghostly blue.

"Wait a minute," his mother said. "Here it comes. It's developing now."

Robert grinned at Ellen and kissed her on the forehead. "I have something for you. Wait a second."

When he came back Ellen handed him the long, thin box wrapped in silver paper she'd been balancing in the crook of her arm. "Here, yourself. Merry Christmas."

Robert pulled the paper off and took out a white clay pipe

with a long stem and an oval bowl. "Far out."

"I got it in Williamsburg."

He put a package wrapped in red and green poinsettia paper in her hands. "I remember you like this stuff. At least you always smell like it."

Ellen unwrapped a bottle of Jean Naté and sprayed it on her neck. Her spiderweb earrings flashed in the cologne mist and the lights on the Christmas tree.

"Look," Robert's mother said. She held out the photo of Robert. He looked self-conscious, like someone about to give a testimonial. "Isn't that sweater nice on him?"

"Gorgeous," Ellen said.

"Let me get one of all of you together."

She linked arms with Jerry and Robert and they posed, squinting at the flash. They watched while the Polaroid disgorged the print.

"It just takes a minute." Robert's mother held it out so they could see themselves forming, in nacreous shades of blue and brown, like spirits appearing.

What if someone invented a camera that went backward, Ellen wondered, that would erase a print after a few minutes, so you possessed the image only briefly. Then after that whoever was in the picture would fade into nonexistence too, the way Martin and Randy Ottley had. You could point it at people and erase them.

The image on the pasteboard solidified slowly: Ellen in the center, looking into the camera, her knees bare under a short red skirt, feet in black satin pumps with huge silver buckles, her hair pulled back to show Jerry's earrings. The red dress and Robert's sweater made twin splotches of color reflected in the lights of the tree. On her other side, Jerry, in a dark t-shirt and jeans, grinning. Both boys' eyes were hidden behind the flash reflection in their glasses.

"Isn't that nice?" Robert's mom said. "You look so nice. Would you like to have it, dear?" She gave her the print and Ellen tucked it in her purse.

Robert pulled off his tie and hung it over the Polaroid. "Get me out of here before she takes my picture again." He kissed his mother's forehead.

"Christmas present?" Ellen asked.

"How could you tell?" His mother was taking a picture of his father in the new recliner.

The three of them went outside, along the path worn in the lawn to the old beauty shop next door. Jerry sniffed the air. "Maybe a freeze tonight." If it froze, the growers would light the smudge pots in the orange orchards.

Robert turned on the lights in The Place and plugged in the coffee pot and the space heater.

"Not many customers," Jerry said.

"Nah. Everybody's scattered. You never come either," he added.

"Working for a living." Jerry held out his hands, callused from cutting trail, scarred with nicks and scratches.

Ellen lit the candles in the chianti bottles and sat on one of the cable spool tables, swinging her legs while Robert made coffee. Jerry pulled a joint out of his pocket and they passed it around. After a few minutes Robert went in the house and came back with a plate of Christmas cookies.

They ate them and watched the smoke twist through the candle flames, and after a while Jerry began to sing,

Go tell it on the mountain,
Over the hills and everywhere,
Go tell it on the mountain
That Jesus Christ is born.

The other two joined in. Then they sang "Oh Come, Oh Come, Emmanuel" and "Joy to the World".

"Damn." Jerry shook his head in amazement at himself. "I don't usually get into Christmas."

"You just like to sing," Ellen said. He'd sat down next to her on the table, and she leaned against him companionably and smiled at Robert.

"You two." Robert stared at them owlishly from behind his glasses. "You two blow me away."

"And why's that?" Jerry grinned at him.

"You make me believe in love, man, honest to God."

Ellen smiled slowly, solemnly. If Robert said that, it must be true.

It did freeze that night, while Apollo 8 circled the moon. Jerry came to Ellen's door early in the morning, barefoot in the cold, face streaming tears.

"What is it?"

"It's Aaron, man. He's dead." He sat down on her doorstep and buried his face in his knees.

"Oh, my God." Ellen slumped down beside him and pulled her blue chiffon robe around her ankles. Her bedroom slippers were padded satin. She could feel the dew soaking through them.

"His old lady called me this morning. They came to tell her last night, on fucking Christmas!"

"Oh, God. How is she?"

"Drunk." Jerry lifted his head. He scrubbed a hand across his eyes. "She's pretty much always drunk."

"How did it happen?"

"I don't know. He was in some kind of firefight. His mom's not too clear. The Army sent two officers to the house to tell her. I think they had to sober her up first. Then she passed out again, and when she woke up this morning, she remembered. She climbed back in the bottle but it didn't help. She was crying when she called me."

Ellen remembered Aaron at his going-away party, solemnly telling her he was going to learn heavy equipment mechanics, learn to be in charge. Her heart felt like lead.

"They're shipping him home. They managed to find enough pieces to bury. The funeral's day after tomorrow. His dad's coming in from Reno."

"Have you told Dreama?"

"Yeah. I woke her up before I walked over here. She was crying into the oatmeal and raving about the military-industrial complex and staging a demonstration downtown in front of the draft board. I couldn't take it. She's right, but I couldn't care."

Ellen wore black to Aaron's funeral, a cocktail dress her mother had thought would be suitable for college dates. Charlene Hawley, Aaron's mother, wore a navy blue suit that Dreama pinned together in the back to make it fit, and dark, sling-back sandals worn down at the heels. His father, Rudy, who was a blackjack dealer in Reno, wore a white shirt with a dark tie and a brown jacket. His eyes were angry, and halfway through the service, he snapped "Bullshit!" loud enough to be heard. The priest paused, then went on with the Mass, Latin prayers incomprehensible to Ellen. She watched the light from the stained-glass windows move across her hands. The ceiling and the Stations of the Cross were dark with years of candle smoke and incense. The pews were old oak, hard and penitential.

Rudy Hawley glared at the altar and the flag-draped coffin. When the pallbearers started to carry it out—Jerry and Robert marching uncomfortably with an honor guard from the Army— he stood and stumped after it. He climbed into his car and followed the hearse, staring furiously through the windshield as the little procession made its way down Ayala Avenue to the Catholic cemetery beside the orange orchards.

A canopy was set up over the open grave, sheltering the lift that would lower the coffin. The pallbearers eased it out of the hearse and into the slings of the lift, and Jerry retreated to Ellen's side. Dreama was with Charlene, one arm around her thin shoulders. Charlene's face was red and slick with tears, her nose running. The Army pallbearers stood at attention.

The priest opened his prayerbook, his vestments flapping in the wind. *"Ego sum resurrectio et vita—"*

"Bullshit!" Rudy Hawley said again. He staggered to the edge of the grave, leaning on his cane. "I'm tired of funerals," he said, glaring at the priest. "Tired of fucking funerals. I see one go by every damn day, long lines of cars, lights on, burying somebody's damn kid. Aaron wasn't no hero. He didn't have time. He was just a dumb kid suckered by his own government."

Charlene pushed Dreama away and stumbled toward him, catching one heel in the hummocky grass. She stared at Rudy across the coffin. "Shut up! What do you know, you were never here!"

"I know better'n to let him join the goddamned Army!"

The honor guard stood at attention, stone-faced.

"They drafted him!" Charlene said, tears streaming down her face.

"Cocksuckers!" Rudy Hawley said. He turned and stalked to his car. The engine started up and it peeled out of the cemetery, spraying gravel across the tombstones and the weeping marble angels.

The day after New Year's, Jerry got a notice, forwarded by Ana, to report for a physical in Oakland. It wasn't an induction notice, so before she went back to school Ellen drove him up to Berkeley to see if he could flunk the physical. She had to catch a plane in Los Angeles the next day and couldn't stay, so she left him with Ana and flew to Virginia with a tight knot in her stomach. Then Jerry didn't call her when he said he would and she cut art class to sit by the telephone, a squat, ugly, black plastic toad that didn't ring. She imagined him inducted, trapped; or alternately—remembering the riots at the Oakland draft board—beaten and jailed.

The next morning her art teacher scolded her for putting her education second to some hippie, then suggested himself as a better choice. When Jerry didn't call that day either, she called Ana's house and he was there.

"Oh," Ana said, "it's Ellen. Jerry, it's Ellen."

There was a pause and then he said huskily into the phone, "Hello, love."

"Are you all right?" The knot was still there, not erased by his voice.

"Yeah."

"Why didn't you call me?"

"I don't know. It's been a scene." He said something unintelligible, presumably to Ana.

"You promised you'd call. What happened with your physical?"

"I couldn't flunk it, babe."

"Oh, no."

"They walked us through the whole building naked, me and a bunch of other poor assholes, while people with clothes on looked at us. They took my blood pressure and asked if I did drugs. I took some speed and gave them a dirty urine, so I said yeah, but they didn't give a shit. There was one guy who was having some kind of convulsion on the floor. It looked real as hell, but they just left him there. They wouldn't even give me my clothes back while I talked to the shrink. Other guys had got dressed again, they were just being shitty because they knew I was trying to get out. I sat there stark naked in front of this guy. Finally I got up and went to the locker room, and put on my clothes and left."

"Why didn't you tell me?"

"I didn't want you to worry about it."

"How do you expect me not to worry? What are you going to *do* now?"

"I thought maybe I could convince 'em I was crazy. You think I'm crazy. Everybody I know thinks I'm crazy." His voice was slurred and weary. "Except the Army."

"Jerry, please go back to school."

"I don't want to go back to school. It's too late anyway."

"What are you going to do then?"

"I thought I might go to Phoenix." He sounded as if that was a logical move.

"What can you do in Phoenix?"

"Be an otter." His voice had a smile in it now. She could imagine him stretched sleepily on Ana's sofa, wrapped in a quilt. "I miss you."

"Jerry, if I transfer to UCSB for senior year, will you go to school, too?"

"You'd do that?"

"Yes."

"Why can't you be here and I won't go to school? I read more books than you do. I know how to cut trail and run a Caterpillar. I bet you don't. Why should I go to school?"

"Because if I do something for you, you could do something for me!" Her voice was tight.

"Then don't, babe."

"And because none of those things will keep you out of the Army!"

"They won't want me." His voice trailed off again, as if he'd turned his head away from the phone. "I just have to convince them they don't."

"I can't hear you."

"Sorry, babe," he said. "Look, can we talk tomorrow? I'm wiped. The scene at the induction center was ugly and I got into Ana's pot a bit to take the edge off. I think I'm about to crash."

"Fine." She didn't want to hang up, to let go, but she could feel the space between them stretching. "All right."

"I love you." His voice was cajoling.

"I love you too."

"We'll take care of him!" Ana's voice called from somewhere in the room, and certain things occurred to Ellen.

"Goodnight, love."

When she hung up she could still see him on the other end of the line, a tenuous tether letting loose at both ends. He wasn't on Ana's sofa. He was in Ana's bed.

The realization she couldn't take it arrived slowly. It had something to do with beginning her senior year the next fall.

Where was she going to go from there? She'd majored in history but had no idea how to make that useful, unless she went to graduate school and got a doctorate and taught it all, all over again, to someone else. That prospect seemed unutterably dreary. She could go back to work for the *Chronicle* and cover the Women of the Moose and hope eventually to get a job in the newsroom; and hope eventually Jerry wouldn't be too afraid, or too feckless, to have children with her. And stop sleeping with other women. Theoretically she could agree sex was not a commodity to be sold for a wedding ring, that love could be free of jealousy. In practice, when he called her a week later and she asked him directly, and he admitted it, thinking about him in bed with Ana made her furiously, torrentially jealous. In practice she didn't give a shit about the revolution. She wanted to kill him.

It just seemed so sad and pointless, and she envisioned them living in some shack in the riverbottom while she waited for him stop farting around being an otter, humiliated while he slept with other women and everybody knew about it. Maybe making a fool of herself trying to do the same thing.

When she flew home for Easter, she told her parents not to bring Jerry with them when they picked her up at the airport. She thought about what she was going to say to him all the way back to Ayala in the car, an hour and a half of repeating like a mantra the speech she'd composed on the plane.

And then when the car pulled into the Callahans' driveway, Jerry was there anyway, waiting for her, asleep in a sleeping bag in her carport. He got up and hopped to the car window, goofy and smiling, feet still in the bag.

She pushed past him blearily. "Jerry, I'm too tired. Go home. I'll see you tomorrow." She fled into the house, while he stood there, entangled.

"Ellen, are you sure this is the way to deal with this?" Daniel Callahan looked out the French doors at Jerry, still standing in

127

the driveway.

She dragged her suitcase into her room and closed the door. "I can't talk to him tonight," she said through it.

In the morning he was at her door at nine. She heard him whistling up the driveway and suppressed the urge to bolt out the back and hide in the cabin.

He peered at her anxiously through his glasses. "What's wrong, babe? Are you sick? Your folks said they had stuff to do all over L.A. yesterday and I couldn't come, or I'd have been at the airport."

"I told them not to bring you."

His face changed slowly, the expectant light in his eyes dimming behind the glasses.

"We have to talk." She pulled him into Daniel's study and shut the door. Her father was somewhere in the back yard tactfully pruning pear trees.

Jerry didn't say anything, just waited for her to do it.

"I'm going to graduate next year," she said frantically. "I keep thinking about what I want to do then."

They'd talked about grad school in Santa Barbara.

"How I want to live." She bit her lip. She poked at the pencils in her father's pencil jar, stuck her fingers between the keys of his electric typewriter. "I don't want a lover. I want a husband. I want children."

Jerry didn't answer her. It seemed impossible to be responsible when something wanted to eat you, to plan for the future when you didn't think there would be one, but he was aware that under the circumstances that was no answer.

"I want to be a real person," Ellen said desperately. "Not live on the edge with people who don't have hot water or privacy or enough money to go to the doctor when their kids are sick."

"That's what's wrong with doctors only being for people with money," Jerry said, unable to resist arguing. "That's why they started the Free Clinic."

"I don't want to go to the Free Clinic! I want to be the kind of person people will rent an apartment to! And give a credit card to!"

"Sure. Buy into the system." He nodded, but it seemed wrongheaded, to buy into the system when the system had gone crazy, and was sending thousands of its citizens to someone else's country to die horribly and kill other innocent people to force them not to adopt the government that the majority of them seemed to want. Ellen wanted to be safe, and that didn't look to him like the way to do it. But she'd always been the optimist. "I suppose we could get married," he said. It seemed like a prescription for doom, but he didn't know what else to offer.

"You don't want to get married!" She jammed a pencil back in the cup so hard the point broke. "You're crazy. I'd be crazy if I let you. You don't want to have kids or a real job, or go to school so you won't be cutting trail your whole life. You don't want *anything* I want!"

"I want you." He looked at her bleakly.

"I care about you," she said desperately, wishing he'd just vanish. "I just can't go on like this."

"Don't cry." Jerry kept looking at her so that she couldn't bear to look at him. "I didn't think you'd stick with me as long as you did, you know." He felt his stomach turning to lead, his mouth forming easy lies. He'd let himself get sucked into hope. He put his hand on the door. "Quit feeling guilty. When you find you a guy, you can invite me to the wedding."

She sniffled. "Would you come?"

"Sure." He grinned at her. It took some effort, but she didn't know that. "I'll even wear a tie."

After he'd gone she kept herself from running after him by imagining what being married to him would be like. She went back to bed and slept as long as she could. When she got up, she called Robert and told him what she'd done. Then she got in the car and drove down to Teak's house.

Brooding in the fast lane, she missed the Laurel Canyon exit and cut across three lanes, cursing, to get off and turn around. An interchange she didn't want coiled around 101 as it headed into Hollywood, encapsulating a thicket of oleander and eucalyptus. As she passed, a white chicken stuck its head out of the bushes and cackled at her. She hit the brakes. Another one farther down was bustling along the shoulder, pecking at bugs. She slowed while a black T-Bird tailgated her. The chickens squawked and scuttled back into the brush.

The T-Bird honked furiously. She pulled over and parked on the shoulder, and pretended to have car trouble. She'd heard rumors of the freeway chickens, descendants of an overturned truckload, but had never seen them before. Despite her dismal mood, they made her smile. She sat on the guardrail and watched them foraging in the brush until a motorcycle cop pulled over.

"Miss, you can't park here." The chickens were reflected in his dark glasses.

"Oh." She stood. "I think something's wrong with my car."

"Let me look at it."

"It just stopped," she said, trailing him.

The cop turned the key. "It's running now, Miss. So get it off the shoulder, hear?"

Ellen smiled at him brightly and nodded. A chicken looked out of the oleanders at her. For some reason it made her think of Jerry and she started crying.

At Teak's house, Teak and Ellen smoked pot and drank cheap red wine all night and tried to decide what made love work.

"I had a letter from Martin," Teak said, sitting cross-legged on the llama-skin bedspread.

"What did he say?"

"Wants me to come up there, live in Vancouver. His papers are going through for legal immigrant status or whatever they call it." Teak looked around the room. "Vancouver. Can you imagine?"

"I'm afraid to go home," Ellen said. "I'm afraid I'll see Jerry." Living in the oleanders by her driveway.

"His parents gave in and sent him his birth certificate and diploma and shit."

"And I'm going to quit taking the Pill. Sex is what got me into this."

Teak poured more wine into the coffee cup she was using. She shook her head at Ellen. "There may be a great truth in that, but I can't see it just at this moment."

"Well, I mean it," Ellen said stubbornly. "I'm not gonna sleep with guys until I can get married and have babies."

Teak held out the bottle. "Have some more wine, dear."

Ellen went back to Carter Randolph and told Linda and Maggie what she'd done. She felt compelled to tell everyone, which somehow made it official.

"You were the first person I know to start talking the Pill," Linda said. "Now everyone I know is taking it, and you're gonna stop. That's beyond avant garde, Callahan. Are you planning to be a virgin again?"

"Sure," Maggie said. "You get it back on a technicality. It doesn't count 'cause you were drunk. Or 'cause he was drunk. Or you'll never see him again, or—"

"Oh, shut up," Ellen said. "It counted. All right? But it's too much trouble. I'm tired of it."

"You have a point," Linda conceded.

"You bet I do."

She got a couple of letters from Jerry—"just friends" letters that said he was going to Phoenix to hang out for a while, a friend had a middle eastern dance troupe, they might go on to New Orleans.

When she came home that summer Ayala felt different. She hardly saw anyone she'd hung out with while she was hanging out with Jerry. Robert had an apartment in Santa Barbara. All the old Ayala boys who'd been Jerry's friends had scattered. She didn't go to see Dreama, even though Jerry wasn't there. Life post-Jerry could be arranged to match the edges of life pre-Jerry, she discovered, and you'd never know anything had been cut from the script.

She ran into Carl Leeman's mother downtown in the drug store. Mrs. Leeman told her how well he was doing, how good the Army had been for him. Ellen said that was nice. Mimi Ottley got engaged. They'd get married when Don finished his degree. Ellen said that was nice too. Mimi didn't mention Randy. He had been eliminated from the script as well.

Ellen started work at the newspaper again, writing endless wedding stories. Married attendants had to be listed by their husbands' names. You couldn't refer to married women as Miss, or use Mrs. with the woman's first name unless she was divorced. The Society editor was firm on that. The black girls were the worst, she said. They just didn't seem to care about doing it properly. And the Hispanic girls were nearly as bad and always had too many bridesmaids. She gave Ellen to understand that it had all been much easier when the newspaper decided whose wedding merited coverage. She tapped a fingernail on a name on the wedding form on Ellen's desk. Ellen needed to call that one, she said, and find out if she was divorced.

It felt surreal to be grilling bridesmaids about their marital status while the newsroom reported on the coming draft lottery. It was supposed to be fairer than the old system; money wouldn't keep you out of it, there would be no deferments for college, and the sons of the men making the decisions would start getting drafted. President Nixon claimed to have a plan to end the war and Ellen wondered if that was it.

In Houston they were getting ready to put a man on the moon. That seemed a magical and hopeful notion. She was startled when Carl Leeman came to see her, an event as unexpected as the moon flight. He looked rugged and muscular in his uniform, and said he was home on leave before going back for another tour. His green eyes rested on her with apparent approval, and his blond hair was neatly clipped despite an endearing cowlick over one eye, like Superman's.

"Do you want coffee?" She tried to pretend she was her mother, an adult woman entertaining company. "Or a beer?"

"Beer, sure. I thought maybe you'd go to lunch with me somewhere."

He drank his beer while she sat primly on the sofa. "When do you have to go back?" she asked him.

"I've got two weeks. I'm a sergeant now," he added, patting the chevrons on his sleeve. "Come on. I borrowed my mom's car."

Carl drove her to the Topa Topa Room and they settled into a booth and ordered pastrami sandwiches.

"It's wild to see you so grown up," Ellen said. "I remember when you got kicked out of Apple Valley for putting a cherry bomb in the toilet."

"That was kid stuff. Randy Ottley was in on that too but they didn't catch him."

"Why do I suspect you talked him into it?" Ellen said. "You know he deserted?"

"Oh yeah, everybody knows." Carl looked disgusted. "I saw him once over there, crying in his beer in the canteen. I told him he was lucky he wasn't in my unit."

"It must be awful over there," Ellen said. "And awful not to be able to go home. Are you really going back for another tour? I thought no one had to do but one."

"I asked for it. We need to be over there. The commies'll overrun the world if somebody doesn't slap 'em down."

Ellen chewed her sandwich thoughtfully. "You think? It's such a little country."

"It looks little on the map, hon, until you're over there. Then it's great big. I'm in a LRRP unit," he pronounced it *lurp*, "that's Long Range Reconnaissance Patrol."

"What do you do?"

"Look for enemy troop movements, signs of Viet Cong in the villages."

"What do you do then?"

"Then we call in the gunships on 'em."

She put her sandwich down. "On the villages?"

"I'll show you a picture of me and my best buddy." He pulled his wallet out and put a snapshot on the table. A large German shepherd, ears up, sat by Carl's boots in a square black and white print. They were both grinning. "That's my partner, Jojo."

"He looks like a nice dog." Maybe they could talk about the dog.

"He's trained to smell out mines and booby traps, VC tunnels. He can tell a gook from an American. The gooks hate him. He doesn't like South Vietnamese any better'n he likes VC." Carl tucked the picture back in his wallet. "Dogs are smarter'n people a lot of the time. He's saved my ass twice."

Ellen took a bite out of her sandwich. She couldn't think what to say but Carl seemed happy to talk.

"One time," Carl said, "we'd just landed and the NVA were all over us. We called in some air power and they dropped the napalm and we thought that would do it, but the gooks kept coming." His face was suddenly intent.

"Picture a river, rice paddy, jungle." He laid it out with forks and a spoon. "I call for choppers and we button up and wait. Finally a chopper comes down but it gets hit with a rocket as soon as we're up. I wake up on the ground with Jojo licking my face, and the chopper's on fire. Jojo starts dragging me by the collar. And now we're here—"

Carl arranged the salt and mustard on the table. "And there's a village nearby, here, and we think they're maybe VC, so we don't make for that, we call in the Skyraiders to flame it, and we start heading back the other way. There's mines all along the trail, and Jojo keeps marking them—Bouncing Betties, the kind that shoot up three, four feet before they blow, so they can take your nuts off."

"You had them drop napalm on the village?"

"Keep 'em busy," Carl said. "When we stop to rest, Jojo's flaked out beside me one minute, and the next he's got this gook by the ankle, and the gook's screaming and my men are all grabbing their rifles. The gook had got right up on us, the sentry was screaming how he never saw him. I give the word to Jojo and he holds him still while I question him. We found out how many VC were in his village and the next village over for good measure."

The table top had green trees on it now, and little houses on stilts exploding into flame. Ellen swiped them away with her hand. "I thought you were going to tell me about the dog."

"I did," Carl said. "That's what it's like."

"What did you do with the man you caught?" she whispered, wishing she could make herself not ask.

"You don't want to know, hon." He stared for a moment at the condiments spread out along the table, as if he could see the little trees too. "You know, what still surprises me after all this time is how quiet it can get there. There's birds and bugs and all kinds of noises hoo-hooing and squeaking in the jungle all the time, night and day. And then it'll just be . . . still. Like death passing by, you know. And you wonder what the jungle hears that you don't."

The waitress asked if they wanted dessert, and Ellen said no before Carl could say he did. He paid and they stepped out into the dusty sunshine on Ayala Avenue. A group of protesters were carrying signs in front of the post office two doors down, where a recruiter had a table set up. Ellen recognized the woman, Judy, who'd organized the vigil Jerry had taken her to. She shied away, crossing the street to Carl's car, afraid Jerry would be there, even though he was in Phoenix.

"Hippies." Carl's mouth tightened. "With their goddamned peace signs and their fag hair. I'd like to get them in my unit for a day."

"What would you do with them?"

"Accidents happen all the time in-country."

"They think the war is a mistake. That doesn't make them traitors."

"It does in my book."

"To think it's wrong to kill people?" She stopped, hand on the car. "Carl, you just told me you ordered a village bombed that was full of civilians."

Carl smiled at her and shook his head. "Life and death doesn't mean anything to those people. That's what guys like that shithead Ottley don't understand. They don't look at it the way we do over here. They're a whole different culture."

"How could life not mean anything to them? They're human beings."

"No, they're not." Carl shook his head again. "You have to remember that or you can't function, like Ottley. You *have* to keep knowing that."

X
LUNAR LANDING

W hen Carl called her again, Ellen pleaded orders to cover the Eastern Star's installation dinner, and said, when he offered to escort her, it wasn't allowed, though she knew they'd have loved him in his uniform. She spent the rest of the two weeks hiding until he went back to Vietnam.

At the end of June the paper hired a new reporter, an affable, ginger-haired man, Gordon Murphy, who was twenty-seven and had a mild birth defect in one foot that had induced the Army to pass him by long ago. He covered the county government beat and appeared to have no strong opinions about the war at all.

"He's going to ask you out," the Society editor whispered to Ellen. "You go. This one's a prospect."

"How do you know?" she demanded.

"Oh, Gordon's a good boy. He worked here a few years ago, then he went on to Las Vegas. If he's back, he's ready to settle down. And he's interested in you."

"Oh, for Pete's sake," Ellen said, "I've just been to the *Yes We're Open* with him." Everyone went to the *Yes We're Open*, a restaurant around the corner from the *Chronicle* that featured 23-cent tacos and had no other name except at night when it was the *Sorry We're Closed.*

It was a slow news day despite war and revolution in the streets, and the men at the city desk were goofing with a copy pencil and a tape measure. "Hey, Callahan!" one of them called. "Come on, we'll measure you."

"What for?" Ellen came suspiciously around the counter from Soc.

"See what your Ape Index is," the police reporter said. "It's Murphy's invention. If your arm span's longer than your height, your Ape Index indicates how close grandma was to the gorillas." They'd drawn their own measurements on the newsroom wall by the AP wire. He applied his tape measure and clucked his tongue. "Jones here is off the gorilla scale. Let's try you."

"Try Murphy," Jones demanded.

"My people have been walking upright for many years," Murphy said.

He's possible, Ellen thought, stretching her arms out. *Possible.*

The police reporter measured her. "Fine stock, Callahan, fine stock. No suspicious ancestry."

Gordon leaned on the counter after she went back to her typewriter. She was supposed to be writing a piece on the County Fair's fashion show. He eyed the Soc editor, who turned her back and pretended she had copy to edit.

"It's like a fishbowl," Murphy said disgustedly. "Want to go somewhere this weekend?"

"Um," Ellen said. That didn't sound very bright. "Where?" That wasn't much better.

"A movie? Dinner? Both?"

Heavens. A date with someone sane. "Sure." She smiled at him.

They went to see *True Grit*. He took her to dinner first at the Sportsman in Ventura, which was good and expensive and dimly lit, and they ordered martinis on the rocks, and the waiter looked at Gordon, in a coat and tie, and didn't ask Ellen how old she was. He kissed her goodnight on her front steps when he took her home, and on Monday there was a note in her typewriter: *Want to go on a picnic Saturday?*

"Told you," the Soc editor said.

"Mmm," Ellen said.

Gordon brought a bottle of wine and a loaf of bread, and tins of paté and caviar. She brought a bag of apples and two pomegranates from her father's trees, and Henry, the poodle-cocker mix who'd begun as hers but was now mostly Lily's since Ellen had gone to college.

"Take him," Lily said. "He doesn't get out much."

Gordon didn't seem to mind him. They put Henry in the back seat of Gordon's Fairlane and drove up Highway 33 to Rose Valley with the windows open and Henry's whiskers blowing in the wind. They passed the turn-off for the otter, but Ellen didn't say anything.

"Have you ever been up here?" Gordon asked her when they got out of the car.

"A couple of times. We used to have my birthday parties at Lions' Camp. My father has horrible home movies of me in my first two-piece bathing suit. Don't let him show them to you."

Gordon put the lunch on a picnic table under an oak tree. They could hear the splash of a stream farther off. "There's a waterfall," he said. "Want to walk up to it?"

The path beside the stream was shady and cool with drifting

mist from the falls. After two years of low rainfall there wasn't much water in the mountains, but what there was made everything around it come alive as if someone had put a green filter on a camera lens. The stream was studded with round white stones and overhung with willow thickets and sycamore. The water was cold snowmelt from the higher ridges, clean and sharp as crystal. Small brown fish darted in the bottom of the shallows. They walked single file up the narrow path with Henry bouncing from rock to rock beside them.

At the end, the falls frothed down a steep slab of brown stone into a pool between yellow boulders. They sat on a rock and watched it.

"What are you going to do after college?" Gordon asked her. "You've got one more year, right?"

"God knows. I have a totally useless major, unless I go to grad school."

"History, right?" Gordon chuckled. "Me too."

"Well, look what it's fitted you for," Ellen said. "Newspaper reporting."

"Only a cut above bank robbery," Gordon agreed, "and not so profitable. Except that I like it."

"I do, too," she sighed. "If they'd let me *do* anything."

"That was a good piece you did on the Free Clinic."

"My point precisely. It should have run news side, and it would have if I hadn't been from Soc."

"Are you going to burn your bra?" He looked interested. "You could do it in Harper's office."

Ellen chuckled. "He's the one who told us we shouldn't be insulted that the Fair press party is stag. After all, they have a tea and fashion show for the girls."

"Tea's no good?"

"We have to cover the damn thing," Ellen said, outraged. "It's a fundraiser. The press party is a freebie—steak and scotch and I don't expect anybody reports on what happens."

"Jesus, I hope not. But that's for news side."

"Helen's news side. And the Oxnard paper has a woman on news side, too. And you know what they said when Helen complained? If they let women in, they'd have to let the guys bring their wives, and then they couldn't get drunk."

"I guess you have something there."

"Will it stop you from going?"

"That would be drastic. But I'll tell the committee the women have a point. Maybe next year they'll see the light."

"Maybe I'll be back next year."

"Well, I hope so," Gordon said. He took her hand. "Caviar?"

He was nice, she thought, climbing off her rock. He seemed to think she was nice. And he seemed to intend to be around when she graduated. They retraced their steps, with Henry hopping along the rocks ahead of them like a fluffy goat. He stopped abruptly before they came out of the last willow thicket. When they passed him he whined plaintively.

"Come on, Henry."

He peered up at Ellen, his whiskers twitching. He looked pop-eyed and worried.

"What's the matter, old man?" Gordon ruffled his topknot.

"Let's *go*, Henry." Ellen went on down the path. "He'll come," she said to Gordon. They could hear him fussing behind them.

As they came around the last bend, they saw their overturned picnic. The basket was on the ground, with a bitten apple and the broken jar of caviar. All that was left of the bread was a few shreds in the dirt.

"*Shit!*" Gordon picked up the basket. "Brazen little buggers. Look at that." There were tracks all around the table, disappearing into the buckbrush. Coyotes.

While they studied the tracks, Henry shot out of the willows and sat on Ellen's feet. When she pushed him away he got in the car, through the window, and refused to get out again.

The tin of paté had been bitten open and licked out. They had left the wine and the pomegranates alone. Ellen peeled one, digging her fingernails into the shiny red skin. Inside it was compartmented, with ruby seeds like beads in a slick pale membrane.

Gordon opened the wine and got a paper cup the coyotes had left unchewed. "I can't believe it. In broad daylight."

"Have some pomegranate." Ellen held out a section.

He took it and they shared the cup. "They're way too smart. Did you see that tin?"

She picked it up. The steel lid and been punctured over and over, and rolled halfway back at the corner. The shards stuck up in jagged splinters, but there was no blood on them. "They're good." She got the can opener and took the rest of the lid off gingerly. There was still paté in the far end. She offered it to Henry but he wouldn't eat it and he wouldn't come out of the car.

In July Neil Armstrong walked on the moon. Headlines proclaimed the achievement in enormous black type, for once eclipsing the news from Vietnam.

THEY DID IT, the *Honolulu Star-Bulletin* trumpeted beside a picture of the lunar lander. Randy Ottley stopped and stared at it. His physical body still functioned but on most days his consciousness was loosely tethered to it. The moon landing was somehow terrifying, in the way that the jungle had been, an alien landscape ready to open and swallow him.

The thought of being trapped in a spacesuit made him choke and he shoved his way out of the crowd around the news stand. A storefront window showed a wavy image of a ghost in clothes stolen from someone's clothesline, of sunburned skin, blank eyes, a haircut grown out from its draftee shearing, ragged where he'd tried to cut it himself with a pocketknife.

Then suddenly behind him the reflection caught fire and the endlessly burning jungle and the blinding white phosphorus engulfed the people in the street. He shielded his eyes and fled back to the box in the alley where he slept behind a coffee shop and lived on their discards. They knew he was there but no one bothered him. He frightened other, worse thieves away. He curled in on himself the way an animal makes itself small, and closed his eyes, searching for home, for the valley, for the place where he'd been someone solid.

His sister Mimi, making up the new guest room—now stripped of its trains and chess club jacket—saw him as a flash of uncomfortable light in the windowpane and closed the blinds.

Jerry hitchhiked home from Phoenix under that full moon, flinching every time a red Volkswagen drove by but drawn by a similar yearning for home. He found Judy in his mother's living room, painting banners for an antiwar demonstration. Another woman was with her, thin, intense, with a pointed chin, pen clutched tightly in her hand, outlining each letter with fierce concentration.

"This is Joelle," Judy said.

"Hey," Jerry said.

Joelle nodded silently. Her hair was sandy blond, tied back

from her face with a scarf. Jerry guessed she was about thirty.

"She's had a bad time," Judy said, cornering him in the kitchen where he'd gone to look for beer. "Her fuckhead husband just moved out." She looked at Jerry as if that might be his fault, as the only available representative of male fuckheadedness.

"Bummer," Jerry said. He squatted on the floor next to Joelle and picked up a brush. "Here, let me do this end."

The moon was round as a saucer of magic when they got into downtown Ventura. It was still afternoon, but it glowed in the sky like a pearl in an oyster. Everyone seemed to be out on the sidewalk looking at it, imagining those weightless footsteps in the lunar dust. Jerry thought that if people could do that, maybe they could quit shooting each other over dumbshit politics. The demonstrators set up shop in the park and lined the sidewalk beside it where the afternoon home-from-work traffic could see them. Joelle clutched her end of the banner tightly and her kids ran around in circles in the park behind them, shrieking. Someone had brought lemonade, and someone else had a guitar to get everyone singing. It was like camp, Jerry thought. Demonstration camp. Tomorrow they'd learn to make peace sign badges. The moon beamed down on them, and the familiar salt smell off the ocean tickled his nose. He felt glad to be home, more hopeful than he had been since he and Ellen had split. There was kinship among the people in the park, a tribal sense of belonging. Jerry's little brother Ben, who was seventeen now, was there. Dreama stood holding the other end of Joelle's banner.

"Looks good," Jerry said to Joelle, because she looked like someone caught on the end of a fishhook.

She smiled, all at once, showing a lot of teeth, her eyes crinkling up. "It does, doesn't it?"

"You do really good lettering."

"I wanted to study design."

"Hey, Joelle, how's it going?" Ben slapped her on the shoulder.

"Pretty good, Ben. You know Dave moved out."

"He's a shithead."

"Yeah." She bit her lip. "The kids don't like it."

"Got enough money?"

"No. I'm gonna try for some kind of job when they're back in school, but Matthew's only in half a day."

Everyone had shifted into new patterns while he'd been gone, Jerry thought.

Joelle smiled at him again. "Want to come by my place afterward with Ben and your mom? I can't go anywhere and leave the kids, but I got beer and a watermelon. Judy's gonna bring burgers, we could cook in the back yard."

"Sounds good."

Jerry let himself get caught in the music, in singing "Ain't Gonna Study War." The Plowshare Center running the demo was a Quaker group and they were trying to keep it peaceful, trying to stay away from the shouted insults, the "Hey, hey, how many kids did you kill today?"

Cars were slowing down, some honking support, others shouting "Commies!" with raised fingers as they passed. Two stopped in the middle of the street and their drivers shouted at each other. The cars behind them honked. "Keep it cool!" Judy called up and down the line of demonstrators. "Keep it cool!"

A man pulled over and flung himself out of the driver's seat. He was young, not much older than Jerry, with a military haircut. Jerry was the first face his eye lit on and he grabbed him by the shirtfront, fingers digging into blue chambray. "What do you think you're doing?" he shouted, spitting in his face. "Our guys are over there fighting for your pansy ass!"

"They aren't fighting for *my* ass," Jerry said quietly. The man's face was red with emotion and his eyes glittered.

"They're fighting, and you aren't, asshole! They're getting cut up with knives by gooks in the jungle, do you know what those people did to my buddy, they tied him down and—and I watched it and I couldn't get to him, and you're out here waving placards for them! You ought to be shot!" His hand tightened on Jerry's shirt. "Rotten faggot *coward*!" The man's fist came back and Jerry stiffened.

Two cops grabbed the guy from behind. "Come on, pal, you can't beat them up here." They didn't sound unsympathetic. They pulled the man away and pushed him toward his car as a TV reporter worked his way through the crowd with a cameraman behind him.

"Faggot *traitor*! He died because of people like you!" The man was sobbing over his steering wheel.

The reporter stuck a microphone in Jerry's face. "Can you tell me how you'd answer that?"

Jerry willed the thudding in his chest to slow down and took a deep breath. "I'd say—" He took another slow breath. "I'd say that we're here to try to bring that guy's buddy, and all the other soldiers, home, because we've sent them over there to do a thing that's wrong, and no one should be dying for it." The cops had got the guy's car moving by now, and Jerry watched it until it turned the corner.

"How did you feel when he called you a traitor?"

"How do you think I felt?" Jerry snarled.

"Plowshare is committed to the idea of peaceful protest," Judy said, inserting herself between Jerry and the camera. "And amicable dialogue."

But it was Jerry who was on the evening news, his ripped shirt displaying a string of beads on his bare chest, and his long hair tousled by the ocean wind. He made better copy.

That was what Gordon said, watching it with Ellen at her parents' house. Ellen didn't tell him she knew the boy with the torn shirt and the beads.

Jerry watched it at Joelle's, summoned from the backyard barbecue where he'd been flipping burgers.

"Hey, Jer! You're famous!"

Jerry wiped his hands on a towel and stared. It was like seeing your own ghost. Then the clip flickered out and the station went back to the national feed. The lumbering forms of the astronauts danced across the screen in slow motion. They seemed more immediate and more real to Jerry than his own face had.

He went back to the barbecue, set up beside a card table under the scrawny pepper tree in the back yard. Everyone had brought all the lawn chairs they could scrounge and a cooler full of beer. He began parceling burgers out to Joelle's kids, who ranged from five to around ten. The two youngest retreated into a play tent on the lawn with theirs, and the two older girls took theirs to their room. They came out again later in shorts and halter tops made of scarves and danced solemnly with their Barbies under the pepper tree.

Joelle sat down on the grass next to the barbecue. "Thanks for cooking."

Jerry put a burger on his plate and sat down next to her. "Can you dig it?" He pointed at the moon. "There're people walking *around* up there."

"Yeah. Weird." She looked at him quizzically. "Ben said you went to Phoenix."

"Just to look around." Let the draft board lose him.

"I've never been anywhere. I married Dave right out of high

school."

"Home is a good place to be." Jerry looked at the mountains that ringed the valley like a coffee cup, the profiles of Topa Topa and the Chief cutting into the stars. He'd missed them. It was hard to say why. Maybe he liked being cupped in them like a hand, and all that talk about freedom was bullshit. He knew he was lonelier than hell. He'd met some girls in Phoenix, but they'd taken one look at his hungry, desperate face and run. "Been hanging out with Judy long?" he asked Joelle, so he could keep talking to somebody.

"Judy and your mom. Especially since my asshole husband left."

"What was his trip?"

"He didn't like having four kids to support."

"It's a lot." He watched the girls dancing with the pepper tree's fronds, draping them about their shoulders like scarves. The little boy and the youngest girl were wrestling in the tent. He could see it bouncing on the grass as if self-animated.

"Yeah. I got my tubes tied after Matthew."

"They're cute little buggers, though," Jerry said because he thought he ought to say something.

Joelle smiled. Matthew burst out of the tent and rocketed into her lap. He bounced off her and into Jerry.

"Whoa, sport, slow down."

Matthew grinned at him, hopping on one foot. Jerry grinned back. He'd figured out in Phoenix, staying with a friend who had four little girls, that he liked little kids, he just couldn't bring himself to be personally responsible for putting one on the planet, to get screwed by the world. It seemed better to just take care of the ones who were here.

Matthew plopped into his lap. He leaned back and looked at Jerry upside down. "I saw you on TV."

The commander of the naval base at Point Mugu, where Raymond Manoury designed missile guidance systems, saw him too, and called Raymond into his office. Raymond went home and waited for Jerry to show up. When he finally did, Raymond sat him down in the chair beside his desk in the living room.

"Son, do you have plans?"

"Plans for what?" Jerry eyed him warily.

"The commander saw you on the news last week," Raymond said. "He spoke to me."

"About me?"

"Gerald, are you aware that I have to have a security clearance for my work? That it can be revoked for dangerous behavior?"

Jerry's stomach tensed. "Whose dangerous behavior?"

"Any member of my family," Raymond said.

"That's bullshit!"

"It may be, son, but I have a job that puts food on the table in this house." The Viennese accent was calm, precise, as if he were explaining it to an idiot. "You have jeopardized it. I do not argue with your political convictions. But I do not have the privilege of sharing them. Not if I want to keep my employment and continue to support you and your brother and your mother."

"Aw, man." Jerry stared out the front window in disgust. Raymond was right. He didn't have any right to shake his father's tree at the base. His father had enough to contend with there, just being Austrian and Jewish. "I'm sorry. I won't do it again. No more speeches."

"Perhaps you could go to school," Raymond said. "It would

give you less time for speeches."

Jerry tried to think about that, envision himself back at Ventura, but he'd gone too far to get back, blown off too much, dodged too many exams and requirements. If he tried, the draft board would notice. And anyway, there wouldn't be any more student deferments. They had something new up their collective sleeve now—a national Selective Service lottery. Jerry thought maybe he could hang on till then, and luck out with a high number. "Yeah, I'll think about it," he said.

Raymond nodded. He picked up his newspaper.

Jerry wriggled his fingers in his pockets: he possessed a pack of cigarettes, a joint and five bucks. Maybe he'd go over to Joelle's. He'd been back a couple of times. It seemed to be where people hung out now.

On the way, he bought a pizza and took it with him. There didn't seem to be anyone else there, but the kids smelled it as he came up the walk and danced out, whooping.

"Hey, guys, get down!" He held it over his head as if they were puppies.

"Dad was supposed to bring us a pizza," Matthew said. "But he didn't."

"Shut up, Matthew." Lauren, the oldest, grabbed him by the neck.

"He's always saying he'll come, and then he doesn't," Samantha said.

"You shut up, too!" Lauren raised her fist.

Joelle came out on the porch. Her face relaxed when she saw Jerry. He figured she might have been expecting her husband.

"Not a cool time?" He raised his eyebrows. "I can come back. Let me leave you this, though, I think the kids are attached to it by now."

"No, stay." Joelle beckoned him through the open door.

"I thought maybe Ma and Ben would be here."

"Haven't seen them today. You stay, though." She pushed a plastic caterpillar tricycle out of the way and put the pizza on the dinette table. The kids descended on it and took their slices to the fading gold couch in the front room, where they were watching *Batman*.

"Look out with that sauce," Joelle called. She shrugged at Jerry. "I don't know why I bother. It's like living in a war zone. The landlord came around today to see if I was gonna be able to pay the rent now that Dave split. Asshole."

"What did you tell him?"

"I told him he was an asshole." She grinned suddenly. "I told him he could wait and see, he couldn't evict me for ninety days. Judy told me that."

"Better eat some of this pizza before the herd gets it." Jerry put a slice on a paper towel for her. Joelle's kitchen reminded him of his mom's. There was a dish drainer full of plastic clown mugs and turquoise plastic canisters for sugar and coffee on the counter. An empty ice cream carton sat in the sink.

"Here." Joelle gave the kids each an apple. "For God's sake, eat some fruit." She picked up her pizza. "Let's go in the yard. I can't take any more *Batman*."

Jerry followed her outside. The sky was ridiculously pink over the western foothills. A coyote was up there somewhere warbling at it, and another answered. He wondered where Randy Ottley was now. He hadn't seen him again. Another one lost, he thought, casualty of the war effort.

Joelle plopped herself down in a plastic lawn chair and motioned to Jerry with the hand that held her pizza. She took a bite, rolling her eyes as the cheese stretched out in a string. "Thanks for the pizza."

"No problem. I think I've had about a case of your beer."

"Want another?"

"Sure."

She got up and came back with two. She sat down again, stretching her legs out. She wore white shorts and a tank top, her hair pulled back in a scarf. She looked at him sideways. "You got a girlfriend?"

"Nope." That was still a raw place. He didn't talk about Ellen except in his head. He saw her in his head all the time.

"I don't know what to do with myself since Dave left," Joelle said moodily. "I mean, I don't want him back, I married him to get away from my old man. But honest, I don't know how I'm gonna make the rent, or cope with all these kids." Her voice caught in her throat. "I looked for a job today."

"Any luck?"

She shook her head. "They keep asking what my skills are, as if I ever learned to do anything but clean the house and make peanut butter sandwiches. I went down to the welfare office yesterday, and they asked me all these questions about Dave, if he was still coming around, then they said I couldn't collect welfare and go to school. I thought maybe I could learn how to do something if I went back to school."

"Bummer," Jerry said sympathetically.

"Jesus, I don't know what I'm going to do!" Joelle started to cry. She put her hands over her mouth.

"Aw, come on, come here." He got up and knelt beside her chair, his arm around her. "You need somebody to talk to."

"I just don't know!" She was crying harder.

A neighbor who was spraying his rose bushes in the dusk stopped in mid-squirt to look over the fence at them.

"Come on. Let's go where there's not so much activity." Jerry put a hand on her shoulder.

"I don't want to talk about it in front of the kids." Joelle sniffled. "They're freaked already."

"Okay. Over here." Jerry got her out of the chair and pushed her toward the kids' tent that was still set up in the yard. The neighbor watched them with raised eyebrows.

"Old fart." Joelle glared at him over her shoulder as she passed. "They heard us when Dave left, and his wife came over to 'see if she could do anything.'" She started to cry again, loudly.

"Let's make like a camp-out in here." Jerry aimed her at the tent.

She crawled inside obediently. The green nylon walls cast aqueous shadows on their faces, like fish in an aquarium. Joelle scrubbed at her eyes with her fist. Her nose was red and her chin wet.

"Here." Jerry wiped them with the hem of his shirt. "You've had a bad time." He put an arm around her, tucked her into his shoulder.

She leaned against him, quieter. "I'm scared," she said after a while.

"What of?"

"How will I make it? I don't know how to do anything. And I'm so damn lonesome."

"You've got friends."

"Where are they now?"

"I'm here."

"Yeah, you are." She snuggled her head deeper in his shoulder. "You always sound like you know what to do. How do you do that?"

"Me?" No one else had ever told him he knew what he was doing. He wondered how big a flake her husband had been.

"Yeah. You always know how to handle things, what to say to people." She shifted a little, snuggling into his arm. "It'd be all right with someone like you."

Jerry didn't ask her what would be all right. It felt good to have someone in the crook of his arm again, telling him he was cool. They sat there for a while, while the bug chorus cranked up outside. "I'm lonesome, too," he said tentatively.

"We're all lonesome. Everybody is by themselves in this little box, and they can't get to each other. You want another beer?"

She got up and went in the house and he went behind the tent to get rid of the previous beer. It was dark now, with stars starting to stick out of the blue-black sky. The neighbor with the rose bushes had gone inside.

"Kids all buttoned up?" he asked when she came back.

"Yeah. I put them in bed." She handed him a can and sat down again in the doorway of the tent, cross-legged. She pulled the scarf out of her hair, shaking it out.

Jerry got the joint out of his pocket and lit it. He handed it to her. "My dad got in trouble over that speech I made on the news. The base commander hauled him in and threatened to yank his clearance."

"It figures," Joelle said darkly. "Their whole agenda is to keep everybody where they are so they don't disturb the assholes on top." She sucked the smoke down and held it.

Jerry chuckled. "You're a bigger cynic than me."

"I don't know what else to be," she said when she blew it out again. "I went and filed for divorce today."

"You sure about that?"

"Damn straight. He never did anything but wax his fucking car."

"How'd you pay the rent?"

"He hauled junk for people. Things like that."

"I got a job painting this guy's guest house," Jerry said. "I'm gonna try to get a truck."

"See," Joelle said.

"See what?"

"You have a grip on things. Maybe you could teach me."

"Joelle, honey, I'm scared to get a real job because the draft board will find me. I had a girl and she tossed me because I was hopeless. I don't have a grip on anything much." He sucked on the joint.

"Yes, you do." She was insistent. "I'm just scared all the time, but you're— you're—"

"Crazy," Jerry said. "I have it on good authority."

The bugs had tuned up and were whirring in the dry grass by the barbecue. Jerry rolled a piece of matchbook cover to hold the end of the joint. In the back of the tent was a pillow in a Mickey Mouse pillowcase. Joelle grabbed it and lay down, propping herself on one elbow. "I keep thinking about what you said about people walking around up there." She pointed at the moon. Her pale hair hung in a curtain over her face. "Isn't the moon supposed to make people crazy?"

"Lunatic." Jerry stuck the roach in his pocket. He leaned over and kissed her and she reached up and grabbed him.

"Hang onto me."

He kissed her some more, and slid a hand into the halter top. Joelle looked into his eyes, the moonlight from the open tent flap glittering in hers. They were gray-green like the sea on a cold day. "I love you," she said.

Oh, God, he wanted to love someone. "I love you, too." He kissed her again.

They stayed in the tent until the sun came up.

"Oh, shit, the kids!" Joelle sat up and pulled her shorts on. "Where's my top?"

Jerry handed it to her. He slid into his jeans. Joelle was running for the house. He came out of the tent buttoning his jeans, squinting in the blue-white light coming over the mountains. The neighbor was up, spraying his yard. Jerry waved at him.

The children looked at him quizzically as he ambled in through the back door. "Came to help your mom fix breakfast. What do you eat?"

"Cereal."

"French toast." Matthew looked at him hopefully.

Jerry looked in the refrigerator. "I don't think there's eggs for that this morning." He held up boxes. "Frosted Flakes? Cheerios?"

"I'll fix my own." Lauren took the Cheerios box out of his hand.

"Frosted Flakes," Liz, the next oldest girl, said. "With a banana."

Jerry threw away last night's pizza box and found a banana on the refrigerator. There was a coffee maker by the turquoise canisters so he plugged it in and put coffee in it.

Joelle came back in a different top, with a scarf in her hair.

"He's been here all night," Lauren said to her mother.

"So? Your father's slept with half the goddamn valley." Joelle slammed a cupboard door open and got out bowls.

"I'm not hungry." Lauren put the Cheerios box down on the counter and left.

Joelle rubbed Jerry's neck, while he stood by the coffee maker wondering what he ought to do now. "She'll come around. She's still pissed at her dad."

"You could move in here," Joelle said a month later. They were in bed, in her room with the door closed.

Jerry felt for his glasses on the floor and put them on, to see if they made anything any clearer. It seemed as good a suggestion as any. He'd been sleeping with Joelle for weeks now and the kids were halfway used to him. Most mornings he was the one who got up and fixed their breakfast. He didn't have anything to move but some tools and his truck.

"Except the landlord came with another eviction notice." She closed her eyes.

"When?"

She pulled the pillow over her head. Jerry poked her.

"I don't know. Yesterday. And he gave me shit about you."

"Hey!"

"I think that asshole next door told him."

"Mr. Bug Spray?"

"He said it wasn't that kind of neighborhood. He didn't care when Dave came home fuck-drunk and hit me." Joelle wormed her way deeper into the covers.

"What do you want to do?"

She didn't answer him.

Jerry put a tile roof on a garage in the Arbolada with Ben and a couple of other Ayala boys. When he got paid, he drove down to a place he'd seen in the riverbottom, with a FOR RENT sign out, and put a month's deposit on it. Then he went back for Joelle and the kids.

"I'm not going anywhere." Lauren stood with her arms folded.

"When I get this bed out, you're gonna have to sleep on the floor," Jerry said.

"Mom!"

"Can I have a dog?" Matthew attached himself to Jerry's shin.

"I don't know, son."

"He's not your son!" Lauren stalked out.

"Get the bed out," Jerry said over his shoulder to Ben, "before she comes back."

"I got to hand it to you, dude." Ben grinned. "When you do something, you go full on. Four kids!" He shook his head.

Jerry grinned back. It was an okay thing, to have someone to take care of.

That month he poured a driveway, wired an addition on a restaurant, and laid a brick patio. He wasn't licensed to do any of that, but he'd paid attention, working construction jobs in Phoenix, and what he didn't know how to do he could figure out from books in the library. He rewired the house in the riverbottom after the bathroom heater started a fire. They stood shivering in the bare yard while the fire department sprayed water over the kids' toys.

With nowhere else to go, they stayed a few days with his parents while he cleaned the house out. The children built a fort in the backyard and Dreama cooked a pan of lasagna and said it was nice to see him settled down. Joelle and her kids were people Dreama recognized. Jerry wasn't sure what Dreama had thought of Ellen. He had seen Ellen in August, at a distance, walking with some guy with red hair. His truck had been stalled by the road and he'd been half under it, so he didn't think she'd seen him.

After dinner the kids got to horsing around and spilled a box of computer program punch cards off Raymond's desk into an unintelligible pile like a disemboweled player piano roll. Raymond spent the rest of the evening stolidly, grimly restacking them one by one, and Lauren retreated to the room she was sharing with the other three and locked the door. While Dreama and Joelle did the dishes, Jerry grabbed the other culprits and settled them on the couch at the far end of the room from Raymond's desk.

"You're a walking disaster zone. Settle down and I'll tell you a story."

"Tell us about Char Man." Matthew bounced on the cushions.

"You want to hear about him? Right after the fire?"

"Yeah. Maybe I'll wake up melted." Matthew curled his fingers into claws and opened his mouth, baring his teeth at Samantha.

"Ew! Quit it!" Liz slid off the sofa and Sam shrieked.

"Char Man!" Matthew yelled.

"Why don't you tell me?" Jerry said. The story had been a fixture in the valley ever since Jerry could remember, but each new set of kids had their own version.

"Okay. There was this guy who lived in the riverbottom and he got burned up in a fire. And his skin was all gooey and he lives on Creek Road and you can't go there at night or he'll eat you."

Liz climbed back on the sofa. "You don't know anything," she said. "His head was messed up from being in the war."

"What war?" Sam asked.

"I don't know. The one with the Germans, I guess."

Any war, Jerry thought. Any war would do it.

"He got burned trying to save his brother," Liz said, "but he couldn't. So then he went crazy and thought he was back in the war and hid down in the chaparral, eating deer and rabbits that burned up in the fire. He's still there. His face is half burned away and where one of his eyes ought to be there's just this gob of jelly."

They shivered appreciatively. "What does he eat now?"

Matthew asked, though they all knew the answer.

"Whatever he can catch!"

Lauren came out of their room, disgusted. "That is the stupidest story ever."

"Want to go down to Creek Road?" Liz asked her. "I dare you."

"No, but because it's dumb."

Jerry thought he'd better get the kids in bed while Lauren had the door unlocked. Joelle had disappeared into the back yard with Dreama to smoke, so he wrestled Matthew into the tub. Matthew's underwear was so tight it was leaving red marks and his shoes were worn through the sole. Once they were in bed, Jerry went out in the back yard too and looked at the stars and tried to figure how to scam a job that wouldn't call him to anybody's attention.

In late September a Jewish summer camp bought the old orchid ranch in the foothills, and the camp managers hired a crew to ferry all the furniture and equipment up there from their old facility. They paid cash so Jerry signed on.

He found himself staring at the double kitchens, the separate sets of dishes for meat and milk, like someone looking through a curtain. No one had ever explained any of that to him and he found it as incomprehensible and oddly alluring as a whisper in a foreign language. The camp staff explained where he could go and where he couldn't and what had to be done. He never told them his father was Jewish.

Afterward, he made a deal to clear out the old site for scrap, and for the rest of that fall he hauled loads of copper pipe and window frames to the junkyard and brought home anything that looked useful. Once he thought he saw Ellen again, and hid behind the postcard rack in the drug store until she'd left, and then remembered it was October and she was in Virginia.

Joelle hardly left the house in the riverbottom, once they

moved back in. She met the kids' bus at the end of the dirt drive and went back inside. Jerry brought home groceries and day-old bread from the bakery thrift store. But she was always waiting for him, happy to go to bed any time. Lauren allowed him to exist and the three younger ones had no problems with him.

"How old are you?" Matthew asked him once.

"Twenty."

"Mom's thirty. She told me."

"Well, then she knows, so it's probably not a good idea to remind her."

He asked Joelle if she thought her folks would be willing to help them some. Four kids ate up a lot of shoes and peanut butter and bread and the summer camp job was nearly done. Her mouth tightened into a white line and she shook her head. "I wouldn't go in the same county with my old man."

"Hon, you got to give up being afraid sometime." He put his arm around her gently. He could feel her shivering. "I guess not right now, though."

He decided to hell with the draft board and went to the Employment Commission, but they told him he didn't have training or a license to do all the things he'd been doing, so they couldn't get him a job doing them.

The employment counselor folded her hands. "Mr. Manoury, the best thing you can do is go back to school."

"I have four children."

The counselor raised an eyebrow.

"Step-children," he said, furious at having to explain himself, to beg for dignity. "I know how to do that whole list of things." He pointed to the paper on her desk.

"How did you learn to do them?"

"Taught myself."

"Well, we have no way of knowing that, do we? There are licenses and training programs. Your aptitude tests indicate you could become a trained technician in a number of fields."

Meaning: a trained seal. Jerry resisted the urge to bark at her, or bite her, or throw her a fish. "I don't have time to get a certificate to prove I know what I already know. I have a family to support."

He left the office grim-faced and went home and had a fight with Joelle. He stalked out and didn't come home until the next morning. When he did he found her huddled in a ball on the kitchen floor in her nightgown.

"Aw, hon." He picked her up.

"I thought you weren't coming back!" She clung to him. Her face was mottled with crying.

"You called me an immature prick," he pointed out.

"Where did you go? Never mind." She wrapped her arms around him and kissed him until he got hard. "Come on. The kids aren't up yet."

He followed her into the bedroom. The bed squeaked, but they always pretended it didn't. If the kids didn't know what was going on by now, they weren't paying attention. Afterward, she lay with her head on his shoulder, looking at the ceiling. Jerry counted the cracks in the plaster. He could fix those. He ought to, before any more pieces fell. He'd already reputtied the kitchen window and planted a garden in the riverbottom silt out behind the house. That was what he was good at, it seemed, taking care of things, of people. He thought he'd make Lauren a shelf for her records. Maybe she'd like that.

Joelle kept on looking at the ceiling. "Why did you leave me last night?"

"Why did you tell me to get out?"

"I was scared. I didn't know how we were gonna make it."

"We'll make it," he said. "I'll figure it out."

XI
SISTERHOOD

C arl wrote to Ellen at Carter Randolph, letters that didn't say much, but she read them furtively, then threw them away as if they might contain lingering traces of explosive. Gordon wrote to her, long funny letters about newsroom gossip and ways to pass the time in county political meetings so you didn't actually fall asleep. Jerry stopped writing, though her father said he'd hired him to bury a sprinkler line.

"God!" Ellen waved the letter at Linda and Maggie. "He's hiring my old boyfriend to do odd jobs."

"At least he's not hiring him to be your lawyer," Maggie muttered.

They raised their eyebrows at her. Maggie looked at the wall. "Shouldn't have said that."

"Lawyer?"

"Not mine, really."

"Maggie, you look like hell." Linda peered at her. "You haven't looked good since we got back."

Maggie was painting her fingernails, a pale luminescent pink like the insides of shells. She bent over her left hand, not looking at them. "Y'all remember those voter registrars who got shot in Mississippi five years ago?"

"Yeah."

"Mag?"

"It seems like my Daddy's involved in that now. He didn't have anything to do with it, we aren't scum. But now they think he knows somebody who had something to do with it and they won't let him alone."

"Oh, no, Mag, how awful."

"It was like living in the middle of the Sunday newspaper when I went home. He's got another lawyer to handle it for him, and he's this man I thought I might marry once, and I just can't bear it."

"Can't he prove—?"

"Nobody would believe your father would—"

Linda and Ellen offered well-intentioned protests while she sat painting her nails.

"Maybe he does know something. Or somebody. There are people he knows that if they were involved he'd never tell. Men he went to school with maybe." Her fingers shook and the polish went down the side of her thumb. "I'm not supposed to talk about it to anybody. Y'all forget I said anything."

"Sure."

"Of course."

"It'll be okay. Nobody would believe your father would—"

But maybe he would. Not murder voter registrars, but know someone who might. Ellen had discovered you never knew everything about anyone. People kept turning inside out, showing things you'd never seen before. What if Maggie's father really was involved? Ellen had met him last Thanksgiving, a tall genial man with a drawl who called her Sugar.

On Veterans Day there were rallies to support the government's policy in Vietnam. The next day Ellen picked up the newspaper and read that the Army was investigating a charge U.S. troops had massacred more than a hundred civilians at some place called My Lai. The New Mobilization Committee was sponsoring its own rally in Washington and Linda insisted that they drive up there for it. She was intense and furious, throwing sleeping bags in the back of her car, ordering Ellen and Maggie about. In Washington they followed her docilely, like bodyguards, other things on their minds. Maggie seemed to be on autopilot. Ellen tried to take notes, so she could write to Gordon about it. The Mall had even more demonstrators than two years before. Linda knew the organizers, and dragged Ellen and Maggie to a stage where a young man in a camouflage jacket was making a speech to the crowd. They were with him, leaning forward, intent, murmuring responses to his exhortations like parishioners in a Gospel church.

A bearish young man in a denim vest bore down on them. "Linda! Good girl. Come on back and help us. We got to get these placards stapled on sticks before the march." He nodded at Ellen and Maggie. "You girls can help too."

"When am I on?"

"On?"

Linda glared at him. "Joey, I told you I wanted to talk. Darren okayed it. Here's my speech." She waved a piece of paper in his face. "Now when am I on?"

"Jesus, Linda. . . . " Joey looked irritated. "We got to get these placards—"

Linda pushed her way past him. Joey looked up at the man on the stage and shrugged. He turned to Maggie and Ellen. "You girls want to help with these?"

Linda was nose to nose with another man, who was adjusting the sound cables at the foot of the platform. He protested as she pushed past him. "Hey! Get offa there!"

Linda spun back around. "I cleared it with Darren."

"Well, you're not on my list." The sound man looked stubborn.

Joey shoved a stapler and a bundle of sticks into Ellen's hands. "Make sure you get 'em on good and solid or the wind'll tear 'em up."

On the stage the man in camouflage, who was apparently Darren, broke off and trotted over. He and Linda had an inaudible conversation while the crowd chanted. Linda braced her feet as if he were a high wind, until Darren threw up his hands and motioned her to the microphone.

Ellen heard the crowd's voice shift as Linda picked up the mike. Nothing overt, just a subtle uncertainty, a break in the momentum. A couple of wolf whistles.

Linda stopped, glaring at them.

"Take it off, honey, take it off!" A man in a leather jacket hooted from the front row.

Linda's eyes dropped involuntarily to her white jersey. She stared at the guy who'd catcalled her. "Women are going to Vietnam too!" Her voice cut through the noise. "We wouldn't be allowed to fight there if we wanted to, but nurses can go over there and die! We can send our men to kill civilian women! Women have a stake in this! We *must* be a part of the effort to stop it!"

"Hey! We didn't come here to listen to some feminist agenda!" someone shouted from the crowd.

"Goddammit!" Darren had got half way down the steps, but now he headed back up them.

"I told you not to let her up there," the sound man said to him as he passed.

Ellen put her placard down. She could feel collective anger coalescing like fog in the air.

"Shut up!" someone shouted at Linda.

"Aw, shit," Joey said.

"Leave her alone!" a woman yelled.

"Get her offa there, man!"

The sound tech pulled the mic cord. He cupped his hands and yelled, "Take her off the stage and fuck her!"

Linda tried to shout over the crowd. Here and there a woman called for the rest to listen, but no one did. They took up the sound man's chant instead: "Take her off the stage and fuck her!" A tennis ball hit her in the shin and bounced across the platform.

"Aim higher!"

Darren took the steps back up to the stage two at a time. He grabbed the mic from Linda and pointed at the sound man. The audio came back on. "Okay, folks, we're here to stop this war, not to push anyone's individual trip. Let's get going on what we're here for!"

The crowd leaned forward, the women's voices drowned. The sound man pulled Linda down the steps while she fought him. Her nails raked his face.

He pushed her away and swung around to scream at Ellen and Maggie, who were gawking from their pile of placards: "You two get her out of here!"

"Well, why don't you just take these and put them up your ass?" Maggie inquired, handing him her bundle of stakes. "Come on, Linda, before Limp Dick here has a hissy." She swept the three of them off through a gap in the crowd.

Linda's face was set in a furious mask. "Goddamn them! Goddamn them!"

"They're just jerks, honey," Maggie said. "Men are just jerks. They want to keep it their party, you know."

"I cleared it with Darren," Linda said between her teeth. "Two weeks ago."

"Honey, you know men don't have that long a memory."

All around the crowd was swaying to the rhythm of the speeches. Women pushing baby buggies waved placards: WAR IS NOT HEALTHY FOR CHILDREN AND OTHER LIVING THINGS.

WHAT IF THEY GAVE A WAR AND NOBODY CAME? WHAT IF SCHOOLS HAD ALL THE MONEY THEY NEEDED AND THE ARMY HAD TO HAVE A BAKE SALE TO BUY A TANK?

"What if they decided not to let men screw them over anymore?" Linda said tight-lipped.

"Now, that would be a revolution." Maggie patted her arm.

"What if they quit making the sandwiches and the coffee and painting the goddamn posters and let the shitheads just go get *killed?*'

"Maybe they'll draft Limp Dick," Ellen said sympathetically. She burst out laughing. "Honestly, Maggie, I can't believe you called him that to his face!"

"Well, if it wasn't before, I bet it is now." Maggie chuckled. "Suggestion is powerful."

Ellen snorted. "Let's hear it for sisterhood!"

"Power to the women! Males to the stud farm!"

Linda snickered, then laughed, hiccupping, her face red.

"Attagirl," Maggie said.

When they got back to Carter Randolph Sunday night they had aching feet and one small triumph. A woman who'd heard Linda had come up to her where she sat putting Band-Aids on her feet in the dusk. People jostled past on either side, weary but still charged with an adrenaline kick, like walking cups of coffee.

"Wow, I never thought I'd find you again in all this." She sat down on the curb by Linda, shaking long blond hair over her shoulder. She wore a parka and a felt fedora. "That was my boyfriend who started whistling at you. I'm sorry. I told him he was an asshole but he wouldn't quit."

"Not your fault." Linda put her shoe back on.

"No," the girl said, "but you know how sometimes something just, like, dawns on you? You think, Wow, why didn't I see that? Well, when I told Jay to shut up, he gave me a dollar and told me to go get him a hot dog. So I took the dollar and left him there."

Ellen looked at her, worried. "How will you get home?" Now they were responsible for this woman being abandoned, and probably raped and mugged, in the middle of a demonstration.

"Oh, it's my car." The blond girl stood. "I drove him and his buddies from Omaha. They never did pay for any gas." She adjusted her hat. "See ya."

On the way home they imagined Jay the Boyfriend stranded by the side of the road, trying to get home to Omaha, and passed by cars full of women who pretended not to see him.

Maggie wouldn't go home for Thanksgiving, and Ellen couldn't afford to, so a week later they both drove with Linda to Davenport, where they reenacted Linda's humiliation and ultimate triumph for her little sister, taking all the parts in turn between them. They made a mess in the kitchen making pumpkin pie, and shopped the after-Thanksgiving sale at Linda's family's department store with Linda's discount, and ate turkey sandwiches and watched the news. The trial of the Chicago Seven, charged with inciting a riot at the Democratic Convention. The massacre at My Lai and the boyish face of Lt. William Calley, looking too young to be a soldier or a murderer either one. The body count for the week from Saigon: Americans—130, South Vietnamese—576, North Vietnamese and Vietcong—3,201. American troop strength in Vietnam—479,500.

On Monday, back at Carter Randolph, they watched the Selective Service lottery in the dorm social room. The housemother put the television on top of two stacked tables so everyone could see, and they filled the couches and the carpet in front of it.

The idea of the lottery, its very randomness, riveted them to the screen. While they waited for it to start, the announcer explained how men born on the first third of the dates drawn were certain to be drafted. The last third would probably never be. The fate of those in the middle would depend on troop requirements in the coming year.

Representative Alexander Pirnie from New York would draw the first number, he said, and the Selective Service System's Youth Advisory Committee the rest. "Sell-outs," Linda said darkly to the young men standing uncomfortably on the stage.

"Be quiet!" someone hissed. Pirnie drew the first number, a round blue plastic capsule like a giant pill. He handed it to a colonel who opened it and read "September 14." Another man posted it on a board with the elaborate gestures of a game-show host.

The Youth Advisory Committee took over. April 24. December 30. February 14. October 18. September 6.

"Relax, Callahan," Maggie said. "You got a new guy they aren't interested in." Another senior was weeping quietly in the corner of the couch behind them. Ellen didn't say anything when the announcer got to number 51 and it was Jerry's.

Jerry watched the first part of the lottery with Joelle and Robert while the kids played Monopoly on the floor. After they hit November 7, he went and got a beer. It was surreal, watching the guy pulling plastic vitamin pills out of a goldfish bowl. He listened from the kitchen for a while, just far enough away to mute the numbers, make the colonel's voice indistinguishable from the birds in the trees outside the window, while his skin slowly chilled. Life and death determined by random numbers at two in the afternoon. He wondered how long it would take the draft board to find the riverbottom address. The newspapers had been full of the plan. No more advantage for the white and well-off over the poor and black. In Jerry's case, it didn't matter much.

The flickering black and white TV made a ghostly square in the dim living room, a floating disembodied head announcing numbers. Joelle's sandy head and Robert's dark one floated in front of it.

"They get you yet?" he asked Robert at 253.

"Not yet." Robert's deferment, like all the rest, would run out as soon as he graduated.

"Far out." He sat back down.

At 312 Robert's birthday came up. Jerry clapped him on the back. "Good going, Ace. They'll take you when they draft your granny."

Robert looked at his feet. "Stupid way to do it. I could have kept the deferment two more years as long as I didn't graduate."

"You have to graduate," Jerry said. "Your old man's not made out of money."

"Neither are we," Joelle said. "Fifty-one. Jesus." She took Jerry's hand.

"Look, guys, they were after me before. This doesn't change anything. I was kind of hoping for a free lunch, but I'm not surprised." The base commander would give his father shit again. He'd have to see that Raymond didn't know where he was, so they wouldn't have a reason to can him.

"I knew they'd do it," Joelle said darkly. "They know which numbers are going to come up."

Robert looked uncomfortable. Jerry knew he was never sure what to say to Joelle, who had not finished high school, much less been to college, and was prickly and easily offended about it. She'd been sewing lace on the collar of a dress for Lauren while she watched the television. Two more dresses were laid out on the couch beside her, all matching flowered prints. "Christmas outfits?" Robert asked.

"There's a party at school. I want them to have something new." She picked up another dress. "I need to measure Samantha."

"Come here, brat." Jerry snagged Samantha from the Monopoly game.

Matthew followed, protesting. "Mom! She took my money."

"Did not. It was mine. Liar!"

"Hold still." Jerry helped Joelle drop the dress over her head. "Wow. It's a princess."

"Can we have the television now?" Samantha asked him.

"You bet. As soon as your mom gets your ball gown pinned up here."

Robert stood up. "Man, I'm sorry."

"Quit it," Jerry said. "You're about to graduate and go into plastics or something. You can't go to Nam."

"What are you going to do?"

Jerry didn't answer him.

"I'll help you get north if you want to," Robert said at the door.

Jerry looked at Joelle, wrestling with Samantha's dress. "I don't think Joelle could handle it." Canada was a frighteningly unknown destination to her, even though she was terrified of his being drafted. She'd spotted the last draft notice that had come to his parents' house and stayed in the bathroom all morning, crying.

When Robert left, Joelle took the dresses into their bedroom and sat down at her sewing machine with them. She stayed there grimly stitching, swearing occasionally, while Jerry fed the kids and put them in bed and walked the shepherd puppy they'd got from the pound.

He picked up the Monopoly game and poked his head into

173

the bedroom. "You about done?"

Joelle shook her head. Her face was wet with tears and she yanked at the thread that had tangled in the machine. "God damn it!"

"What's the matter?"

"I can't get it right. I keep sewing the skirt to the piece under it by mistake, and I just put the goddamn sleeve in inside out!" She jerked the cloth out from under the foot and he heard something tear.

"It's eleven. Why don't you go to bed?"

"Because the goddamn party's tomorrow. I have to get these done."

"You aren't gonna get them done in that state."

"What state?" Joelle twisted in her chair, snarling. She reached for the scissors.

"That state. You sound like a rabid baboon." Jerry moved the scissors out of her reach. "Go to bed and give me the dress."

"You're going to finish it, right?"

"You bet." He glared back.

"*You're* going to sew them?"

"I am if you'll shut up and give me the machine."

"Fine! All right!" She jerked her chair back and stood. "Finish the goddamn things if you think you can." She stumbled to the bed and flung herself face down on it.

Jerry sat down and picked up the dress. He knew how to sew a straight line, so he didn't see why he couldn't figure out the rest. Pattern instructions were like a recipe, just another kind of assembly. You did the first thing it told you, then the next thing.

When he had finished the first dress, he went over and pulled the blankets up over Joelle. She didn't move. Her breathing was the deep rattle of exhaustion. Jerry looked morosely at the crumpled fabric on the sewing machine. The dresses were something to do. Taking care of Joelle was something to do. With something to do, he had purpose, and could not afford time to sweat over lottery numbers. It was so easy to fall into the silent puddle of fear that was always waiting at the end of the hallway, the bottom of the road. The ditch you fell into when your life was not in your hands, like that poor bastard Ottley. He'd been careful to put the phone here in Joelle's name, not to open a bank account, to get his mail at his parents' house.

Robert would graduate in the spring. Robert knew where he was going. Jerry knew he was supposed to know what he wanted to do, and was defective because he didn't. But the idea that kept surfacing, of running a bookstore, the next best thing to living in one, was ridiculous because where would he get the money to start one? Ellen had had a plan for him. His father might once have had a plan. Joelle's plan was to survive tomorrow.

What's your plan, Manoury?

Sew three dresses, save the princess.

He sat back down at the sewing machine.

In the morning Robert's mother called to say he'd signed an enlistment agreement to train as a combat medic as soon as he graduated. His father was proud of him, but did Jerry really think he'd done the right thing?

"He what?"

"He enlisted. Or deferred enlistment, something like that. Yesterday. As a medic."

"Oh, Christ." Jerry put the phone down.

Lauren came out in her dress, pirouetting like a ballerina. "Mom made me a new dress."

"No, she didn't. I did."

Lauren held the skirt out in front of her. "You did?"

"Yep." Jerry picked up the phone again. "I'll talk to him." He hung up and got cereal out of the cupboard.

Liz came out of the bedroom. "Mom finished our dresses," Lauren told her.

Jerry put bowls on the counter. "Fix Sam and Matthew some cereal and tell your mom it's time to get up."

"Why? Where are you going?"

"Out. Walk the dog, too."

Robert was in class by the time Jerry got to UCSB. He bumbled through crowds of purposeful students until he found the right apartment block. The air was crisp, blue-white and salty, and Christmas wreaths hung on the lamp posts and doors. Jerry sat on the front steps of Robert's building and waited, smoking a cigarette and looking at the girls. Randy Ottley's sister Mimi walked by, so he said, "Hey," to her, happy just to see someone he knew. She stared at him as if he were an apparition and hurried down the concrete walk, books clutched to her chest.

Robert never showed. Having enlisted in a fit of guilty bravado, he'd gone and gotten drunk in a bar until it was too late for anyone to talk him out of it. He appeared at Jerry and Joelle's house on Christmas Day, with a fruitcake and a bottle of brandy.

"You asshole, you had 312." Jerry glared at him. "And your eyes are like a bat's."

"So are yours. They didn't flunk you. I couldn't see sitting on my deferment and my degree and watching every poor brother and Chicano kid get sucked out of the projects while I get on with my life."

"You didn't need the deferment. You got 312. That was the *point* of the lottery," Jerry said, exasperated. "And if I hadn't got 51, you wouldn't have done it. And they aren't going to get me, so you wasted it!"

"Well, if they get you, I'll be there to sew you back together. All for one and one for all. Maybe I could have sewed up Aaron."

"Nobody could have sewed up Aaron. He came back in pieces." Jerry looked morosely at Matthew playing with the new G.I. Joe set his dad had sent. The floor was littered with shredded paper, like little scraps of greed. He'd done his best for the kids, but he hated Christmas and staying stoned was about all that got him through it.

Robert handed him the brandy bottle. Joelle made eggnog, and some more people came by and gradually it turned into a party, which made her happy. Jerry drank straight brandy and smoked enough pot to stay cheerful, and watched dusk fall outside the window to see if he spotted Randy Ottley, last heard of in Hawaii.

On January 2, he got an induction notice. He studied it for a long time, the new address neatly typed across buff paper.

From the President of the United States to Gerald Manoury, GREETING...

He put it in the glove box of the truck, where Joelle wouldn't see it.

The induction center in Los Angeles was a huge stone edifice like someone's tomb. Jerry stood in the front lobby with his manila envelope full of papers, waiting for someone to notice him. Someone was yelling from somewhere down a hall. Feet thudded on a staircase. The desk in the lobby was empty. It held a still-steaming cup of coffee and a mug full of pencils, but no person. Jerry felt cold and stupid. He'd come prepared to fight, to resist, to mess with the system, and then if he had to, if it got that far, to just refuse induction and run. But there was no one here to mess with. They were all working on whatever hapless soul was down the hall screaming, and throwing file cabinets too, from the sound of it.

Jerry weighed the envelope in his hand. It was like going to the dentist and having him unexpectedly cancel your appointment. You didn't know what to do with the adrenaline. He supposed Desk Person would be back soon, as soon as they'd subdued Hapless Soul. The front door flew open and two cops ran past. Jerry put the envelope in the exact middle of the desk and smoothed it out with his hand. Then he turned and marched out the door, down the street, and got in his truck.

"Jerry was working on this," Daniel Callahan said to Ellen and Gordon while he showed them his new sprinklers. "But he moved, so we're only half done. I haven't found anybody else who wants to let me pay them to dig a hole."

"The county has the same problem," Gordon chuckled. The county had started a new courthouse when the contractor had been caught pouring inferior concrete on another job and fled to Mexico, leaving a partially dug foundation in his wake.

Ellen walked behind them, picking leaves off the pear trees

and shredding them while Gordon and her father talked about county government. When had Jerry moved? Why hadn't her father said anything? She glared at his back. She'd been so careful over this Easter break not to go anywhere that she might run into Jerry, and he wasn't even in town. She felt like an idiot.

"So where did Jerry go?" she said casually, linking her arm with her father's. Just a casual question about the handyman.

"Petaluma, I think. One of those Bay Area towns. He's got all those kids, he said he had to go where the work was."

Kids? I will not call Robert and make a fool of myself. But, not the Army.

"It's all a crap shoot," Gordon said. "The county's trying to hold the line against L.A. Creeping suburban sprawl. But there are too many pressures to rezone. Did Ellen tell you the *Chronicle* wants her after she graduates, if she'll promise she won't take off for grad school in the fall?"

Ellen went back to Carter Randolph and got ready to graduate, with Linda and Maggie and three hundred other girls who'd gone to college expecting to have fun and then marry and raise kids, and now were emerging with the suspicion they might have to support themselves, even that they ought to, but with no real clue as to how to do that. Earn a living, stop the war, fight injustice. It seemed like a lot to ask. The *Chronicle* was going to pay her half what Gordon made.

Her history orals were interrupted by a white-faced professor who flung herself through the doorway of the department chair's office. "They're shooting students at Kent State."

The chairman turned a radio on.

"—Four dead and nine wounded after a weekend of rioting that began with the President's pledge to send troops to Cambodia. National Guardsmen called out to quell the protest fired live ammunition into the crowd—"

The professor stood in the doorway with her hand pressed to her mouth. "We've gone mad."

"Someone has," the department chairman said. He stood, shakily, fingering his collar. "Callahan, you'll have to come back tomorrow. I've forgotten everything I meant to ask you."

The next day they patted her hand, gave her a cookie, and told her she'd passed on yesterday's questions. The newspapers and television played and replayed the scenes of tear gas and fleeing students, and the single arresting image that burned itself into everyone's retinas: the girl kneeling in the street, arms outflung, screaming endlessly over a motionless body.

At the end of May they graduated, in caps and gowns and green-and-gold Carter Randolph hoods. Daniel and Lily flew from California and took pictures of Ellen standing under a sycamore on Front Quad, diploma clutched to her chest. Linda joined the Peace Corps and Ellen went home to work at the *Chronicle*.

Robert took her out to dinner before he went to basic training at Fort Sam Houston in Texas, and she told him he was crazy.

He smiled. "That's what Jerry said."

"He was right about something for a change," Ellen muttered, and that was the last time they mentioned Jerry.

"They draft my folks half again as often as white boys," Robert said. "Maybe I can even out the survival rate."

"The lottery was supposed to fix that," Ellen protested. "And you had a high number!"

"I know, babe," Robert said, "It just seemed like something I had to do. Don't ask me why. I'm not sure I know myself."

He wrote to Ellen from Texas that he was practicing debriding wounds on anesthetized goats. He learned to crawl under razor wire while someone fired a machine gun over him, and how to put a gas mask on. A few months later he wrote from Vietnam, graphic descriptions of cutting leeches out of skin and treating heroin withdrawal and immersion foot, the horrible scaly swelling caused by standing for days in bacteria-laden water. The medics had stopped wearing the Red Cross armbands, he wrote, because the NVA aimed for them first. He put tourniquets on the arteries of men who'd had their feet blown off and stabilized booby-trap victims with shards of steel in their skulls. Then he put them on the medevac chopper and it took them somewhere he never went, lifting off through the smoke of white phosphorus rounds and the orange-red bloom of napalm. Later, on the radio, he might hear whether a man from his platoon had lived or died, but sometimes they came and went so quickly he never knew. He lay awake at night and thought about them, he wrote.

Ellen's fear that some horrible change would come over him, as it had Carl and Randy, seemed unfounded. Maybe Carl and Randy hadn't really changed. Maybe the war took what you were to start with and just doubled it, again and again. She wrote back often, trying to tether him to home and wondering if anyone had written to Randy besides his family, and if that would have helped.

In Hawaii, sometimes the ghost's wandering mind merged with the physical being that was still Randy Ottley and the world righted itself for a few hours, grew three-dimensional and solid—the tourists, the street vendors with carts full of leis, the troops on leave from whom he hid in case they knew him. So did the woman who ran the bakery where he now swept the floor and washed the bread tubs. She was blond and Swedish so he never feared her or feared his harming her when the world shifted again. That was when the tourists on the beach transformed into burning figures on a muddy riverbank, and the lush green growth that was everywhere shriveled to black as orange flame poured over it, and he ran to the shed behind the bakery and buried his face in the cot. If he kept his eyes closed he could imagine he would open them again on the dusty sunlight of home and the tawny lion-colored hills above the valley. Imagine his mother and father running to welcome him, his sister throwing her arms around him. Imagine them saying, yes, we understand, we are sorry we sent you there, come back to us now.

XII
THE PERFECT WEDDING
FACE

*D*ear Ellen,
If my parents ask you where I am, don't give them this address, please. They have been driving me crazy, and Devi and Sita Dasi told them I left. My father was roaring and threatening Guruji with lawyers. Lakshmana says that often happens when someone Surrenders and I shouldn't worry about it. Well, it's nice not to worry.

Ellen reread the paragraph in Maggie's neat boarding-school handwriting. It still said the same thing.

I just love it here. It's almost like being back at Carter Randolph except I've given up meat and sleeping around. I learned to make curry today, and killed a mouse in the kitchen with a broom. (Maybe not supposed to do that? But I wasn't going to eat it. I'll have to ask Guruji.) Krishnas keep women separate from men. The men are all in charge, of course, Guruji explained that women need to be protected and sounded just like my father. But they all call us "Mataji," which means "mother," and nobody messes with us.
Here's what we do all day:
Go to Temple and chant japa

Greet the Deities and Guruji
Breakfast prasadam
Class — I'm learning Sanskrit
Sell books at the airport
Lunch prasadam
Class
Hare Nam—chant on the street
Dinner prasadam. Some nights we have a feast and invite people who might want to join.

You should try it. It's like Krishna knows everything and we don't have to. I tried to explain that to Mother when I first got here, but all I could hear was her screaming into the telephone. I could have heard her without it if I put my head out the window. She kept saying, "Oh, the one thing I was praying you wouldn't do," as if she'd be happier if was in New York pregnant on drugs.

Tomorrow we're going to bake bread and learn how the soul transmigrates into the next body. Maybe my parents will come back as armadillos.

Hare Krishna,
Mahema (previously known as Maggie)

"Everybody's gone crazy." Ellen slapped Maggie's letter down on the table at the *Yes We Are Open* the next day. "My friend from Atlanta's handing out Hare Krishna literature in airports!"

"Everybody has different ways of dealing with the times," Gordon said, reading it. "Is this the one whose father is, um?"

"Yeah. I wasn't supposed to tell you that."

"My lips are sealed." Gordon opened them around a taco.

"She sent me pamphlets."

"Are we in danger of losing you?"

"If I'm going to take up religion I'll go back to church." She doubted they'd have any answers though. Nobody seemed to. A few days after Kent State, police had shot two students at a college in Mississippi and construction workers in New York had beaten students with crowbars. Three members of the Weathermen had accidentally killed themselves with their own bomb and yesterday someone else exploded a bomb at a military research center at a university and killed a physics professor. "We're all monsters," she said miserably.

"People are pretty much idiots, on any side," Gordon said with the resignation of a journalist. "Present company excepted. Can I cheer you up and take you to the antique show in L.A. on Saturday?"

"Mmm." She put her fork down. "You're a very strange date."

"Howzat?"

"You haven't tried to take me to a football game yet."

"Hate football. Hate sports. Did your previous boyfriend take you to football games?"

"No." *He took me to riots and weird houses in Berkeley.* "No, but that was all anyone I dated at college wanted to do. That and get drunk."

"Date much in college?"

"No."

"See. You've been waiting for someone who'll take you to antique shows."

Ellen and Gordon furnished hypothetical houses at antique shows, and had a special category reserved for guest rooms for guests you wanted to go away.

At the L.A. show, she pointed at a four-poster bed with carved crocodile heads. "That. I couldn't even sleep in that."

"With a Victrola." Gordon pounced on a piece in the next booth. It was a Victrola-and-lamp combination on legs, with a huge fringed green shade and the motto HAPPY HOME carved

185

around the case. "For the 'Relatives from Omaha Who Don't Leave' suite."

Gordon loved anything that smacked of outrageous excess. He took her to Solvang and they ate meatballs and gravy and waffles with whipped cream in Swedish restaurants with pointed roofs, and bought painted horses for good luck.

They went to San Luis Obispo and had dinner at the Madonna Inn, an accretion of stone and chalet-style woodwork where they sat in pink leather booths under a gold candelabra tree. The Inn's rooms were displayed on brochures in the lobby. The Old Mill Room had cuckoo clocks in the headboard of the bed, and the Cloud Nine Room had a conical red ceiling and a gold cherub holding up the chandelier.

"It's a shame we can't stay the night," Gordon said wistfully. He looked sideways at her.

He hadn't actually asked her to sleep with him. This was the closest he'd gotten. She envisioned them making love under the cherub chandelier. "I tell you what. You can show me the men's room."

Gordon chuckled. There was one man outside it already, standing guard. From inside they heard shrieks of female laughter. "Go on." Gordon grinned.

Ellen joined the women already there.

"It's a fountain!" Two women in pastel sun dresses inspected the urinal. A rock wall rose above an elaborately tiled floor with a drain. When the women stepped up to it, water flowed down the wall.

"Oh, my goodness!"

"Oh, my goodness, look at that mirror!"

It was like Disneyland, she thought. People came to California and stopped at the Madonna Inn to see just how bad it could get. She wondered how Jerry would have reacted to it.

By the end of June Gordon asked Ellen to marry him. It

seemed like a possible thing to do, more possible than the Peace Corps or the Hare Krishnas. She was always the unimaginative one; all she wanted was the life her parents had. Gordon wanted children and he didn't expect her to wait on him, despite having been brought up an only child like Ellen by a mother who waited on him hand and foot. "I always say a man needs a haven of peace to come home to," Mrs. Murphy said. She was always telling people what she always said.

Gordon brought his parents to meet Ellen's parents after they were engaged and the announcement had been in the *Ayala News* and the *Chronicle*, and the people at the *Chronicle* had given them a drunken engagement party at which two people locked themselves in the darkroom by mistake and couldn't get out.

Tom Murphy was a lanky Midwesterner who worked for the electric company, and Marie had a tight poodle perm and thought it was time Gordon got married.

"Well," Lily said, "isn't this lovely?" They tried to think of things to say to each other while Daniel cooked dinner, which Ellen could already tell the Murphys found odd. "My mother can't cook," she told Gordon. "I can, though."

"We had dinner at that new restaurant at the harbor last night," Marie said. "Tom had the pork chops but they were overdone."

"They were fine," Tom said.

"Your father had to send them back," Marie told Gordon.

The doorbell rang and Gordon looked expectant, as if he knew what was out there. He'd been hinting at some surprise all evening.

Ellen went to the door and opened it to find Jerry on the steps. She looked frantically over her shoulder at Gordon and his parents and her mother, who'd paused in their conversation. Daniel appeared in the kitchen doorway with a spoon. "Out here," Ellen hissed and pushed Jerry back down the front steps.

She closed the door behind them. "What are you doing here?"

He smiled ruefully. "I saw you're getting married. I just wanted to say good luck."

Her stomach clenched. "Jerry, that is so sweet of you." He was barefoot, in a pair of jeans. No shirt. His only other garment besides his glasses was a blue glass earring. "You got your ear pierced," she said inanely.

"Yeah."

"How have you been? Daddy said you'd moved."

"Up to Petaluma. I just came down for the weekend to see my folks."

"Oh. Daddy said you had kids." She hadn't meant to say that but it had emerged in spite of her.

"Stepkids; I live with somebody." He smiled again. "Four of them."

Four. Jesus. "Well, this isn't a good time," she said desperately. "My prospective in-laws are here for dinner. So—"

"So will you send me an invitation?"

"Sure. Of course." *Just go away.*

"Is this guy okay? Are you happy with him?" Jerry stood with his hands in his pockets, looking at her earnestly.

"Yes. Very happy."

"Well, okay, that's good. Don't forget that invitation." He sauntered back down the driveway to the truck parked in the street, and Ellen leaned her head against the warm plaster wall until she was reasonably sure she wasn't going to throw up or cry.

"Jerry," she said to her mother between her teeth as she sat back down in the living room. "Guy I used to date," she added to Gordon and Gordon's mother, who were politely attentive.

"Was that an earring?" Gordon asked.

The doorbell rang again and she flinched.

Gordon stood. "I'll get it this time. Defend the castle from rival suitors." When he opened the door he stood for a moment talking to whoever was out there, then came back with a package. "Special delivery." He put it in Ellen's lap.

She opened it. A jeweler's box, with a ring inside, on dark blue velvet.

"If you don't like it, we can trade it in. But I wanted to give you one tonight."

The ring was enormous, a diamond that probably came close to six months' pay.

She went to her mother's doctor in Ayala, virtuously engaged this time, to get birth control pills again, but Lily had forgotten Dr. Malone was Catholic. He gave Ellen a book on the rhythm method and charged her two dollars for it. Ellen drove back to the clinic in Los Angeles.

Linda said she would be a bridesmaid, but Maggie couldn't leave the ashram. Ellen asked Mimi Ottley instead, with Teak as maid of honor. She pondered what kind of outfit would suit all of them. Maybe a nice A-line with go-go boots, Gordon said.

Ellen suspected she'd fallen through a hole in the real world into a copy of *Bride's Magazine*, which she consulted without result. "I spent a whole morning worrying about my dress," she told Gordon. "How long the train should be and whether I want pearls on it. I think I'm losing it."

"S'okay. You're supposed to. Do you want outriders and an elephant?"

"I think just a simple coach with footmen."

Gordon grinned, and she thought, *What a blessing the man is*. She suspected he was actually enjoying himself during her agonized deliberations over The Dress. Jerry would have been rigid with outrage over the excesses of consumer culture and the display of the bride as goods for sale. If he'd agreed to get married in the first place.

When she stopped thinking about flowers and the cake and what kind of shoes to wear and thought about real things, she wondered what sleeping with Gordon would be like. Fun, probably. They'd come close, but he seemed to understand her urge to wait. For her it had become an unspoken formula, a spell and an incantation: She'd slept with Jerry and it hadn't worked. She wouldn't sleep with Gordon, and it would.

She felt pleased with herself, as if she had figured something out. "You can arrange things," she told Teak the night before the wedding. "You don't have to just let the wind blow."

"Maybe," Teak said dubiously, painting her nails. "Is Jerry coming to this wedding?"

"No! Oh God, no." She hadn't sent him an invitation because handily she didn't know his address. He wouldn't have actually expected one.

"No? It might have been wild."

"Ellen doesn't want wild," Mimi Ottley said, sitting at Ellen's dressing table rolling up her hair. They were all spending the night at Ellen's house so they could leave for the church together the next day. It was like a seventh grade slumber party where two of the guests hated each other. Ellen had briefed Teak before she could mention Randy and make it worse. Like almost any male who'd ever met her, Randy had had a thing for Teak. The family hadn't heard from him at all. The Army was still looking for him and hounding the Ottleys about it, which must be awful no matter how awful they had been to him.

Linda sat cross-legged on Ellen's bed, the stranger and distant observer of Ellen's childhood. "We never thought you'd be the first, Callahan."

"Well, we thought it would be Maggie," Ellen said. "Hare Krishna."

"That's a cult," Mimi said.

Teak gave her a look, wide-eyed. "I thought it was a religion."

"Well, it's not."

"How do you tell?"

"For one thing," Mimi said, "they don't believe in God."

The church was full of white and yellow flowers tied with ribbon, the garden outside serene under a blue California sky. Nodding rows of lilies-of-the-Nile bloomed against the stucco foundation. No one ever got rained on in September in Southern California unless they'd been very wicked. That was what Jerry had said. But there was still a drought and they needed the rain, and why was she quoting Jerry, even in her head, that was bad luck, don't quote Jerry. Ellen carried her makeup case across the church lawn, with Lily bearing The Dress in a plastic bag. The bridesmaids had theirs, and the flower girls darted and shrieked across the lawn like dragonflies, their mothers behind them, spike heels sinking in the grass.

The dressing room had the air of a high school drama department, full of crinolines of the sort no one had worn since grade school, the air thick with hair spray. The fresh flowers for Ellen's hair were sitting in a box. Ellen blotted her lipstick with powder the way *Bride's Magazine* had showed her in its article, "Put on the Perfect Wedding Face." Teak leaned in the doorway to the garden, smoking a joint.

"This is a church!" Mimi was rigid with disapproval.

A flower girl buzzed by and Teak ducked out into the garden with her joint. Ellen saw Linda slip out after her.

"Put your arms up, dear." Lily dropped The Dress over Ellen's head.

Ellen stared at herself in the mirror. The Dress was a cloud of lace and organza with a stiff skirt. It was like standing in a cake, or in one of those pincushion dolls immobilized in the depths of their satin skirts. Lily began to brush out her hair. Ellen blinked at the apparition in the glass while Lily pinned her veil to the wreath of flowers and settled it on her head.

"Nearly ready!" The church lady assigned to keep them on time popped her head around the door. "The organist is starting up." She wrinkled her nose. "What's that smell?"

"Ready, darling?" Lily touched Ellen's cheek with a fingertip, sniffled suddenly and burrowed in her purse, stopping to dab at her eyes with a handkerchief. "Girls?"

Teak, Linda, and Mimi lined up obediently. The flower girls jiggled their baskets, shedding rose petals. "Now, remember, scatter the petals on the floor as you go. Don't throw them at people." Lily handed Ellen her bouquet.

Her father was waiting in the hallway outside. He smiled down at her. He had a rose in his buttonhole.

Wait. Ellen stopped in the doorway, teetering in unfamiliar shoes, lost behind a bouquet of gardenias. What was she doing? She felt the way she had when her cousins had enticed her to the top of the high dive when she was ten, and she'd frozen, too terrified to jump off, or even stand up. Finally she'd backed off again, on hands and knees. She envisioned herself doing it now, in a wedding dress. But her father held out his arm, uncomprehending, since she'd told him specifically she wanted to get married. She took his arm because the flower girls had started down the aisle. Once the music started, you couldn't stop, that was probably a rule.

A sea of faces turned around to beam at her. What if Jerry had come anyway? She scanned them, panic-stricken. What if he showed up, like Dustin Hoffman in *The Graduate*, and grabbed her?

Jerry wasn't there. Jerry had moved to Petaluma and it was not his day for rescuing brides. Gordon was waiting at the altar, smiling, looking so happy it wasn't clear whether he was tethered to the ground or not. Gordon wanted to get married. Gordon knew what he was doing.

"Dearly beloved," the rector said.

What if she just ran off by herself? Screamed "NO!" and ran down the aisle? What would they do?

Gordon would be heartbroken.

And where would she go, she couldn't drive in this dress and her purse was in the dressing room and she didn't even have her keys anyway, her car was at her parents' house.

She envisioned herself flying from the nave, her veil wild behind her. Lily, who knew that nice people didn't let things get this far before they broke an engagement, would die of embarrassment. Her father would ask if she'd thought things through. She would be notorious in Ayala forever and no one else would ever want to marry her, and anyway where the hell would she *go*?

"Do you take this man?" the rector demanded of her and Ellen jerked her head up, horrified.

Someone said, "I do," and she wondered if people about to be executed had that same sense of starring in a show that had got out of control.

She couldn't see behind her, could only dart her eyes sideways at Teak and Linda, who looked stoned and cheerful, and Mimi who was getting married herself next month and looked saintlike and ethereal. On the other side, the ushers and Gordon's best man, the photographer from the paper, looked hungover and were standing slantwise, like people in a high wind.

Teak handed Ellen a ring. Ellen stared at it. Oh. Gordon stuck out his finger, so she put the ring on it.

Oddly, the queasiness vanished once the ceremony was finished. When the rector said they were actually married, and there wasn't any way out of it but a divorce, Ellen blinked and looked up at Gordon. He looked cute. He grinned at her. The organist began to play again and they started down the aisle. The ushers and bridesmaids woke up and followed them. Now she felt light, the fairy princess in her triumphal procession. This would be all right, she thought. It just took concentration.

She concentrated on cutting the cake, and drinking most of a bottle of champagne, and not passing out on her wedding night. Then she concentrated on her honeymoon, and coming home to the house they'd rented at the beach in Ventura. A huge bougainvillea grew up one side and over the flat roof, and sand drifted in through all the doors and windows. She planted a little garden behind it and brought home a pair of Siamese kittens. Somewhere on the other side of the television screen, soldiers were murdering other soldiers at the dinner hour, but there were carrots in Ellen's garden and a kitten in her lap, and her husband could cheerfully ignore mayhem, rape and murder because he paid attention to it at work.

The kitchen was minuscule, cheerfully lined with cracking green and yellow tile, with a refrigerator that froze beer and thawed ice cream, and a stove that had to be lit by hand. They made breakfast together in the mornings and actually invited people over for dinner parties, two at a time. The only thing wrong with the house was the cockroach who lived under the toaster. He appeared a week after they moved in and Ellen, horrified, swatted him with a newspaper, and a wooden spoon (which she threw away afterward) and a brick, but she never quite caught him square and he always came back. The next night he would be there again, sauntering out of a crevice under the window sill.

"It's just a water bug," Gordon said.

"It's a *cockroach*." Ellen's upbringing did not allow cockroaches, particularly one that skittered under the toaster while she watched it.

"Maybe the cats will eat it." Gordon looked hopefully at Yin, who was perched on the counter staring fixedly at the toaster. Yang had found a chunk that had fallen off the brick and was trying to eat that instead.

Ellen upended the toaster and banged it down on the counter in a flurry of toast crumbs. The cats flew off the counter and the cockroach disappeared inside his crevice.

In October a conglomerate bought the *Chronicle* and implemented its anti-nepotism policy regarding employing relatives of staff members, so they fired Ellen.

"I'm afraid there isn't anything I can do about it," the editor told her, shaking his head. He gave her an avuncular smile. "Unless you want me to fire Gordon."

Gordon made twice what she did. They couldn't do without his salary, so it was probably a bad idea to tell the editor to screw himself. But she didn't know how to do anything else. "What am I going to do for a job?"

"Aw, honey, you'll find something. Go out back and see what's in Sunday's classifieds, get a jump on the competition."

Ellen could see the other people in the newsroom watching her interestedly through the glass walls of his office. Gordon was out on assignment. He would love this. She stalked out and sat back down at her desk, trying furiously not to cry.

"God, I'm sorry," the Soc editor said. "I didn't know he was going to do that today."

Gordon hadn't either, and roared around the house that night, cursing the conglomerate and making empty threats to quit, which they couldn't afford.

"This is what Linda was talking about at the reception," Ellen said grimly. "When she said women get shafted on a routine basis, and Jones just kept drinking punch and telling her to prove it."

"Maybe the reception wasn't the best place for a speech," Gordon said, distracted from his fury. "Harper told you he could fire me instead if we wanted him to. It's just an asshole policy."

"And you make twice what I do so we can't do that." She doubted that Gordon would have been inclined to, either, if it had actually been an option. She took her advance copy of the Sunday classifieds to her chair and stuck her nose in it, gloomily perusing the HELP WANTED MALE OR FEMALE section and the dismal HELP WANTED FEMALE column, which clearly wanted help they could underpay. When she went to the kitchen to get a red pen, the cockroach had got married, too, and was scurrying around a lettuce leaf in the sink with his wife. She pounded the bottom of a plastic bowl at them and they ran.

She interviewed for a copywriting job at an advertising agency, and another at a radio station. She took an examination for eligibility worker at the Welfare Department, which looked like an utterly depressing prospect, and was relieved when KENO, the station, offered her the job, at two-thirds of what she'd made at the *Chronicle*. She wrote ads for local clients in an office where the monitor played Top 40 rock all day and the all-night disc jockey shot speed in the control room during the news. The DJs adopted her as Little Mother, sent her out for aspirin for their hangovers, and left her to screen their groupies on the telephone.

"I found a girl asleep in the ladies' room this morning," she reported to Gordon and Gordon's parents. "The all-night guys let them in when they're on the air."

"Ellen, there must be some other place you could work." Marie looked disapproving. "Why don't you just have a baby instead?"

"Mother," Gordon said.

"Not yet. Have some more pie." Ellen felt rebellious. She wanted children, but everything seemed to be conspiring to push her into having one now, since there wasn't anything else to do.

She felt pushed to make a stand, but how did you make a stand when you had a living to make at the same time? It wasn't any big thing that drove her finally, but a series of small ones. She discovered that the previous copywriter had voiced the station editorials, but she couldn't because women's voices weren't held to carry authority on the air. She sent a letter to a gasoline company asking them to add Gordon to her credit card and found the next month that they'd switched the entire account to his name. She agreed to model for a *Chronicle* fashion page on Women at Work and the cutline identified her as Mrs. Gordon Murphy.

"I want my name back." She felt as if she could see it vanishing, like disappearing ink.

"Ellen—" Gordon looked hurt.

"I am not invisible!"

"People will think we split up."

"I'm living with you."

"Don't you think you're overreacting a little? You worked for Soc."

"How would you like it if people kept referring to you as Mr. Ellen Callahan?"

"It doesn't mean you're not your own person."

"That's what you think," she said darkly.

"It's a lot of trouble to change your name," he said.

"It wasn't when I changed it to yours."

"That's because that's how people do it. The system isn't set up to go back the other way."

"Then it needs resetting."

"What about when we have children? You won't have the same name they do."

"Have you thought about giving the girls my name and the boys yours?" Ellen asked him.

"No."

She brooded about it at work. "You look down in the mouth, Murphy," Harry Hart, the afternoon drive jock, informed her when she went in the control room to rearrange the commercial cartridges and pull the dead ones.

"I'm changing my name back to Callahan."

"Splitting? Didn't you two just get married?"

"We're not splitting. I just want my name back."

"That's going to screw up your W-4," the office manager said. She slapped the next day's log book down in front of Hart. "Tomorrow's. Remember? Don't start this one till you finish the old one." She tapped with a long pink fingernail on the log in front of him. "We're still on Thursday."

"Yeah, yeah." He watched her disappear through the door. "Christ. I only did that once." He flicked the mike on and the red "On Air" light came on. "That was Sonny and Cher, 'I Got You.' Heartless Harry Hart comin' at ya this *gorgeous* fall afternoon. I'll be giving you a chance to qualify to win the new CCR album in just a minute here, and we've got some Carpenters comin' up and some Stones, right after this." He punched up Chevrolet's afternoon drive spot and shook his head at Ellen. "Names don't matter. You know how many names I've had my personal self?"

"Yeah, and I bet none of 'em was your wife's." All the disc jockeys had air names. Heartless Harry was really Joe Willets.

"Aw, come on, Ellen, give the guy a break. Why do you care?"

"For the same reason you would," Ellen said, but Joe shook his head, uncomprehending.

She went ahead with the attempt anyway, with no real notion of how much trouble it would cause until the bank and two department stores canceled their accounts due to the divorce.

"There isn't any divorce."

"You said in your letter you were taking your maiden name back."

"Yes, but there isn't any divorce."

"Well, we can't put two names on the same account."

"Why not?" Ellen felt herself growing more stubborn.

"It is not Framingham's policy. So you'd have to have your husband sign any time you bought anything."

"Then just put my name on it."

"I am sorry, but it's not our policy to issue married customers accounts that do not include the husband."

"Then how *do* I get my name on this thing?"

"Use your husband's name, dear. Legally you're Mrs. Gordon Murphy anyway." The voice was smug, as if it took satisfaction in putting her in her place.

"I am not," Ellen said, but the voice was not to be convinced.

Gordon's mother called him up and told him that all her friends thought he let Ellen go too far.

"I don't *let* Ellen do anything," he said, exasperated, and called Lily.

Lily said Gordon was hurt and why did Ellen want to make an issue of this when it wasn't really important?

"It's important to me," Ellen said.

"Well, darling, you're not the only one involved here."

Finally she gave it up, because it would have been a constant irritant to Gordon if she did it, a constant explanation to people they met that they were married, they just had different names. Gordon sent her a bunch of roses to the radio station, addressed to Ms. Ellen Callahan Murphy.

At Thanksgiving the *Chronicle* promoted Gordon to assistant city editor. They had the cats neutered and called an exterminator about the cockroaches. In December the FBI came to KENO to see Ellen. They were looking for Jerry this time.

Agent Brown wore a dark suit and ignored the disc jockey in surfer shorts who was opening boxes of promo records and singing "Bad Moon Rising" along with the monitor. "When was the last time you had contact with Mr. Manoury?" he asked her.

"Last winter." She tried to make it sound like a long time ago.

"And where was he living at that time?"

"I don't know. He just stopped by for a minute."

"What was the purpose of his visit?"

She could see Harry Hart and the news director looking at her through the production studio's glass window. Harry mimed a conversation via Dick Tracy wrist radio. She turned her back on them. "He came because I got engaged."

"Did he ask you to conceal his whereabouts?"

"No, he asked me if I was going to get married."

"What was the nature of your relationship with Mr. Manoury?"

"I used to date him," Ellen said between her teeth.

"Did he ever discuss with you his intention to evade military service?"

"On our dates?" She gave him a vague smile. "No, I don't believe he did."

"Do you know his whereabouts now?"

She pondered. "No."

Agent Brown gave her his card. She took it by the corner. "Will you contact us if you hear from him?"

"I don't think I'll hear from him."

"If you do."

"I won't," she said firmly.

Over dinner, Gordon said, "You didn't warn me the Feds were after you."

"Oh, God, they came looking for me at the paper, didn't they?" She couldn't tell if he was upset.

"Been leading a double life?"

"No, they're looking for my old boyfriend." She wondered if he already knew that.

"The one with the earring?"

"Uh huh." She picked up her plate. "Do you want pie? I bought blueberry at the bakery."

"I always want pie."

She made a grab with a paper towel at a cockroach in the sink. There was another under the window sill. So much for the exterminators. Her plate, balanced precariously on the counter, fell off.

Gordon came in from the next room. "Darling, would you relax? Here, sit down, put a cat in your lap. I'll make coffee. Was the FBI guy a jerk?"

Ellen stroked Yin's cream-colored fur. Yin crossed her eyes ecstatically. She closed hers. "No. I'm just worried about Jerry."

"Is this guy important to you?" He rattled the coffee maker. "Goddamned bugs are still here."

"Well, I don't know what he's likely to do." She decided that that didn't sound reassuring. "He's a little crazy," she added. Worse.

The coffee maker burbled and after a while Gordon put a

mug on the table beside her. He sat on the arm of her chair. "My darling, leave crazy old boyfriends behind." He kissed her and Ellen leaned against him while Yin kneaded her knees. "We could go to bed," he said hopefully.

The telephone rang at 2:00 a.m. Ellen reached out an arm for it, knocking it off the nightstand. Oh, God. Jerry? Something awful.

"Murphy, is that you?" The all night jock's voice was carefree. "Murphy, I just erased the California Milk spot. What do you want me to do?"

"What do you mean you erased it?" She propped herself on an elbow, balancing the phone. The cats shifted sleepily on her feet while Gordon muttered something from beside her.

"I stuck it in the bulk eraser. I thought it was the tape I was dubbing to for the FM station. Can I run the old one?"

"No! It's dated. Some damn contest. Oh, shit. Just scratch it. I'll call around and find another copy in the morning."

She hung up the phone. Twenty minutes later it rang again. This time there was only silence but she could feel some desperate yearning at the other end of the line. She froze, staring at the receiver. There was a click and a dial tone.

"Ellen, what the hell?" Gordon rolled over. "Who was that?"

"The station," she said slowly. "The night guy. He does his production while he's on the air and screws it up."

"And then he calls you? Twice?" He peered at the luminescent dial of the clock. "Jesus."

"The paper calls you. They called you last week."

"That was important."

202

"Oh."

"Someone firebombed a draft board office," Gordon said patiently. "Anything down there on fire?"

Ellen put the receiver down in the cradle. "I don't think so," she said.

XIII
RED DOG FARM

Jerry read Ellen's wedding story, which Dreama sent him from the *Ayala News,* and thought the guy looked like a dork and she looked like a coyote caught in the headlights. But maybe that was just wishful thinking.

After he got sick drunk and drove clear to a pay phone, he was ashamed of himself. He hid the clipping in a jacket pocket in the closet. It wasn't until he and Joelle were leaving Petaluma—he'd packed it in the bottom of his duffel bag with his clothes—that he dug it out again and put it in the garbage. New start, new life, he thought, pushing it down under the coffee grounds and banana peels where she wouldn't see it. He wasn't going to be Randy Ottley, beating his head against some place that wouldn't let him in.

He and Joelle were going to take part in changing the world, putting his butt where his convictions were. There wasn't any room for Ellen. He pulled the neck of the duffel tight, slid the keeper down its cord, and slung the bag on his shoulder.

The kids were dancing around outside, piling their things in the back of the truck and taking them out again, and running up and down the dirt drive with the shepherd, Pete, on a rope. Joelle came out of the house smiling, swinging an old gray hard-sided suitcase. She looked young and excited, with the breeze blowing her hair in wisps over her forehead.

Jerry put his arm around her and hugged her shoulders hard. Here was someone willing to take chances with him. What did he need with a woman who wanted to get married in a long white veil and an aura of fictional virginity, and be given away by her father like a prize cow?

"How long will it take to get there?" Joelle asked him.

"Couple of hours, depending on potty stops." They never got farther than twenty miles at a time before someone had to go. The kids scrambled into the back of the truck, hauling Pete up with them. Jerry slammed the tailgate. He climbed into the cab and Joelle got in beside him. The engine caught on the first try.

At the start of winter, the people at Red Dog Farm had invited them to move in, to join seven others living communally, they said, self-sufficiently, outside the culture that fueled the military juggernaut and the sucking dry of every resource to spew out bigger and faster machinery. Outside the culture that had pushed Jerry farther and farther to its fringes. After beating himself to death in Petaluma doing odd jobs for cash, trying to make ends meet and still stay anonymous, a non-person, Red Dog Farm felt like a haven. Joelle had liked the women there and Jerry could make himself useful—they didn't have anyone who did plumbing or knew how to fix a generator. He could opt out and still take care of Joelle and the kids. The nearest school was ten miles away, but Blue Jay said Sue was teaching the Red Dog children, and she'd be happy to have four more, so that might work out.

It took two hours to cross the border, even if the border was totally self-defined: a long dirt road north of Sebastopol. The house was old and electricity-less, a farmhouse on the edge of a long-neglected apple orchard. Two women were knitting on the front porch when they drove up and children exploded from the apple trees at the sound of the truck. A tall man with a long blond ponytail and a handlebar mustache came out of the house and held his hand out to Jerry.

"Welcome, man."

"Thanks." The kids were climbing out. "This is Blue Jay," he told them. "These are my kids—Lauren, Liz, Samantha, and Matthew."

Lauren and Liz eyed Blue Jay, reserving judgment. Samantha and Matthew were on the ground, inspecting the children who'd come out of the trees. "This is our dog," Samantha said.

"He's his own dog," the boy said. "We don't own living things. But we'll help you feed him."

"He's our dog!" Lauren said from the truck.

"Stop it," Joelle said.

Blue Jay grinned. "It takes a while. We don't rush things, guys," he told the tree children.

A blond woman in a blue caftan got up from her chair on the porch and hugged Joelle. Sue, Jerry remembered, Blue Jay's old lady. Blue Jay introduced the other, a frail girl with frizzy brown hair and wide blue eyes, as Daisy, Yoshi's old lady. They went in the house and found two men on the floor in the front room, working on a bike, and two women in the kitchen beyond, cooking rice on a woodstove. "You remember Stephen," Blue Jay said. Stephen raised a bearded head from the bike and said, "Hey." The man on the other side didn't look up. His sandy-brown ponytail was tied with red feathers.

"That's Yoshi," Blue Jay said, stepping past them into the kitchen. "And this is Wolf, and Yoshi's other wife Daphne." Wolf had a dark braid and her hands in a pan of dishwater. Daphne was brown skinned and zaftig with a billowing cloud of hair tied up with a strip of red cloth. Jerry smiled at her and she smiled back, wrinkling nose and eyes.

They went on through the kitchen to a room on the other side that might have been a hired hand's when the place had been a farm. It had another little room beside it that had once been the pantry. Jerry thought he and Joelle could take that for themselves and put the kids in the big room.

"There's a litter of kittens outside, honey," Daphne said to Lauren, who was standing in the doorway, arms crossed across her chest. Liz had vanished with the younger two. "And some chickens. Want to see if you can find me some eggs?"

"Are those your kids outside?"

"Rain is Sue's, and Salamander is Daisy's. Daisy has a baby, too."

"Are there any more?"

"There are now." Daphne smiled at her. "Four more. That's cool. Go find me some eggs."

"All right."

"Look out for the poison oak," Wolf said without turning around.

Jerry dragged their mattresses in from the truck, with his duffel and Joelle's suitcase and the kid's clothes in black plastic bags. Joelle hung their clothes on a line strung across the room and packed everyone's underwear into her suitcase. She'd brought fabric to make curtains with. They'd brought no other furniture since it wouldn't fit in the truck and hadn't been worth much anyway. Jerry figured they could acquire some when someone threw it out, or he could make it.

The first night he lay on the mattress, eyes open, after the kids had crashed, full of rice and beans, and Joelle was asleep beside him, and watched the moonlight from the one high window travel across the faded ivy-patterned paper on the far wall. In the morning he'd get his tools out and see what he could do for the place. The women mostly made the food runs, Blue Jay had told him. People with a surplus they might donate didn't trust men. Stephen went along to drive the farm truck and make sure nobody messed with the women.

Jerry watched the moonlight flow across the ivy like a slow river. He imagined the pantry walls lined with glass jars of preserves and apple butter and the deep green of beans. Sacks of potatoes and onions, tops sprouting pale green shoots. Peppers ripening in the kitchen window, and the smell of his mother's fried green tomatoes.

They needed a garden. Maybe that would be the first thing.

When he woke Lauren was demanding to go home rather than use the outhouse.

"It's better than plumbing that always backs up," Joelle said sleepily. "You can't clog up a privy."

"It was dark last night," Lauren said in a furious hiss. "I couldn't see. I'm not staying here. It's gross. And the door doesn't shut good."

Jerry decided that should be his first project. He pulled his jeans on under the blanket and kissed Joelle. "I'll do something about that."

He found Daphne in the kitchen making coffee, snagged a cup, and ambled out on the porch to see what the morning looked like. The low winter sun was just shining through the apple trees. A flock of crows settled in the yard, cawing, then rose again, streaming against the sky. The spirits of the place, making him welcome, he thought. Pete came lolloping around from behind the barn with Matthew behind him.

"Morning, sport."

"We found the chickens!" Matthew announced.

"I hope Pete behaved himself."

"He likes chickens. He tried to lick one but she pecked his nose."

"Cool." A chicken lover, not a chicken killer. Jerry looked at Pete affectionately.

"There's a big spider in the potty."

Jerry thought uneasily of black widows and decided to check out the spider while he fixed the door. He went to his truck to get his tools and found the box open on the tailgate. Pieces of his socket set were scattered in the bed and he found his pliers and hammer on the ground.

Yoshi was using the socket set when he tracked it down.

"Uh, man, I'd like it if you asked first."

"You weren't around."

"You always work on your bike before daylight?"

"We don't have private tools here. Tools are to use."

"Well, mine just got here and they don't know that yet. So I need to know where they are if I'm gonna fix anything."

"I'm fixing my bike."

"Everybody rides your bike?"

"Like hell."

"I figure everybody uses the shitter." Jerry fitted the sockets back in their case. "You're welcome to borrow any time you want to ask, man."

Daphne caught up to him on the porch. "Don't mind Yoshi. He's an asshole."

"I thought he was your asshole."

"He's good in the sack and I figured Daisy needed backup, you know? But we don't have an exclusive thing."

"Oh." Jerry considered that while he went out to the privy and poked around for the spider. She turned out not to be a black widow so he took her to a promising corner of the barn, then came back to fix the hinges. The privy stank and he looked around for some lye, but didn't see any. He put it on his mental grocery list. They'd probably have to move it anyway. The ground here was low and muddy and way too close to the well. He fixed the door and put a hook-and-eye latch inside, and went to look for a good spot to move it to.

He was digging a new hole on the far side of a rise behind the house when Daphne came out with a bowl of granola and apples and a thermos of coffee.

"Far out," she said. "I've been trying to get Blue Jay to move that thing for two weeks."

Jerry looked hungrily at the granola. "I need to wash."

She looked at his hands. "It's just dirt. One of the things we try to get away from here is obsessing on cleaning."

"Pin worms," Jerry said. "You get 'em from eating dirt."

"Really?"

"Really. Not to mention the things you can get from people's shit."

"I'll bring you some water," she said.

Jerry looked at the granola and tried not to wonder what she'd had her hands in before she fixed it for him.

"Silly hippies haven't got any sense half the time," Blue Jay said when Jerry told him he wanted help to drag the privy up the hill. "Yoshi and Stephen put it there while I was in town. They didn't want to carry it any farther than they had to. I told them it would stink, that close to the house."

"It's not good to get it in the water table," Jerry said. "When the ground's wet, bacteria spreads and you get it in your well."

"Oh, man, I never thought of that. Wow, it's good you came."

Jerry took the truck into Sebastopol with two dollars from the communal fund. He bought a sack of lime and poured it down the old hole to kill off what he could. He told Stephen to scrape wood ash out of the stove and put it in a can to dump in the new one when it got smelly. Lauren fussed at him about having to climb the hill to use it and he gave her a science lecture on *e.coli* until she stomped off. Yoshi and Stephen were in the kitchen and he made sure he was loud enough for them to hear.

By the time spring came he'd fixed everything that leaked or stuck or squeaked on the farm and had put a hook-and-eye latch on the inside of his and Joelle's room, too. Wolf borrowed his needle-nose pliers and forgot where she put them, and Stephen left the lid off the toolbox and it filled up with rain water. Jerry thought about a padlock on the box but figured it would make trouble, so he put a loaded mousetrap in the top tray and didn't say anything.

"It's possessive-obsessive shit like that Red Dog people are trying to end," Stephen said, nursing his finger.

"Jerry's not ready to give up ownership." Joelle gave him a patient look from the other side of the room. He had thought the farm would be good for her, and in a way it was, but lately she'd begun to treat him with a self-righteous superiority that emphasized the gap in their ages.

The younger kids were all in bed, being sung to by Sue, who was pregnant again and going to have the baby at the farm with a midwife. Lauren was rebelliously holed up in Joelle and Jerry's room listening to her transistor radio on dying batteries. The rest were sharing an after-dinner joint and a jug of wine by the light of a kerosene lantern. Blue Jay said it was important to do that; it made community. "When the whole material culture goes down in the revolution, ownership will be universal," Blue Jay said. "We'll all be owners, so nobody will be. That's what the counterculture is all about."

"Who's going to run the power stations after you've taken over the state?" Jerry asked him, feeling argumentative.

"The people," Stephen said.

Jerry looked at him over his glasses. "You know how?"

"Man, you are just trying to bring us all down."

"I don't know. The sink drains now," Daphne said. She got up and drifted into the kitchen, brushing her fingers in Jerry's hair as she passed.

She came out the next day while he was digging the garden, glasses in his pocket and his hair tied back with a rubber band. He peered at her, a foggy and indeterminate shape in his field of non-vision.

"It's Daphne. Why don't you put those things on?"

"One side's loose. They keep falling off." He balanced them on his nose and she came into focus, breasts looming out of a low-cut peasant blouse, hair blowing around her face. She was barefoot. A gold toe ring peered from under an Indian skirt. Some burden was slung over her shoulder, knotted into a scarf.

"I have something to show you." She smiled at him. "You told me about the otter, remember?"

"The rock carving? Yeah."

"Well, there's one up here too. Want to see it?"

"Can you wait while I get these in?" Jerry patted the last pepper seedlings into the ground. He'd started them in a cold frame made out of window glass, kept in the kitchen by the woodstove. Beyond them were tomatoes and onions and watermelons. The stiff green bristles of corn stuck up at the back of the garden. He watered the peppers in and stood.

Daphne led the way up a slope of apple trees. The gnarled limbs blossomed with clouds of white flowers, blooms thick with the buzz of bees. New grass covered the hillside like emerald fur, patched with splashes of yellow mustard flower and orange poppies. Above the hill the sky was brilliant blue, laced with wisps of transparent cloud. Beyond the orchard the hill rose abruptly. She scrambled up it with Jerry behind her. From the top they could see the farm house below them, the residents in miniature. Unidentified children chased each other around the barn with Pete galloping between them. A cat sunned itself on the porch roof.

Daphne took him higher, and then down over the crest through a stand of mustard and knee-high grass, her skirt trailing in the yellow flowers. An outcropping of stone was nearly buried in the mustard. She knelt and pushed the stems away. Near the base of the rock the dirt had been dug out and a board propped over the excavation.

"I found it last week." She settled cross-legged in front of the board. She patted the ground beside her and unslung the bundle from her shoulder. It proved to be a bottle of hard apple cider. She took a drink and set the bottle in the grass. She moved the board to one side. "Cool, isn't it? The old man at the hardware store in town told me it was out here."

Jerry stared at the sunwheel on the rock and the figure of a deer that raced across it. They'd been half buried by time before Daphne had dug them out again. The deer seemed to move as a cloud ran over the sun, racing eternally on his rock.

She handed him the bottle and he took a swig. It had a potent kick, like alcoholic essence of apples.

"I figure it's some kind of hunting magic. You think?"

"Probably." He touched the little figure with a fingertip. "I wonder how long he's been out here."

"Five hundred years maybe. I asked the local Indian folks and that's what they said. They said I should give it something."

Jerry poured a little of the cider at the base of the stone. "They like tobacco smoke, too." He lit a cigarette and blew smoke gently at the rock. The little deer looked appreciative, or maybe that was just his glasses. He needed a new prescription, but they didn't have any money for it. Daphne leaned down to look at the carving. Her breasts were nearly out of her blouse. She eyed him in obvious invitation. He put his hand on one and she smiled happily and scooted closer.

Joelle was looking for him when he got back and it seemed prudent not to come in the house with Daphne, since Joelle was unlikely to be ready to give up that particular ownership, so he let himself be diverted by the strange truck parked beside the barn. Unknown wanderers regularly fetched up at the end of the dirt road, guided by local rumor or friends of friends. Sometimes they stayed a few days or a few months. Jerry ambled across the yard to see who these were.

The newcomers proved to be an artist named Rabbit and his wife Annabelle, who had the most stupendously ugly face Jerry had ever seen, and the most beautiful body. She modeled one day a week for the Art Institute in San Francisco and bought Rabbit welding tools with the money. Rabbit was little, hardly five-feet-six, sandy-haired, with a face like an Irish tough. Someone had broken his nose at some time and chewed his ear.

The Red Dog people took them in and fed them, and after a few days it was decided they would stay. Rabbit had a rifle and proved to be a better shot than the other residents. He began to bring in deer regularly, with a fine and complete disregard for hunting season.

It was warm now and most of the household went more or less naked, with no outsiders to hassle them. Rabbit and Annabelle slept in a tent in the yard, with Rabbit's welding equipment in back under a canopy. Jerry, fascinated by any new tool, convinced Rabbit he wasn't dangerous and Rabbit let him weld a pipe to run from the well to an outdoor shower. When the sun went down they sat by a campfire and traded songs. It was spring and the night air was magical. Jerry felt it seeping through his skin. On nights like this he was convinced the farm had been a good idea.

"Man, what is that pile of crap behind the barn?" Rabbit asked him.

"Mostly junk," Jerry said. "I haven't been able to sort it out yet." The pile was slowly being devoured by an aggressive bougainvillea.

"I'm gonna clear it out, okay? I've got a stash of lumber in the truck I want to make a lean-to with, against the wall. I've got to get this stuff under a roof. It's gonna rain eventually."

Jerry looked at the sky, spattered with flung stars. It had rained in February, but since then he'd been watering his garden with a bucket. Sometime it *would* rain, though. And Joelle had been looking at him suspiciously. A project with Rabbit would keep him out of trouble. "I'll give you a hand," he said. "There might be something useful in there. Yoshi was burrowing through it for a while but he gave up."

"Man, it would be paradise here," Rabbit said, "if anybody knew what they were doing."

Rabbit went after the bougainvillea with a machete and Jerry found a pile of copper tubing tangled in it that he could use for the shower, and three cast-iron skillets black with grime. He blasted them clean with Rabbit's torch and gave them to Wolf. When it was cleared, he went to town overnight to get manure for his garden. To Joelle's fury, Daphne hitched a ride to pick up a box of bees the Digger commune on the coast had promised them. No one else wanted to ride with bees.

"You can use chicken shit from the hens," Joelle told Jerry. "Stephen can get the bees."

"You've got to mix chicken shit with something," Jerry said, going into lecture mode, which always annoyed Joelle, "or it burns the plants. Horse manure amends the soil. And I need to go to the library." He tossed his sleeping bag and a shovel in the back of the truck beside the wicker hamper Daphne was bringing for the bees.

They came back in the morning to find Rabbit raging because Yoshi had taken his stash of wood, cobbled it into a precarious lean-to himself and installed his bike under it while Rabbit was out hunting.

"It's free space, man," he'd told an infuriated Rabbit.

Rabbit told him to sod off and went to Blue Jay, who had decided they should vote on it and everyone in the main house had voted for Yoshi because they were tired of having his bike in the living room.

"If he doesn't get his bike out of there I'm gonna melt the sucker," Rabbit told Jerry.

Jerry looked at Joelle. "Did you vote for this?"

"Everything should be free," Joelle told him. "We're a free people, so we don't hoard our possessions."

"It's not a possession if you clean out a dump and then someone moves in on you," Jerry said to Joelle. "Yoshi could have built himself something there last fall if he wasn't too lazy to move his butt."

"You could have been in our room last night instead of wherever you were," Joelle said pointedly.

He dropped it. "Never mind." He wasn't in charge anyway, although he didn't understand why Blue Jay hadn't thrown Yoshi out before now. On account of Daisy and Daphne maybe. He saw Daphne go by outside the window, the hamper of bees balanced on her hip, giving them a taste of the local air. A couple of loose ones zoomed about her head. They were a new swarm with a young queen.

"You'd understand if you were older," Joelle informed him. "All your focus is still directed inward."

She stayed pissed, so Jerry spent most of the next week outside, making a mulch out of the kitchen compost, the manure, and chicken droppings from the barn. He built a hive for Daphne's bees, and watched uneasily as Yoshi and Rabbit refined their feud. The day after Rabbit threatened to melt his bike, Yoshi ran it over Rabbit's tools outside his tent. The next day Jerry saw Yoshi saunter under the lean-to, whistling, and erupt a minute later, shrieking.

"Snake!" Yoshi danced around the lean-to. "Snake!"

Rabbit appeared from his tent in a pair of hiking boots and nothing else, his customary costume. "Snake? Where?"

Yoshi skidded to a halt in front of Rabbit, still looking uneasily over his shoulder between words. "You. Son of a bitch. You know where. In my bike!"

"In it?"

"Behind it! Next to it! Rattlesnake!"

"Well, calm down, man. It ain't gonna chase you." Rabbit gave him a big grin. "You just get you a forked stick and haul it on out of there."

"I'm not going in there!"

Eventually Blue Jay and Jerry killed the snake, a sizable rattler. Daphne wanted them to let it go in the hills, but Sue and Joelle vetoed that idea because of the kids, so Wolf cooked it instead.

The next day Yoshi just happened to leave the barn door open and the wind trashed the elaborate and delicate metal structures Rabbit had assembled to take to an art fair. Jerry heard him howling with rage, then an ominous silence.

Jerry ignored them and shoveled mulch in the garden until Yoshi came out of the house wearing his riding leathers. Yoshi went under the lean-to and came back out again, face twisted in a furious grimace, and headed for Rabbit's tent.

Rabbit peered out, looking expectant. He held a sack that gave off an ominous buzz. *Jesus.* Jerry started toward the house. They confronted each other, Yoshi with a knife out and Rabbit

217

waving the writhing sack on the end of a stick.

Jerry flew down the slope and got between them. "Stop it, you assholes!" Yoshi's eyes glittered and it crossed Jerry's mind that this might not be the best idea, but they didn't have any antivenin. On the porch, Daisy scooped up the baby and her knitting and vanished through the front door.

"You messed up my stuff for the last time!"

"You poured crap on my bike, man!"

"Your goddamn bike needs to find another place." Rabbit cradled the end of the stick carefully and waved the bag in Yoshi's face. Yoshi batted at it with the knife.

Jerry screamed at them, "Goddamn you assholes! You motherfucking morons! Give me that before some kid gets bitten!" He rounded on Yoshi, still screaming, louder and crazier than Yoshi. Yoshi's hands wavered. Jerry spun around. "Rabbit, give me the goddamn sack, where the hell are you getting snakes?"

Rabbit did. Jerry clutched the top of the bag and snatched Yoshi's knife out of his fingers when he waved it at him again. He held one in each hand and backed away from them.

They stood like dogs at the ends of their chains, quivering with constrained anger. Jerry backed up another couple of feet. As soon as he was clear of them they dived for each other. Jerry turned and went up the steps to the house.

On the porch he stopped to let his breath out. Rabbit and Yoshi were rolling in the dirt, growling, entangled with each other.

Jerry banged on the door to Blue Jay and Sue's room and it popped open. Blue Jay was sitting on the end of the bed, tying a piece of leather thong around his arm, just above the elbow. His hair was matted and greasy. A syringe lay on the chenille cover beside him. It had rolled down into the depression his body made and was snuggled against his thigh.

Oh, man. Jerry laid the knife on the bed beside Blue Jay anyway. "Yoshi and Rabbit were trying to kill each other. With a knife and snakes." The sack made an angry buzz. "Now they're out there fighting."

Blue Jay looked angry and displeased, like a parent whose children suddenly refuse to follow the rules. The rules of Red Dog Farm were that there were no rules. If everyone did what he wanted to, it was supposed to make it unnecessary to step on anyone else.

"How long have you known Yoshi?" Jerry demanded.

Blue Jay's expression sank into blankness. "I don't know. He just showed up one day, you know?"

"I thought you said you'd known him from the beginning!"

"Since we moved in here, a year ago maybe. The girls came, and kinda scouted it out, then Yoshi came."

Was that before you started doing junk or after? Jerry almost asked him, but it wouldn't have made any difference. He'd never known a junkie who gave a shit what anyone else thought. Maybe he wasn't a junkie yet. Maybe he was just chipping. Jerry didn't feel like he had a pulpit to hold forth from since he personally had tried a lot of things, mostly whatever was handy, though not that. "Acid's a lot more fun, man," he ventured.

Blue Jay took the knife and put it under his bed. "Jerry. Go away."

"Yessir."

Wolf met him in the doorway with a kitchen knife in her hand, looking exasperated, and took the sack.

On the porch, Daisy was painting Yoshi's lip. It was split and puffy, his chin bloody. His riding leathers were shredded across the chest and one arm. Daphne appeared to be unconcerned. Jerry could see her at the shower, Daisy's baby at her feet, soaping bare breasts. The baby was playing with the water. Jerry didn't see Rabbit.

"Tell him not to touch my bike," Yoshi said to Jerry. The puffy lip made him lisp.

Blue Jay came out on the porch. His skin was pasty but he looked functional. "Council meeting tonight," he said.

When the residents met in council, they sat around a fire in the yard, and passed a painted stick from hand to hand. If you had the stick you could talk. If you didn't, you listened. It worked reasonably well. Jerry watched them assemble, their eyes cautious, quick looks moving from Yoshi to Rabbit, who had two skinned knees but was otherwise unmarked. "Asshole bit my leathers," Yoshi said, glaring at Rabbit.

"Talking stick." Sue held it up.

Yoshi subsided. Blue Jay had given him back his knife and Wolf had dispatched the snake. Jerry hoped rattlesnake wasn't going to be a permanent menu item just because Rabbit had decided they were his private arsenal.

People tended to dress up for meetings, one way or the other. Yoshi had fresh feathers in his hair. Daisy wore an elaborate collar of body paint and a crown of vines. Daphne wore her Indian skirt, with spirals of red paint on bare breasts. Stephen and Wolf and Blue Jay were naked, with shiny stone amulets on cords around their necks. Sue, vastly pregnant, was enveloped in a caftan covered with yellow flowers.

Jerry put on an Indian vest sewn with little mirrors he had found at a garage sale and Joelle sat beside him in jeans and her best blouse.

Rabbit and Annabelle sat side by side in the lotus position, hands folded in their laps. They wore matching white garments like penitents, but Jerry doubted they were.

Blue Jay put out his hand and Sue laid the talking stick in it. "We came here to redefine the culture," Blue Jay said sorrowfully. "To throw out hating and embrace loving." He looked at them. "How many of us still feel they can love the rest of us?" He put the talking stick on the ground so they could answer him.

"I do," Stephen said.

"I do."

"For sure."

There was a chorus of assurances.

"When someone isn't poisoning the air," Wolf said.

"Free people have a *responsibility* to love," Sue told her.

"Okay, I love you." Rabbit reached across Blue Jay and patted her hand.

Blue Jay looked at Yoshi until he said, "Yeah, man, all right."

"So then why are people angry?" Blue Jay waited for them to sort it out.

Wolf picked up the stick. "It poisons the air when people become attached to possessions. Attachment gets in the way of freedom."

Yoshi held out his hand and she gave him the stick. "We ought to have everything free, man. Everything. Put all the tools in one place in the barn. Hang all the clothes up on a line and let people wear what they want to."

Stephen took the stick out of his hand. "We already share the food and the trucks. Why not? It might keep people from getting obsessive."

Jerry held out his hand. "Sure. But whoever takes a truck out has to bring it back full of gas. And we need a list and a sign-out sheet for the tools, so no one loses a crescent wrench down the privy." Stephen looked sheepish. "I like it though," Jerry said. "I want to take the bike into town tomorrow. It uses less gas than the trucks and I can wire stuff on the back."

"Me, too," Rabbit said. "I could weld a basket on it."

Yoshi opened his mouth but Wolf had the stick back. "What Yoshi said. I think it ought to go for people, too. Monogamy is poison in a free society. People get into jealousy bags and they can't get out." She glanced at Joelle. "We could say no one can spend more than two nights with same person, so people don't get into coupling and jealousy trips."

Daphne held her hand out. "You want a sign-up sheet for that, too? If we want freedom, we have to be free, not make more rules."

Jerry scratched his head. He didn't want a turn with Wolf. The woman scared him to death. "I think people ought to be free to choose monogamy if they want to."

"I think you'd put it in a knothole, that's what I think!" Joelle snapped at him.

"Hey, whoa. Talking stick." Blue Jay held up his hand and they quieted.

"I didn't mean like that," Yoshi muttered.

"Why not? You can't demand exclusive rights to *two* women in a free family," Stephen said.

"I didn't mean the women."

"Well, what if they go with other men?" Blue Jay asked. "Would it be all right?"

"I'm not a goddamn crescent wrench! I'll go with anybody I want to." Daphne glared at Stephen.

"I think we ought to stay out of everybody's sex life," Sue said. "People will do what they want to do. We wanted to keep the establishment from telling us who we could sleep with. Telling people who they *can't* sleep with or *have* to sleep with is the same thing. So shut up."

"Yes, Mama." Stephen grinned at her.

"I don't want that jerk on my bike." Yoshi glowered at

Rabbit.

"I thought we were a free family," Rabbit said. "You had a lot to say about that."

"Yeah, well I don't want you wearing my underwear," Jerry told him. "Some things are sacred."

"You don't wear underwear."

"Talking stick!" Blue Jay said and they subsided.

"If we're going to be free, we have to redefine the concept of *owning*," Annabelle said. "If I don't own Rabbit and Rabbit doesn't own me, it doesn't matter who I sleep with. If I don't own my clothes, then they don't own me, and I become free to wear them or not."

"Giving up is freedom." Wolf reached across the circle and patted Joelle's hand.

Blue Jay tried to put it to a vote, but everyone had his or her own definition of "free" and they couldn't get consensus. Finally they voted to renounce the *idea* of ownership, while retaining some rights to monogamy and underwear for those who weren't completely cool with that. No rules were ever proposed on *how* to share all these things and when Blue Jay passed a ceremonial hash pipe around the circle, the idea gradually dissipated in a drift of smoke. Rabbit and Wolf got their guitars and Jerry his flute and the night moved on, carried on a tide of music. Joelle and Daisy got up and danced in the firelight. Jerry passed his flute to Sue and began to slap his fingers on a drum made of deerskin stretched over a section of the hollowed trunk of a dead apple tree. Daphne produced a jar of cider and Annabelle a bottle of elderberry wine and they got drunk on fruit and music. When the sun came over the ridge, they got up and staggered into the house and fell asleep as the children were waking.

Blue Jay had gone to sleep on the floor so Sue gathered the children into bed with her and they worked arithmetic sums in soft voices while Lauren coached them and Sue dozed dreamily, but after a while, she poked Lauren and said, "Go wake up Blue Jay for me, hon, and get Wolf and your mom."

Lauren shook Blue Jay and he opened one eye.

"Whatsit?"

"Sue says to go get the midwife."

"Auugh!" Blue Jay sat up, wild-eyed.

Lauren went to shake Wolf and Joelle but they were inert. "Sue says to get up!"

"Can't." Joelle rolled over.

Jerry sat up.

Lauren looked panic-stricken. "Sue's having her baby and Mom won't wake up."

Jerry didn't think Mom was going to wake up. He had no idea what she'd been into last night. He had stayed drumming with Sue while Joelle had disappeared into the night with Stephen and Wolf. He looked angrily at her inert form, ignoring the fact he hadn't cared last night.

Blue Jay's truck started up out in the yard.

"Go get Daisy and Daphne."

Daisy and Daphne were half asleep but functional. "Sue's having the baby," Jerry said.

"Well, come and help," Daphne told him.

Daisy had already gone to Sue and chased the children out. "Lauren, you watch the baby. Liz, you take the little ones and go look for eggs. Rain, you and Sal get some wood and get the fire in the stove going. Now, then." She turned briskly to Daphne and Jerry. "Jerry, sit there. Let her squeeze your hand as hard as she needs to. Daph, you rub her back like you did for me."

Jerry blinked at this transformation in Daisy, and sat down obediently. "Blue Jay's gone for the midwife," he said to Sue.

Sue's fingers clenched around his hand and she breathed in and out in sharp, short puffs like a toy train. Daphne rubbed her back, crooning a lullaby. Jerry remembered it from some hazy moment of his childhood and joined in.

Baby's boat's the silver moon
Sailing in a starry sky,
Out upon the sea of sleep,
While the stars roll by.

"Come on, Sue, sing."

Sue gasped as the contraction released its grip. She picked up the melody. Jerry beat his free hand on the bedstead, making a bouncing rhythm. They sang in harmony, luring the baby into the world with music. It didn't matter whether more babies were a good idea or not. This one was one its way.

Periodically someone woke and stumbled in to peer through the door. Daisy would give them a job and they would go away again to heat a pan of water or make Sue a hot tea. Sue got up and walked up and down the room, dancing to Jerry's drum beat, doubling over when the contractions hit. In an hour, the contractions were nearly on top of each other. Sue's water broke and Jerry panicked.

"Where's the midwife?"

"Not here," Daisy said. "Baby nearly is, though. Hang on, Susie."

Sue's fingers compressed Jerry's like a vise. She was drenched in sweat, hair plastered to her face, the yellow flowered caftan soaked through and hiked above her belly.

Daisy bent over, inspecting her. "Okay, push."

Sue grunted and the baby slid out between her legs into Daisy's hands.

Jerry stared at it, awestruck, while Daisy cradled it, a tiny blood-covered form with improbably enormous testicles. The baby screwed up his mouth and wailed. Daphne washed him with a wet cloth and tied off the umbilical as the afterbirth came.

She handed Jerry a pair of scissors.

He looked into the baby's eyes. They were a deep impenetrable blue and at any moment they would tell him something important about the universe. He cut the cord and kept staring as Daphne wrapped the baby in a blanket and handed him to Sue.

XIV
BOB AND HOLLY SUE GO NORTH

G ordon stuck his head through the bathroom doorway. Ellen was wrapping a towel around a river of wet hair. "Some guy's here to see you."

"Who?" Her heart thudded.

"I don't know. Tall. Hispanic-type. He said, 'You must be the husband' to me."

Not Jerry then. *Martin?* She flew into the living room, the sleeves of her cotton kimono flapping around her, bare wet footprints trailing her down the hall.

It was Martin, rumpled, in faded jeans. He looked weary and road worn and his hair was longer than she remembered it. A knapsack lay at his feet.

"Oh, God, Martin!" She threw her arms around him. He rested his chin on the top of her head. "What are you doing here? Does anybody know you're here?" She pulled away and closed the curtains with a swift, frantic jerk.

"Take it easy. I don't think there're any G-men in the driveway."

"They were looking for you," she said.

"You must be Martin Alvarez." Gordon held out his hand.

227

"Ellie's talked about you."

"I hope it's all right to be here, man."

"It's fine."

"I didn't want to go back without seeing Ellen." He eyed her curiously. "Mom told me you'd got married."

"I'm Gordon," Gordon said.

"Did you see your parents?" Ellen asked Martin. "What about your father? Wait a minute. Let me put some clothes on." She disappeared into the bedroom and grabbed a caftan out of the closet. She pulled it over her head and combed her hair. Martin and Gordon were sitting in the living room looking at each other when she got back. She sat on the sofa beside Martin, tucking bare feet under the caftan.

"I saw Mom," Martin said sadly. "She thought we'd better not let Dad know. She'll tell him after I leave. She's afraid we'll argue and he'll call the cops."

"Want a beer?" Gordon offered. He got one for Ellen, too, and sat opposite them. "Did you drive from Vancouver?"

"I hitched. Canadian plates might not be a good idea. And my car's a junker. I was afraid it'd die somewhere conspicuous."

Ellen looked at the drawn curtains again. She envisioned FBI men stopping him, asking for his ID, checking for warrants. She saw them in her mind, endlessly chasing Martin, chasing Jerry, chasing Randy Ottley, chasing all the boys on a perpetually moving track, like ducks at a carnival shooting gallery.

"I went to see Teak," Martin said. "I don't know how glad she was to see me."

"Surprised, maybe," Ellen said carefully.

"She had some guy there in a safari jacket and desert boots. He looked like a goon." He rubbed the back of his neck wearily. "Or maybe I did."

"Occupational hazard with Teak," Gordon said. "She's constructed to make men look like goons." He smiled at Ellen.

Besides Jerry, Gordon was the only man Ellen had ever met who hadn't forgotten her existence when he saw Teak. Gordon said Teak was a walking invitation to psychosis.

"She sent the guy off," Martin said to Ellen. He flicked an eye at Gordon, but Gordon didn't seem inclined to leave. "I spent the night, but it was like she was half there. Very up, very manic. She drank enough to topple an ox and never showed it."

"She can." Ellen grinned. "Remember the night we went to that house in L.A. with— Anyway, remember the guy who was mixing tequila with organic guava juice?"

"And he claimed it counteracted the toxins in the tequila?" Martin started to laugh.

"And we all got soaked." She snorted into her beer. "Except Teak, who said you just had to believe in it!" They both leaned forward, butting heads, laughing.

Martin sat back first and she looked up and caught Gordon eyeing her thoughtfully. She said to Martin, "One of the ushers at our wedding tried to get her to go out with him, practically in front of his girlfriend. When Gordon asked him what the hell he was doing, he said, 'I lost my head.'"

"It happens to lots of us," Martin said wistfully. "I guess I'll just slink around Ayala a little more before I head back. I want to go see Day Logan, but I don't like to just show up. Is it okay if I call her from here?"

"Sure." Day Logan was a sculptor who'd been Martin's teacher at Apple Valley. Ellen listened and pretended not to while he got on the phone with her.

"She's got some hotshot gallery people up there tonight," he said uncertainly, "but she said to come tomorrow."

"Well, stay here tonight." Tomorrow was Saturday. "I'll feed you and drive you up there if you want me to. If she doesn't mind."

"I don't want to take you away from anything."

"Gordon has to work tomorrow," Ellen said blithely. "But I don't."

"Gordon is a wage slave," Gordon said.

"Are you sure you don't mind my staying, man?"

"My house is yours. Just don't get my wife arrested."

Ellen thought Gordon was just glad Martin wasn't Jerry. They were both carefully not mentioning Jerry. She made a salad and enchiladas for dinner and brought out a bottle of tequila and margarita mix, which made Martin laugh. After dinner, they sat with elbows on the table, playing the Ayala version of Whatever happened to him?

"That was bad about Ottley," Martin said. "Could have been me if I'd gone in, I suppose. What about that guy his sister Mimi was dating?"

"They got married. He got a high number." Ellen poured a shot of tequila, straight, into her water glass. "She's pregnant already."

"Barefoot, too?"

"Not Mimi. Sensible pumps. She joined the Junior Women's Club."

Martin reached for the bottle. "She told me she was going to be a nun once, at your birthday party. That was the night I met Teak."

"She was twelve. I wanted to be a secret agent."

"I wanted to be Evel Knievel."

"I remember your motorbike. You took me for a ride down Foothill Road on it, and I wet my pants I was so scared." She poured another shot. There was still a lot left in the bottle. "You know who I saw last week? Nicky Madsen from eighth grade. She calls herself Rainbird Dragonsong now and she runs a health food store in Santa Monica."

Martin tipped a little more tequila into his glass. "Is Carl Leeman still in the army?"

"Yep." At least she thought so. "I'm not entirely sure he's changed much. More so, if you get my drift."

"Remember the time he took Ottley on a snipe hunt on the upper school camping trip and lost him?"

"Wasn't it you who finally found him? I felt bad for him."

Martin raised his glass to her. "To growing up, fer Chrissake."

"To growing up." Ellen reached for the tequila again. She noticed Gordon seemed to have gone to bed.

"You see Jerry?" Martin asked her quietly.

"No."

"I'm sorry."

"It wasn't in the master plan." She drained her glass.

"You happy?"

"You bet."

"I didn' think Teak would come to Vancouver. Not really." Martin tipped his head back and drank the shot in one swallow. "Jus' wiffle— wishful thinking."

"I'm sorry I didn't write." Ellen sniffled guiltily. "You know Robert Hutchinson joined the Army? He's a medic. An' my friend Maggie from college is a Hare Krishna. And Carl actually came to see me while he was on leave, it was awful, he kept talking about killing Vietnamese."

"Hell of a career plan."

"What about Maggie? Sitting around all day in a sheet, chanting. An' you can't drink."

Martin held the tequila bottle to the light. "We can't either. This thing's empty."

"Well, thass a sign." Ellen got up and staggered down the hall to the linen cupboard. "You can sleep on the sofa if I can unfold this sheet."

Martin took the other end of it and between the two of them they got it untangled and stuffed it down around the edges of the sofa cushions. She tripped over her shoes and he grabbed her before she went over. "Good night," he said. She kissed his cheek and he fell down on the sofa.

In the bedroom, Gordon was asleep with the cats curled against his chest. Ellen crawled under the blankets without brushing her teeth.

In the morning she had the queen of hangovers. Gordon had already gone to work when she stumbled into the kitchen to make coffee. The cockroaches waved their feelers at her from under the coffee maker and she smacked at them half-heartedly with a spoon.

Martin sat up and looked at her over the back of the sofa. "Are you alive?"

Ellen picked up the tequila bottle and the wreckage of dirty glasses from the table. "Oh, lord, I haven't done that in a long time. Maybe I'm too old. There's aspirin in the bathroom."

When they had had coffee and aspirin, though, things began to look better and so they climbed into Ellen's bug to go see Day Logan. She needed an adventure, Ellen thought. Day might be one. Day wore saris and heavy Indian jewelry and she'd had a string of famous lovers. Her studio was at the top of the grade in the Upper Valley, a brown Craftsman bungalow in a eucalyptus grove. A series of slate steps led from the road to a porch shaded by an arbor of wisteria. Ceramic wind chimes hung from its cross ties, making silvery notes in the breeze. A fat black and white cat was sunning itself on a faded velvet cushion in a chair on the porch.

Day was a substantial woman nearly as tall as Martin, big boned and angular, with long black hair streaked with gray, pulled into a bun at the nape of her neck. She wore a red sari, an armful of silver bangles, and a ring on her big toe.

"Martin!" She hugged him joyfully. "And I know you." She peered down at Ellen.

"I went to Apple Valley," Ellen said. "But I never took art."

"Well, why not?"

"I was afraid of you." She held her hand out. "Ellen Murphy."

"And are you still afraid of me?"

"I hope not." She looked around Day's house with awed interest. In the foyer was a four-foot ceramic goddess who might have been Guan Yin in a bad mood. Or one of the Furies under an eastern influence. Her string of prayer beads was made of tiny skulls and she held a pomegranate in the palm of her other hand. The piece was finished with a soft blue-green glaze like ocean water.

"That's Mother," Day said. "Come in the studio. I'm just putting things away. The people from *Art World* were here to take pictures."

The studio, down two steps and a hall from the foyer, was lit on three sides by louvered windows and full of the rustle of the eucalyptus behind the house. Pieces of ceramic and stone carving sat on the work tables, backed with artistically draped squares of cloth and Chinese embroidery. Day began folding up the cloths.

"Wow." Martin was squatting on his heels, nose to nose with a little mustard yellow jug. Out of the side of it peered a warty face like a frog's. It was hard to tell where the face stopped and the jug began; there was something froglike about the jug and juglike about the frog.

"He's my favorite," Day said. "At the moment. Mother likes him. I may let her hold him for a while. She can keep souls in him, I think."

"I'm doing stuff with stone," Martin told her. "When I can get the stone."

"Keep on getting the stone," Day said. "Don't slide into self-pity up there in Canada."

"No."

"I mean it, Martin. Self-pity is too easy. Now come and sit in the living room and talk to me. I've been talking to photographers all day yesterday, and idiot magazine people. They asked me what my beauty secrets were."

"What did you tell them?"

"I told them chocolate and young men." She picked a pile of newspapers off the velvet sofa and stacked them on a brass tray. "Sit down. I asked Dottie to make us tea." Day vanished into another room and came back followed by a short gray-haired woman in a serviceable apron, carrying a teapot on a tray. Day carried a plate of brownies. "I'll pour, dear, thank you." The woman disappeared and Day sat down in front of the pot in a jangle of bracelets. "Be careful with the brownies. There's a little something in them." She handed Martin and Ellen each a cup of tea and sat back with a sigh. "Martin, is everyone looking for you? Should I not say I've seen you?"

"No, you probably shouldn't. It's not legal to aid draft evaders." He smiled. "Or feed them tea and pot brownies."

"Pah! We've come to a disgusting state in this country."

"I'm a Canadian resident now," Martin said. "A landed immigrant."

"What does that mean? You have land?"

"No, it means I've landed. Legally speaking. They can't throw me out."

"Did you renounce your citizenship?"

"I can't quite make myself do that. Maybe in another four years, when I'm eligible for Canadian citizenship. I'll decide then."

While they talked Ellen nibbled the edge of a brownie, gauging its potency, and stared around her at the array of Indian gods, paisley scarves, Chinese boxes, Mexican pottery, and the collection of wire and wooden cages with papier-mâché birds in them. The tea was hot and smoky and tasted of ginger. Day asked Martin how he was getting back to Vancouver, and Ellen heard herself saying, "I'm driving him," as if it had just been settled.

Martin blinked at her. "Are you sure you should do that?"

"Well, they can pick you up, can't they?" she asked him. "If you're still a U.S. citizen?"

"They could pick me up anyway if they felt like it."

"Well, then. That's an excellent idea," Day said. She gave Ellen an approving look.

"She just got married," Martin said. "Is your husband going to want you to do that?"

"I'm not going to let you hitchhike."

"Martin, when a woman offers to go to Canada with you, don't argue."

He chuckled. "You're a dirty-minded old lady. We went to kindergarten together."

"And you are a new bride," Day said solemnly. "Of course. What do you do the rest of the time?"

"I write radio commercials," Ellen said, wishing she could claim something more serious.

"I saw you looking at my sculpture. Were you afraid of me or of art?"

"I took art in college. I had more nerve then. My family are all writers, though, one way or another. I didn't think I could make things."

Day raised an eyebrow. "Writing can be art."

"Maybe," Ellen said. "But it's . . . ephemeral. I started to want something I could—" she lifted her foot and put it down again on the Turkish rug—"put my foot on, you know, before it got away again."

"Well, come and see me when you get back from Canada and I'll show you how to make something you can put your foot on. Even if it's just for you."

"Do you think she meant that?" Ellen asked Martin when they'd left and were driving down the mountain.

"Day doesn't say anything she doesn't mean. I think she likes you."

"She likes you. I'm your transportation."

"If you think that would make Day offer to give you art lessons, you're nuts. She's the most ruthless woman I know. Go see her."

"I'm going to take art lessons," she told Gordon at bedtime, while his mouth was full of toothpaste. Martin was asleep on the couch, or pretending to be. "And I'm going to drive Martin to Vancouver. I don't want him to hitchhike."

Gordon paused. "Don't you have a job?" he asked after a moment.

"I'll tell them my grandmother in Vancouver is dying."

"This blatant lie doesn't trouble you?"

She picked up her own toothbrush, eyeing Gordon warily. "I'm afraid some cop will stop him and ask him for his draft card. They do it all the time if you're young and long-haired or they just don't like your looks."

"Perhaps this should have occurred to him before he left Canada?" Gordon looked irritably at his own reflection in the medicine cabinet—hair cut short and too old for the draft.

"Gordon, he didn't ask me to drive him."

"'Scuse me." Gordon spat his mouthful of toothpaste into the sink. The bathroom barely held two. He rinsed his mouth and stood back, regarding her dubiously. "This isn't like you.

Even with a hangover."

"I don't have a hangover."

"We don't have any tequila left either. That bottle was two-thirds full."

"I don't have a hangover *now*," Ellen amended. "We just got to talking."

"And drinking. Is that when you decided it would be a great idea to drive to Canada with a draft dodger?"

"No, it was at Day Logan's place." Ellen didn't think she'd mention the pot brownies. She squeezed a strip of toothpaste onto her brush and stuck it in her mouth.

"Oh, yes. You mentioned something about art lessons." Gordon leaned against the shower stall, looking amused. "Isn't she the one who makes the incomprehensible stone carvings with names like 'Maladroit Relationship Two'?"

"Gordon, she's famous."

"Half the people in Ayala are famous. Mostly for bad movies and nutty religions. Nutty art is a change, at least."

"You're being a jerk," she said through the toothpaste.

"Look, Ellie," he said, "I just think you're getting into something unwise. Let Alvarez go back the way he got here. You can take all the art lessons you want to."

"Does that mean you're going to tell my boss I'm lying?"

He looked uncomfortable. She figured he wanted to say he would, but it was just too Victorian-husband and he knew she'd call him on it. "Do you expect him to check up on you with me?" he asked her.

"No."

"Then it won't come up."

"It won't take more than a week."

He didn't say anything.

She rinsed her toothbrush, put it away, and buried her face in a soapy washcloth. When she surfaced she said, "I promise I'll be careful." He was clipping his toenails, one foot on the edge of the toilet. She leaned around him to hang up the washcloth. "Gordon, I've known Martin forever. I can't just abandon him."

"Well, I suppose you think you can't," he said finally, still clipping his nails. "If you're going to do it, take my car. I don't trust yours."

Ellen thought that was the best she was going to get. She wanted him to say he agreed with her, that she ought to go, but she could tell he was damned if he would.

She called KENO the next morning with a suitable tale of a grandmother on the brink, and she and Martin left in Gordon's Fairlane after breakfast. Gordon took Ellen's VW to work.

"I don't think he's happy about this," Martin said as the red bug turned the corner.

"He'll be all right." Ellen slid into the driver's seat of the Ford. "You have a Canadian license, right? You can drive some of the time?"

"Sure." He turned the radio on. "Where's your station?"

"1300 AM. I'm afraid to listen. Someone will play the wrong spot and I'll feel guilty."

"*I* feel guilty."

"I won't if you won't." She turned on the air conditioner and grinned. "My car doesn't have air conditioning."

"I want to hear one of your commercials."

"There's one." The new Last Sandwich Stand spot came on. The Singing Pickles were Heartless Harry Hart singing four-part harmony with himself, speeded up.

"Oh you must be a lover of your landlady's daughter
Or you don't get a second piece of pie!"

Martin hooted with laughter.

"I got that line out of a book, but mostly they sing classics with new lyrics. At Christmas we did 'Hark the Herald Pickles Sing'—*Welcome in the Sandwich King, mayonnaise and mustard mild, two for man and one for child."*

"Hey, can I write for them?"

"Sure. I'm running out of lyrics."

Martin beat time on the dashboard with his fingertips. "*I come on the sloop Roast Beef—*"

"*With my grandmother's false teeth—*" Ellen pulled the Fairlane onto the freeway. "Um. I'm not sure where that one's going."

"Straight down the tubes."

"Well, not every one's a Grammy winner."

They sang all the real songs they knew, up the coast past Monterey, and came up with one usable Pickle song, based on "Clementine." They saw a few Highway Patrol cars but none looked interested in them. By the time they were in Sonoma County, they were both too tired to drive. Ellen insisted on staying in a motel, because camping was likely to get them rousted by the cops.

"You're more paranoid than I am," Martin told her.

She registered them at the Russian River Motel as Mr. and Mrs. Gordon Murphy and put the room on her credit card. As a sop to her conscience, she called Gordon. At ten o'clock they fell asleep in their clothes on the beds, beneath a blinking neon sign in the shape of a dinosaur in a bathing suit. The next morning they ate a greasy road breakfast at the House of Pancakes and filled the Fairlane with gas again.

"I've got enough money, damn it," Martin said when Ellen tried to pay for that, too.

She put her gas card away. She felt sneakily guilty—she was having too much fun. The sun coming through the windshield was warm and the road went on through dusty orchards and brown velvet hills until it wound back to the freeway. "Remember the time we all went to San Francisco together?" she asked wistfully.

"Yeah. You got pissed off at me for sleeping with Ana."

"I had some idea you were Teak's, I think."

"Maybe I was."

"Well, as far as I can tell, Ana sleeps with everybody who comes through. It seems to be a requirement."

"Uh oh," Martin said.

"Yeah. It was kind of the last straw. One of them, anyway."

"Shit. I'm sorry."

"Doesn't matter now," Ellen said.

"You sure?"

She felt tears sliding down her cheeks. Damn it. "I am from one standpoint. I love Gordon. But I'm scared to death the Army's going to get Jerry, and he won't survive it. Whether he gets sent to Vietnam or not, he won't survive."

"Um." Martin tapped his fingers on his knees. "I wasn't going to bring this up, but maybe I should so you won't worry. Teak says he's living in some commune up here."

Ellen looked wildly at the sides of the highway, the dusty trees flashing past, as if Jerry might step out of them, like a freeway chicken, thumb extended. "She didn't tell *me!*"

"She thought you didn't want to know. But her goon in the safari jacket is an archaeologist, and she came up here with him looking for rock art and they ran into Jerry in a store."

"Oh, God." It was worse than thinking the Highway Patrol was after them, seeing Jerry behind every bush. She felt untethered from Gordon and dangerously adrift now. "How far do you think we can get tonight?" How far from Jerry?

"Oregon maybe. Want me to drive?"

"Yes." Ellen pulled over on the shoulder and got out. With Martin driving, the car wouldn't automatically go where Jerry was, diving down some unknown back road, through some salt-bitten coastal town where Teak had seen him in a store.

For the rest of the trip they didn't talk about Teak and Jerry. Instead they pretended they were a vacationing couple, Bob and

Holly Sue, and they picked their motels for their weirdness factor: a cluster of cabins incongruously shaped like wigwams on the Oregon coast, and the English Manor with Tudor cabins south of Seattle. The English Manor had a lighted pool open till 10 p.m.

"Holly Sue, you want a swim?"

"Grab me one of them towels, Bob."

She floated on her back in a pair of Martin's boxers and a t-shirt, staring at the night sky. Tomorrow she would drive Martin across the border, and the next day she would start the drive home. She had called Gordon again as soon as they stopped, and he sounded less grumpy, and as if he missed her. The cats were lonesome, he said. "I'll be home soon," she promised, grateful for the sea anchor of Gordon. Without that who knew where she might float off to? Martin dived into the pool and she rocked on his wake, her hair floating around her like seaweed. When she got out she was cold and she put on her nightgown and crawled under the covers. The room only had one bed, and Martin crawled in with her, cradling her against his chest, one lonesome traveler to another.

The next afternoon they crossed into Canada. She let Martin drive so they would look more normal. She gawked at the Peace Arch that straddled the border while her heart fluttered in her chest, waiting for recriminations and arrest. The customs officer on the U. S. side said to have a nice stay, and didn't question the car's registration, or Martin's American driver's license or draft card. It seemed better to show those and hope the officer didn't run an ID on the name than to admit emigrating to Canada. There was only one reason young American males emigrated to Canada. On the Canadian side, Customs passed Martin through with his Canadian papers, and smiled at Ellen, assuming her to be the girlfriend. She changed a twenty into Canadian dollars and told the teller brightly how she'd always wanted to see Canada.

In the car she put her hand against her heart. "I don't know how we had the nerve to do that. I was stiff with terror."

Martin smiled shakily. "I don't either. It seemed like an idea to go see everyone, you know. I get so lonesome it's indescribable. But when we got to the border, I thought, Alvarez, you moron. You got here all right, why did you have to be stupid enough to leave?" He put the car in gear and they drove through the Canadian side of Peace Arch Park, where an elaborate bed in the center of an emerald lawn displayed the Maple Leaf flag in flowers.

"I ought to call Gordon and tell him I didn't get arrested."

"That'll thrill him," Martin said.

She chuckled. Unarrested, it felt satisfactorily daring to be the wild half of the couple for a change. With Jerry, there'd never been any question. He had the territory staked out. To be wilder than Jerry she would have had to be insane.

Martin drove them to the apartment he rented in a shabby old Vancouver Victorian and unlocked the door. A month's worth of mail splattered the floor under the mail slot. He scooped it up and piled it on a table.

"Here's the phone."

While she gave the operator the number, he opened the windows and turned on lights.

"I'm here," she said when Gordon picked up the phone at the *Chronicle*.

"Is your grandmother dead yet?"

"We're expecting her to expire this evening. I'll start home tomorrow. Will you call KENO for me and tell them that, or are you too pure of heart?"

"As long as you're coming home, I'll call them." He sighed. "I miss you, Ellie."

"I miss you too," she said, and did, at the same time she looked forward to the drive home, alone in the car.

When she hung up Martin was standing on a chair, rooting in a cardboard box on top of a block and board bookcase. He climbed down with a smaller box in his hand. "I was afraid to cross the border with this, so there ought to be something in here if my landlady hasn't found it." He put the little box on the table and took out rolling papers and a plastic bag of pot.

"I'll cook dinner if you'll tell me where there's a grocery store," Ellen said.

"Down at the end of the block. Turn right out the front door."

She walked to the store craning her neck to look around her. Traveling with Martin had some of the same illicit kick that hanging out with Jerry had had, with someone a little saner and without the complications. She bought steaks and boxed rice pilaf, lettuce and tomatoes, French bread and a bottle of wine. She took them back to Martin's apartment and they opened the wine and smoked a joint while she cooked. Gordon didn't smoke pot, so she'd given it up except for unauthorized excursions to places like Day Logan's house. She wasn't sure Gordon would disapprove, but she wasn't sure he would approve either. All he'd said on the subject that she could recall was that he belonged to the martini generation.

It was like putting a foot back into a previous life to hang out with Martin. Ellen had a faint sense that it might be dangerous, but it was also seductive and giddy, like a spring day. Martin got his guitar out while she cooked, and they sang "The Midnight Special" and "Chilly Winds" and "The House of the Rising Sun" and all the Riverbottom Ramblers' old songs. He started to do "Sloop John B" and gave up on it when he got to "I want to go home," so Ellen got him another glass of wine and he rolled another joint and they sang the version about Grandmother's false teeth instead.

They ate the steak and bread ravenously, and Martin showed

her his sculptures. He'd made a little studio out of the one bedroom in the apartment, and slept in the living room. The stone shapes in the studio were four-footed, not quite deer, not quite something else. They leaped from their stone into air as if they had just emerged from the ground.

"They're elk," Martin said. "Dream elk. The elk of the world-making when all the animals and people came out of the earth. It's an old Indian legend."

"They're beautiful." These weren't hippie unicorns, but creatures of magic from the beginning of the world, shaking soft earth from their antlers, muscles of loam and grass hardening into flesh. Their metamorphosis hung, fluid and frozen, in front of her.

"I found a gallery that'll take some of my smaller pieces. I haven't had the nerve to show her these yet. They're so damn big."

"What do they weigh?" She looked yearningly at the stone elk.

"God knows. I nearly killed myself getting the blocks up here on a dolly."

"Oh, Martin, I want one. Sell me one."

"You'd bust the suspension on Gordon's car taking it back to California."

"Do you think it would?"

He scratched his head. "Hell, I don't know. I won't sell it to you. I'll give you one if you think you can get it home."

"I'll get it home." She stroked the stone backs and wild heads. There were three of them. One had its head thrown back and she knew the antlers wouldn't fit. What would Gordon say when she brought home a stone elk? She settled finally on the smallest, still nearly chest-high at the antlers.

Martin made her up a bed on the couch where he usually slept, and rolled himself in a sleeping bag on the floor. She dreamed the elk were running beside her car, hooves like muffled drumbeats on the shoulder of the freeway.

In the morning they went to a thrift store and bought a lot of ratty blankets to pad the carving with. Martin got out his dolly and they maneuvered the elk out his door and into the back seat of the Fairlane. Its head stuck up as if it were trying to look out the window. She pulled the blankets back from its face so it could see, and it looked then as if it were wearing a babushka with an elaborate headdress inside it.

When they had the elk packed, Martin put his arms around her and they stood, Martin resting his chin on her head again, Ellen leaning hers against his chest, while the morning traffic went by.

"Take care of yourself," she said finally. "I'll write."

"Drive safe."

He stood on the sidewalk and watched until the Fairlane, its back end sagging, turned the corner, heading back where he couldn't go.

At the border Ellen declared the elk and the customs officer told her, worried, "You're gonna wreck your shocks."

"I'll be careful," she promised. "I won't drive very fast." The back end of the Fairlane did feel as if it had rocks in it. It crunched ominously at speed bumps until she learned to crawl over them. Once on the freeway, however, it seemed to do all right.

She and the elk took their time on the way home. They stopped to see the whales in Puget Sound and the seals at Morro Bay. The only place they hurried through was Sonoma, because everywhere she stopped she saw Jerry out of the corner of her eye. When she turned to look at him he was always a fat farmer in overalls or a woman with a toddler by the hand.

When she got home she convinced Gordon to put the elk in the living room, where it looked as if it had fallen through the roof from somewhere else. Gordon drove his car around the block and then straight to the repair shop, but he didn't complain. He just looked at her oddly, as if she might have grown antlers herself.

XV
LOBSTER QUADRILLE

The ghost heaved another armful of sugar cane onto the truck bed. After this harvest it would be time to move to a different island, always moving because to settle anywhere eventually invited curiosity. The farm workers were migrant, from harvest to harvest, and he drifted with their tide. At night, in whatever bunkhouse or room-for-rent he slept, he went home, a spectral apparition above the ocean and the Channel Islands and then inland, yearning, stubborn in his flight, to hover over the valley, pleading with it to take him in. Sometimes in the daytime he thought he was there already in the orange and avocado orchards where his teenaged self had worked summers in the dusty sunshine. At other times he was aware of the cane fields, the pineapples he loaded into boxes, the lush greenery that turned in the worst times to the jungle he had fled, the fire and the burned dead who followed him everywhere. Only the fierce concentration that took him home to the valley of his childhood could blot out that vision, but his fragmented form could never stay.

The compulsion for body to follow mind was growing. His mother's letter to the *Ayala News* had made the AP wire for its timeliness and its viciousness and talking heads on television had debated it, multiplied endlessly in a department store display in Honolulu. Still his feet drew him to the little airfields of the islands, or the great ones on Oahu and the Big Island where the planes lifted off in their true bodies and flew homeward. Someday, when fear couldn't hold him back any longer, he would get on one.

Robert was supposed to have been back in the States in a few months but he'd volunteered for another tour; they needed him, he wrote to Jerry, he was the old man of the outfit now, and afraid to leave them. Jerry wrote back that he admired that, and meant it, and wondered how any of them were going to get home. The road to the Ayala Valley was printed in his head like a map but he couldn't travel it either; he'd seen to that himself.

A coyote trotted up the road past the garden, its tongue hanging out, and he threw it a tomato. The coyote caught it and gulped it down, squirting juice. Jerry had been tying the tomato vines to stakes, their hairy branches pungent smelling and heavy with fruit. He spotted a huge green tomato worm on one and picked it off. The coyote was sitting expectantly in the road, so he threw it that too and it vanished in a snap of jaws. Jerry looked around guiltily. Wolf had caught him feeding the coyote once before and was certain that it would eat her chickens. He'd seen it catching mice in the upper meadow where the rock carving was. He didn't think it would be above chickens, but Pete was on guard at the farm and Pete was twice the coyote's size. The coyote swiveled its ears now, listening for him.

Something else was coming up the road in a cloud of brown dust.

"You better scram," he said.

The coyote disappeared in the tall grass.

He squinted against the afternoon sun and recognized the arrival: Teak's archaeologist in a Jeep with the back fitted out in a fancy set of metal boxes. The archaeologist himself wore khaki shorts with multiple pockets and a camera around his neck. As he watched, a long, tanned leg appeared, and Teak climbed out the other side and surveyed the house. Yoshi and Rabbit, apparently tuned to the same radar, both came around the barn. Jerry had built the chickens a coop so that Rabbit could put his welding equipment in the barn, but it hadn't stopped their feud.

He started down the hill. Sue was on the porch nursing the baby and talking to Felix, a gigantic, bearded garlic farmer who'd known her in some other life and was staying at the farm for a week or two. Neither of them looked like they wanted to move. Jerry waved his hand to indicate that he would deal with the new arrivals. Yoshi and Rabbit didn't appear to be armed with anything but their dicks this time.

"Jerry." Teak brushed her hair back from her face. It was still long, a heavy mane that fell to her waist. She wore a suede miniskirt and a fringed suede vest over a thin blouse.

"Hey," he said.

"You remember Ray."

"Sure." He held out his hand.

Ray shook it. He pushed his sunglasses up on his head. "The locals tell me you have some petroglyphs up this way. I didn't realize that when we were talking to you in the store."

"Really? I haven't seen any." *If I'd wanted you stomping around up there, I'd have mentioned it to you.* He wasn't entirely sure why he didn't like Ray. Maybe it was the safari shorts.

"Wow." Teak looked over the house and garden and the gaggle of children hanging upside down in the apple trees. "This is too much. I didn't realize this was where you lived."

Resigned, he motioned them toward the house. "You better meet everybody."

"I'm Rabbit," Rabbit said, intercepting them before they got to the porch.

"Yoshi." Yoshi kept his hands in the pockets of his leathers, and nodded at them intently.

"Can we camp here tonight?" Ray asked. "We've got our gear. We won't put anybody out."

"Yeah, sure, man," Yoshi said before Jerry could answer him.

"I'm Ray."

Yoshi didn't appear to care if he was Allen Ginsburg. "You his old lady?" he asked, eyeing Teak.

Teak gave him a vague smile and began looking for something in her purse, a huge suede shoulder bag.

Jerry got in between Yoshi and Rabbit and wished Annabelle and Daphne would show up. Then he thought the hell with it, and let it roll. Blue Jay came down the porch steps, and the rest trailed after him. Jerry introduced Teak and Ray.

At dinner everyone took stock of the newcomers. Rabbit, Stephen and Yoshi addressed their attention to Teak with an intentness that made Wolf sit up with narrowed eyes and Daisy look forlorn. Blue Jay welcomed Teak officially to Red Dog Farm, and Felix yearned toward her silently. Even Pete the dog lay down on her feet.

Daphne, on the other hand, watched Ray with interest. She wore a peasant skirt and a top of cream-colored gauze thin enough to see through. Teak left men speechless, but Daphne scooped them up and took them home with her. Ray's eyes kept returning to the nipples showing through the gauze as if they were spiders crawling dangerously close, which he pretended not to watch and couldn't make himself ignore.

Joelle had figured out that Jerry knew Teak from someplace

else and glared at them both.

"Friend of a friend," he whispered, bending around the corner of the long table to talk into her ear.

"Mmm. Eat your spaghetti," Joelle told Samantha.

Daphne had cooked that night and there was no meat in the sauce. Liz picked the zucchini out of hers, and Sam and Matthew poked at the squash as if it were toads. However it was considered self-centered and non-contributing not to eat what was served for dinner, so slowly and surreptitiously their plates emptied themselves. Pete's tail brushed by Jerry on his way from Teak's chair to Matthew's.

Perhaps as a defense against Rabbit and Yoshi, who were jockeying for position and glowering at each other, Teak sat by Felix and listened with her usual appearance of complete attention—which might or might not denote actual attention, Jerry knew—while he talked about his garlic farm in Gilroy.

"Important carvings," Ray said to Daphne. "Ought to be catalogued."

Jerry wiggled his eyebrows at her, trying to say, *Don't tell him*, but she just looked perplexed.

"These people are pretty canny about not letting you know where carvings are when it's a sacred site, but there's usually someone sensible you can slip a few bucks to." Ray adjusted the various pockets and epaulets on his khaki shirt. "We don't do any damage, just photograph them *in situ*. Otherwise a site's liable to be lost when the last local Indian dies off."

Jerry could tell by Daphne's expression that she was going to show him.

While Joelle and Wolf and Lauren cleared the table, Ray and Teak went outside to put their tent up. Blue Jay helped Ray unpack it, a Swedish modern igloo of aluminum and canvas. It looked like a spaceship about to take off beside Rabbit and Annabelle's warren of old flags and paisley canopies.

"It's way cool to see you," Jerry said to Teak, while Rabbit circled them, obviously trying to figure out how to detach her. Yoshi stood on the porch watching.

"Yeah. Long time." She squinted her eyes down the road into the darkness. "You see Martin?"

"No. Is he around?"

"He came back. Just for a visit, you know."

"That took nerve."

"Yeah. Martin has nerve." Teak twisted the fringe on her vest.

More nerve than he had. He wondered how long he could stay out here without asking about Ellen. "I gotta go get my kids in bed."

"Kids. You. Wow." Teak shook her head. She picked up her bag and disappeared into the tent.

When he woke in the morning, Daphne and Ray were in the kitchen drinking coffee and getting ready to hike up to the rock carving.

"Where's Teak?"

"Zonked," Ray said. "She's not a morning person." He shook his head. "I've been up two hours, and had a hike around the orchard."

Jerry poured the last of the coffee into a mug and put some more in the pot. He took it out on the porch and watched Ray and Daphne climb the hill. Ray's pockets were stuffed with notebooks, tape measures, a trowel, and a whiskbroom. Jerry put his bare feet up on the porch railing. A redwing blackbird perched on a tall spike of grass at the edge of the road. He whistled at it and it cocked one eye at him.

Felix lowered himself onto a chair beside Jerry's, and Teak crawled out of the tent and stood stretching. She had on a man's white shirt that came mid-thigh, buttoned askew. Felix watched her wistfully. She started up the hill to the privy and the blackbird flew up off his grass stalk and winked into the sky.

"You known this lady a long time?" Felix asked.

"Friend of a friend."

"She and that Ray guy? Are they—?"

"Probably not permanently."

When Teak came back down the hill, Yoshi and Stephen materialized from the house. Teak sat down by Jerry, and Felix handed her a cup of coffee.

Rabbit bounded up the steps. "Expedition! Some people at the Art Institute are having a solstice festival, we've got to go to it." He grinned at Teak. "No kidding, on the beach, it's gonna be out of sight."

"What are they going to do?"

"Set fire to a lot of art."

Teak looked as though the idea had promise. "Let me get dressed."

When Ray came down the hill at noon with Daphne, he found the tent empty. "She went with Jerry and Rabbit and Annabelle in the truck," Sue said cheerfully.

"In the truck?" Ray looked from the road to the tent.

"They'll be back in a few days."

Rabbit drove, with Annabelle in the truck cab and Jerry and Teak in the back. Teak had put her leather skirt and vest back on. She didn't seem worried about Ray. Rabbit's wooden sculpture, a three-piece edifice that could be assembled into a fifteen-foot human figure, was tied down in the truck bed with rope. Jerry and Teak were supposed to lean on it so it didn't shift.

Rabbit was an explosive driver, taking curves on two wheels, sliding to a tire-screeching stop to inspect a toppled beehive, its white wooden slats collapsing in a field of foxtails. "I can use that." He dragged most of it to the shoulder and stuffed it in the truck bed. He took note of an isolated pasture with three goats in it, slowing to stare at them hungrily, and Jerry checked the cab to make sure Rabbit didn't have his rifle.

Then they were careening down the road again, through dusty apple orchards, and over the Golden Gate through the fog caterpillars, down 101 to somewhere on the south coast. No one else from the farm had decided to go. Joelle had demanded to, and then refused. Yoshi had said he would ride his bike, but no one had seen him on the road.

Rabbit pulled the truck up on a bluff overlooking the beach. Cars were parked bumper to bumper along the shoulder. A crowd of people milled on the sand below, their hands full of ribbons that snapped in the wind and flowed along the beach in rainbow streamers. Black shapes basked on the tumble of rocks beyond the surf and the seals' barks punctuated the sound of drums.

They carried the pieces of Rabbit's sculpture down a footpath that might have been worn by foxes. At the foot a girl with a bowl of fruit put a piece of melon in Jerry's mouth. A group of Hare Krishnas chanted at the water's edge and farther up the beach a ring of people danced around a fire.

They sank the base of Rabbit's statue in the sand above the water line and began to put the top pieces on it to the beat of a drum that might have come out of the air, thick with the bite of salt and the gray surf spray. When the top was on, it was a man, or maybe a woman, standing with arms upraised. Rabbit piled driftwood around it, arranging the sticks until he liked their look. A woman dragged a gigantic wire sculpture past them down the sand. Heaved upright, it was another human figure, antennae sprouting from its head and bug's wings on its back. It stood with one foot lifted as if about to take flight. Jerry thought with a sudden ache of the wooden figures they'd found on the Oakland mud flats, on the way to Ana's. All down the beach, more fanciful shapes were rising, all vaguely human, none quite, with wings or extra arms, horse's heads or shovels for hands. They pranced and tumbled and danced their way down the sand. A gigantic praying mantis stalked by, arms folded, head turning slowly from side to side. It took Jerry a moment to be sure it was a costume. The Hare Krishnas followed it, chanting.

Hare Krishna, Hare Krishna, Krishna Krishna, Hare Hare, Hare Rama, Hare Rama, Rama Rama, Hare Hare.

They swayed to the chant, finger cymbals clinking, bare feet leaving delicate prints in the sand. A sari-clad girl handed him a pamphlet and a flower.

"Hare Krishna." She peered at him intently. "No charge. We love you. You can make a donation if you wish." Her voice was startling, a thick Southern drawl.

He stared back, bemused. She wore a little string of wooden beads around her neck but she still looked more like someone who did her shopping at Bullocks Wilshire.

Her eyes widened on him. "Wait a minute, I know you!"

"No, you don't."

"No, I've seen your picture!" She smiled from ear to ear. "You're Ellen Callahan's hippie boyfriend!"

He shook his head, wincing. "Not now."

"No, but you were, weren't you? I'm Maggie. It's Mahema now, but I used to be Maggie. I went to school with Ellen."

He imagined Maggie as she must have been in college, a blonde with big hair and a string of pearls, metamorphosing into the sari-clad avatar now trying to convert him to Krishna Consciousness. The salt air around both of her wavered like old glass, bubbly and distorted. Jerry saw the blue god dance past her, graceful hands lifting a flute. Other people began to part the thick air along the beach in his wake, over the water from the horizon: Aaron, his wild hair hidden under a bloody helmet. Randy Ottley, almost transparent, in badly fitting civvies. Randy's feet kept trying to step on the beach but with every step the tide drew him back again.

"We have the answer," Mahema/Maggie told him, jerking Jerry's attention back to the chanting Krishnas. "Krishna loves you. We're serving a feast tonight at San Francisco State. You should come. The food's really good." She tucked her arm through his, friendly and relentless. "I'm here on a trip with Guruji. He asked for me especially, to do public relations," Maggie's cheerful drawl nattered on. "Do you know Ellen's here?"

"Ellen?" He spun around as if she too might come walking out of the water.

"Up the beach, that way. She's with an old lady in a sari. Not a Krishna devotee, she was drinking wine."

"Mahema!" A disapproving voice pushed through the chanting. It was attached to a tall man with a shaven head, who looked at him suspiciously.

Maggie smiled at Jerry. "I have to help Guruji. Hare Krishna."

She vanished before he could give her back the pamphlet, so he stuffed it in the pocket of his jeans and put the flower behind his ear. There were probably five hundred people on the beach. If Ellen was here, he didn't know how he'd find her, so that made it easier not to look. He wondered what Annabelle had put in the quiche she'd brought them to eat in the car, but no one else seemed to be stoned. Rabbit was complaining because he wasn't. While he stood bemused Martin Alvarez walked by him on the sand. The dead and the maimed and the exiled, trying to tell him something. He wished he knew what.

Someone began drumming, drowning out the Hare Krishnas. A man and a woman painted head to toe with green vines began to dance among the figures on the beach, pulling other people into line with them. The sun was heading down the sky and the water turned orange as the fire bubbled into it.

The line of dancers began to weave between the statues and he hooked onto the end of it, between Annabelle and a girl with a pair of goat's horns tied to her head. He thought he actually saw Ellen, putting a cloak of bones on one of the horse-head statues, but he couldn't be sure, and maybe it was only because he wanted to, and the dance dragged him on. When the line spiraled back that way she was gone.

Day Logan sat cross-legged on a bale of hay, a wine glass in one hand. "They'll light the fires after dark, I'm told. What do you think of letting our horse women go up in flames?"

Ellen frowned. She hadn't got used to the idea yet of throwing things away, or setting them on fire. It seemed wasteful.

"We won't have to take them home if we do," Day said.

Ellen had a secret yearning to put a horse-head woman up in her back yard, but she could make another one if she wanted it. Day had made the first one, but the bones had been Ellen's idea. Gordon had found her boiling a washtub of turkey carcasses on the stove, attended by cats.

"All right," she conceded. They might look wonderful, leaping in the flames. A man danced by, naked, his chest painted with blue spirals. Her eyes followed him into the dance.

"Are you having fun?" Day asked. "You should go and join the Lobster Quadrille down there."

The sand sloped down to the flat edge of the beach, giving her a bird's eye view. The lead dancer had antlers and was naked too, a torch in her hand, flame and smoke streaming behind her.

"I just want to watch them."

Day chuckled. "They're a little much. Are you glad we came, though?"

Ellen grinned. Gordon had gone to the County Fair Board's annual men-only steak dinner. He hadn't had the moral high ground when he'd objected to her going to San Francisco with Day for the weekend, and he'd known it, particularly since Maggie was going to be there. All the same, she knew her lessons with Day were annoying him. He never knew what to say to Day, and disliked her as a result. She sat down on the hay bale and wrapped her arms around her knees. The Hare Krishnas were chanting in their white and yellow robes. Maggie had given her a flower and tried to get Ellen to come to a feast in San Francisco. She still sounded just like Maggie. Beyond the Hare Krishnas, the dancers on the beach were silhouetted against the setting sun, black figures prancing and leaping like the statues on the sand. Sparks flew from the torch.

"That is the artist's instinct," Day said. "To watch."

"Writers, too. My father always listens in on other people's conversations."

Day refilled her wine glass and handed one to Ellen. "On the other hand, it doesn't do to become too sedentary. One must participate in life or one can't make art from it." She looked pointedly at Ellen.

"Are *you* going to dance?"

Day shrugged noncommittally. She wore a purple sari and an anklet of bells that chimed when she walked. Her heavy black hair was knotted in a bun spiked with a silver prong and her hands were heavy with silver rings. She waved them vaguely. "I may just sit here. Someone I know is supposed to be coming."

Oh, Ellen thought. Day's dark, arched brows lifted in amusement, but she didn't say anything. *She wants me to go away for a while.*

She slid off the hay bale. The sun was nearly gone, a bright egg yolk in a pool of fiery water. She started down the slope, balancing her glass in her hand. The parade of dancers had moved down the beach toward a bonfire at the north end. Just past it a bluff dropped straight down in a tumble of rough stone slapped by the surf, with the black jumble of the seal rocks beyond. Their voices carried across the water, eerie and half-human. The line of dancers spiraled around the bonfire and back down the beach. More of them had torches now. They stopped at a trio of straw figures, and a thin woman in a white caftan ceremoniously touched her flame to them. They rose in columns of fire, showering sparks into the darkness. The line of dancers cheered.

They danced their way down to the next statue and set it alight. They skipped the metal bug people, but lit the wooden figure with the raised arms, and Day's horsehead people. Ellen saw Day take the torch and push it into the cloth stuffed inside a wooden ribcage. A dark man with a gold hoop in his ear stood next to her. The statue burst into flame and the cloak of turkey bones swirled in the fire.

Whooping, the dancers made a ring around the last statues, a wooden circle of forms holding hands. They set one alight and the fire ran around the ring. The vine-covered man and woman danced around it, and other people were starting to take their

259

clothes off too to dance in the light of the leaping flames. The sky was completely dark now, with only the flaming pyres up and down the cove to cast a red glow on the sand. Ellen had lost her wineglass. She untied her top, a flowered black halter with matching harem pants, and tossed it on the sand. It felt like someone else doing that. It would never have occurred to her to do it while she was going with Jerry. Jerry would have thought of it, and he would have done it.

She pulled off the harem pants, too, and then her underpants because they looked so silly. When she dropped them she felt light, as if her feet had lifted an inch or two over the sand. Her hair came out of its knot and flowed out behind her like the flames. She joined the naked, dancing circle around the burning statues.

Jerry watched Rabbit's statue burn. It raised its arms, silhouetted against the black sky, and looked wildly triumphant, as if this consumption was what it had craved.

"You give it all the things you don't want," Teak said, coming up beside him. She had acquired a wreath of seaweed on her head. "Letters you wish you hadn't written. People you wish you hadn't slept with."

He nodded, but the thing he wanted to get rid of, he couldn't make himself put on the fire. "Have you seen any people who aren't here?" he asked her.

Teak didn't ask him what he was talking about. "Yep. Borders are kind of thin out here. I think I saw Ellen too," she added.

He looked at the ring of naked dancers in the firelight. A girl with long hair was spinning, raised arms outstretched like the burning statue. He saw her flanks and breasts silhouetted in the fire. He didn't need to see her face.

Sirens wailed along the road above the beach. Ellen froze. She flung herself frantically at the sand, digging for her clothes, trampled under scores of bare dancing feet. The drumming faltered and picked up again and people kept on dancing past her, while a few halted, caught in the spinning red light that wasn't from the fire.

"Who's in charge here?"

"Hard to say, man," someone answered to a ripple of laughter.

Ellen pulled her pants out of the sand. No one else seemed to be in a hurry to get dressed. She slid them over her hips and tied the halter around her neck.

"You folks got a permit?" the cop asked.

To burn statues on the beach? To take their clothes off? To levitate? She slid through the shadows toward the dying embers of the horsehead people. Something gleamed in the sand. Her wineglass. She picked it up and ran to where Day was waiting for her. The man with the gold earring had gone.

Day was packing their picnic hamper and held it open for the wine glass. "Here, Cinderella. Got your clothes?"

Ellen looked back dubiously at the fire and the park police on the slope below them. The man with the vines was gesticulating expansively, explaining what it was all about. Her hair fell in her face, smelling of smoke. There was sand in her pants. "I can't believe I did that."

Day chuckled. "Places like this are conducive to things you don't think you'd do."

They climbed the trail to the bluff and Day backed her truck around while Ellen hung out the passenger's window to watch the dying fires. The road was a jumble of cars trying to maneuver around the green Park Police truck that sat sideways on the shoulder. The lights of a fire truck came down the beach road from the north. The sculptures were still smoldering, fiery patches on the dark sand, reflected in the breakers rolling out of the inky ocean. The glowing waves tumbled onto the beach and slid away again leaving patches of white foam and strange, luminous creatures.

A car careened by going the other way, the back seat filled with sooty, sandy revelers, and then a pickup with Jerry and Teak of all people in the back. Ellen stared through Day's window at them and they stared back at her, and were gone. Day slipped the truck into the stream of cars heading south.

XVI
SUICIDAL TENDENCIES

When Jerry got back to the farm, his toolbox was gone. No one seemed to know what had happened to it.

"Ray probably took it." Joelle's lips were compressed in a disapproving line. Ray had left with Teak as soon as they got back from the beach.

"My toolbox. My rusty old toolbox that half the stuff is missing out of. A guy who practically has his Jeep chromed."

"Maybe not, then." She looked uncomfortable.

Jerry cocked an eyebrow at her and went to look for the toolbox. He found it in Yoshi's room under a pile of dirty clothes.

Joelle pulled at his arm. "Don't."

"Don't what?"

"Don't make a scene. It'll spoil the balance. Come out of there before he comes back."

He raised his eyebrows again. She looked determined. Her hair was skinned back from her face in a tight pony tail. The apron over her cut-off shorts was businesslike. "We're here to give up ownership. Wolf says he'll learn he doesn't have to hide things if we're all open to him."

Jerry put his toolbox in their room and drew a skull and

crossbones on it with a marking pen.

"Yoshi drove your truck while you were gone," Liz volunteered.

"He had to go to town," Joelle said.

"He came back drunk," Liz said.

"*Liz!*"

"He did."

Jerry went out to the yard and took the rotor out of the distributor cap while Joelle was lecturing Liz on group wholeness. The next morning she told him, puzzled, that the truck wouldn't start.

"You want to go somewhere, babe?" He sat up and began to turn yesterday's t-shirt right side out.

"No, but Stephen's making a garbage run. He tried it and it wouldn't start."

"Nope." He rolled out of bed. "I'll start it for him." As he passed Yoshi's room where Daisy was nursing the baby, now a year old, he noted that his flute seemed to have migrated in there.

"Tell him the next time he touches this I'll shove it up his butt," he told Daisy and tucked it under his arm. Daisy nodded.

Joelle glared at him but he pretended not to notice. Joelle didn't like Yoshi anyway. Nobody did but Daisy and Daphne, and Jerry wasn't too sure about them. Blue Jay was sitting on the front porch with a cup of coffee when he came out. There was a plate of eggs in his lap, but his eyes were closed and his skin was pasty.

"Yoshi's stealing stuff," Jerry said to him as he passed.

Blue Jay opened his eyes. "I know." He looked miserable— gaunt and sick.

It wasn't considered polite to question anyone's drug of choice, so he put the rotor back in the distributor and watched while Stephen drove the truck away. He was damned if he was going to let Yoshi drive it again. So much for giving up ownership. He looked back at Blue Jay on the porch and then at his garden, noting that he still thought of it as *his* garden.

Joelle seemed to be happy here, as happy as she was anywhere, but Red Dog Farm was beginning to feel like ants under his collar. It had seemed like such a good idea, once. The trash Stephen was hauling to the dump was mostly kitchen garbage that was supposed to be composted for the garden, but nobody had bothered to separate it from the meat scraps and glass, and now it was worthless. The house was sinking in a clutter of useless and broken objects that no one would throw away because it was too much trouble. The revolution hadn't allowed for the necessity of taking out the garbage regularly.

When he found his jack in a pile of junk Yoshi had scavenged to sell, and thought seriously of beating him senseless with it, he knew the end was coming. Yoshi was outside the shed door when Jerry came out with the jack in his hand.

"What's this doing in your stuff?"

Yoshi scratched his ear.

"My jack, man. What's it doing here?"

"You sure it's yours?" Yoshi looked as if he'd never seen it before.

Jerry felt the little tic in his cheek that started when he got seriously angry. He thought about taking this to Blue Jay, which was house procedure, but Blue Jay was nodding out on the porch again. Even Sue had diverted enough attention from the new baby to take note of how much smack was going into Blue Jay's arm, but she didn't know what to do about it.

Jerry grabbed Yoshi by the collar of his riding leathers. They smelled like old grease. He pulled Yoshi up close so his face was in Jerry's. "If you take anything else, I'll kill you, got that?"

Yoshi's eyes were dark slits like the rattlesnake's. "Better watch your ass, Manoury. You aren't in charge here."

265

"That isn't going to matter," Jerry said. He let Yoshi go and he staggered back. Jerry stood in the shed door until Yoshi walked away, then he went through Yoshi's for-sale pile and pulled out Joelle's hand mirror and Rabbit's rifle.

In the morning Yoshi was gone, with his junk from the shed, Blue Jay's typewriter, Lauren's radio, and the tires off Jerry's truck.

Daisy and Daphne were still there. They appeared to have no idea where he'd gone. Daisy wandered forlornly around the house, nursing the baby, while Salamander clung to the hip pocket of her jeans, thumb in his mouth, until Daphne scooped him up and took him off to look for berries. Rabbit rummaged furiously through his camp like a terrier counting bones to see if anything else was missing. Jerry gave him back the rifle, with the small, secret hope Rabbit might find Yoshi and shoot him with it.

Blue Jay called a meeting in the living room that night. Nobody bothered to dress up for this one.

"We're all here to make sure Daisy and Daphne know we don't hold them at fault," Blue Jay said. "And that they're welcome here at Red Dog Farm."

"Of course they're welcome," Wolf announced to everyone. "We are free people."

"Maybe we ought to be a little less free in the future about who we let in," Annabelle said wryly.

"That's a plastic idea." Wolf sniffed. "If we say, 'You're an okay person, and you're not,' that's a total value judgment. How do we have the right to do that?"

"I'll start with the next one that steals my stuff," Jerry said.

"That's what's wrong with you," Joelle snapped. "You don't think about the *group*."

"The *group's* turned this place into a pigsty." Jerry eyed Blue Jay uneasily. "With respect, man, if we don't get our act together we aren't going to last the winter."

"That's counterproductive egocentrism," Wolf told him. "Thinking for the group."

"Then let me know when the revolution's complete." Jerry stood up. "I'm dying to know who's going to fix the busted windows before the weather gets cold."

Blue Jay looked weary. "We'll assign tasks. Can you make a list of what needs doing?"

"Yeah, as long as nobody wants to vote on it." Jerry stalked off.

He went around the farm the next day with a pad and pencil, gloomily making notes. Blue Jay posted a repair committee list on a paper in the kitchen. For a few days, everyone consulted it religiously and Jerry began to think they might survive. Then it lost its appeal since it wasn't actually raining into the house at the moment. In fact the summer weather was so beautiful Stephen moved outside next to Rabbit and Annabelle's camp, and Daphne dragged her bed up on the hill above Jerry's garden and made herself a bower there of brush and downed apple limbs.

Jerry appointed himself a one-man fix-it crew again for a few more days, but in the end it was easier to quit trying to swim upstream and just go with the current. Blue Jay's list fell off the wall and nobody put it back up. In the warm evenings, Jerry sat in the garden and smoked a joint rolled from homegrown pot and listened to the tomatoes grow, while Pete tried to catch rabbits in the orchard and the house fell down around their ears. After dark he'd sneak up to Daphne's bower and they would make it on her mattress in the moonlight, sheltered by a pre-Raphaelite collection of diaphanous scarves and leafy branches. Daphne was busty and ample-hipped and sometimes Jerry would pretend she was Ellen. Then he'd slink back down the hill and slip into bed while Joelle slept. Joelle put up with that for most of the summer, occasionally sleeping with whoever she thought would piss him off the most in return, until September.

He'd disappeared up the hill again to Daphne's bed in the crisp, apple-smelling darkness. He was sitting astride her, breathing hard, when Joelle came stalking up at midnight holding a lantern.

"Goddamn you!" She hovered over them both in a faded thrift store kimono like a vengeful ghost.

Jerry toppled off Daphne. He sprawled in the grass while Joelle circled him. She clutched the hem of the kimono to her chest, like a farmwife with an apron full of apples. Her hand shot out and a rock smacked into his chest.

"Hey!"

"Asshole! You think I don't know what you're doing?" Another rock clipped his ear.

"Quit that!" He grabbed at her kimono. She appeared to be carrying an arsenal in it.

"You don't care anything about me!" Joelle shrieked. "You just want to—" another rock went past his head— "tell everyone what to do because you think you know everything, and—" another rock— "screw anything that moves—" another rock— "and—"

He made a dive at her and yanked the hem from her hand, tumbling her ammunition in the grass. "Listen, quit it, I—"

"You *what?*" Joelle shrieked.

Daphne was collecting her possessions and stuffing them behind the mattress, out of harm's way. Jerry saw wavering light beginning to glow in the windows of the house below them.

"I'll kill you!"

He got to his feet and grabbed her as she ran at him. He lifted her and flung her over his shoulder, holding on while she kicked him. He walked down the hill naked with Joelle crying and beating on his back with her fists. At the front door he set her down on the porch. She began hitting him in the chest.

"We'll talk about this tomorrow," he said, trying to fend her off. He could hear interested movement in the front room.

"Asshole!" She was crying with rage, her face slick with tears.

"It doesn't mean anything," he said.

She hit him again.

The door opened and Sue stood in the rectangle of gold light cast by her candle. She set it on the hall table and held out her arms and Joelle fell into them, sobbing. Feet pattered on the porch steps and Annabelle appeared on Joelle's other side.

"You need to work out your boundaries," Sue told Jerry.

They took Joelle inside and left him standing on the porch. He sat down glumly on the railing. Theoretically, the boundaries included pretty much anything anybody wanted to do. In practice they overlapped unhappily and occasionally violently with other people's. He felt simultaneously irritated that the promise of sexual freedom hadn't been upheld, and ashamed of himself. He also knew that if they stayed at Red Dog Farm he wasn't capable of being faithful to Joelle unless she did kill him.

When the house had quieted down again he got off the railing and walked slowly back up the hill, silently skirting Daphne's bower. He went up through the orchard and the steep slope above it to the top of the ridge. The night was crystalline, like black glass. Below him he could see the lights of the distant coastal towns strung along black water. He walked down through dry weeds to the meadow where the deer carving lived.

Jerry sat down cross-legged and stared at the antlered form in the moonlight. Teak's archaeologist didn't seem to have done him any harm. "Do *you* know what I ought to do?"

The deer was enigmatic. Jerry lit a cigarette and thought about the kids and what kind of example they were setting them. He'd been scared to death to have children, and now he had four. Or they had him. He was still trying to be an otter but you couldn't be an otter with four kids.

Grow up, Manoury. Sue couldn't teach them forever; in a couple of years they'd be beyond what she knew about math. And they weren't getting any history at all. The past had been declared irrelevant, but Jerry could see it attached to the present with tendrils entwined like clematis. They'd never figure out how to change the world if they couldn't see how it had got this way. Wolf was teaching them biology, but what about a language? Jerry could teach them some trail-camp Spanish, but he didn't know much, and most of that was dirty.

He thought about Joelle. She wasn't getting more self-reliant, she was getting brittle and insistent on the predominance of groupthink. Her sense of self was focused on adherence to the party line and on keeping him under control. Ellen hadn't liked his sleeping with other women either, though she'd never thrown rocks at him. Maybe if she'd lived with him, she would have. The new freedom was supposed to have redrawn the rules of sex while it was redesigning the world. Now he wondered if, like the problem of taking out the garbage and running the electric plants, they hadn't assumed that things were simpler than they were. How could you work out your boundaries with eight other people trying to work out theirs?

To his surprise, Joelle made no complaint about leaving. The pattern at the farm was already shifting, prodding their exodus. Wolf was going south to study herbal healing with a witch who lived in Angels Camp. Sue was taking Blue Jay somewhere a Miwok medicine man had told her was a place he could get off smack. Rabbit and Annabelle were staying on over the winter and Daisy and Daphne were going to stay too and take care of

Sue's kids. Stephen seemed to be a permanent fixture.

The morning they left Jerry loaded their possessions, the little that they'd come with or acquired since, in the back of the truck. He cuddled Sam, who was crying because she didn't want to leave.

"Shut up, stupid," Lauren said. "Don't you want to live in a house with a bathroom?"

"No." Sam stuck her thumb in her mouth and snuffled into the pile of sleeping bags in the truck bed, one arm around Pete's neck.

Jerry had driven down to L.A. and found a house in the San Fernando Valley that one of his mother's friends was renting and would let them have free for a month in exchange for fix-it work. There was time to get the kids registered for school so they wouldn't start the year late and on the wrong foot. And a month would give him time to find a job. He didn't know what he'd do about the draft, but it seemed possible to take things only one at a time.

Things still seemed that way to him in the smoky neon haze of an L.A. night, wandering forlornly along Ventura Boulevard past the Safeway, wondering what to do next. The bedding was unloaded in the tiny living room of the little stucco house, and the kids were asleep in their clothes. Joelle was putting things away in the kitchen, intent on order among thrift store plates.

It was Friday night and a few blocks later he found himself suddenly in the middle of a crowd of well-dressed strangers milling on the sidewalk outside a modernist brick building with big plate-glass windows. Not a church; Jerry tilted his head to read the words over the door: TEMPLE BETH-EL. Some of the men wore yarmulkes, and one very old one's shoulders were draped with a blue-and-white prayer shawl, fringed at the ends with elaborate knots. They smiled at him, friendly, not like the Hare Krishnas, but still as if they might let him in.

Jerry looked down at himself. He was barefoot, in ragged jeans. It didn't seem right. He backed away, yearning after the gold light that spilled out of the temple doors.

What would his father think if he told him he'd been to a temple? He doubted Raymond had ever been to temple in this country. No, that wasn't right. His grandmother's funeral had been in a temple in Los Angeles, this one maybe. There'd been a service in Hebrew and old men in prayer shawls. Grandmother must have been a member; it was Raymond who'd given up being Jewish. But Jerry had noticed his father knew the prayers by heart.

He watched the people filing in for Friday night services. Were things easier if you belonged somewhere? He'd always been scornful of that sort of belonging, of being tethered by tradition instead of free choice. Now the smoggy dusk felt lonely and the people in the temple's doorway seemed purposeful, as if they might be going to do something that mattered.

He gave it up, went in the Safeway and bought Joelle a six-pack of Fresca and the kids some gum. They needed shoes before school started.

Before the month was up Jerry had a job, as maintenance manager at an auto parts warehouse in Pacoima. Queasily he gave them his Social Security number, because he had to.

Social Security records were supposed to be untouchable and untraceable, but the FBI found him before he cashed his first paycheck. He answered the door just as the kids had left to catch the school bus, and stood blinking in the early morning sun, holding his glasses with one hand because the tape was coming off the hinge.

"Gerald Manoury?" The agent on the doorstep was pale, blue-eyed and crewcut, with a briefcase. Jerry closed his eyes. He thought about claiming to be Ben, who looked enough like him to match a description and had a high number. When he opened them the agent flashed a badge. "You've been ordered to report for induction."

Jerry's stomach clenched but he stepped back and waved the agent into the room. "Look, man." He spread his hands desperately. "The Army doesn't want me. I'll make trouble, I'm not good with authority figures. Can't you tell them that? You'll be doing them a favor."

"Sir, you only have two choices here. You can report to the induction center and the U.S. Army can cut you a set of orders." The agent paused, regarding Jerry with an impassive stare that conveyed both righteous disapproval and a curiously electric physical pleasure in the ultimatum. "Or I can take you into custody right now."

Jerry shook his head. "Tell them I'll report," he said wearily.

"You've made the right decision," the agent said.

"I don't know what we're gonna do." Joelle paced the kitchen, teary-eyed, face splotched with rising panic. They'd been up all night talking, and decided nothing. "They're gonna take you away somewhere, what am I gonna do?"

Jerry looked at the envelope in one hand, his truck keys in the other.

"You won't come back!" she wailed.

"I'll come back." He put his hands on her shoulders, made

her look at him. "I'm not going to let them induct me."

"They'll send you to jail!"

He kissed her forehead and held her to his chest for a moment. "I won't go to jail either. Don't freak out and scare the kids, okay? I *promise* I'll come back."

"How?"

Actually he had no idea. He left her huddled in her nightgown by the kitchen counter and went out into the thin sun. The truck coughed but started.

The induction center on Wilshire still looked like a ziggurat, stair-stepped and faceless. Broad shallow concrete steps led up to the front doors, which were bordered with flat slabs of stone, like table tops. Inside the walls were institutional green, with brown linoleum and doors with frosted glass. At the center of the lobby this time the desk had two corporals in khaki behind it. He presented himself and they wrote his name on a folder and handed it to him.

"Room 102."

In Room 102 a sergeant was explaining the procedure to fifty draftees sitting behind rows of school desks. Jerry slipped into the back.

"You will carry your folder with you at all times and present it at each station."

Jerry peered into his. It held a sheaf of papers, mostly white, with a few pink ones mixed in. He pulled out every other one and slid them under his chair.

"The intelligence test will be given in Room 107." The sergeant gave them all a fatherly look. "Don't sweat it. Your country can use you however you score. Just relax and do the best you can."

Peaches are to nectarines as horses are to:

a. apples

b. donkeys

c. dogs

d. stallions

Jerry applied his sharpened number 2 pencil carefully to (d), deciding that (a) and (c) were too stupid.

There were sentences with missing words to fill in from a list of possibilities, and paragraphs to read and answer questions about.

The final statement in the passage chiefly suggests which of the following?

a. Helga had strongly disapproved of the author's stories.

b. The author's homeland was no longer as charming as her memories of it were.

c. The weather was milder on the mountain than it was in the valley.

d. Few people realize how the world appears from a mountaintop.

Sometimes it took a minute to find the dumb but not obviously cheating answer. There was a section of arithmetic problems which he worked carefully so as not to hit any correct answers by mistake. It was like taking the SATs in reverse.

He waited until everyone else was finished and handed his test to the corporal at the head table. The noncom laid it face down on a stack and held out his hand for Jerry's file. He flipped through it and looked puzzled. Finally he made a note on the inside of the file jacket and gave it back to him. "Physical   next. Third floor. Just follow everyone else."

Jerry palmed three hoarded tablets of Dexedrine out of his pocket and swallowed them. Everyone was filing into a locker room. This time he was ordered to strip only to his undershorts

275

and given a plastic cup. They were herded into a bathroom with a row of urinals and instructed to pee in the cups. He bit down hard on the inside of his lip until he tasted blood. When the sergeant in charge wasn't looking, he spat in the cup.

In the medical room things bogged down. A long line of guys in their shorts reached out into the hallway. Through the door Jerry saw rows of cafeteria tables with the line snaking between them. He waited, feeling the Dexedrine working. When he got to the door, a doctor with a stethoscope asked to see his folder and looked irritated when he looked in it. He put the stethoscope to Jerry's chest. "Breathe."

Jerry waited for his turn at the next station while a clerk asked the kid in front of him if he'd ever had chicken pox, measles, mumps, diphtheria, or polio. When they got to him, Jerry claimed to have had none of them in the hope they'd decide he was an infection risk. The clerk looked bored so he also claimed asthma, hives, and an allergy to wool. "You need a doctor's letter for that," the clerk said. "Next."

A hand closed around his balls. "Cough."

The line inched forward. Most of the boys in it looked as if they didn't know what hit them. A few seemed eager to pass. One or two looked wildly at the windows but no one made a break for the door. Jerry wondered briefly what had happened to the screamer the cops had come for two years ago. Probably doing time. His stomach hurt again. He felt about prison the way he felt about the army.

The next technician took his blood pressure and frowned. Jerry brightened. The light outside the windows was fading. He was standing miserably while someone poked and prodded his spine when a sergeant appeared in the doorway.

"The following names get dressed and come with me: Aguilar, Baker, Esparza, Gutierrez, Howes, Jackson, Manoury—"

Jerry picked his folder up off the table, looking suitably bewildered.

"The office is closing for the day," the sergeant said, collecting the folders. "We'll put you men up overnight and finish your exam tomorrow."

"But they just told me to get dressed. My blood pressure's high."

"We'll check it again," the sergeant said. "Sometimes we need to do it twice."

The Army put them all on a bus, declining Jerry's suggestion he drive himself. It unloaded them at a barracks-like YMCA and someone brought hamburgers. When the others had gone to sleep, Jerry stood looking out the window. He was older than the rest now, nearly twenty-three, a fact that merely depressed him. It was hard to say where he was going, if not into uniform. Thinking they could remake society on a communal farm had been an immature daydream.

He flexed his fingers, staring at them. Martin had gone to Canada but Joelle was afraid to go to another country. The Army wouldn't let go of him at this point anyway. If nothing else worked, he'd have to call Joelle and tell her to come get his truck. He knew only that he wasn't going where Randy Ottley had.

In the morning they loaded everyone up and took them back to the induction center, starting with Medical again. Jerry's blood pressure was normal. The doctor gave him an irritated look and shoved his folder at him. It seemed to have reacquired its missing papers overnight.

The sergeant was checking names at the door. "Manoury. Fourth floor. 408."

Jerry noted he was the only one headed up the stairs. 408 turned out to be the psychiatrist.

The desk had a name plate that said CAPT. STEVENS on it.

The man behind it looked depressed, as if he'd given up expecting things to work out. He motioned Jerry to sit, and shuffled the papers in Jerry's file.

"Look, man. Captain." Jerry tried to find the words that would animate him, make him give a damn. "Please understand that they sent me up here because you really shouldn't draft me."

"They sent you up here because you flunked your intelligence test and your urine sample was suspicious."

"I smoke pot," he said hopefully.

"We'll cure you."

"Look, really, I'll just be trouble." No one ever believed that. Or they wanted to punish him for being trouble. "You don't want people who can't take orders. Ask anybody at my high school. They'll tell you not to take me."

The psychiatrist pushed his file back at him. "I can't do anything for you."

"Come on, man. You've seen what's in there. You know I'm not a good candidate."

The psychiatrist shrugged. "You're not insane."

Jerry wondered how long it would take before he was. He could see a sergeant waiting for him in the hall. The psychiatrist scribbled something on a piece of paper and held it out to the sergeant, not to Jerry. The sergeant took it. "Ninth floor," he said. "947."

In 947 there was another captain at a desk. He looked stern and folded his hands in front of him. Jerry waited to see what he would say.

"All right, Mr. Manoury. We know you flunked your IQ test on purpose. We know you contaminated your urine sample and boosted your blood pressure. We know every way you've screwed with us and we're tired of it. Now you will proceed down to the first floor and take the oath in good order and get on the fucking bus to Fort Ord and become a fucking soldier. Is that crystal clear?"

Jerry thought he saw Randy Ottley outside the window. "Yes, sir."

"Good," the captain said.

Jerry went down the stairs. No one followed him. It was understood that he would now do the expected thing. He went out the front doors. He wasn't sure he could get his truck out of the parking lot, so he walked to the first bus stop he came to. He felt in his pocket. Less than three dollars, mostly in change.

He gave twenty-five cents to the driver when the downtown bus came by, and rode it until it got to Alameda. He got off, knees feeling like rubber, on autopilot, the last-resort script finally written in his head. All he had to do was follow the script. He found what he was looking for in half a block, among dubious cafes and one-night hotels: Sam's Army Surplus, with a department store's cast-off mannequin in the window, modeling a Navy peacoat. He went in, passing his reflection in the window, eyes startled, glasses crooked on his nose.

He fingered piles of olive drab pants and web belts, a row of flashlights and pup tents. The most serviceable hatchet was $1.79, the price permitted by the cash in his pocket, less bus fare. He took it to the counter and they put it in a brown paper bag.

He held it in his lap on the bus ride back and climbed the induction center steps with it tucked under his arm, inconspicuous, its weight a statement of inevitability. Three Greyhound buses were just pulling out with the day's crop of recruits, oaths taken and bound for Fort Ord. Jerry waited until they'd turned the corner, then sat down on one of the tabletop slabs that edged the steps.

He was mildly startled to discover he was still carrying his file folder. It now seemed reasonable to lay it out on the slab before he spread his right index finger across it, knuckles and other fingers curled well down. Follow the script, Manoury, and don't think. A quick glance around. No one on the steps. He slid the hatchet out of its sack. Don't take a lot of time, someone may come and stop you, just lift it and swing, take the end off the trigger finger, just between the last two joints.

The hatchet comes down, it's impossible not to wince, the eyes close for a fragment of a second, the hatchet bites skin.

His eyes shot open as the blade sank through bone into the file folder. His index finger was severed at the knuckle, hanging by a strip of flesh. Oh, shit. He stood, the steps spinning around him, and took a deep breath. Breathe, damn it. He clenched his muscles, all of them, abdomen and legs and shoulders, to keep his blood pressure up. The body goes into shock when it cannot contemplate its own dismemberment. Robert had written him that. Nausea and lightheadedness rocked him. He tightened his other hand around the wrist to keep the blood from spurting and climbed the steps to the lobby.

There was no one inside but a boy with pfc's stripes, tall and beefy, with freckles and sandy hair. Jerry stuck his mutilated hand in his face. "All right, let's go through this again. I want Captain Stevens to tell me I'm still acceptable."

Color drained from the boy's face, leaving his freckles standing out like a rash. He stammered but no words came.

"Medical's on the third floor," Jerry said as the room started spinning. "The elevator's over there. Let's go."

The boy closed his mouth and ran for it, stabbing frantically at the button.

The third floor was empty, the examining rooms all locked. The kid blanched. "Recruiting!" he said. "Recruiting's on the ninth floor."

They got back in the elevator.

On the ninth floor three sergeants and a corporal blanched too and called the police. Jerry sank into a chair and bled on the desk.

An ambulance came. Attendants put a tourniquet on his wrist and wrapped the hand in a towel and carried him down the elevator on a stretcher. They drove him downtown to UCLA Medical through the rush-hour traffic. Flat on his back, he watched the street signs go by the window, the siren howling around them while one of the attendants kept his hand elevated. They unloaded him at the Emergency entrance, where someone peered at him and pronounced him stable. So they took the gurney away and left him to stand in line at Admitting. Jerry propped his towel-wrapped hand on the counter while he waited. The room spun in and out, appearing to expand and contract with his breath. A clerk asked him if he had any insurance.

Admitted at last, they sent him upstairs with an escort. A pair of nurses came to prep him. They took his clothes and scrubbed the hand with Betadine and pushed a rolling table with a telephone on it toward him while they gave him a shot of Valium. "You better call somebody," the older one said sympathetically.

He had to call collect. He could hear the panic in Joelle's voice when she accepted the call.

"It's okay, I'm all right." Even in the same room with himself, his voice sounded as if it were coming over long distance.

"Where are you?"

"I'm in the hospital."

"What happened?" Her voice rose in a frightened rush. "What did you *do*?"

"They kept me overnight and I had to go through their processing and they wouldn't believe me. I tried to tell them and they weren't going for it. Finally they said to get on the bus for Fort Ord and I bought a hatchet and chopped my trigger finger off, and I'm here getting it sewed up."

The nurse with the Valium paused, eyes widening. "Well." She patted him. "You'll be going in for surgery pretty soon, as soon as we've got a room. You just relax until then."

Jerry cradled the receiver under his ear. "Can you come and get my truck? Bring me some books?" He could hear Joelle crying on the other end.

He hung up the phone and stared at it for a while. He ran Ellen's number through his head, but it was long distance too. So he had a conversation with her in his head, aided by the Valium, until two residents came in to see him.

"Mr. Manoury." The shorter one unwrapped the hand and clucked. "I'm Dr. Henning. How did you do this?"

"With a hatchet."

"Accident?"

"The nurse says you cut it off on purpose," the second resident said disapprovingly. "I should tell you that my father is an admiral currently serving in the Tonkin Gulf. I have no sympathy for a so-called American who would evade his duty in this fashion."

"You were very lucky, Mr. Manoury," the first resident said. "You missed an artery and a nerve, so the finger isn't dead. We might be able to reattach it."

"Unh unh." Jerry shook his head. "Take it off."

"You really should have it reattached."

"Take it off."

"We can't." The second resident looked pleased. "If we can save the finger, we're bound to do so."

Something beeped in the hall and he left. Jerry looked after him. "Fine. Sew it back on. Admiral boy wants to make sure I'm still cannon fodder."

Henning chuckled. "See you in surgery."

Jerry drifted with the Valium until they came and got him and strapped his arm to a board so they could work on it.

When the sodium pentothal hit the anesthetist's voice ballooned and distorted like someone singing underwater. He woke in a room full of monitors, then again in one with a window and an ancient gray-bearded black man in the other bed.

"Missed breakfast," said the ancient man.

"Oh." His head felt foggy and stuffed with glue.

"Isn't no good anyway," the old man said.

He went to sleep and when he woke up Joelle was there, with his brother Ben and his mother.

"I can't believe you did a thing like that." Joelle sniffled and kissed him.

"They called me to ask if you had suicidal tendencies," Dreama reported. "I told them I thought hell, no, just the opposite."

A nurse came in and wheeled the old man out. When they all left, Jerry went to sleep again. He woke to find a candy-striper standing over him.

"Hi. Want a shave?" She looked about fifteen, with long sandy-red hair and bangs.

Jerry rubbed his chin. "Sure, if you want to."

She inspected him. "I bet you'd look good with a mustache."

"You think so?" Anything seemed possible.

"Yeah. And I'm not very good with upper lips."

"Go ahead, then."

When they discharged him he had the beginnings of a respectable handlebar and looked, he thought, vaguely like Wyatt Earp. His hand had a wire through it, holding the tendon together, linking what had been severed with what remained.

XVII
THE WOMEN'S JOURNALISM
COLLECTIVE

The cockroaches seemed to like fog. Ellen had thought maybe it would make them dispirited, but it didn't. The beach was overcast for days at a time, spitting a mild drizzle while the cats stomped around yowling for the sun. Sometimes they ate a bug, but it didn't dent the population. Gordon called an exterminator again, and a man in a mask sprayed insecticide everywhere, until she thought only the fact the house was badly insulated kept humans and cats from asphyxiation. The cockroaches put on their little gas masks and hunkered down in the crevices behind the sink. The next day Lily found one in the bathtub and embarked on a campaign to get Ellen and Gordon to move.

Gordon got a raise, so they went looking for something cockroachless as a Christmas present and found a house on the bluffs, which he said cheerfully were probably too high for cockroaches to climb. They settled in, admiring the Craftsman bookcases flanking the fireplace and the arch between the living and dining rooms, which Ellen plastered with Christmas cards. The sun came out, and she sat at the dining room table in a pool of December light, wrapping presents and trying to figure out why she still felt disgruntled.

Ellen couldn't decide what was the matter with this Christmas. Ordinarily, she loved the holidays. There was a huge tree in their living room, presents spilling from under its branches, and a record of medieval carols on the turntable. Teak was coming up to Ayala with her parents for Christmas Day. Martin had written a long, funny letter that made Ellen think he might be all right up there. Robert had sent her a Vietnamese *ao dai*, which he said he'd had a nurse who looked to be Ellen's size try on for him. Ellen had made a punch bowl in Day Logan's studio that Gordon actually liked, with three human feet supporting its base and a ladle that was a cupped hand. She even had four days off because Christmas was on a Saturday.

Ellen tied and retied a red bow, fretfully smoothing its folds. The packages under the tree were neatly sorted into piles for the Murphys and the Callahans and their friends. The elk looked over her shoulder and seemed to like the new house. Gordon had hung a Santa Claus hat from its antlers.

"Ho, ho, ho," she told it.

Gordon came home, cheerily juggling grocery bags and oblivious to her mood. "I thought we could take some champagne to my folks," he said, setting bags on the kitchen counter.

"Sure."

"They want us to come over on New Year's Eve too." Bottles clinked as he unpacked. "My aunt from Columbus is going to be there. And my cousin Bill. We were buddies when we were little."

She bit her lip. "Gordon..."

"Hum?" He was opening cat food for Yin and Yang, who'd come to twine around his ankles.

"I told Day I'd spend New Year's Eve at her place. Remember? She's having a party that night, and before that we're going to fire some pots with a new glaze we've been working on."

"Well, can't you get out of it?"

"I don't want to get out of it."

He sighed. "Look, hon, I work all week, and I hardly have time to say hello to the folks. On holidays, we need to give them a little time."

"Well, I work all week, too, and I work just as hard, despite the fact I only make half the money."

"Do we have to go into that again?" He looked pained. "I'm not responsible for the unfairness of the universe."

"No, but you're responsible if you act as if my work isn't as important as yours."

"Half price underwear sales at Framingham's may not exactly be breaking news," Gordon suggested.

"I meant important to me. In terms of what I put into it. Just because *you* think it isn't important to the greater world doesn't mean I don't bust my ass, too, and on my off time I need to do something *I* want to do." Ellen stabbed her finger at the bow and pulled its loops tight. It flopped crookedly on the wrapped package. "Ah, the hell with it."

"Hey, hon." He came over and put his hands on her shoulders. "What's the matter? You aren't usually so cranky."

"I don't want to go to your parents' house on New Year's Eve," she said. "I want to spend it at Day's. In fact, you told me you'd come to her party."

"I really want to see Bill. Day isn't going anywhere. Bill's going back to Columbus."

"Then go see him. I'll go see Day."

"They're going to wonder where you are."

"Tell them."

"I'll tell them you were too exhausted from writing copy for Framingham's."

"That's a cheap shot, Gordon."

He sighed. "Maybe. I'm sorry. I just like for us to do things together."

"Me too." Ellen gave up on the bow. It looked like a weed growing out of the corner of the package. "We've got Christmas to spend together." She tilted her head back and looked at him upside down, encouraging him to kiss her. He did and pottered on into the new kitchen to put the groceries away, while she wondered how she could be discontented with a man who went grocery shopping. All the other married women she knew were lucky if their husbands agreed to dry the dishes after they'd both worked all day. Gordon did half the chores.

They dutifully spent the day of Christmas Eve at Gordon's parents' house, where Marie kept the television on all the time whether anyone was watching it or not, which drove Ellen crazy because then she couldn't help watching.

"Your cousin Cheryl's having a baby," Marie told Gordon. Her eyes slid speculatively to Ellen's stomach. (On the television, Rachel on *Another World* was scheming to ruin the reputation of her rival.)

"That's nice." Gordon scooped up a handful of nuts from the bowl on the coffee table.

"I don't see how Ellen stands listening to that radio all day. I turned it on in the car and it was just gibberish. That isn't music."

(National Airlines offered a post-holiday getaway to the islands. A blond stewardess smiled breathily from the screen. "I'm Lisa," she said. "Fly me.")

"It isn't to everyone's taste." Ellen didn't care for KENO's playlist either, never turned on the radio in the car, but she would have been boiled in oil before admitting it to Marie.

"I always think young people shouldn't wait too long before starting a family." (The television screen offered a pressure cooker to please the little woman at Christmas.)

"Congratulate Cheryl for us," Gordon said.

The next day they drove to the Callahans' house, where Teak and her parents were just pulling into the driveway. "You look good," Teak said. "Are you knocked up yet?"

"Shut up. Everyone wants to know. No, not yet." They couldn't really afford it, not with the new house. And Ellen, now that she'd achieved a man who didn't mind having children, felt herself in no hurry. Plenty of time. "I had a letter from Martin," she said.

Teak looked sad. "He didn't write me."

"Well, you don't write him."

"Sometimes." Teak sighed. "Everything gets too complicated." She eyed Gordon's back, a safe distance away. He was unpacking presents. "I talked to Jerry again."

Ellen swallowed. "Yeah?"

Teak lingered, letting Gordon and her parents go in the house ahead of them. "He cut his finger off on the steps of the induction center in L.A. so they wouldn't draft him."

Ellen put her hand against the wall outside her father's office. The wall swayed under her palm, as if it might be made out of foam. "When?"

"Last week. He called me. He says he's moving back up here while he gets well."

"Oh my God. His finger?"

"Trigger finger. With a hatchet. They sewed most of it back on."

"Ellen?" Gordon was calling from inside.

"He called you and told you?"

"I think he figured I'd tell you. It didn't seem like something to tell you on the phone . . . Ellen?"

She opened her eyes.

"You don't look good," Teak said.

"I'm okay." She went in the house and hugged her parents and let Henry Poodle lick her face. Gordon was making a drink in the kitchen and Teak's parents were unpacking their own sacks of presents.

"So," she said brightly to Teak, "What have you been doing?"

"Planting garlic." Teak grinned.

"Back to the land?"

"Sort of. This guy has a garlic farm in Gilroy. He asked me up for the weekend. I met him at that farm Jerry was living on."

"Oh." Ellen wondered what Teak would do on a garlic farm.

"I thought maybe it would, you know, keep the vampires off," Teak said.

The vampires seemed as real as not. She could close her eyes and see Jerry in a wave of blood, hand outstretched on concrete, a hatchet in his other one. She got up and made herself a drink and got so drunk she didn't remember Gordon bundling her into the car when they left, or going to bed.

"We had a little too much Christmas, didn't we?" Gordon said when she woke. "Want some aspirin?"

Ellen buried her face in the pillow until she thought she probably wasn't going to throw up.

He was cooking eggs when she appeared in the kitchen. He said, "At least you got drunk with me this time instead of a draft dodger from your sordid past."

Ellen swallowed. "I found out somebody else I used to know cut his finger off so he wouldn't get drafted."

"And that got you drunk? What somebody?"

"Jerry."

"With the earring?" Gordon raised his eyebrows. "What a moron. How'd you find this out?"

"Teak sees him."

"And keeps you up to date?"

"Not exactly." She pulled a carton of orange juice out of the refrigerator and drank out of it.

"Sounds like he still has a screw loose."

She didn't answer. She envisioned a screw holding Jerry's trigger finger to his hand.

"Was this guy always such a flake?"

"He's not a flake."

"Your mom told me that's why you broke up with him."

"My mom told you? My mom discussed Jerry with you?"

"I assumed he was ancient history," Gordon said.

"That's not the point. I don't ask your mother about your old girlfriends."

"Go ahead." He grinned. "She doesn't know anything."

"Well, neither does my mother," Ellen said. "She just thinks she does." The egg Gordon put in front of her looked back glassily. She pushed it away. "I'm going back to bed."

When she woke her head felt better. Gordon wasn't home and the cats were yowling in the kitchen for dinner. There wasn't any cat food so she got dressed and went out to see what was open on the Sunday after Christmas.

A store on Telegraph was doing a brisk business with shoppers out of cat food and milk. Across the street the Buena Center parking lot was jammed, the ritual day-after-Christmas exchange of presents. Ellen was putting the cat food in her car when she saw the crowd of women outside Framingham's. They weren't shoppers; they were shouting something and handing out flyers to passing cars. Some drivers took them; others honked angrily and shouted back. Ellen saw the local NBC affiliate's truck, and a cameraman with his camera balanced on his shoulder. They were all standing under a giant National Airlines billboard, and she noted with amusement that the billowy blonde who'd had been saying "I'm Lisa, Fly me," was now saying "Fuck me," a correction made in spray paint. She put the cat food in the car and crossed the street.

When she got closer she saw that the billboard was a joint promotion for the airline and Framingham's: FRAMINGHAM'S MIDWINTER GETAWAY: TWO WEEKS IN HAWAII FOR YOU AND YOUR FAMILY! The stewardess appeared again in the background on a sandy beach, wearing a bikini. The women below her carried placards: THIS AD DEGRADES WOMEN. WE ARE NOT PRIZES. Behind them, a Framingham's employee was trying to climb a ladder to the billboard but they wouldn't let him. Every time he went up a few steps, three women would shake the ladder from below. Ellen recognized the Framingham's ad manager, clinging to the swaying ladder. A woman with a placard handed her a flyer.

VOTE YOUR POCKETBOOK. DON'T SHOP AT FRAMINGHAM'S UNTIL THEY RESPECT WOMEN. DON'T FLY NATIONAL. JOIN US TOMORROW AT THE NATIONAL AIRLINES TICKET COUNTER, LOS ANGELES INTERNATIONAL AIRPORT.

Ellen put the flyer in her jeans pocket. A sea breeze was blowing. Her headache was gone. "I hate that ad," she said to the woman with the placard.

"Here, join up. We've got some spares." The woman handed Ellen one that said THE FRAMINGHAM'S CUSTOMER: BAREFOOT AND PREGNANT. She was cheerful and muscular with dark salt-and-pepper hair and hammered silver bracelets on her wrists. Ellen had seen her shaking the ad manager's ladder. He appeared to have given up. A row of women were sitting on his folded ladder.

Ellen waved her placard. Someone gave her a stack of flyers and she began handing them through the windows of passing cars. The NBC cameraman was walking up and down the line of women, with a reporter beside him. Ellen held her sign up high.

When the scene was shown on the local evening news, the "Fuck me" had been tastefully brushed out, but the local anchorman informed his listeners that the protesting women had replaced National's slogan with "an obscenity." A leader of the group, the dark-haired woman who'd given Ellen her placard, was interviewed on the spot. She said they considered the ad itself an obscenity. The ad manager informed the public that Framingham's respected and loved its lady customers, and spoke sadly of destruction of private property and an unruly element who did not represent the Framingham's clientele. Ellen saw herself waving her placard just below the airbrushed "Fuck me."

Gordon still hadn't come home, which she thought was fortunate, since that way he hadn't seen the news either, although the protest would no doubt be in the paper the next day. When he did come home around nine, he climbed into bed beside her without comment and Ellen decided not to ask where he'd been.

On Monday, Sam Benson, the station manager, called her into his office on what was supposed to be a day off.

"Al Aldrich from Framingham's called me at home last night," he said. He folded his hands on his desk and looked exasperated, as if she were a cat that had peed on the carpet.

"What about?" Ellen was pretty sure she knew.

"That juvenile display outside the store. He's demanding an apology."

"From whom?" Juvenile?

"From you," the station manager said. "And that was after he demanded that I fire you, which I talked him out of because he likes your copy. He says no one else understands junior women's fashion."

"Don't I have a right to opinions on my own time? That's a disgusting ad, Sam. *Fly me*," Ellen breathed. "Ugh."

"It's just a play on words," Sam said. "You girls have got so sensitive no one can talk to you. Now you go call Al and make nice. Tell him you were just passing by and someone stuck a sign in your hand."

"You want me to call him and apologize. For something I did on my own time. When his ad insults the actual people he's trying to sell clothes to." She could feel herself getting furious, like a kettle on the boil.

"Yes." Sam looked at her expectantly.

"No."

"Ellen—"

Ellen blinked, because along with being furious, maddeningly, she wanted to cry.

"Look," Sam said patiently, "Al has a right to complain. Your bunch of bra-burning lezzies made him look like a fool. They wouldn't even let him up his ladder. NBC got it all on TV. Now we need to salve his pride a bit. It won't hurt you."

His face blurred into the *Chronicle*'s editor, firing her for being married, and the city editor, tossing her film in the wastebasket, into the boy in the camouflage jacket, throwing Linda off the stage. "Ever since I was old enough to take notice," she said carefully, "I have been told that I needed to give up things that I was entitled to, or apologize for things I didn't do, or laugh at jokes that made fun of me, or put up with having my butt grabbed by creeps, all so I wouldn't hurt some guy's feelings. I'm not going to do it again."

"I don't want to give any ultimatums here," Sam said, "but you need to think carefully about that."

"I have." Ellen knew she was just going to get madder if she thought more about it.

293

"God damn it."

"Al will get over himself," she suggested.

"This is a radio station, not the revolution," Sam said. "Go clean out your desk."

Ellen drove home behind a cascade of furious tears, wishing she had bulk-erased all the next day's spots instead of leaving them on her desk, their cartridges carefully marked with color-coded labels.

"Jesus," Gordon said when she told him. "It made the City page, we're just lucky Jones didn't spot you. Can't you just do it? Everybody'll forget about it in a week if you apologize."

"He already fired me," Ellen said.

"He'll hire you again too, if you say you're sorry. He's not an idiot. He needs you, and it'll make him look good to Aldrich if he can get you to apologize."

"It is not my function in life to make men look good."

"God damn it, Ellen, don't start in on me. And have a sense of humor. I don't see what's wrong with that billboard."

"It makes women look like whores. 'Fly me.' We aren't really people, we're here to be your conveniences. Anyone with the money for a ticket can have us. Do you know they fire stewardesses who weigh too much or get too old? They aren't professionals, they're decorations, and that billboard makes that perfectly clear."

"Okay," Gordon said. "Okay, I see what you mean. But do you have to lead the revolution? We need your salary, and you can't work for the paper, and that pretty much uses up your possibilities."

"I can find something else."

"No other station's going to let you in the door now, much less an ad agency. What something else?"

"Anything. I can wait tables."

He grinned. "Honey, you wouldn't last a week. Waiting

tables is work."

"And I can't work? You watch me."

"If you think you have to put up with crap from men at that radio station, just try waiting tables."

"They won't tell me what I can do on my own time," Ellen said stubbornly.

"It's not exactly intellectually stimulating either," Gordon said.

"It's honest, at any rate." She did her best to look saintly while it occurred to her, irritatingly, that that was what Jerry had said to her about cutting trail and pouring concrete.

The next day, ignoring Gordon's dire warnings about bunions and boredom, she found a job at a truck stop on Rincon Beach. Nicer restaurants were hiring, but the prospect of waiting on her mother's friends, and possibly her own, was more daunting than she would admit. She doubted she knew anybody who'd eat at the Rincon Diner.

"All right, hon. Now you gotta keep your hair pinned up, you don't wanta forget that. The pocket hanky goes like this." The head waitress stuck a starched white handkerchief, folded into a cone like a calla lily, into the breast pocket of Ellen's yellow uniform.

Ellen peered at it with loathing. Gordon hadn't mentioned stupid uniforms. She might have listened to him if he had.

"Keep the coffee coming unless somebody tells you otherwise, and nobody will."

She nodded. She could see herself reflected in the diner window, a yellow cap stuck on top of her head, in front of her bun, pencil behind her ear. ("Not in the apron, hon, them leads make black streaks that won't come out, and you gotta launder your own uniforms.") The other waitresses wore similar pastel uniforms in aqua and pink. The head waitress's was lime green, and her pocket handkerchief said "Lucille" in green script. Ellen's was blank. Lucille had promised her a monogrammed one by next week.

"Your husband okay with you driving yourself home at night?" Lucille asked her. "We don't get outta here till one, one-thirty."

"He'll have to be," Ellen said.

If Gordon wasn't okay with it, he didn't say so. He was ostentatiously asleep when she dragged herself home after her first shift. In the morning, he left for the paper while she was still in bed.

Everyone else had something to say. Lily called at eight to ask why she couldn't substitute teach. Day Logan said it would do her good, and art blessed troublemakers. Gordon's parents said those places on the Rincon were dangerous and they'd heard of some girl who'd been found murdered there, or maybe a few miles up the road, but around there anyway, and it wasn't a nice clientele. Teak said that was wild.

On her third night at work, the woman with the salt-and-pepper hair who had been at the protest came to see her.

"I'm Jenna MacIntire. Day Logan said we got you fired," she said, sliding into a booth. "I'm sorry about that."

"I could have apologized," Ellen said. "I was just too stubborn. It was the ad manager from Framingham's, the one who kept trying to climb up the ladder. I just wasn't going to grovel to him."

"Attagirl. I'll have coffee and the tuna melt. And maybe you'll come to our group Saturday. We're sorry about what happened. We aren't trying to make things worse for anybody."

Two truckers in cowboy hats were waiting for Ellen's coffee pot in the next booth, and Jenna didn't say anything else, but Ellen took the little card she handed her and slipped it into her apron pocket.

CONSCIOUSNESS-RAISING SESSION
SECOND AND FOURTH THURSDAYS
6:00 p.m., VENTURA COUNTY LIBRARY MAIN BRANCH
VENTURA COUNTY WOMEN'S LIBERATION

Jenna had written *New Year's Day, 3:00 p.m., 133 North La Luna* in pencil across the corner.

"You're going to Day Logan's tonight, instead of to my parents', and tomorrow you want to go get your consciousness raised by the same idiots who got you fired? Where do I fit in all this?" Gordon glared at her across the table at the *Yes We're Open.* "It's nice you could meet me for lunch."

"I wouldn't be able to get to your parents' house until after midnight," Ellen said. "I have to work a short shift at least. I'm lucky they'll let me off a couple of hours early. Day's party will still be going. You could come with me."

"I feel strangely disinclined to," he said. "You could quit that job."

"We could starve."

"You'd have to quit if we had a kid. We talked about that."

"And you're the one who said we couldn't do without my salary when the station fired me." Ellen bit into her taco and gave ostentatious attention to the drips that oozed out the other end.

"I don't like having my wife working in a truck stop." He looked stubborn, and slightly embarrassed.

Jones, the photographer from the *Chronicle*, leaned over Gordon's shoulder. "Hey, Ellen! How's the job? Got the six-plate carry down yet?"

"Just about," Ellen said.

Jones grinned. "I dated a waitress once." There were very few professions open to women of which Jones had not dated a specimen. Ellen refrained from asking for further details. He slapped her shoulder. "Watch out for those truckers. They get lonesome on the road." He headed for the take-out counter while Gordon sat stiffly, poking a fork through his napkin.

She gritted her teeth. "I suppose you're getting a lot of that?"

"I suppose so," he said. "I'd like to see my wife once in a while, which is becoming difficult since I work days."

Ellen found herself getting irrationally stubborn, clutching her aching feet and her loathsome hair nets, even her monogrammed handkerchief, to her as personal property, not to be maligned or taken away from her by males. "After a month I can apply for the day shift." She didn't tell him that Lucille said that was about as long as the new girls lasted.

Gordon declined to meet her at Day's party, so she changed

her clothes in the ladies' room after her shift and went by herself. She stuffed her uniform in the back of her bug and slid behind the wheel, transformed in slinky black velvet. "You look real good," Lucille told her. "You drive careful now."

She took the back road to Ayala, through avocado orchards and a tiny valley where bananas grew in a microclimate that occurred only in hidden folds of the coastal hills. The sky was black and spangled with stars. Coming into Ayala she stopped and waited for a half dozen teenagers on horseback to clatter across Highway 33, ghostly emanations of her youth. Going up the grade into the Upper Valley toward Day's place, the air that whistled through the wind wing was chillier, but not cold enough to freeze. She saw no glow of smudge pots among the orange groves.

Day's house was lit with strings of Chinese lanterns and candles in bowls on the porch. Dottie met her at the door and gave her a glass of champagne, with a motherly pat. "Everyone's in the living room. You're just in time."

Day lifted her glass when she saw Ellen. "Lady Midnight."

Ellen sidled in, self-conscious under the glances of the others in the room. Day seemed to know everybody. Ellen recognized the mayor, and several other artists, and a man who usually slept under the oak trees in the park. Day's mantel clock chimed twelve and everyone raised their glasses and drank.

"There, that's done," Day said, coming over to Ellen. "We've turned the year around and now the sun will come up in the morning."

"I thought that was the solstice," Ellen said.

"Well, the calendar has slipped a little maybe. But it's the effort that counts. I hear you're going to Jenna's consciousness-raising."

"Maybe," Ellen said. "Will you be there?"

"Probably not. You should, though. Come back and organize

the truck stop waitresses."

"I don't think they want to be organized, and definitely not by me." The other women made Ellen feel the way Jerry had, as if she'd led a sheltered life and they knew things no one had ever told her. She suspected they might also know things Jenna's group didn't, mostly about survival.

"Well, it'll do you good." Day didn't look inclined to go herself. As far as Ellen could tell, Day had taken care of any liberating she needed some time ago.

There were twelve women at the house on La Luna when Ellen got there, including a girl she recognized after a moment as Carl Leeman's little sister Bunny.

"I know you," Bunny said. "You used to be my brother's girlfriend."

"In high school," Ellen said quickly. "For a couple of weeks, I think."

The rest were a mixture of ages and apparent inclinations. Ellen tried not to stare at the two who were holding hands. Jenna MacIntire waved her into the living room—it seemed to be her house—and took her coat.

"We're just getting started. Everybody, this is Ellen Murphy. She used to work for KENO radio. She helped at our protest at Framingham's and got fired for it."

There was a general murmur of sympathy and indignation. "What are you going to do?"

"I got a job as a waitress," Ellen said, feeling uncomfortable. Most of these women looked as if they spent more time at the country club than in truck stops. "My husband hates it," she added.

"Attagirl," Jenna said briskly. "We're just starting to share. Want to go first?"

"I don't really know what to say."

"That's all right. We'll just go with our discussion topic for the day, and you can chime in when you feel like it. Have a cookie and some punch. Because this is a holiday, today's topic is leisure time."

Ellen put two cookies on a plate and perched on the arm of Jenna's overstuffed sofa. A thin blond girl in a poncho and a leotard smiled up at her and scooted over to make more room. "I'm Liv," she said, for Ellen's benefit. "How do you define leisure time?" she asked Jenna. "As time when you don't have to do anything you don't want to, or just time when you aren't doing your regular job?"

"I'm Lupe," a woman in a blue pantsuit said. "My husband defines it as time when I'm not doing my regular job. Which is cooking meals and cleaning the house. He thinks it's leisure time if I'm mending his shorts."

The rest chimed in, hands waving, eyes rolling.

"I washed six loads of laundry and the dog, and my husband said, 'Why are *you* tired? *I've* been at the office all day.'"

"Leisure time is watching football with him so you can bring him a sandwich at half time."

That got a hoot of laughter.

"I work," a dark-haired woman with nervous hands said. Lupe and the woman who washed her dog glared at her and she corrected herself hastily. "In an office, I mean. And leisure time is when I come home and cook dinner."

I'm lucky, Ellen thought guiltily. Then, mildly indignant, why should a husband who'd do what Gordon did be so rare?

"Leisure time is when he's in a good mood," a quiet voice said. Ellen found the source—Bunny, whose dark eyes peered

301

doubtfully from under her shag haircut.

"Are you still letting him come around?" Lupe demanded.

Mary Nell and Valerie, the two women holding hands on the other couch, leaned forward solicitously.

Bunny sighed. "It's not that easy." She looked apologetic, as if she shouldn't have brought it up, as if she was exhibiting a bad habit other people would have gotten rid of. "My fiancé has a bad temper," she said to Ellen.

"You're not still going to *marry* him?" Jenna demanded.

"He's been doing better," Bunny said.

"That's not what it sounded like a minute ago."

Bunny bit her thumbnail. "My mom's already bought my dress. And paid for the church. She says he'll settle down once we're married."

"Pigs like that don't settle down." Mary Nell folded her arms. "I've got two false teeth to prove it." She was soft-looking, as if she'd been designed to be a placid person, drifting through sunny meadows in feminine hygiene commercials, until something irreparable had happened to change that. "He'll just get worse."

"Does he know you're here?" Liv asked Bunny.

"No."

"What would he say if he did?"

"Well, he wouldn't like it. But your husband wouldn't like it either," Bunny pointed out.

"My husband doesn't hit me," Liv said. "He just sulks."

"A distinction without a difference," Valerie said.

"The hell it is," Mary Nell retorted. "You sulk all the time. If you hit me, I'd have broken your neck."

"I do not sulk."

"You do."

"Ellen, what about you?" Jenna's voice slid between them with the practiced air of a woman who'd run Cub Scout packs

302

and PTA meetings.

"I guess leisure time is when I can do whatever I want to. Or my husband and I can do something together."

They blinked at her. "We all feel like that at first," Valerie said kindly.

"No, I..." Gordon's failings seemed so mild in comparison as to be unmentionable. "He's good about chores and cooking, and stuff. I don't think I'm a good example. I..."

"The personal is political," Mary Nell said.

Ellen flushed. All she could find to complain about was that Gordon didn't like her to write to Martin or hang out with Day, and had given the *ao dai* from Robert a raised eyebrow; that he went to the County Fair's stag dinner, agreeing that it was sexist but not willing to stay away to make the point. That he was embarrassed she worked at a truck stop. Of course, so was her mother.

"You got fired," Jenna said. "It sounds to me like that's where the system has really screwed you."

"It was the second time," Ellen said. "I got fired when I got married because we both worked for the newspaper and there's a rule against that."

"The newspaper. Now there's an issue." Liv pointed a finger at Ellen. "How come they still run those stupid wedding stories about the bride's dress, as if she was the wedding present. And how come women have Miss or Mrs. tacked on their names and men don't? And how come women are Mrs. Male Pig, not their own names?"

"That's just in the women's pages," Ellen said. "They don't do that on the news side anymore."

"They don't cover women on the news side," Lupe said. "Unless she chops someone up with an ax and they have to."

"Then it's news," Ellen explained. "Female ax murderers sell more papers than male ones because they don't do it as often."

"The women's pages," Mary Nell said with deep loathing. "Did you see last Sunday's? How to entertain your husband's boss and the Little Mrs.? An entire page, *with recipes*, on how to be a corporate whore."

Ellen said, "When I was there they made me write a piece on women's auxiliaries. You know, Women of the Moose, Elks, whatever, and how they didn't mind not being able to join the real thing because the auxiliary was much comfier. It drove me crazy, because they wouldn't let me ask how they felt about not being allowed in the Jaycees or the Rotary or anything that would do women who worked any good. They said news side covered those groups."

"And you think you haven't been put down?" Lupe asked her.

"Sure I have. Just not by my husband."

"And what did he say when you got fired?"

"He was furious the first time."

"And the second time?"

"He thought I ought to apologize. They would have taken me back if I'd apologized to Framingham's."

"So. He was angry when it affected him directly." Mary Nell seemed to be working this out in her head. "When he married you and that got you fired. But when it only affected you, he thought you should take it."

"Thank you. I can figure this out for myself," Ellen said.

"Okay, let's move on." Jenna waved her hands briskly. "Liv has a point about the newspaper. Maybe that should be our project. We won't make our voices heard talking to each other every other Thursday."

"Let's make a list," Lupe said. "Of what we want them to do. We'll present it to the editor."

"What do you think he would do, Ellen?"

Ellen remembered her film. "Smile. Then throw it in the

trash when you leave."

Liv grinned. "Let's make it more memorable."

They headed their petition WOMEN'S JOURNALISM COLLECTIVE, which Ellen knew would piss off Harper, who had a thing about communists plotting to take over the free press. She wondered if she ought to warn Gordon, or let it be a surprise. There was no way she was going to go with them to present this thing. That would probably get him fired too, which they definitely could not afford. Jenna wrote their demands on a poster board at the next meeting.

1. All women will be referred to by their own names, not by their husband's.

2. When the use of an honorific is required, women will be referred to as 'Ms.'

Jenna lettered those carefully across the white board.

"3.," Mary Nell said, "This will only be used in circumstances in which a man would be called 'Mr.' and not just when some pig thinks the reader should know he's talking about a woman."

"4.," Liv said, "Women's achievements will have a central place in this newspaper outside of the Society pages."

"5.," Ellen said. "This newspaper will hire fifty percent women on its reporting and editorial staff. It will hire a man to work on the Society page." She'd worked there; she felt she should make a contribution.

"I like it," Liv said. "Make him write about the groom's clothes."

"Girls' sports will be given as much coverage as boys' teams," Lupe said.

"What girls' sports?" Valerie asked.

"The newspaper will sponsor a girls' team in at least three city sports leagues."

Once they got going, they filled the poster board and had to start on another.

"Female staff will receive wages equal to those of male staff."

A faint hoot of laughter.

"Employees of this newspaper will neither cover nor attend civic functions that are not open to women."

"This newspaper will accept no advertising demeaning to women."

"No women in bathing suits advertising cars."

"No women with their boobs hanging out advertising beer."

"Women in the news will not be described in terms of their weight, hairdo, or clothes."

"Or whether they are married or have children."

"Pregnant employees will not be fired, and will be guaranteed their jobs back after the birth."

"Would they really do all that?" Bunny whispered to Ellen.

"When pigs have wings," Ellen said. "But you don't get anything if you don't ask for a lot. Then they can have something they can *not* give you, to make them feel better when they give you some of the rest of it." She had noticed that was how the civil rights activists and the anti-war people had managed to get somewhere.

"Okay, we'll meet tomorrow morning at ten outside the paper. Ellen, are you with us?"

"I can't," Ellen said. "My husband is the assistant city editor. They're likely to fire him too."

"Oh, for God's sake!" Mary Nell exploded. "Are you protecting some man who's probably responsible for the oppression of women there in the first place?"

"I told you I'm not," Ellen said stubbornly. "It isn't Gordon's fault and I'm not going to jeopardize his job. We can't make a living with both of us working at truck stops."

Mary Nell snorted. "So it has to be you. Well, lie down on your back."

"Mary Nell," Jenna said. "Ellen has to do what she's comfortable with."

"That's what comes of fucking men," Mary Nell said darkly.

"Leave her alone," Liv said. "I wouldn't stage a march on Bob's office either."

"Then maybe the both of you should join the PTA," Mary Nell said.

"I have to go to work." Ellen picked up her purse and the canvas tote with her uniform and tennis shoes.

"Are you going to warn your husband?" Mary Nell demanded.

She thought about it. "No."

Valerie caught up to her at the door. She was tall with a stiff brush of short hair. Ellen thought she looked tougher than Mary Nell, but had learned she was a kindergarten teacher. They lived in fear of the school finding out anything at all. "Don't mind Mary Nell," Valerie said. "She's had some bad experiences with men. It's affected her outlook."

"Well, I can't jeopardize my husband's job."

Valerie patted her. "Of course you can't."

When Ellen got home, Gordon was still up, reading the L.A. *Times* with both cats in his lap in a pool of lamplight, and she almost warned him anyway. Then he said, "How was the Lesbian Ladies Aid Society?" so she let it be a surprise.

He was waiting up for her when she got off work the next night too, eyes narrowed and what looked like his third or fourth drink on the end table beside his chair. "No wonder you weren't home this afternoon."

"I guess they showed up." She fell into the other chair and kicked her shoes off.

"You might have warned me. Or were you just interested in having me look like a total ass?"

"I didn't go with them so you wouldn't," she said wearily. "And if I'd warned you, you'd have warned Harper and then you would have had time to think up lots of ways not to let them in the door."

"You bet we would."

"Well, we had things that needed to be said."

"We? And there are, let us say, less strident ways of doing it."

"Why is it women are always strident when they want something, but men are just assertive?"

"Oh don't give me that feminist bullshit. You aren't abused. I shop for the goddamn groceries, I do half the chores around here."

"I didn't say it was your fault personally."

"Then why did you make such a fool of me?" Gordon looked hurt.

"I didn't! Nobody even knows I belong to the group."

"Is that why they were shouting at Harper about firing you?"

"Oh, God. Did they?"

"Then they handed him a dress and a pair of high heels— and a Kotex pad!—and dared him to wear them for a day."

Ellen looked up. Her mouth twitched. She put her hand over it. It wasn't any use.

"It's not funny!" Gordon said.

"It's hysterical."

He glared at her. "It won't change anything."

It was going to though, Ellen suspected. They were headed somewhere new, and it was going to be a mess.

XVIII
GARLIC

In January Nixon announced another troop pullout and peace talks in Paris. Jerry regarded both developments with a mixture of hope and suspicion. By the time a doctor took the wire out of his finger, he could move it a little. When medical personnel asked him what kind of moron tried to chop his finger off, he found himself explaining he'd only meant to take the end off, and finally gave up, sitting in sullen silence while they worked on it.

He couldn't hold a hammer or drive a car, so they packed the kids and the dog into his truck again and Joelle drove them to Ayala where Jerry's brother Ben had a friend with a friend with a house that was free. It didn't occur to him at first to wonder why. The friend was going somewhere vague (Tucson? Mexico?) and wanted someone to live there and see that it didn't fall down any more than it already had. Dreama said The Coffee Pot was hiring waitresses and Joelle could probably work there. Judy had some clothes the kids could probably use.

The house was a ramshackle cabin in the East End, on the edge of an orange grove, and might have been a caretaker's cottage once. Jerry could drag a lawn chair out under the trees, read in the dusty sunlight that filtered through the leaves, and brood. What he'd done had seemed straightforward at first.

Something plain and unarguable to put up the draft board's nose. A statement for all downtrodden draftees. On this end it looked somehow different. Self-mutilation seemed to carry a price, some shift in the balance, a wound that went deeper than tendon and bone.

The house was always full of people, just dropping by to bring a casserole or a joint, see how he was doing. A man he remembered vaguely from the Art Center came by to offer him a job laying a rock wall after his hand healed. He gave Jerry fifty dollars; an advance, he said. Mrs. Rosenbaum, his high school English teacher, asked him to walk her fat black lab along Shelf Road, something he could do one-handed, for two dollars a day. Mrs. Levine, the librarian, who remembered him as a twelve-year-old bookworm dreaming his summers away in the science fiction section, gave him a clerk's shift on Tuesday nights. The other waitresses at The Coffee Pot gave Joelle food to take home.

It slowly began to dawn on him that there were people who thought he'd done the right thing. Who thought he wasn't a fuckup, but something along the lines of a local hero. It made him uneasy, as if the Eye of God might notice and do something about it.

When the envelope from the draft board came he was sure that the Eye had opened, but the letter just read, *You have been reclassified. Your new draft status classification is 1-H.*

"What the hell is 1-H?" he asked Ben.

"Don't push it," Ben said. "Don't even ask."

That was Jerry's inclination.

"I thought they'd give you a 1-Y," Dreama said.

Joelle read and re-read the notice, searching for clues. She was convinced it was somehow a trap, something Jerry also suspected.

Raymond Manoury did what no one else was inclined to and

called the board. "It is a new classification, son. It is for people with whom they do not know what else to do. They will only let you into the army in the case of a national emergency." He smiled. "When the Vietnamese attack Santa Barbara, you can get out your gun. In the meantime, if you do not get in the newspaper, I will be grateful."

"Pow," Matthew said. He fired his finger at Raymond. Then he folded it under, pretending it was gone, and waggled his knuckles at Jerry.

"That's disgusting," Lauren said. She was nearly thirteen now, and most things were disgusting, although she showed signs of warming to Jerry as adolescence began to pit her against her mother.

Joelle fingered the letter, creasing it between her fingers as if she could wring some hidden meaning from it. "How did they know where to find you?" she demanded.

"Hospital has my address." Jerry closed his eyes. He doubted the hospital really thought he was going to pay their bill. They might as well have asked him to walk on the moon. They were feeding the kids on government surplus cheese and powdered milk. But he tried to send them five bucks when he could, until he thought his finger could get by with the Free Clinic in Ventura if it had to.

That was what he thought about when he was alone in his lawn chair, or walking Sybil Rosenbaum's lab, or when he saw what might have been Ellen's red bug and dived behind a telephone pole: how living on the margins was only simple if you were single, and childless, and uninjured. Even at Red Dog, where they'd tried to form their own society to replace the one they'd left, it had held together only so long as everyone could stay static, and resist the urge to redefine their domestic arrangements, contemplate their jealousies, redirect their addictions, or hoard their possessions. As long as no one cared very passionately about anything, or wanted anything. About five minutes, in other words.

"You should go to school," Mrs. Levine told him while he shelved books. "You were always a smart kid. What the hell happened to you?"

"If you want to make God laugh," Jerry told her, "tell Him your plans."

"You had plans?"

"Maybe not. I thought the world was going to end."

"So for a cosmic joke, God doesn't end the world." Mrs. Levine had frizzy, salt-and-pepper hair and tortoiseshell glasses on a chain. She pointed a red fingernail. "He may yet, but in the meantime, you've got to figure out something to do with yourself. Only crazy people sit around waiting for the End of Days."

"I've got four kids to support."

Mrs. Levine rolled her eyes. "You married to their mother?"

"No."

"Maybe you better decide about that too. If you're planning to stick around."

"You think I should get married?"

"I think you should figure out what *you* want to do. I'm a librarian, not Dear Abby. Librarians don't tell people what to do. We give them information so they can make their own decisions. That's our product—information. And we don't even sell it. It's free." She went back to her own pile of books, drawing Dewey Decimal numbers on their spines in white ink. All information had a house number.

Jerry balanced the book he'd been shelving. The library binding snagged the edge of his bandage, just a faint tug, a pinprick of pain. The finger tingled sometimes, and sometimes it ached, where things were growing back. He imagined the book's cover growing over it, a layer of grafted skin, sealing in new and foreign information. The end of his finger would know things the rest of him didn't know, about—he opened the book— wildflowers of the High Sierras. Or—he touched another on his cart—Fibonacci numbers. Or breeding the English cocker spaniel.

He remembered his fantasy of life in a bookstore, worshipping at the shrine of Ferlinghetti in City Lights, a devotee walking the paths of hip. The library was the universal bookstore, where all the books were free. It was all just information, whether it was how to cook a pot roast or the life of Jesus. All of it—Jesus, pot roasts, cocker spaniels—always had three or four versions, mutually contradictory in places. If you gave people all of it, everything they wanted to know and then some, then in the long run, they'd have power. They'd probably do all right. Maybe that was what the denizens of Red Dog Farm had missed.

When Jerry pulled out the job openings list for the county library system, Mrs. Levine pretended she didn't notice. The next Tuesday night, a note was tacked to the desk with a pushpin: *To be hired as permanent, full-time, you need two years' college. For my exalted job, a master's degree.*

"To feed kids," he told her, "I need to make money."

"Half time," she said flatly. "That's all, with no college."

"Yes, ma'am." He hung his head meekly.

"You can drive the Bookmobile. Minimum wage. When that hand heals."

On Wednesdays the Bookmobile stopped at Gray Gables, a nursing home where retired teachers went to roost. They were avid readers, fighting each other over the stock of large-print mysteries. On Thursdays it went to the hospital, and on Fridays to the little towns of Foster Park and Casitas Springs. On Tuesday nights he still took the evening shift, dispensing assistance to the lost souls who inhabited libraries at night. There was a woman who knew all the foreign dictionaries in the Reference section, and came in, he thought, just to touch them, and read the words softly aloud to herself. She always spoke of them as if they were edible. "I think I'll have Portugal tonight."

To Jerry the books began to take on a certain life as well, particularly at closing, when they settled on their shelves like chickens roosting. He would run his fingers along their spines, lightly straightening, feeling all that information stilling itself, dozing in dim moonlight, but ready to wake if he needed it, to tell him how to sail a boat or mend a wall or make bourbon. He stayed later than Mrs. Levine knew, doors locked, lights off, stretched on his back on the rug in the children's corner, hands behind his head, thinking, waiting for the books to tell him something. They had something to say, he was sure of it, but the words were always filtered through the Portuguese dictionary, or encoded in the Fibonacci numbers.

He found himself going to the Art Center again to dance. He half thought he might see Ellen there, and fantasized that she came alone, without her husband, who didn't look like the dancing type. She didn't. He did see Daniel Callahan, who was directing a play there. Ellen was living in Ventura, Daniel said. He needed someone to build a set of stairs for the third act. Did Jerry have any time?

His own parents got divorced, an event that was not, in retrospect, particularly surprising, but which surprised him anyway, leaving him feeling dangerously at sea.

"What would you think about getting married?" he asked Joelle while she was clearing the table.

Joelle stared at him as if the tuna casserole had proposed to her. "You don't want to get married."

"I don't know." He wanted to belong somewhere.

She eyed him with exasperated suspicion. "I did that. It was messed up. It would be more messed up with you."

"Okay. It was just a thought." He felt relieved. He'd made the gesture. He touched her face hopefully.

She slid away and stacked the dishes in the sink. Jerry came up behind her and breathed in her ear. She stiffened.

"What's the matter?" he said.

"You're never here. Now you want to get it on?"

"Well, not this minute." He did, though. Desperately. "What do you mean, I'm not here?"

"You're at the library. You're at the Art Center. Now you're building a wall with that old geezer."

"We need the money."

"The Art Center isn't paying you anything."

"I need those people, babe." He leaned closer to her, ignoring the stiffness of her spine, her clenched fingers on the dishrag. "You could come with me." Maybe dancing would loosen whatever had clamped down in Joelle.

Her lips tightened. "You don't get it."

"No," he conceded.

"I thought we were coming home. I thought it would be better. I thought you wouldn't screw around on me. I don't know why."

"I haven't."

"Yet." She glared at him.

"You just said you don't want to get married. You have every right do anything you want to do. You always have. We started off that way."

"*You* started off that way."

"You never said—"

"Yeah, well it wouldn't have mattered. All that bullshit about freedom, it's just bullshit. You can make it with anything that comes along. Good old Jerry. But I'm a tramp, or a bad example for my kids. I even catch shit for living with you."

"From who?" Every busybody in town, he supposed. "Look,

I haven't been—" He knew he'd thought about it, but he hadn't done it.

"You went to the PTA," she said resentfully.

"Somebody needed to."

"They're my kids."

"Then you go."

"The hell with you." She spun around. "I don't need this. I don't need some kid telling me what to do with my own kids! I don't need you prowling around the PTA like a tomcat. You stay away from the PTA. If they notice us, there'll be someone from Social Services coming around telling me I shouldn't be living with you. You think I'm kidding? I'm not. People with no money, no power, they get fucked over. It's not going to happen to me."

"What's not going to happen?"

"No one's going to take my kids."

"Of course they're not. What makes you think they are?"

"What makes you think you know anything? You're too busy following your dick around! And that's another thing. I'm sick of all the people hanging out here. I don't know these people. Get them out of my house."

"You know Ben." Jerry felt for solid ground. New people seemed to feed her anger, as if they might make impossible demands of her. "You know Judy."

Joelle glared at him.

"We haven't seen Judy in a while, anyway," he said.

A pot sailed across the kitchen, clipping his eyebrow. The back door slammed behind her, rattling the dishes.

"You're a paranoid bitch!" he shouted after her.

When Joelle came back he was in the lawn chair, reading. The dishes were washed, and the kids all in bed, except for Lauren who was studying. The house was vacuumed and the kitchen floor mopped.

Joelle's fingers balled into fists. "What the hell did you do that for?"

"Apology," Jerry said, reading. He'd done it to make it clear he hadn't gone anywhere while she was out.

Joelle gave him a long look. She turned around and went in the house. When he came to bed she was asleep, or pretending to be.

Since no one wanted him to, except maybe Mrs. Levine, he went to Ventura and signed up for a night class.

The cockroaches scrambled over the top of the bluffs and set up housekeeping in Ellen's blender. She landed a day shift at the diner, which didn't mollify Gordon as much as she'd hoped, and in July Teak married the garlic farmer.

Ellen was a bridesmaid, crowned with a wreath of roses, in green sandals and a long green dress that matched the crop in the field behind the groom's house.

"Interesting," Gordon said, surveying the wedding tent, also decorated in green and white. "I never knew anyone who picked garlic as their wedding theme before."

"Good for werewolves." Ellen craned her neck so that she could see if any were coming up the drive. Teak was drifting among the guests with a champagne glass, in an off-the-shoulder white dress that dripped old lace. She didn't seem to mind the groom seeing her before the wedding. Or the guests getting into the champagne, which was stacked in a clawfoot bathtub full of ice.

"Is old Four-Fingers going to be here?" Gordon inquired.

"Gordon, stop it. I don't know." That was what Ellen had been wondering, but she had been at great pains to convey to Gordon her complete lack of interest in the subject. She wondered if the woman Jerry was living with would come. A lot of women would probably be willing to turn out to watch Teak get safely married.

The other bridesmaid was a friend from Teak's high school. The ushers were a tall blond man named Blue Jay, decorated with a formidable handlebar mustache, and a bearded man, as big and bearlike as the groom, who turned out to be his brother Gene. A small man in a clerical collar was trying to herd them without success.

"We'll start pretty soon," Teak said, smiling gently at her mother over her champagne. "Everyone's always late, you know? Give them a little longer."

Ellen abandoned Gordon to her own parents on the pretense that they really were going to start, and took Teak by the elbow. "Is Jerry coming?" she hissed.

"I invited him." Teak paused. "Have you heard from Martin?"

They looked at each other for a moment. "This is great," Ellen said. "You talk to Jerry and I write to Martin."

"Works for me," Teak said. "Have some champagne, he's coming up the driveway."

"Oh, God."

Felix appeared behind Teak and put his arms around her. She disappeared in his tuxedoed embrace. "They're restless. Come on and marry me."

"Might as well." Teak smiled sweetly at him, then at Ellen, then at Jerry as he came through the open gate.

Ellen tried not to stare. He had a mustache. It was the first thing she saw. It hid his mouth and made him look as if he might be someone else, or in disguise. He was wearing an embroidered Mexican shirt, jeans, and boots. A thin, sandy haired woman in a flowered skirt was with him.

Teak handed Ellen her champagne glass. Ellen emptied it in one gulp and set it in the grass, where a dog licked it out. She clutched her bridesmaid's bouquet with both hands.

"Dearly beloved..."

The wedding guests beamed appreciatively at Teak in her flowing dress and spindrift veil fluttering from a crown of white roses. The groom looked as if he was still surprised but prepared to take fortune and run with it. Teak's mother and Ellen's mother sniffled into their handkerchiefs. The afternoon sun pooled on the waving shoots in the field until it shimmered like a green lake ready to cast up mysterious fish. A faint scent of garlic lingered on the wind.

"The ring!" Teak poked Ellen and she realized she hadn't been listening. She'd been trying to see Jerry out of the corner of her eye. She fished the ring out of the crocheted bag around her wrist.

The wedding dissolved into the reception. A table had been set up on the lawn in front of the farm house, laden with plates of sandwiches and various contributions from the guests. A huge cake decorated with nasturtiums rose from the middle. Lanterns on poles were ready to be lit when the sun fell. Someone brought out a fiddle. Children shrieked and chased dogs and each other in and out of the house and the barn. Adults depleted the tub of champagne.

The minister rounded up the wedding party long enough to get them to sign the marriage license. Blue Jay had a bottle of champagne under one arm. He took a drink and passed it to Ellen. By the time they got their signatures straightened out, she had had a good deal of it. She wandered back outside, shedding her shoes, and drifted across the grass, noting that Gordon was sitting with her parents and Teak's, looking like an inspector taking notes, and that Jerry's wife, or whatever she was, was talking to Felix and Teak. Neither looked like a good group to join.

Behind the house the barn rose solidly, its hay loft doors open. A barn cat sat thoughtfully in a pool of late sun by the door, disappearing into the growing shadows whenever children tried to pick it up. Past the barn was a lean-to with the shadowed silhouette of a tractor lurking inside, and three low-roofed buildings that might be packing sheds. A kitchen garden appeared as Ellen drifted past them. Beyond it was an apricot orchard that the barn had hidden from view, heavy with fruit. A buzz of bees hummed in the kitchen rows, and one zoomed past her hair, drawn by the wreath of roses.

Jerry was standing between the corn rows like an apparition. He had an open bottle of champagne in one hand.

She stopped and he said, "You look like a grass fairy in that dress."

The driveway that ran past the house diverged into a fork of dirt roads. One ran out into the garlic fields, the other into the tall grass between the apricot trees. Jerry held out his free hand and she walked with him into the trees. He gave her the bottle and she tipped it up. The fact that every time she thought about Jerry she seemed to get drunk probably wasn't a good sign. She took a modest sip.

"I'm a figment of your imagination," he said, seeming to read her thoughts.

"You are in that mustache. Where did that come from?"

"I couldn't shave for a while. The candy-striper in the hospital said she didn't do upper lips so well."

Ellen made a small noise in her throat. "Your—"

Jerry held it out. An angry red line ran from the base of the knuckle clear across his index finger. "It's all right now."

"It's not." It made her cry just to look at it.

"I told you I wasn't going to get drafted. How about you? Are you all right?"

"Yeah. I've got this awful job I hate, I got fired twice, for getting married and then for being in a demonstration, but I'm taking art lessons with Day Logan and I joined this women's group that invaded the newspaper and handed the editor a dress and a Kotex. They started printing women's first names anyway." That had been vindication of a sort.

"Here, let's sit down." He folded up cross-legged in the shadow of an apricot tree and motioned her down beside him. He took a long drink from the bottle. It was nearly dark, and the bees had begun to lumber away. They could hear fiddle music from the other side of the house.

"Does Martin know she got married?" Jerry asked quietly.

Ellen nodded, her face streaming with tears.

"Are you crying for them?"

"I suppose so."

They passed the champagne back and forth. "Are you—?" they both said at once, and stopped.

"Happy?" Jerry said after a moment. "I'm working at the library. I like that."

"I'm waiting tables at a truck stop," Ellen said. "I could have found something else by now, but Gordon hates it, and I've gotten so stubborn."

"Gotten?" Jerry chuckled behind the mustache.

"All right, fine. I always was as stubborn as a pig."

He made an oinking noise and she laughed.

"I have to pee."

"It's dark. Go behind a tree."

She got up and stumbled into the orchard. When she came back, he was lying on his back under the low-hanging branches. She stretched out beside him, leaning on her elbows.

"Am I different?" she asked him.

"You're feistier."

"You think? I figured I just finally got fed up."

"You got fed up with me a long time ago."

"That was with you personally."

"The personal is political," Jerry said.

"That's what everyone says. The personal still feels personal to me."

"Then what's political?"

"Political is when a woman does something, the first thing everyone notices about it is that she's a woman, not what she did. Political is restaurants that look at you like you're a hooker if you go in there at night alone."

"Sounds pretty personal to me."

"Personal is when my husband tells me then don't go in there alone if I don't want people to get the wrong idea."

"He said that?"

"He was pissed. I was raving."

Jerry scooted a little closer, still on his back. He was smiling, teeth glinting under the mustache. "I always thought you were beautiful when you were raving. And that was you at that beach festival where they set fire to everything, wasn't it?"

She nodded. Gordon hadn't liked that much either. "I can't even see you behind that thing."

"Try it out." He lifted his head and kissed her. It tickled, like nuzzling a wire-haired terrier or a scrub brush.

She pulled her head back. "Oh, no, I'm not going to kiss you. That's the first step on the road to hell."

"Then why are you out here lying in the grass with me?"

"Because you're imaginary."

"I imagine you all the time," he said softly. His arms slid around her shoulders. Their faces disappeared in the curtain of her hair. "I imagine wrapping up in that hair," he whispered in her ear. "Like a blanket."

It was too easy, like sliding back into an old bad habit, one you had really enjoyed. Jerry rolled them over so that he was on top. She felt him through her dress. The mustache nuzzled her neck. One hand pulled the top of her grass fairy dress down, the other tugged its skirt up.

She could feel the long orchard grass tickling her legs, and Jerry's breath in her ear. The champagne bottle reflected a half moon of light from somewhere, like a heliograph with one message on its mind. Jerry slid her underpants down her thighs.

"Well, I don't know where she's got to," Lily's voice said in the shadows. "Maybe she's with Gordon."

"Oh my God." Ellen sat up, pushing Jerry off her, pulling frantically at her dress. "It's my mother."

"Hide," Jerry whispered. "It's dark out here. Just be still."

"I can't. I can't make love to you in the orchard at Teak's wedding with my husband looking for me."

"Sounds like a great idea to me," Jerry said. "How do you know he's looking for you?"

"I must have been crazy. My bra's unhooked. Jerry, fix it!" She sat frozen, quivering with anxiety while he fumbled with the hooks, peering at them in the dark, the mustache brushing her back. "Come on!"

"I'm only good at undoing them," he said. "And this finger's still tricky. Settle down, I've got it."

She stumbled to her feet. "Where are my shoes?"

Jerry handed them to her. She took them and fled, and he rolled over, face down in the grass. After a while he picked up the champagne bottle and drank the rest of it.

"There you are." Lily popped out at her from behind the kitchen door as Ellen tried to sneak through it. "We've been looking for you. Teak and Felix are about to leave." The wedding couple were retreating to a hotel in Big Sur, leaving the house and the party to their friends. "What have you done to your dress?"

Ellen brushed away bits of grass. Gordon stood behind Lily, watching with grim interest.

"Where's Teak?" Ellen asked.

"Changing her clothes. You're supposed to go help."

She fled up the staircase, a massive edifice with a carved oak banister. Teak was pulling on pantyhose in the master bedroom, a gray silk suit spread on the Victorian double bed.

Ellen sagged in the doorway. "Mother says you're taking off."

"Yep. I am a married lady on my honeymoon." Teak sounded pleased, as if this was a state of respectability she hadn't expected to achieve. "All due to you, too."

"Me?" Ellen caught sight of herself in the mirror. The roses dangled over one eye.

"Well, I never thought it would work, you know, marriage, but you did it first, kind of blazed the trail. You guys got it together, so I figured I could, too." She shrugged into the silk jacket.

Felix stuck his head in the door. "Teak? You ready, doll?"

Teak picked up an overnight bag. "Absolutely." She kissed Ellen on the forehead. "Keep in touch, Good Example."

XIX
SHORT

Gordon didn't say anything much on the drive back down to Ventura, but it was a long drive and there was a certain air of tight-lipped non-questioning in the car. Ellen kept her eyes closed and tried to ignore the fact she wasn't wearing any underpants. She hoped it wasn't true, as her mother had always maintained, that people could tell when you weren't wearing underpants.

The next day Jerry called. "I almost didn't have the nerve," he said, "but Robert's mom just called me."

"Oh, no." Ellen collapsed on the couch, dragging the kitchen extension with her on its long cord, ready for it to be the worst. Calls like this were always the worst.

"He's lost a leg. He stepped on a mine, trying to get to somebody else. They're shipping him home."

"Oh, my God. When?" She pushed her hair out of her face. She was still in her nightgown. Gordon was in the kitchen.

"He's in a military hospital in Can Tho. His mom had an address." He was silent while she wrote it down. "Kind of makes a finger look not so bad, huh?" he said after a while.

Ellen sat staring at the address despairingly.

"Uh, I don't know how much you want to hear from me,"

Jerry said, "but you said last night, about hating your job? Bern's Books wants to hire somebody."

"Um."

"Just thought I'd mention it. Take care of yourself." The receiver clicked before she could say anything else, if she'd been going to.

She hung the receiver back in its cradle on the kitchen wall and slammed open a cupboard, looking for coffee. "You can chalk up another one for the forces of darkness!" She banged the pot on the counter.

"Indeed?" Gordon turned from the sink.

"Robert! He's lost his leg!"

"Robert?"

"He went to Vietnam before we got married. He sent me the *ao dai*. You know perfectly well who Robert is. You've seen me write to him."

"Should I ask who else you've been writing to?"

She tore the coffee open. "What is that supposed to mean?"

"You'll note I haven't asked you where you were last night. I'm not a moron."

"I wouldn't bet on it." She was gripped by seething anger. Not necessarily at him. She smacked it down. "Sorry. That was a cheap shot, but what are you implying?"

"What do you feel impelled to deny?"

"Gordon, what exactly do you think happened?" She pulled her hair back from her face and tied it in a knot while the coffeepot filled.

"You tell me," he said stiffly.

"Nothing." She tried to appropriate the virtue happenstance had granted her. "We sat in the orchard and drank champagne and talked."

"You looked like you got your head caught in a hedge."

"I always do. My hair never stays combed."

"Especially under trying circumstances."

She banged her fist on the counter and a cockroach dropped off the bottom of the cupboard above. "I just found out one of my friends lost his leg, and you're needling me about this! What do you think we did? Made love in the grass at Teak's wedding?"

Gordon looked thoughtful. "Let's say it made me wonder."

"He's just an old boyfriend. I never see him. He was just at the wedding."

"And who just called you about Robert?"

She compressed her lips. "Jerry."

"Just how intimate were you with this guy? When you were going with him, I mean?"

"Gordon, that's none of your business."

"Since you wouldn't sleep with me, I do feel a certain curiosity about whether you slept with him."

Ellen glared at him. She kept envisioning Robert with one leg gone, and Gordon kept grilling her about Jerry. She desperately did not want to talk about Jerry. "I thought we would do better if we didn't sleep together," she said primly. "It didn't work out very well for me when I did that. And I know for a fact you weren't a virgin either."

"I never pretended to be."

"You think *I* did?"

"What else do you call it?"

"Well, pardon me. Should I have said, 'Oh Gordon, you must forgive me, but I have to confess to you that I am not pure?' I thought if other people could learn from their mistakes, so could I. I slept with him and he slept around, so I thought I'd try a different approach."

"Things aren't that easy to rearrange," Gordon said. "Especially when you're rearranging other people."

"Well, I've slept with you more now than I ever slept with him."

"That is strangely small comfort."

"It's all I've got." The cockroach looked out at her from under the toaster and waggled its feelers. They would follow her permanently, Ellen thought. They were karmic marriage cockroaches, the cockroaches of guilt, who invaded the houses of people who made stupid decisions and screwed up other people's lives.

"Are those things back?" Gordon asked. "They must have hid in the packing boxes. Didn't you check for them?"

Bern's Books inhabited an outdoor courtyard under a motley collection of live oaks that grew through gaps in the concrete. The shelves formed a warren of aisles and dead ends, like a maze under corrugated fiberglass roofing. The best things were in the small house at the center of the maze, and the cheapest were outside the fence, in shelves that fronted the sidewalk. Anyone who wanted a book after hours could take it and throw a nickel through the gate. Bern's 5-cent shelves were the haunt of Ayala insomniacs with nothing to read.

Bern hired Ellen for minimum wage to run the cash register and realphabetize the books after they'd been scrambled by the day's browsers. His standards weren't high. As long as all the A's were together and most of the B's came after them, that was as far as he felt the need to go.

She knew Gordon didn't like the job because it was in Ayala, where Jerry was, and felt mildly furtive about her daily drive to work. She spent her time thinking of ways to undo the messes she'd made, realphabetize her marriage, as it were, but none of them seemed to work. She arranged a weekend at an inn in Big

Sur and surprised Gordon with it, hoping for a romantic re-set. She stopped taking birth control pills. Then they had a fight on the way back because she mentioned Teak, which brought up the wedding, which was a mistake, and she started the pills again.

The women in her group were no help. Half thought she shouldn't have quit the truck stop, as a symbol of solidarity with her blue-collar sisters, and half thought she shouldn't be trying to placate Gordon.

"We'll never get anywhere as long as women have to have their husbands' 'permission' to work," Mary Nell said disgustedly. "What are you apologizing for?"

"He doesn't mind my working. He doesn't like my working in Ayala," Ellen said.

"You'll never get your head clear as long as you're motivated by trying to please men."

"I'm not trying to please men."

"Then why are you sleeping with them?"

"Because I don't like girls," Ellen said.

"Really, Mary Nell, we can't all be nuns just because we aren't lesbians," Lupe said.

"It might simplify your life."

"No, it wouldn't," Valerie said.

In between they tried to get Bunny Leeman to leave her boyfriend before he killed her.

"I'm worried to death about her," Jenna confided while they were lettering placards to picket Bank of America. (HOMEMAKERS DESERVE TO BE HOME-OWNERS. GIVE WOMEN THE CREDIT THEY'RE DUE.) "Her mother's still acting as if he just has a bad habit or two that'll change when he marries him. Bunny says her mother thinks she needs someone to take care of her. Can you imagine? So she should marry this jerk?"

"Her brother's coming home from Vietnam," Ellen said. The president was pulling all the ground combat troops out, a miserable consolation at this point. "Maybe he can do something." She wondered if Carl would feel the same way Bunny's mother felt. He might. She doubted he'd approve of the women's group. Not that it had succeeded in raising Bunny's consciousness yet. Bunny seemed to inhabit a kind of self-perpetuating Easter egg, the kind you looked into and saw little rabbits and lambs frolicking in sugar grass. Then you hit it with a hammer and the lambs and rabbits turned out to be cardboard.

When Ellen got home, Gordon was pacing up and down, muttering, and Maggie, of all people, was huddled on the sofa, clutching Yang. She had on a plaid blouse and a long skirt, and a little traveling bag lay on the floor by her feet.

Gordon glared at the door, as if someone else might be out there. "Those sons of bitches are going to be sorry they were ever born. Them and their sorry fucking swami."

"What happened, Mag?" Ellen asked.

"I couldn't figure out anywhere else to go." Maggie sniffled and managed a Southern smile. "Gordon's been real sweet, considering he's never met me."

"Where are your Krishna people?"

"In Santa Barbara. They asked me to leave. Guruji wanted me to admit it was my fault, and it was like they didn't even blame him."

"Blame who?"

"She was raped," Gordon said.

"Oh, Maggie." Ellen dropped onto the sofa beside her. "Your guruji?"

"No." Maggie's lip quivered. "I don't know his name. I was

trying to convert him. And they all said it was my fault because I wasn't supposed to be alone with him, as if I'd give five minutes of my time to that— I just wanted him to see that Krishna loved him."

"Who said it was your fault? Did you call the police?"

"They didn't want me to. It would make Guruji look bad. He said I used bad judgment."

"Maggie, I can't— *I'm* calling the police."

"No, no. I already did. That's why they threw me out. Even the women. They said it was because I hadn't let Krishna take care of me."

"The police—"

"They took my statement. They asked me what I'd been wearing, and said my top was too tight." Maggie plucked at the bedraggled sleeve of her blouse. It looked like she'd slept in it. "I was wearing a sari. He pulled it all the way off, they just wrap. The cops said men are excited by that kind of thing. By then he'd been gone for hours. I don't know if they even looked for him, they probably didn't, they don't like us, but I was afraid to stay there, and Guruji said it would be better if I left, so I took a bus."

"Have you been to the hospital?"

"He didn't hurt me." Maggie picked at the folds of her skirt.

"He raped you!"

"I know, but he didn't, you know, hurt me. Maybe a bruise or two. I took about three showers."

"Have you called your parents?"

"No." Maggie hung her head. "I can't stand them to know."

"Mag, this isn't like you."

"They'll just blame me too."

They put her to bed in the spare bedroom that might be going to be a nursery eventually. Ellen sat by her until she went to sleep. The moon flooded the bedspread like water, like some current you could sail out onto if you just knew where you were going, which unfortunately none of them did. Gordon had gone to sleep. Ellen wanted to wake him up again and tell him this was why there was a women's movement: because women got raped, then everyone told them it was their fault. She didn't, because it would be pointless, and he'd been furious at the ashram people and Maggie's guru and said Maggie could stay as long as she wanted to. Ellen supposed that was really more useful. Gordon seemed to like Maggie, so it was all personal to him, but it wasn't personal in the larger sense because he wasn't female and no one was likely to rape him, and if they did he could beat them to a pulp. What made things personal was being vulnerable, Ellen decided. And oh, God, what if Maggie got pregnant?

In the morning she gave Maggie a packet of her birth control pills and told her how many to take. Jenna had taught her that one. It was one of those useful things that the doctor who prescribed them had never mentioned.

The women's group took up Maggie's cause. They had a great many things to say about it and said them to the Santa Barbara police, who said, well, little lady, they were working on it, but half those Hare Krishna girls were turning tricks on the side, everybody knew that, so in some sense the girl had been asking for it. Even if she wasn't turning tricks, that kind of clothes was an invitation.

"And the Berringer girl hasn't got any witnesses."

"If she had witnesses, she wouldn't have been raped," Jenna explained.

"Well, the court can't simply take a woman's word for anything she feels like saying," the captain explained back kindly, as if Jenna might not understand. "You wouldn't believe it, but a lot of women get mad at a guy because he won't date them, and they accuse him of something like this to get back. Happens all the time."

"I told you all it wouldn't do any good," Maggie said morosely. Her nose was red and she clutched a handkerchief (being Maggie, it was a cloth one) in her fist. "They aren't even going to look for him. I shouldn't have been in the hotel alone talking to strangers."

"You said *he* came up to *you*."

Maggie sighed. "He did. It doesn't matter."

Ellen persisted in the idea that it did matter. Jenna said it did, and she thought Jenna was right.

"Rape is an endpoint on a continuum that begins with marriage," Mary Nell said. "Marriage is merely legalized rape."

"Well, how can you rape your wife?" Lupe asked her.

"He wants sex. You don't. He holds you down," Mary Nell said.

"Oh." Lupe pondered that. "I hadn't thought of it that way."

"We're getting sidetracked," Jenna said. "The question is what are we going to do for Maggie? Now if Maggie would just agree to sue the guy in civil court—"

"Oh, no." Maggie put her head in her hands.

"We'd have to find him first," Ellen said. She put an arm around Maggie. "No one's going to make you go to court, Mag."

"I just couldn't."

"Well, why the hell not?" Mary Nell demanded.

Maggie sat up, "Well, because I'd die of shame, for one thing."

"That's our whole point," Jenna said. "It shouldn't be shameful. You are the victim, not a criminal."

"Would I win?"

"No," Jenna admitted.

"Then I'm not going to be a hero of the revolution," Maggie said.

Ellen tried to get Maggie to take a part-time job at Bern's. Bern had decided to add soup and outdoor movies to his product line and needed someone to ladle minestrone and run the projector. But Maggie had begun to hyperventilate every time she left the house for anything except to go to the group at Jenna's. It seemed to Ellen that Maggie had been gradually evaporating since they'd graduated. She'd joined the Hare Krishnas for the simplicity they promised: chanting, making flower garlands, not worrying about what your father was mixed up in. The old Maggie wouldn't have needed anyone to take up for her, but she seemed to have faded entirely from view.

"Give her time," Gordon said. "She's been through the mill. And the Lesbian Liberation Front poking at her about going to court isn't helping any."

"It's not good for her to sit around in her robe all day watching *Another World*, either," Ellen said. "She won't even kill the cockroaches."

"I guess that Krishna stuff gets a grip on you," Gordon said. He stamped on one that had ventured out from under the cat-food dish.

"Leave her alone," Bunny said when the group met again. "Not everyone's made out of solid brass." They looked at her, surprised. Usually it was Bunny whose resolve they were trying to stiffen.

"I need to tell you something," Bunny said. "Jim's gone. My brother stabbed him with a fork and now he's in the hospital."

"What?"

"We had a welcome home barbecue for Carl," Bunny said. "Jim got mad because I didn't bring him a beer and Carl stabbed him with a kitchen fork. Then his dog knocked Jim down and wouldn't let him up and my dad and some men got Carl and took him to the VA hospital."

"It's Carl in the hospital, not Jim?" Ellen asked.

"Yes, and Jim broke off the engagement, so I don't have to, and no one can get mad at me about it. He said Carl was crazy and he ought to call the cops but the doctor says not to worry."

Ellen remembered Carl the last time she'd seen him, wound like a too-tight spring. He hadn't rescued Vietnam or democracy, but apparently he'd saved Bunny.

"They gave him something to calm him down."

"Thorazine," Jenna said knowingly.

"My dad asked if this was because of him being in Vietnam, but the psychiatrist said he just needs rest."

"He stabbed a guy with a barbecue fork," Ellen said.

"He's afraid of helicopters too," Bunny said. "And he scares Mother to death whenever he takes the car out. He just drives for hours and he goes way too fast. But the doctor says he'll be fine, it's just a big adjustment, coming home."

The ghost sat staring into the window of the plane, his own face looking back at him in the dark. He willed himself into his body, into the physical self that had bought a ticket with his hoarded cash and filed on board, obeying without protest the compulsion that drove him. The self who still had Randy Ottley's driver's license and Randy Ottley's military ID. The president was pulling all ground troops out of Vietnam, so now he was short. "You're short," they would say when someone's time in-country was nearly up. Short on days in-country, good on the odds of getting home. He would go home now.

When the plane landed in Los Angeles he took a taxi to the bus station. The bus took him to Ventura and a second one homeward past the landmarks he'd conjured on his nighttime voyages. The refinery stark now in the daylight, and the apple orchard at the top of the grade. The Post Office tower where he got off, shouldering his duffel bag. The flagpole in his mother's yard.

He stood staring at the house until a barking dog summoned his mother to the window. She stared back, open-mouthed, and screamed, and he ran away again, blindly, stumbling down the road until it turned toward the East End orchards and the half-remembered trails into the foothills where they'd gone camping when they had still loved him, when the valley had been home and its gates always open.

He kept climbing until he came to the campground where he and Mimi had held their childhood birthday parties. After years of drought the swimming hole was almost empty, the stream dried to a trickle, but he pushed his way through gates barred with CLOSED signs. The night was getting cold and the wind whistled in the dry scrub and the cottonwoods that shaded the camp, little voices from those distant parties. He collected sticks for a fire to cook the hotdogs he'd stolen and set about building it in an empty firepit under the picnic shelter. When it began to burn steadily he held the hot dogs over it on the end of a stick. The warmth was welcoming but he kept his eyes averted from the flames because it was too easy to see things in flames, even here.

After a while he slept, and the wind picked up.

The sparks settled first in the blanket he'd wrapped himself in. When he sat up, choking on the smoke, it was burning. He flung it from him reflexively. It tangled in the brush and the brush caught. Randy staggered to his feet, pulling on his boots while the flames ate into the dry brush, parched by five years of drought. He flailed at them with his jacket while the smoke stung his eyes. The wind blew the flames into the drought-starved cottonwoods overhead and he dropped the jacket. He began to run but the smoke roared into his lungs, acrid and choking. The wind fanned the flames around him. When he tried to breathe the burning air, his lungs burned too. He ran, gasping, until he couldn't and fell, fighting for air while his vision clouded.

The coyotes had smelled the fire when it began to eat its way into the brush and they moved away from its path to watch cautiously from the ridgeline. They saw the still body in the dry brush as the flames passed over it. They waited to see if it would move, but it didn't.

"The psyche takes a long time to heal," Jerry said when Ellen went, guiltily, to the Ayala library after work looking for books on rape. The subject appeared to be nonexistent.

"Apparently rape is just a minor inconvenience." She glared at the card catalog.

"Maybe, but I read a good article by Susan Griffin a couple of years back in *Ramparts*. Do you want me to see if we can get it?"

"I don't know." What would be the consequences of allowing him to woo her with articles on rape? "How are the kids? And Joanne?"

"Joelle," Jerry said.

"Right. And the kids?"

"They're fine."

"Four, is it?"

"They were prepackaged," Jerry said.

"Boxed set?"

"The contents are unreliable. I've figured that much out. So how come you aren't pregnant yet?"

"You sound like my mother-in-law."

"Mother Murphy hankering for grandchildren?"

"In spades. She doesn't see why I want to spend my time showing those peculiar movies instead of raising her namesake."

"You're planning to name it for her?"

"I'm planning to name it for Che Guevara to piss her off."

He chuckled and Ellen gaped at him, horrified. She was actually complaining about her mother-in-law to Jerry. That way ruin lay. Her stomach felt queasy. Everything was wrong.

"I have to get home." She looked at her watch as an afterthought. "Gordon will worry."

"Especially if he finds out you were here."

She pretended she hadn't heard him. And what was he doing making bibliographic passes at her when he had four kids and Joanne—Joelle—at home?

The house was dark when she pulled up. She wasn't that late. She wasn't even as late as she'd called and told Gordon she was going to be. Maybe he was making a point about that. Or maybe Maggie just hadn't had the energy to pull the lamp chain.

Ellen unlocked the front door and flicked the light switch. She dumped her purse on the dining room table and inspected the mail. Two bills and a sweepstakes entry. Mr. and Mrs. Gordon Murphy might have already won their dream home. The cats yowled at her. She could hear a murmur of voices from somewhere, but no one appeared to be feeding cats, so she went in the kitchen.

She turned on the kitchen light and opened a cupboard, banging its door against the wall while she scrabbled for cat food at the back. There was an answering bang from the back of the house. She set the can down.

She heard another bang and a thud from the end of the hall and a light went on in the spare bedroom, a light that hadn't been on before. Gordon bolted through the doorway in his undershorts and fell over a cat in the hall.

"Goddammit!" He stumbled to his feet. Yang clung to the top of the door above him, like a gecko.

Ellen opened her mouth but she couldn't think of anything to say. Maggie erupted through the door after Gordon, clutching an unwrapped sari around her, and said, "Oh, Lord, I'm so sorry, I just don't know what got into us, I was feeling so sad, and Gordon was bein' nice, but we didn't really mean to, it's all my fault, you've just got a prince of a husband, Gordon just loves you to death, he was just bein' sweet to me because I felt so low and no one's ever going to want me again and he said of course they will, and I am just so sorry, I am leaving right this minute."

Gordon turned back into the guest room. He emerged again zipping his pants. "Mag, go get dressed, you don't need to go anywhere. Ellen, we need to talk."

Ellen felt herself developing a galloping, towering, shameful rage. "I can figure out what's going on without your confession," she snarled.

"You can't figure out shit!" Gordon snarled back. "You can't even figure out how to be married."

"*I* can't? Oh really?" Ellen glared pointedly at his zipper. "I decided to marry you because I don't know what I'm doing?" she inquired acidly.

"You decided to marry me the same way you decide to do whatever you want to do, with the bit in your teeth," he said. "You just don't have a clue where to take it from there."

"What's that supposed to mean?"

"You decided I'd *do*, didn't you? I auditioned better than the other guy. And it helped that I'm not a raving nutcase. It's a shame you forgot to mention a few of the rewrites you did along the way."

"Gordon, that's not what I said." Maggie clutched her sari to her and looked pleadingly at Ellen. "I didn't say that. I said she thought you were a responsible person."

"How flattering," he said between his teeth. "I could be a new superhero—Responsible Man."

"You told him things I said to you?" Ellen demanded.

"Well, I just said you thought Jerry *wasn't* responsible," Maggie sniffled. "You know you told us that's why you broke up. And you said Gordon was someone you could depend on."

"Anything else you want to make public? My bra size? My medical records?"

Maggie sniffled again. "I'm sorry. I was just trying to encourage Gordon."

"He seems pretty encouraged." Ellen felt humiliated tears starting. "He'd have to be to sleep with a house guest and tell his wife it's *her* fault." She spun on her heel and snatched her purse from the table before Gordon or Maggie could say anything else. The glass in the bookcases shook when she slammed the door.

Ellen backed the bug out of the narrow driveway, grinding the gears and dropping the front wheel off the curb. Ahead, the sky had developed an ominous orange glow.

XX
REHABILITATION

A t first the burning sky seemed to Ellen some kind of manifestation of her fury at Gordon, although it seemed unlikely she'd acquired that ability. She turned on the car radio, which said there was a fire in the foothills feeding on the dry brush of Los Padres Forest, where the years of drought had taken their toll. Gordon would have remembered to tell her that if she'd come home half an hour later. Another wave of fury rolled over her and she bit it back because she knew she'd asked for it. Half her anger was with herself for the messes she had made so blithely. She would have noticed the sky when she left Ayala if she hadn't had Jerry on her brain.

When she got out of the car in her parents' driveway, she could taste the ash in the air. She let herself in through her father's office door, which no one ever locked, and stumbled over Henry Poodle in the doorway of the room that had once been hers. She pulled the covers back from the bed and got in with her clothes on.

In the morning her mother listened to Ellen's account of the situation, and called Gordon to tell him where Ellen was. "It's not right to let him worry."

"He's not worrying. He's probably back in bed with Maggie."

Daniel turned the radio on. The fire had moved closer. They could see flames on the ridgetop in daylight this morning.

"Well, stay here for now," Lily said. "I may need you to help with the cats. But don't do anything rash about Gordon."

Ellen helped Bern cover the outdoor bookshelves with plastic, then called Gordon herself, ostensibly to make sure he took the cats to the vet for their shots. "I made the appointment last week. They'll charge us if you skip it and don't cancel."

"I can handle the cats' schedule," Gordon said.

"Is Maggie still there?"

"You were expecting me to throw her out?" He sounded icy.

"No! I want to be sure she's okay. She was raped and now you go and sleep with her! You don't know how much damage you may have done."

"Your concern is touching."

"Maggie's my friend. I've known her longer than I have you!" Ellen slammed the phone down. That hadn't gone very well.

The air was hotter now and full of ash. Every twenty minutes a helicopter flew overhead carrying a load of flame retardant. The fire ate its way slowly along the ridges. Ash clouded the sun and coated everyone's lips and nostrils and stung the eyes. The coyotes made their way down dry streambeds into town where they took up residence in the drain pipe that ran beneath the Bank of America.

The smoke veiled everything like static on a television screen.

Randy Ottley's mother thought she saw him again, just for a moment, in front of the flagpole in the front yard, then he dissipated into a whirl of ashen air.

The fire went on burning, eating the hillsides, engulfing trees in billows of red flame. The peacocks in the foothills flew down to congregate on the roof of the Ayala Inn, screaming imprecations at the departing guests. Orchard owners wet their trees down while fire crews came in by helicopter and staggered out again black-faced and soot-begrimed for a few hours' sleep at the Capri Motel while new crews took their places. The fire crawled down the overhang above Shelf Road and heat-driven wind blew the sparks to the live oaks in the riverbottom. Everything was tinder-dry. The trees in the riverbottom exploded in gouts of flame like fireworks.

Jerry wet down the cabin in the orange grove and loaded anything he thought they might want into the back of his truck. Joelle watched him, grim-faced, her mouth pulled tight, hair skinned back from her face. At night they could see the whole ridge burning, a flickering orange glow, while the choppers roared overhead.

The Fire Department got ready to evacuate the residents at Gray Gables, and the elementary school in the Upper Valley closed. Day Logan and Dottie wet down the roof, loaded her best pieces onto Day's truck, and took them down the hill to the Art Center's back room. Everyone stood in the street watching the flames, clutching transistor radios. Two minutes after a bath their skin was gritty again, and the air was like a blanket of nettles. Everything felt feral and hungry.

"Coyote weather," Day said.

Joelle wrapped the caustic air around her like a barbed-wire cloak, leaving Jerry on the outside. When the fire had been burning for a week she dragged everything she and the children owned out of his truck and piled it in the driveway again.

344

"What the hell are you doing?" Jerry peered at her myopically through his glasses. These days they hardly did any good, but he could still read if he squinted.

"Get out," Joelle said. She slapped at a cinder on the back of her neck.

Jerry looked at the pile in the driveway. Matthew's Halloween ghoul mask sat on the top, slavering rubber drool. "What?"

"Just go away," Joelle said. Her face was tight.

"What about the fire?" He could feel it in the air, using up the oxygen. Maybe Joelle could, too.

"Dave'll come get us," Joelle said. "I called him." Her ex-husband.

"Dave?"

"I put up with your screwing around for three years. I thought you were going to grow up. If I'm going to hang out with an adolescent, at least I can make it my kids' dad." Joelle stared away from him at the ridgeline, where the fire glowed red-orange along the top.

Jerry peered at the back of her head. Maybe he should have been paying attention to something else. It had seemed more important to give his concentration to the fire, to what he might need to do to get them out; to being the local hero. It appeared Joelle didn't want a local hero.

She turned around, her eyes narrowed. "You came home from the wedding with some girl's underpants in your pocket. I'm tired of you."

Jerry's hand went automatically to his pocket, then he drew it back, shamefaced. Black lace. They'd had been under Felix's apricot tree.

"Just go, all right?"

He got in his truck. Joelle stood in the dirt driveway with her hands on her hips. Pete the dog sat beside her, ears pricked, brown eyes sympathetic. The kids were in school. Pete would hop in the truck if Jerry called him, but he was the kids' dog. It wouldn't be fair. Jerry put the truck in gear, looking at Joelle through the rearview mirror. Her eyes were squinted against the sun, or maybe just against him.

Jerry spent most of the day just driving around, seeing what the fire was doing. The choppers whirred overhead and the radio news said they were getting a hold on it. A campfire had started it, they thought. He looked at the black hills and grimaced. In the dead places you could still see wisps of smoke rising from the rubble. He'd seen a bobcat and a skunk in the orchard that morning. They didn't have any place to go either. It was his night at the library. At five o'clock he could go there.

He drove over to Robert's house to see if Robert's mom had heard anything more from him, and found Robert there.

"Hey, man." Robert was propped in his dad's recliner. His prosthetic leg leaned against the chair. "I tried to get hold of you, but nobody answered the phone. I was going to hunt you down at the library."

Jerry sat down on the couch next to the recliner. "No phone, no home. Joelle threw me out this morning."

"Permanently?"

"Probably." He cracked his knuckles, awkward. "You all right, man?"

"Yeah." There were faint lines in Robert's face that hadn't been there before. His military haircut was growing out. "I hobble around on this thing." He gestured at the leg. "I can't stay on it too long, though."

"Hurt?"

"Like a motherfucker sometimes. I'm still on pain meds. Other times it's OK. Nerves are funny. Sometimes I can feel the damn foot."

"The one that's not there?"

"Yeah. They told me I tied a tourniquet on and gave myself some morphine and called in the dust-off chopper. I don't remember any of that."

Jerry looked at the leg. It was plastic, an incongruous pink like a Barbie doll. "Jesus. Can't they at least give you something that matches?"

"Apparently not. I told the nurse I was getting a can of spray paint and she said I couldn't deface military property." He looked at Jerry's hand. "I heard about your adventure."

Jerry folded his fingers down under his palm. "I guess it doesn't really compare."

"It's not a competition. You've got your head on tighter than some. I saw Leeman when they were loading me on the transport home. He was trying to bring his dog and the stewardess wasn't having it. She kept saying it was Army property. He told her not to fuck with him and after a minute she decided not to. I wouldn't have either."

"I thought I saw Ottley," Jerry said. "The one who went AWOL. He was walking up Reeves Road. I'm not even sure he was real."

"He may not be sure either. I guess he wants to come home," Robert said. "Poor bastard." He yawned. "Sorry. Percodan makes me sleepy."

The Valley of the Lost, Jerry thought. Ottley sobbing over it like some disembodied shadow, Robert home minus a piece of himself. And what about Jerry Manoury, the local hero? What exactly was *he* going to do with himself? Since it appeared the world wasn't going to end. The country might even actually

347

extricate itself from Vietnam. Nixon said he would, and though Jerry trusted Nixon about as much as he did the coyotes who were living under the Bank of America, he'd probably make good on that before there was a national revolution. Public opinion was beginning to veer, having seen all it could stand of burning children and corpses in living color. Even television had proved to have a purpose after all.

"I'm taking freshman comp at City College," Jerry said sheepishly.

"Well, I expect you scare the shit out of the teacher," Robert said. He yawned again.

"I'm sneaking up on a degree, I guess. I like the library. I could stay there, I think."

"Mmm." Robert nodded. His eyes were closing. Jerry left him and told Mrs. Hutchinson he'd be back later. The clock on the living room wall said 4:00. He could be a little early at the library.

When Mrs. Levine pointed out exactly how early he was, he was forced to tell her Joelle had thrown him out.

She sighed. "You can park your truck behind my house if you want to. I've got a guest cabin. It's not much, but you can have it for a while if you'll fix it up. I've noticed you do that." Every squeaking chair and rattly windowpane had healed itself since Jerry had been coming in on Tuesday nights.

"Are you sure?"

"It'll keep you from moving in with some other woman," Mrs. Levine said. "Which you need like a hole in the head. Also you can help me get my stuff out if we have to evacuate."

"I think the fire's almost contained." A chopper went over the library as he spoke. "Maybe."

"Well, since you're here, I'm going to go water down my roof." She picked up her bag. "Just pull into the driveway when you get in. It's in the back. I'll leave the door unlocked."

Jerry nodded, grateful. He was still startled to find there were people who liked him, who would offer him things. He was getting used to it with Mrs. Levine.

It was probably going to be a slow night. Most people didn't go to the library when they were afraid their house was going to burn down. A few teenagers, reluctantly doing research for papers due tomorrow, clustered at a table. He heard the screen doors creak, and then the main doors, closed against the ashy air. A man came through and Jerry caught a glimpse of a German shepherd, ears pricked, motionless outside the screen.

The dog's owner wore blue jeans and a sweatshirt which had the odd, rumpled air of having been folded in a closet for a long time. His blond hair looked like another Army cut growing out. He stood as motionless as the shepherd, eyes uneasy.

"Nice dog," Jerry said.

"That's Jojo."

"Can I help you find something?"

The guy cocked his head, listening to the choppers lifting over the fireline. "I'm supposed to dig my mom a fish pond," he said finally. "I don't have a library card."

"Library cards are easy." Jerry got a form out of the drawer.

The guy filled out the slip with precise print: Carl Leeman, a Signal Street address. Jerry produced a selection of how-to books and they pondered the relative merits of brick and concrete linings.

"I like the free-form ones myself," Jerry said. "They adapt to the terrain better. But the brick gives a tidy look. Lots of people like that. And it's pretty stuff, brick."

"It doesn't matter," Carl said. "It's therapy. I'm supposed to dig a pond so I won't stab some asshole with a barbecue fork again."

"You did that?"

"Sister's boyfriend. I don't remember doing it."

Jerry whistled. "Heavy duty."

"Want me to leave?"

"Got any barbecue forks on you?"

"No."

"Then you're probably okay."

Another chopper went over, and paused, seeming to hang in the air. Carl vibrated to its rumble, a string tuned to the same note.

"You're in the library, man," Jerry said quietly. "We're gonna build a fish pond. That's a Fire Department helicopter, with a load of flame retardant."

"You been in 'Nam?"

"Not me."

"In the Army?"

"Draft resister."

Carl studied him carefully. "I'd like to have had you in my unit for a week," he said finally.

"No, man, you wouldn't," Jerry said. "And neither would I. You want to build a fish pond?"

"Just give me the books. I'll take them with me."

He put them under his arm and pushed his way through the doors. The dog outside stood. Jerry watched them go in a fine shower of falling ash.

In the morning Mrs. Levine woke him, banging on the guest house door. He stood blinking in the morning light, in the clothes he had slept in. "They're evacuating the East End. Don't take the bookmobile out, I want you around the library."

Jerry pulled on socks and boots and got in the truck. He floored it out to the orchard, but the cabin was empty of everything but the odd detritus that stays behind when someone moves: a solitary plastic fork on the kitchen table, a pair of torn underpants on the bathroom floor, a piece of jigsaw puzzle on the windowsill. Bereft of human habitation. Apparently she'd meant it when she said she didn't need him.

He could see flames in the foothills just to the east of the orchard, and when he turned around on the dirt road, a police car was there, its driver waving him back toward town. He turned west obediently. In the center of town, a cattle trailer rattled onto the road ahead of him, black and white Holsteins from the Creek Road dairy peering mournfully between its slats. The sky was uncharacteristically overcast, leaden clouds reflecting the dull glare of the fire. *Rain, damn it,* he thought.

Ellen spent the morning counting cats, retrieving them from kitchen cupboards and under beds, passing them to Lily, who was stuffing them all in Ellen's bedroom in case they had to evacuate.

"I don't see why you can't just take them to Ventura," Lily said.

"Because I'm not going to Ventura," Ellen said. "If you want to take five cats to Gordon, go ahead, but I'm not doing it."

"Darling, aren't you being unreasonable about Gordon?"

"No." Ellen got queasy every time she thought about him. She was an idiot. He was right. She'd picked him out because he would do. Now what? She bent down to haul a cat from under her mother's bathroom sink and her head swam. She let the cat go and lay down on the cool linoleum, pressing her cheek against it. Her stomach knotted painfully and she felt a sudden wet rush between her legs.

"Ellen?"

Oh, God. She sat up, head still swimming. The cat had departed and the bathmat was soaked with blood. She'd felt odd since the Big Sur trip. She'd stopped her pills for three days before it, trying to make Gordon happy, then thought better of it. Apparently her body was thinking better of it too, divesting itself of the last remnant of her marriage.

"What's the matter with you?"

She closed the door. "I'm fine." She found a box of Kotex under the sink. Her stomach cramped again. Whatever was leaving her hadn't been there but a couple of weeks, but she felt shivery and miserable at its loss anyway. She stuffed the bathmat in the washer and stumbled into her bedroom to change.

Lily had incarcerated the last cat by the time she emerged. "If they evacuate us you'll have to take Henry," Lily said hopefully. She would force Ellen home to Gordon with something if she could.

"I'm going to work," Ellen said. "If they evacuate you, they'll evacuate Bern's first, it's closer to the fire."

"I have to do something for Jean Ottley," Lily said, "but I can't think what would be any comfort. They found Randy."

Ellen's stomach heaved again. "Where is he?" She imagined him being dragged from some dingy apartment by the military police. "What will they do to him?"

"He's dead," Lily said.

"Oh, no." Misery washed over her again, for Randy, for

everything.

"Apparently he was here, maybe all along, no one knows. They found his body up in the foothills."

"He only wanted to come home." That was what Jerry had said. Ellen started to cry.

"It's awful," Lily said. "He burned to death. They think he caused the fire too, with a campfire that got away from him."

"And you're going to take Jean Ottley a goddamned casserole after that letter she wrote?" Ellen scrubbed at her eyes with her shirttail.

Lily twisted her hands together. "I don't know *what* to do."

Ellen's stomach cramped again and she grimaced while her mother looked at her suspiciously. She said, "I'm not going anywhere near Jean Ottley but if you have to take the cats to Gordon, I'll drive you."

When she backed down the driveway, the sky was dark with ash and storm clouds. Ellen put the emergency brake on by the street and got out. She huddled under the acacia tree and threw up her breakfast while it started to rain.

It does not rain in October in Southern California, but now, as if called up by collective yearning, by stinging eyes and scorched flesh, it did. The firefighters went home, the last choppers lifting over the sodden black hills like wet bugs, and water sluiced down the burned earth where there was nothing left to hold it. It filled the dry washes that threaded the valley, driving the coyotes out of the drainpipe and into people's garages. The gully in the Callahans' back yard filled and overflowed, carrying debris that flattened against the wire fence at the far end until Daniel unclogged it with a shovel. Lily turned the cats loose but they wouldn't go out. Ellen and Bern tacked the plastic sheeting tighter over the bookshelves and stacked the contents of the lower ones on tables, out of reach of the water that pooled on the concrete floor. Jerry and Mrs. Levine did the same with the bottom shelves in the library, watching the street uneasily as the gutters filled and overflowed.

The air smelled like wet ash, like a campfire put out with dishwater. Where the fire had gone now the water went, uprooting blackened stumps and carving channels for itself in the sandy soil. Little creeks filled and flowed into the riverbottom, flooding the dairy and the campground at Camp Comfort, scouring chicken coops and sheds off their footings along Creek Road. It rained for three days. On Halloween the trick-or-treaters squelched through it in rain slickers, umbrellas grazing their fairy wings and cowboy hats.

"Thanks, but you've overdone it," Jerry said to whoever had heard him ask for rain. Whoever it was didn't answer, and the rain didn't stop. Cars slid off the road, nosing into street signs, or stalled at intersections, their drivers bewildered by water.

The fire had stopped just short of Day Logan's house. Ellen drove up there to help after Bern gave up and closed. The cops were letting cars through now, but the water was pouring down the road and they were plainly worried about mudslides. Day had filled her truck with sandbags and Ellen and Dottie helped layer them along the slope of the garden just beyond the back patio.

"If that hill starts to slide, you ladies get out of here, you hear?" the cop said, rain pouring off his hat.

"Who by fire?" Day said. "And who by water?" She shivered.

The road above the house was slick with rain and wet leaves. They could hear cars slide as they came around the curve, tires squealing, until Day got a can of paint and a piece of board and painted *Slow Down, Dammit!* on it. Ellen dragged it up the road and propped it against a manzanita bush, working the bottom edge into the mud.

She saw Carl Leeman's mother's Caddy come up the grade with Carl at the wheel, the dog in the seat beside him. Carl's face looked frozen in the few seconds it took the car to pass her. Why on earth was he out in this? But Bunny had said that he drove for hours, that he hadn't wanted to come home, that her mother worried about him.

The rain kept pouring down and she helped Day and Dottie load Day's car with more art and essentials like toothbrushes and clean clothes, just in case.

The *Slow Down* sign washed loose from its moorings and Ellen nailed it to a stake and pounded the stake into the mud. As she gave it a last whack the Caddy came back down the curve, faster than before.

She yelled "Slow down!" but the car slewed sideways and fishtailed. The passenger door flew open. The dog scrabbled at the seat covers and landed with a thump in the wet road. The Caddy plunged on. It straightened and then slewed around again and buried its nose in an oak tree while the dog disappeared into the chaparral on the hillside.

Ellen sat sobbing on Day's porch steps while the sirens wound up the grade and the ambulance and fire trucks came. The rain slackened and Dottie brought her a cup of tea. Ellen drank it numbly while the fire crew put out the oily flames and the ambulance crew loaded the body into a bag. Who by fire and who by water?

When she got back to her parents' house Yin and Yang were howling in cat carriers in the living room.

"Gordon brought them," Lily said. "He wasn't very nice and this came for you." She held out a fat envelope with a lawyer's return address.

Ellen weighed it in her palm. "I'm surprised he didn't hand

deliver that too."

"I wouldn't blame him," her mother said. She looked at her more closely. "You're covered with mud."

"I tried to catch Carl's dog." Ellen slumped down on the rug beside the cat carriers. "Carl Leeman drove into a tree outside Day's house on the grade. The road was wet but it looked like he meant to." She started to cry again and Lily knelt and put her arms around her.

When Lily said, "Is he all right?" Ellen just shook her head.

After a while Lily said, "I went to see Jean Ottley but she wouldn't come to the door. Herb looked like death. I asked about the funeral and he just shut the door in my face. I don't know what I thought I could have done. Or for Carl's mother either but I'll have to go see her."

Ellen unlatched the cat carriers and let Yin and Yang out. "I'm sorry," she said miserably, waving an arm at the cats, the envelope, the mud on the rug.

Lily closed her eyes. "I feel lucky to have a live child. Those poor boys."

Three days later the town assembled to bury another of its children. Ellen mumbled the proper responses from the familiar prayer book, in the church where she'd gone to Sunday School, and married Gordon, and where she'd let Carl put his hand down her blouse once behind the parish house.

Robert, in uniform, balanced awkwardly on his prosthetic leg but insisted on standing for the hymns. He'd seen Carl on the plane home, he told Ellen, and it seemed like he should be here.

"What was he doing up there in the rain?" Ellen asked for

the third time because no one had an actual answer to that except for the obvious.

Jerry, on Robert's other side in a jacket and tie, said, "He came in the library. He just wanted to build a fishpond, poor bastard." Ellen thought he was crying.

Lily was sniffling into a handkerchief, her arm around Carl's mother. The women's group was there, hugging Bunny who was red-eyed and teary in a black dress that was obviously someone else's. Bunny said Carl's dog had shown up at her parents' back door and they didn't know what to do with it.

The pallbearers carried the coffin, the flag draping the smooth shiny wood, down the aisle to the hearse outside.

"Your husband left a stone deer on my lawn," Jenna said to Ellen as they walked to their cars to follow the procession to the cemetery. "I can't lift it."

"Is that Martin's elk?" Day emerged from the congregation in a dark dress and shawl.

Ellen nodded. She seemed to be leaving immovable detritus everywhere.

"I'll lend you my truck. Dottie and I can help."

"It was nice of you to come today," Ellen whispered.

"The poor boy died outside my house," Day said.

"He's the third," Ellen said. "Of the boys I knew. I don't know. . . I don't know what to do with it. In my head, I mean." With all the boys swallowed by war, all the dead and broken. With the shreds of her marriage.

"Take sorrow and make art of it," Day said. "And salvage what you can." She looked pointedly at Jerry, ahead of them keeping pace with Robert. "Come see me and we'll make something. For that poor Ottley boy too."

"Does that help?"

"It's all we have."

The cemetery, nearly as old as the town, was enclosed by a wrought-iron fence under ancient live oaks. Randy Ottley had been buried there in a private service a week before, two rows from where they gathered now around a new grave, its depths already filling up with mud. The coyotes watched from the trees as the living and the dead passed between the tombstones. Randy's grave was still raw, a wet fresh mound of earth with one bedraggled vase of carnations. Carl's was ringed with wreaths of lilies. A spray of roses tied with white ribbon lay on the coffin. Carl's mother had the dog with her, his leash clenched tightly in a gloved hand. The dog pricked his big ears and bared his teeth, but neither the coyotes nor the ghosts offered him anything to bite.

Standing at the edge of the open grave, Ellen remembered burying Aaron. His grave would be grown over now, a green blanket covering it. Her throat ached. She leaned around Robert to Jerry. "Why did he want to build a fishpond?" she asked him.

"Therapy," Jerry said.

"Oh, God."

"In the midst of life we are in death," the rector said.

"Oh, God." Ellen's face streamed with tears.

"The earth and the sea shall give up their dead; and the corruptible bodies of those who sleep in him shall be changed..."

"Oh, shit."

They began filling in the grave, each shovelful of damp earth splatting on the coffin's lid.

Jerry traded places with Robert to stand beside her. "I heard you split up with your husband," he said quietly. "Is this a bad time to tell you Joelle threw me out?"

"Why?"

"Probably for not loving her."

"We've made an awful mess," Ellen said. "What do we do now?"

Carl's mother turned away from the grave, the flag from the casket tucked under one arm. "Ellen. Thank you for coming." Her face wavered, as if whatever was beneath the skin was unstable.

"I'm so sorry." Ellen hugged her and put out a tentative hand to the dog. "Is that Jojo?"

Jojo considered the scent of her fingers and allowed her to rest them on his head. "I don't know what to do with him," Mrs. Leeman said. "He's very protective. And he hates Asian people. I can't go to Mr. Wong's gas station if he's in the car. The Army wants him back but I told them he ran away. I'm afraid they'll put him down and Carl loved him. All he does is pace around the house looking for Carl."

"We need a dog," Jerry said.

Mrs. Leeman blinked at him. At them.

"This dog needs—" Jerry wiggled the finger he had tried to cut off— "rehabilitation."

"Do you know how to do that?"

"There'll be a book on it," Jerry said. If not in his library, then in someone's.

"Ellen? Are you—" Ellen knew Mrs. Leeman was about to say, "Aren't you married to someone else?" Mrs. Leeman stood uncertainly, twisting the leash between her fingers.

Jerry took it gently from her hand. "Carl used to come in my library. We'll take good care of his dog."

Saving a dog might be like making art, Ellen thought, all anyone had. She nodded. She would explain later, to her parents, and Robert, and Bunny and the women's group. They walked between the rows of tombstones under the live oaks and out between the wrought-iron gates, the dog's leash clutched in the fingers of her right hand and his left.

The coyotes watched them go leading the dog, and watched Carl drift away over the valley's rim and out to sea above the Channel Islands along the ancient path. The other had gone too, out of the raw grave beneath the vase of carnations, back to the foothills.

The coyotes thought he would probably stay there, drifting among the broom and sage, and the oranges, the white stones and the little horned toads, in the dusty light of the valley. They wouldn't mind him. On the fire-blackened land there would be new growth soon. In spring seedlings of manzanita and Matilija poppies would cover the ground; they were fire followers, sprouting on burned earth. He would sleep there, cradled in the manzanita, its red limbs wrapped around him like hands. In a while he would be part of their landscape.

AUTHOR'S NOTE

This book is a love letter to a beloved place, the Ojai Valley of California, where I grew up, here very thinly disguised as Ayala.

I owe endless thanks to the people who have shepherded this book on its way. Particularly I have to thank Liz Rosenberg, Ellen Kushner, Candice Ransom, and Lisa Rowe Fraustino, all of whom read drafts of this, most of them awful, at the various stages of biting and chipping it into shape; my endlessly patient husband Tony Neuron; my equally patient editors, Lenore Hart who saw what was wrong with the manuscript that I sent her and not only told me in a lengthy rejection but offered to read it again if I fixed it, and David Poyer who reined in my love of "that" and other authorial bad habits; my brother-in-law Michael Neuron, for putting me on to Char Man; Enrique Silberblatt for walking me through the finer points of swearing in Spanish; and Robert Campbell, who vetted the Vietnam scenes for me - any mistakes there are my own and not his.

Much of Ellen's experience at work mirrors my own and that of my friends and contemporaries, though Ellen has more adventures than I ever did. For a description of the idealism and pitfalls of communal living, I recommend Peter Coyote's *Sleeping Where I Fall*. For information on the life of a medic in Vietnam, an excellent book is *Doc: Platoon Medic* by Daniel E. Evans Jr. and Charles W. Sasser. And for a comprehensive account of the war and its effects on a generation of men, *...and a hard rain fell: A GI's True Story of the War in Vietnam* by John Ketwig. The conversation that Ellen has with Carl is a memory of my own of a visit from a childhood friend. I don't know what happened to him. I wish I did.

This book is for the Ojai boys who went to war and didn't come back, or came back someone else, and for the ones who didn't go and were marked by it nonetheless.

READY FOR MORE GOOD READING?

If you enjoyed *Coyote Weather*, you'll like *Deep River Blues* by Tony Morris, also from Northampton House Press.

When the body of a young woman washes up on the shores of the French Broad River, Cord McRae, newly elected sheriff of Acre County, Tennessee, suspects her death might be connected to the Glad Earth Farm, a commune just outside the small town of Falston. Guru/leader Levon Gladson and a group of a hundred and twenty-five followers have moved into an old farm that butts up to the Smokies, and Cord suspects they may be growing something more profitable than sorghum cane up in the hills. The mystery's complicated by Cord's investigation into a second recent murder, of an Afghan vet; the growing power of a local "hillbilly" mafia operated by the wily Thorn Reevers; and Cord's own marriage, which is teetering on the edge of divorce over past violence and his on-again, off-again love affair with liquor. With echoes of *Winter's Bone* and the novels of James Lee Burke, *Deep River Blues* is a worthwhile addition to the regional crime thriller genre.

Available online or through any independent bookstore.

NORTHAMPTON HOUSE PRESS

Established in 2011, Northampton House Press publishes selected fiction, nonfiction, memoir, and poetry. Check out our list at www.northampton-house.com, and Like us on Facebook – "Northampton House Press" – as we showcase more innovative works from brilliant new talents.